Anna's Family

Anna's Family

Nancy Austin Church

Anna's Family

This book is a work of fiction. Named locations are used fictitiously, and characters and incidents are the product of the author's imagination. Any resemblance to actual events or places or persons, living or dead, is entirely coincidental.

Published by
Lighthouse Christian Publishing
SAN 257-4330
5531 Dufferin Drive
Savage, Minnesota, 55378
United States of America

www.lighthousechristianpublishing.com

Dedication:

Anna's Family is dedicated to my eight wonderful grandchildren and all my family and friends whose prayers made this book possible.

Part One: The Journey

Matthew 5:4 Blessed are those who mourn: for
they shall be comforted

Genesis 12:1,b Go forth from your country, and from your
relatives and from your father's house, To the land, which I
will show you.

Chapter One

Savannah, June 1886
The clamor of the brass doorknocker disturbed the
hot muggy night as the large grandfather clock chimed four
times. The rich deep tone of the clock resounded throughout
the otherwise stillness of the townhouse. It was summer in
Savannah. The air was sultry, with both the humidity and
temperature hovering around a hundred. A diligent army of
mosquitoes hummed menacingly, as they craftily sought a
hole in the netting that surrounded the large four-poster bed.

Doctor Joseph Warren usually responded quickly to
being summoned during the night; it was a common enough
occurrence. But this time, he felt as if he was struggling up
through a thick fog. He had been up late delivering a baby

that had stubbornly delayed her appearance into the world and Joseph had crawled into his bed exhausted, only three hours earlier.

The commotion outside continued relentlessly, while Joseph struggled to push back the black depths of sleep.

"Doctor," a hoarse voice called insistently from below. "Doctor are ya there?"

Reluctantly, Joseph threw the sheet back and slipped from under the mosquito netting. He groped his way toward the window of his third-floor bedroom, crying out in pain when his great toe collided with a misplaced stool.

"Hush man, you will wake my household not to mention the neighbors for blocks around with such noise." He leaned out over the windowsill to see who was summoning him in the middle of the night.

A smallish, slightly hunchbacked, man stood on the front stoop of the four-story townhouse. As he gazed up at Joseph, his large bulbous nose and the dark cap perched low over his forehead nearly obscured the rest of his face from Joseph's view, but nonetheless, Joseph was fairly certain the man was not a regular patient of his.

"Sorry," the man called. "Name's Jake Cane. I'm Caretaker at Fort Pulaski out on Cockspur Island. Light keeper got hisself snake bit. Leg was gettin' to look real bad, so figured I had better come to get ya."

"What kind of snake?" Joseph called down. He hastily began pulling on his clothes, as he continued to fire questions at the man. "How long ago? What does his leg look like?"

"Rattler," the caretaker continued. "Said he was walking by the edge of the swamp, through the tall saw grass." The man's gnarled hands moved nervously around the brim of his well-worn and markedly sweat-stained hat.

He had hastily removed it for a better view of the doctor, as he peered upward.

"Got the boat tied up at the dock," he stated.

"I'll be right with you. I need to get dressed, leave a note and grab my medical bag," he called, making sure his voice only carried to the man below. He turned from the window and finishing dressing. Joseph quickly pulled on his shirt and pants. Disregarding the shoes he normally wore, he pulled on a pair of high leather boots he saved for the swamps around Savannah. If he was going among snakes, he wanted as much protection as possible.

Quickly he scribbled a note to Sheba, his daughter Anna's nursemaid, to inform her he had been called away and did not know when he would return. Isaiah, a former slave who assisted Joseph very competently in the clinic, would see to most of the needs of the patients. Those with emergency ailments beyond Isaiah's ability would be sent to another physician. And the patients who could and wanted to wait for Joseph would return another day.

Joseph, slightly rumpled, joined his nocturnal visitor. He carried his black bag in one hand while adjusting his suspenders with the other, as he walked wearily and reluctantly down the front steps of his home and office.

The two men hurried through the quiet city. The only sound as they made their way toward the river was of their feet crunching over the white shells that covered the streets of Savannah. They passed through several of the small park-like-greens the city fathers had carefully laid out throughout the thriving southern coastal town. With only the moonlight to guide them, the numerous trees and shrubs moving in the slight breeze took on eerie shapes and appearances.

"How long ago did it happen?" Joseph asked again.

"Just 'fore dusk."

"Good heavens man, that was nine hours ago

"Yep," Jake muttered. "Didn't come get me right away. Waited till his leg was swelled near double. Had to get hisself into his boat.   Rowed up the South Channel near half mile. Don't know how he made it. Put him to bed at the Fort. Didn't look good a' tall. Took me five hours to get here," he added as an afterthought.

* * *

The Fort was six and a half miles down stream along the South Channel of the Savannah River. When they reached the dock, the caretaker held the small rowboat steady for Joseph to climb in, before untying the rope and gingerly stepping into the wobbly craft.

After several attempts to engage the reticent man in conversation, Joseph gave up and silently rowed, praying they would have a safe trip. There were only brief snatches of conversation between them. If Joseph asked him a direct question, the man responded in the same kind of short choppy sentences he had used to tell Joseph about the plight of the light keeper.

The two men fell into a good rhythm. With both of them rowing and the swift current carrying them along, they covered the distance quickly. Joseph regretted not taking the time to pull on a pair of leather gloves. He could already feel the blisters forming on his hands, which were more accustomed to sewing up cuts than performing manual labor. They were fortunate the moon was full. Its light glimmered off the water in shinning ripples and was just enough to help them avoid obstacles, but not enough to enable Joseph to identify them—for which he was grateful.

They made good time and arrived at their destination just as the red glow of the sun could be seen rising over the Atlantic.

Joseph glanced around cautiously as they disembarked. He knew some of the history of the fort and had always meant to visit it one day. The present fort, Fort Pulaski, was the third fort to be built on Cockspur Island. The first fort, Fort Green, had been built to protect the new colony of Georgia. It had been destroyed by a hurricane around the turn of the century. Fort Pulaski had been built as a coastal fortification after the war of 1812. Joseph was aware that it had been named after a Polish Count, who had been killed defending Savannah during the American Revolution.

The rustle of the saw grass was intimidating and their boots squished in the boggy salt marsh as they moved stealthily toward the fort. Joseph was unceremoniously roused from his reverie when he almost ran over Jake, who was lumbering down the trail in front of him and stopped suddenly when something raced across their path. He was relieved to see it was only a opossum, but his relief was short-lived.

"Gater's prob'ly after him," the caretaker muttered.

Sweat was dripping from Joseph's brow and he murmured prayers with each step, thankful when they finally reached the fort. It was hot and muggy already and the sun had barely peeked over the horizon; however, Joseph was more inclined to attribute his discomfort to the wildlife than the heat from the sun. He had counted seven snakes in the short distance they trudged. The assurances of his guide, that the reptiles were all harmless yellow rat snakes, did not particularly comfort him—especially given the purpose of their mission. He vowed to study reptiles more thoroughly so he could tell the dangerous from the harmless in the future.

They entered, what had once been the officers' quarters and found the light keeper lying on a cot. His leg was swollen and grossly discolored. The man's breathing was shallow; his heart rate slow and irregular--his color waxen.

Joseph elevated the man's leg and asked Jake to heat water for him. After examining the swollen mottled limb carefully, he placed hot salt compresses over the damaged area. When he had finished, he gave the injured man a strong dose of laudanum and a cup of Chamomile tea. Both would help to relieve his pain and the tea would help reduce the swelling in the limb.

He worked over him for several hours before the swelling began to diminish. Joseph hoped his patients were not waiting for him at the dispensary. Some of them traveled quite a distance and were usually grievously ill when they made the arduous trip into town. Others would have dropped by just for assurance concerning age-related ailments; those Isaiah would be able to tend to without any assistance. He did not envy Isaiah's job of trying to console the more irritable patients.

The trip from the island to Savannah was much too far for him to go back and forth to see about the unfortunate light keeper. It would take more time away from his other patients and be exhausting for him. They would have to take him back to Savannah.

"Jake, we have to get him to Savannah Hospital. I'm going to have to watch him closely."

"All that's here is the row boat. How we going to get him up river?"

"We'll have to put him in the bottom of the boat with his leg elevated on the thwart. We have really no other choice; no one knows I'm here. We're on our own. Unless of course there are others on the island," he added hopefully.

"Nope," Jake replied. "Just the two of us this past six years. There's talk won't be none here much longer." The dejected look on the man's face made it evident that he was not pleased about the situation.

"Well then," Joseph replied, with more confidence than he felt. "You and I will row him back to Savannah."

The larger boats used the North Channel of the Savannah River, but it would be much farther that way if they were not picked up. They would also take the risk of being run down by one of the massive steamboats, especially if dark over took them before they were safely secured to the dock in Savannah harbor. They decided to row back up the South Channel, the way they had come. Neither of them entertained any delusions about the trip; it would be long and hard rowing upstream with their heavy load.

Laboriously, they carried him using a sturdy blanket. They made their way cautiously through the tall grass, down to the boat. Each held tightly to two of the corners of the impromptu litter. They laid their burden down on the bank and Joseph gripped him under the arms while Jake carefully picked up his legs. Joseph moved cautiously into the swaying boat, trying not to joggle the injured man any more than necessary.

The light keeper groaned at every step. Because of his precarious grip under the man's arms, Joseph's hands slipped a little with each step. Jake was attempting to steady the boat while holding fast to the man's legs. They finally positioned him between them, in the bottom of the rocking boat. But when Jake attempted to row from the center thwart, the light keeper's legs were knocked about. The man cried out in agony each time he was bumped; they quickly repositioned him so neither of them collided with his injured leg while they rowed.

As the hot sun beat upon their heads and sticky bodies, Joseph wondered if they could possibly make it all the way up the channel to Savannah. After several hours, his muscles ached with excruciating pain from the terrible strain of rowing against the strong river current. Sweat ran into his eyes and mouth. He periodically splashed the cool river water on his face, in an attempt to cool off. That unfortunately only seemed to produce steam, which rose from his shirt like mist over the salt marsh.

Jake spoke very little. Joseph felt as though he was talking to himself whenever he tried to engage Jake in conversation. Eventually he discovered what Jake had known all along; it took all of his energy and concentration to keep his body straining at the oars. The blisters he had gained on the trip down river had now popped and begun to bleed. If they drifted too close to the river's steep banks— where the water was calmer, they put themselves in danger. They might hit a stump, or one of the many snakes dangling from the tree branches hanging over the river could drop on top of them. Or worse yet, a sleeping alligator might be disturbed, or a regiment of the most enormous mosquitoes Joseph had ever encountered might swarm them, instead of their relentless individual assaults.

Fish frequently broke the water, forming whirlpools, which rippled out, into ever-wider circles. Alligators bellowed like great bulls, as they called to their mates or warned off encroachers. Once something large bumped against the bottom of the boat and raised it ever so slightly, in spite of the combined weight of the three men and the sturdy boat. Joseph did not want to know what species of aquatic life had accomplished that feat and kept his mouth tightly closed as he pulled on the oars even harder. *It is amazing the extra strength that comes with a shot of adrenalin coursing through your body*, he mused.

Joseph gave repeated thanks to his precious Savior that they had brought the injured man with them. He knew he would never have been able to make this trip again. *Not while I have any sanity left anyway.* When he thought he could not raise his arms again, Jake made one of his few comments. No news could have been welcomer.

"Savannah's 'round the next bend." The statement was made dispassionately, as he continued the rhythmic churning of the oars.

"Hallelujah!" Joseph shouted, unable to contain himself.

They docked at Savannah seven and a half grueling hours after leaving Cockspur Island. Joseph hailed a wagoner by staggering out in front of him. The man helped Jake and Joseph transfer the light keeper to the back of the wagon and Joseph climbed wearily in beside him.

Jake sought rest and solace at the Pirate's House and decided to wait until morning before making the return trip to his lonely job at Fort Pulaski.

Joseph arranged to have the light keeper admitted when they reached Savannah Hospital. After assuring himself he had done everything possible for the man, he wearily trudged home the five blocks from the hospital.

Relieved to find the waiting room empty, he entered through the dispensary on the ground floor. Joseph practically crawled up the stairs to his living quarters. In the past thirty-seven hours Joseph had only gotten three hours of sleep and had rowed a boat thirteen miles with the round-trip to Cockspur Island—almost all of it against the tide. Jake had informed Joseph half way back to Savannah that they were on a tidal river and the tide was "agin" them. His lack of sleep and the grueling day had taken a steep toll.

Chapter Two

Isaiah, Joseph's butler and friend, was quickly at Joseph's side. His brow furrowed with concern, as he noted the dark smudges under Joseph's hazel eyes and the weary droop to his shoulders. His face, sunburned to a scarlet hue, was streaked with sweat, dirt and two day's growth of blond whiskers; his hands oozed blood from the many large puffy blisters.

"We were very worried about you Doctor Joseph. Sheba awoke when she heard a ruckus outside, during the night. When she peered out her window to see what was causing it, she saw you leave with what she described as 'a disreputable sort of fellow.' Sheba said that he looked like one of the ruffians who worked along the docks. Since it was very early morning and knowing patients would be arriving with the dawn, she checked to see if you had left a note. Unfortunately, the note didn't reveal your destination." The concern in Isaiah's tone brought a fleeting smile to Joseph's cracked lips. "Nor did it state when you thought you might return home."   This time the concern changed to censor.

A twinkle in Joseph's sleep deprived eyes and his characteristic slanted grin, eased a bit of the fatigue in his face. It had been an exceedingly long two days.

"You should have awakened me to go with you. You know how dangerous it is moving about at night with all the riffraff around the docks." Isaiah, his once ebony hair graying and his shoulders stooped with age, moved slowly across the room to fluff the pillows in Joseph's favorite chair. He took Joseph's arm and slowly eased him toward the chair, as he continued to talk. "You sit down and I'll get you some food. Esther kept your supper warm."

"You weren't the only ones worried," Joseph replied with a chuckle. "And I am famished. I-I don't believe I have eaten all day, now that I think about it." He looked a bit startled at the revelation. The day had been so arduous that food had not crossed his mind. He smiled, as he wearily settled back in his chair and propped his feet on the ottoman. On examining his hands, he was not surprised to find them raw and bleeding. Carefully he picked up the well-worn Bible resting on the table beside his chair. It opened, seemingly of its own accord, to the twenty-third Psalm. "Even though I walk through the valley of the shadow of death, I fear no evil: for Thou art with me; Thy rod and Thy staff, they comfort me." Not since his terrible tragedy had the verse meant so much to him. This had undoubtedly been the most fearful and harrowing experience since the night Beth had left him with only Anna and his God to comfort him.

He began to chuckle softly. He must have been a sight—cringing from alligators he couldn't see and harmless snakes that he could. *The Lord must have gotten a good laugh at my expense for such lack of trust,* he mused.

When Isaiah returned, he bore a tray with a plate piled high with beef stew and cornbread—lavishly buttered, along with two cups of hot steaming tea. He settled the tray in Joseph's lap and retrieved one of the cups for himself. Quietly Isaiah made himself comfortable in the chair opposite Joseph.

Isaiah had been born a slave on Three Oaks Plantation, where Joseph's wife Beth had been born and raised. Beth, the only daughter of the Earl's of Three Oaks, had always been a special favorite of the household staff. She had quickly won the hearts of everyone with her mischievous ways and pert grin. Isaiah and his family had served the Earl family faithfully for many years, both as slaves and freemen. They had always been more family then servants. The Earls treated those who served them kindly and with respect. Family integrity had always been preserved on Three Oaks.

The children of the household slaves had been educated alongside the Earl children in the small gray-brick schoolhouse. Mr. Earl had been convinced that slavery was wrong and would soon end. When he had inherited the plantation at his father's death, he had begun systematically freeing the young adults and insisted that the children receive a proper education to prepare them for their freedom.

On Isaiah's twelfth birthday, as was the custom, he was evaluated for his future occupation at Three Oaks. He had proven himself to be intelligent and resourceful, a good student in the classroom and diligent in carrying out tasks assigned to him. At his request, he had been apprenticed under Caleb, the Earl's longtime butler.

After the war, when all the slaves had been freed, all but a few had remained on the plantation. Three Oaks Plantation could only be reached by water through the swamps, so most of it had been spared during the war, unlike so many plantations that had been razed to the ground and their fields salted to make them worthless. The treacherous coastal swamp with its alligators, snakes and huge mosquitoes had not appeared in the least enticing to the Yankee invaders.

Isaiah had chosen to work for Joseph and Beth after their marriage and had proved to be an able assistant in the clinic, after Joseph had requested his help with a difficult amputation.

The two men laughed together as Joseph recounted the episode of the opossum and her presumed pursuer. It was much more humorous sitting in his parlor, in the middle of Savannah--miles away from the treacherous swamp, then it had been at the time.

"I feel like I've lost a day or two." His sigh only emphasized how weary he was. "Thank you for sitting with me Isaiah. It has been a very long day." He was pleased Isaiah had stayed. He always seemed to miss Beth the most in the evenings. She had always waited for him to finish his day, so they could sit and review the day's events and have their devotions together. Tears filled his eyes, as he considered how much he missed her. Beth had been his wife, helpmate and best friend.

His beautiful Beth had died tragically only five months earlier from complications of a long difficult delivery. He was continually haunted by his loss. With all his medical skills, he had been unable to save the one he held so dear. He had devoted his life to saving the lives of others, but had not been able to save his precious Beth. *What good is it having medical knowledge, if I couldn't use it to save my wife?*

He could close his eyes and visualize her gliding across the lawn on her father's arm, as she walked toward him on their wedding day. He had waited for her under one of the massive live oak trees that had inspired the plantation's name. Her flowing white-satin and lace-wedding gown had a train so long and wide it had taken four children on each side and three at the end to keep it from becoming tangled. The young children on the plantation had vied for the privilege to be one of Miz Beth's 'train bearers', thinking about it made him chuckle. The laughter in his eyes turned to tears, as he thought again of Beth. *She was so lovely.*

The minister had asked—"Elizabeth Kathleen Earl, do you take this man…" and his Beth had responded, "with all of my heart and for all of my life, I do."

In one short year, she was gone. Many nights Joseph dreamt of her floating across the lawn toward him, but just before she reached him, she would vanish and he could not find her anywhere. He usually awoke drenched in perspiration, frantically calling her name. Being awakened to make a house call in an emergency was more often than not a blessing.

"Esther left buckets of water on the stove for your bath," Isaiah said, gently pulling him back from his sad reminisces. "Finish your meal while I fill the tub in your bathing room, then I'll bandage those hands. Can't have our doctor laid up with infected blisters, now can we?" He smiled as he glanced at Joseph before leaving the room.

Isaiah helped Joseph out of his clothes and into the tub filled with hot water. He retrieved bandages for his hands while Joseph soaked much of the soreness from his aching muscles and cleaned away the grime from the grueling trip. He sat in the tub until the water began to cool and he found himself dozing off.

Isaiah assisted Joseph from the tub, when it was obvious Joseph's muscles were too sore to sustain him any longer. He was unaccustomed to the long hours spent rowing the boat and sitting hunched in the cramped position necessary to avoid bumping the injured man. His muscles cried out with each movement he made. Isaiah helped him into his nightshirt and then expertly smeared a lanolin cream on his hands before swathing them in bandages.

"What happened to my patients?

"I told them you had been called away on an emergency and they should come back tomorrow," Isaiah informed him. "Old George came in to have his wound redressed. I took care of him and told him to come back next week, so you could look at it. He was the only one that wouldn't keep."

"Good—good," Joseph said, yawning and stretching. He felt the fatigue of the grueling day rolling over him like fog coming off the ocean. He struggled to keep his eyes open.

"Sounds like I have a big day facing me tomorrow, I guess I'd better get some sleep."

"Miss Martin came by. She seemed vexed that you weren't here. She asked that I notify her as soon as you returned." Isaiah grinned, as Joseph's fatigue lined features became a grimace.

"Well, we probably won't have to tell her. I feel sure she will appear at the office tomorrow."

Isaiah nodded and chuckled.

Katherine Martin had been popping in to the clinic every day or two with the excuse that she was fascinated with the care of his patients. When it was obvious to everyone that it was really the handsome young widower she was there to see.

"Sheba has Anna waiting to say goodnight, if you aren't too tired."

"I'm never too tired to see Anna, although I am not sure I could keep up with her tonight." Joseph moved slowly toward the door.

Sheba stood in the hall holding a wiggling five-month-old. Anna smiled and squealed, struggling to reach her father.

"Anna!" Joseph called, a gentle smile penetrating his fatigue.

"She missed you today, Doctor," Sheba said, as he reached over to kiss his wiggling daughter on her fat rosy cheek.

"I missed her too, but I don't think I am up to her energy level right now. I'll see you in the morning precious," Joseph remarked. "You're far too much for me tonight." He brushed her cheek with one of his bandaged hands and Anna leaned toward her father and kissed the bandages.

Sheba, carried the wiggling Anna, up the stairs to the nursery on the forth floor of the Townhouse. Sheba's room had a connecting door to the nursery, so she could hear Anna if she awakened during the night. The baby's mother had been her best friend and taking care of Anna was both a pledge and a joy.

Joseph was asleep almost as soon as his head hit the pillow. Tomorrow would be another busy day; he only hoped it would not prove as adventuresome as this one had.

****

Joseph visited the light keeper frequently during the man's hospitalization. The swelling in his leg eventually diminished, but his skin began to slough off, first on his leg, then over the remainder of his body, leaving pink scaly patches.

Several days after bringing the light keeper to the hospital, Joseph ran into Katherine Martin. He was cutting across the beautiful Forsyth Park on his return to the dispensary from a house call and had paused for a moment to enjoy the serenity of the fountain and the lovely fragrances. Flowers bloomed in abundance throughout the park. His reminiscence was abruptly broken when he heard Katherine hailing him.

"Joseph, I declare, if I didn't know better I'd think you've been deliberately avoiding me." Katherine pouted coquettishly, drawing out her slow southern drawl. Long auburn ringlets peeked out from a stylish bonnet, which enticingly framed her creamy complexion.

"I have been very busy trying to catch up after being gone a whole day." He resumed his stroll in the direction of Gaston Street. The park had been a favorite place to walk and dream of their future and Joseph had been reminiscing about Beth and the plans they had made for their life together. He was not happy that Katherine had intruded on his thoughts.

Holding her parasol to shade her fair complexion from the hot summer sun, she fell in step with Joseph.

"Mother wanted me to be sure and invite you for Sunday dinner," she purred, again exaggerating her southern drawl.

"Thank your mother for me," Joseph responded politely. "But, Anna and I are expected at her grandparents for dinner after church. They don't get to see her as much as they would like with us living in the city. They would be terribly disappointed if we didn't come on Sunday. I am sure you understand." He quickened his pace, but Katherine increased her step to keep up with him.

"Well maybe some other time," she said with a pout. "Would you like me to come in and assist with your patients this afternoon Joseph? Maybe with me helping you will be able to get done more quickly and we could go on a picnic or something."

He started to decline the offer, but reconsidered when he noticed Hank Brown's tall, angular frame, perched on a bench in the dispensary. He knew Hank had come in for his periodic dressing change, unfortunately periodic for Hank usually meant monthly. His stump was healing slowly and was frequently infected by the time he got into the dispensary. Submitting to an unaccustomed streak of roguery and knowing that nothing phased Hank, Joseph decided to accept her offer.

Katherine beamed as she strolled across the room, with her silk gown swishing enticingly. She smiled benevolently at the patients in the crowded waiting room, like a queen greeting her subjects.

"Hank, Miss Martin has offered to help me this afternoon. She's going to clean your wound for me. Hank lost his leg in an accident on the docks," he explained to Katherine. Hank was probably only in his mid fifties, but with his deeply lined face and gray hair he appeared much older. He leaned heavily on a homemade wooden crutch; as he followed them slowly back to the examining room.

"Roll his pant leg up and then remove the dressing with those scissors." Joseph assisted Hank onto the examining table and indicated where the instruments were waiting on the counter. "When you have the stump washed

I'll be back to check it before you redress his leg." He winked conspiratorially at Hank before turning to leave the room. A mischievous smile spread across Joseph's handsome face.

Katherine looked at the patient, took a deep breath and advanced toward him with determination. Her nose twitched at the unpleasant odor coming from the old man's direction. Katherine held her handkerchief delicately over her nose and stared at the man with distaste.

"Pull your garment up, so I can change your dressing." She flipped her fingers impatiently in the direction of the tied up pants leg and all hint of sweetness disappeared from her voice.

Hank untied his pants leg and tugged on it until he exposed the grungy dressing. Katherine's creamy complexion turned a little gray, but she set her jaw and determined to complete the task and make a good impression on Joseph.

She picked up the scissors gingerly, inserted them in the thick dirty bandage and began cutting away the dressing. She held the scissors carefully, to prevent her hand coming in contact with the offensive material. When the dressing fell away, the ugly inflamed flesh was exposed, along with the rotting grayish-yellow tissue. The odor and sight were more than she could stand. She had never before come in close contact with rotting, dying flesh and never wanted to do so again. *There has to be a better way to get Joseph's attention*, she thought with disgust. She dropped the scissors, not giving a thought to them bouncing on the floor and made a hasty retreat. Katherine picked up her skirts and ran from the room and out of the dispensary.

Isaiah saw her departure and quickly took her place. He cleaned the stump and gently removed the dead tissue.

Isaiah explained to the startled Hank, that Miss Katherine seemed to be coming down with something. Later, he confided to Joseph that he did not think Miss Martin would want to help him in the dispensary any more. The incident gave the men a good chuckle. Joseph had been busy in the other examining room and had missed her hasty exodus.

"I hope she didn't startle Hank too much. She has been making such a pest of herself and I just couldn't think of another way to discourage her."

"Well Doctor Joseph." Isaiah looked at Joseph with a twinkle in his dark eyes. "I think you just might have succeeded this time."

***

The Light keeper's convalescence took many weeks, but eventually he was well enough to leave the hospital. He spent several more weeks at a boarding house before he was able to return to his job on Cockspur Island. When Joseph finally pronounced him fit to resume his Lighthouse duties, he sent word by a fisherman going down river and Jake came to collect him in the rowboat.

Joseph walked to the dock with the two men.

"Thank you Doc. I know you saved my life, you and Jake. I'm mighty grateful for your troubling yourself."

"Thank me by watching closely where you place your feet," Joseph cautioned. "I don't relish the idea of making that trip again."

He turned back toward his house, as the rowboat pulled away from the dock. His daughter and friends waited for him in his comfortable home. He hoped he would never make that particular trip again, at least not in the same way.

Chapter Three

Joseph saw very little of Katherine Martin during the following month. His practice kept him busy during the day and Anna's antics filled his evenings. Anna was growing so fast and Joseph was reluctant to miss any of her new accomplishments. She pulled up on everything and had begun to climb anywhere she could get a foothold. Most of her teeth had erupted through her red swollen gums and nothing was safe from her tiny exploratory bites.

Everywhere he looked he was reminded of Beth. The Sunday trips to Three Oaks only compounded his grief, because the talk always came around to their loss of Beth and her "poor motherless baby."

Joseph finally realized he could no longer continue to live with such overwhelming grief and give his child the life and love she needed to grow, both physically and spiritually. He would have to get away from Savannah—the beautiful port city situated on the Yamacraw Bluff. He had considered Savannah the most wonderful city in the world when he first arrived as a young physician. Her charming public squares, elegant brick homes and the enchanting Savannah River that meandered around the foot of the bluff, all held wonderful memories of his courtship and marriage. Unfortunately, these reminders of his life with Beth only intensified the excruciating pain he still felt at the loss of his vivacious young wife. He was sinking relentlessly into a depression that threatened to engulf him.

He had made a valiant attempt to establish a comfortable home for Anna and himself. Friends and relatives had tried to console him, including an ever increasingly persistent number of eligible young ladies from Savannah's best families. Katherine Martin was but one of the young maidens who came to his office with pretensions of harboring a desire to nurse the sick. They appealed to him to allow them the privilege of assisting him in the dispensary, or to take Anna for a stroll in one of the many nearby city squares. The handsome widower continually declined their advances, as politely as possible.

Joseph worked from early morning until late at night and frequently was called back out on emergencies, such as the trip to Cockspur Island, although most were not as exciting, dangerous or arduous as that house call had proved to be. Savannah, a thriving seaport, had grown rapidly. The city had nearly tripled in the quarter century prior to Anna's birth and there was an abundance of patients, but more doctors were also moving into the area to care for them.

His only reprieve was his early morning devotions followed by a visit with Anna in the nursery. His greatest joy was to read to her while he held her in the large wooden rocking chair. Anna was all he had left of his wonderful Beth—the precious bond that continued to unit them. Throughout the dark hours he had been forced to stand by helplessly while she lay dying, he had promised her he would always do what was best for their infant daughter.

His years of medical training had seemed worthless to him when he had been unable to save his precious Beth.

***

"Sheba! Sheba! Where are you?" Joseph had considered his options carefully and had concluded that he and Anna would have to leave Savannah. There must be someplace where he was needed. Somewhere that he could begin to build a new life—for both of them.

Sheba appeared at the top of the stairs holding a wiggling Anna. The infant held her arms out to her father with all the trust of the very young. It was as if she knew if she could just get loose, she could fly down the stairs separating them—right into her father's arms.

"Sheba, we are leaving Savannah. We are moving west. I'm not really sure where we will end up, but I am ready to go." Joseph made his startling proclamation and then turned toward the library.

The announcement took Sheba completely by surprise. She stared at him, transfixed by his unexpected announcement. "But Doctor Joseph, how can we leave Savannah? Your patients are here and the Earls live here. How can we just leave?"

"I have to Sheba," he called over his shoulder. "I must get away from here for Anna's sake, if not for my own." Preoccupied with his plans, Joseph sat down at his desk. He began systematically listing tasks he would need to accomplish before the move.

Sheba had moved quickly down the stairs and followed Joseph into the library. "But Doctor Joseph, how can you take Anna away from her heritage?" Sheba's voice was filled with shock.

"Sheba, I have prayed and prayed about what we should do. It seems all I can hear from God is 'go.' Going somewhere new seems to be His answer. I need to do it for Anna. I need to start over somewhere else.

Sheba began to cry and wring her hands. Visibly confused and shocked by the unexpected announcement, she did not know how to respond. She had never been outside Chatham County and then only to Savannah or the plantation. Moving to an unknown destination was a very frightening prospect to the young woman of color.

"What's wrong Sheba?" He looked up at Anna's distraught nursemaid, perplexed by her reaction. He ruffled his rather long blond hair with one hand while he distractedly moved things around on his desk.

"It will be all right. If you don't want to go with us you don't have to," he assured her. In his preoccupation with his plans for leaving, he had not realized how irrational his behavior might appear to someone else. "It will certainly be more difficult without you," he considered thoughtfully.

Joseph got up and began pacing around the room, as if mentally cataloging the contents. "I'll just have to find someone else to care for Anna if you don't want to go. Anna's so very fond of you and I'd hoped you would want to go with us," he added pensively. "But I do understand. Your family is here." Joseph's shoulders sagged as he contemplated this new problem. Sheba would be hard to replace. She had cared for Anna from the moment of her birth.

"Oh Doctor Joseph! Go where? Where is it you want to go? What can you find somewhere else that isn't already here?" Her voice trembled, as she wondered what had ever possessed her employer to go off on such a tangent.

"West," he stated. "We're leaving Savannah and going west. Oh, not all the way west, not into Indian Territory, but there are thousands of miles of country to see and new people to meet. We'll build a new life somewhere else.

"Don't you see," he added passionately, entreating Sheba to understand. "I just can't cry anymore." His voice broke as he stood in the center of the room with tears glistening in his eyes.

"Yes, I can see that a new place might be better. Of course, I want to go. I would never leave Anna." She straightened her shoulders and bounced Anna, snuggling her closer. The five-month-old had begun to fret at the raised voices and tension in the room.

"Thank you, Sheba." Joseph moved to where she stood in the center of the room and put his arm around her shoulder. "We'll make this work. I know we will."

Hearing a gasp from the doorway, Joseph looked up into the horrified expression of Miss Katherine Martin. Her striking rose-colored gown, with its low neckline and tight waist, was obviously meant to impress the handsome young widower, but the expression on her face was anything but charming. Her complexion was almost the same shade as her dress.

Katherine stabbed her parasol on the floor, as she stood transfixed and glared at Joseph and Sheba from the doorway to the library. The scene before her visibly scandalized her rigid southern sensibilities. Beyond Katherine, Joseph could see the massive frame of Beth's brother Ben.

"Katherine! Ben!" Joseph stammered. He realized how incriminating the scene must appear to them. "Sheba was upset. I...I was trying to console her."

Ben looked amused as he obviously enjoyed Joseph's discomfort and Sheba's flushed face.

"Upset about what? What were you doing?" Her eyes flashed as she repeatedly stabbed her parasol at the floor in her agitation. "Joseph, I am appalled at your behavior." Katherine glared at the two standing before her.

She whirled around so quickly; she collided with Ben and dropped her parasol. Slipping around him, she ran from the house—out into the hot Georgia sun. The dropped parasol was forgotten in her haste to separate herself from the scene of her ruined aspirations. Her dream of becoming Mrs. Joseph Warren—like Humpty Dumpy—was clearly shattered beyond restoration.

Sheba quietly slipped from the room. As she retreated to the tranquility of the nursery, Ben's robust laughter followed her through the house. Seeking the sanctuary of Anna's room, Sheba cuddled the baby close to her body and walked up and down the room until she finally settled into the rocker.

"Oh Anna! What if your papa won't take me now?" she cried gently. "I can't bear to think about being separated from you. I've loved and nourished you from the day you were born and I promised your mama on her death bed that I would always be there for you."

In the library, which also served as the gentleman's parlor, Joseph and Ben faced each other. Joseph's face was scarlet, as he confronted his brother-in-law. Ben was laughing so hard his tall slender frame was bent nearly double. He clutched his aching sides, while tears streamed down his cheeks and soaked into his neatly trimmed black beard. He was obviously having the time of his life at Joseph's expense.

"Gater! For heaven sake, shut up. I can't think with you carrying on like that. It was certainly not that funny." But the infectious laughter was more then he could resist, Joseph began laughing himself. Each time Joseph was about to regain his composure, he would picture the look of shock on Katherine's face and the laughter bubbled up again. They finally lay back exhausted, but Ben nearly started it anew with a seemingly innocent remark.

"Well now we know why Savannah's fair maidens find themselves suffering from unrequited love."

"Quiet you reprobate! You know perfectly well that Sheba is like family to me. Why she was like a sister to Beth. What a spectacle I've made of myself. I wonder what my patients would say if they could see me now?

"I'm sure the servants think we've gone absolutely mad," he groaned. He had caught the click of the library door being closed, ever so discretely.

Joseph would have been surprised to see the look of satisfaction on Isaiah's face at the laughter that was coming from the parlor. "About time that man learned to laugh again," he told his wife, Esther, as he described the laughter that was pouring out of the parlor. "He has served this community day and night in gloomy solitude since Miss Beth's passing. It's time he remembered he's human. I'm going to latch up the dispensary, so no one can disturb them."

He moved quickly to the dispensary, placing the closed sign on the door and fixing the lock to assure that the men would be able to visit privately.

"What brings you here, Gater?" Joseph looked at his brother-in-law, curious as to what had brought him to his doorstep at the same time as Katherine Martin had arrived.

"Well, Joseph," intoned Ben in his slow, deep, southern drawl. "I've been sent by my parents to talk some sense into you."

"That's kind of role reversal, wouldn't you say? It seems to me; I've spent a good portion of the last couple years attempting to talk sense into you, at your parents' fervent request. What have I done to merit a visit from the original rogue?"

"Well, it's like this! It seems that mother heard you are planning to depart our fair city." Ben noted Joseph's look of surprise, as he began to pace up and down the room. "I have been dispatched to talk you out of the crazy notion. Failing that, I am to persuade you that it is in Anna's best interest for you to leave her with her doting grandparents until you have come to your senses and come back to Savannah where you belong." Ben turned and looked at Joseph to see what reaction his proclamation would have on his brother-in-law.

"But I don't understand! How did they ever find out so soon? I've just decided and I planned to tell them on Sunday at dinner." Joseph looked completely perplexed.

"Joseph, you should know that you couldn't keep a secret in this town. It appears that when you visited the railroad station to make inquiries regarding schedules Mr. Jud overheard you. He just happens to be the uncle of Katherine's sister-in-law, Julia Howard. Mr. Jud mentioned it to Julia's mother, who told Julia. Julia naturally ran to Katherine with the tale. Mother was at the mercantile shopping and Katherine cornered her there.

"She pointed out that mother would probably never see her granddaughter again and she must do something." Ben paused for breath while clearly enjoying Joseph's growing discomfort and astonishment.

"Anyway, I really did not come to talk you out of going, but to persuade you to take me along. Of course if you tell mother that, I will certainly deny it." He grinned wickedly and punched Joseph lightly on the shoulder.

"I'm not even sure where I'm going." Joseph was bewildered with all that had happened since he had begun making plans to leave. He thought he would have time to prepare himself before making explanations to the family. "I simply want to get away from Savannah and memories. I'll never forget Beth—I don't want to forget Beth, but this constant state of depression, I have found myself in, is not good for Anna or me. I have to find some place where I can make a home for us without being constantly reminded about what we have lost. Beth has gone on to heaven--nothing can change that. Anna deserves a happy home and a happy father and right now she doesn't have that."

"I know Joseph, but I do want to go with you." Ben enthusiastically picked up a chair, turned it around backward and straddled it. He faced Joseph and rested his arms on the back of the chair. Joseph laughed at his exuberance.

"Things are happening in this country and no one in our family for generations has been any further west then Atlanta, with the exception of during the war." His pensive mood was replaced by his customary mischievousness. "Of course, there are rumors of a great-uncle who was disowned and headed west with the law close behind him in the late 1700's."

"In that case, it certainly makes it appropriate for you to go west," teased Joseph, chuckling.

"Look who's talking?" Ben accused in mock indignation. "I've never been caught by the daughter of the biggest gossip in town, in a compromising situation with my daughter's nurse-maid."

Joseph snorted and grinned at Ben. "That's just because you don't have a daughter." Joseph grew serious once more. "You know I wouldn't.... Sheba is family. She was upset."

"I know that Joseph. I was just teasing you. Of course now you will have to leave town. When the gossips get through with this story your reputation will be in tatters. When are we leaving for the great untamed west to fight fierce Indians and chart new trails?" Ben added dramatically.

"Ben, you are impossible, but it would be great having you come with us. We may not go very far though. I've been talking to a gentleman from Pennsylvania, who has a plantation in Thomasville. He stopped by the dispensary with a minor infection and we began discussing the prospects available in Thomasville. The gentleman said people with pulmonary problems are flocking to the resort city and gave me an article about it. It claims that scientists are experimenting with a theory about the gases given off by the Long Leaf Yellow Virgin Pines. It seems their research is demonstrating they are beneficial in the treatment of respiratory problems.   The gentleman seemed to think it would be easy for me to set up a medical practice in Thomasville. He offered to help in any way he could. The way he explained it, Thomasville is the most beautiful city in the world, with tall pines, enormous live oaks and fragrant flowers blooming everywhere. He claimed he had been to nearly every city worth visiting in the world and considers himself quite the expert.

"Anyway, I thought it wouldn't hurt to make Thomasville my first stop." Joseph hesitated before adding, "Even if it's not where I end up."

"Sounds great, when do we leave?" Ben jumped up almost turning over the chair in his haste, as if he was ready to go that minute.

"Actually I planned to leave pretty soon. He told me I could live in one of the cottages on his plantation, until I decide whether or not I want to stay. You may know him Ben. His name is Theodore Joiner. I believe your father's done some business with him. Hamilton may be able to arrange a position for you in Thomasville, if you are serious about going with us.

"I am sure Anna would be delighted to have her disreputable uncle Ben accompany us."

"Then you do plan to take Anna? That will be hard for mother—losing Beth's baby so soon after losing Beth. She thought you were crazy when you insisted on keeping her here with you instead of letting them keep her at Three Oaks. I declare Joseph, she will surely have you committed to a hospital for the mentally impaired if she thinks you're serious about taking Anna off into the wilderness somewhere."

"Ben, I made a promise to Beth." His jaw was set and his voice betrayed a hint of steel. "And even if I had not promised Beth while she was dieing, I would never leave Anna behind. I am doing this more for her than I am for myself. We are going. You can go or stay, that's up to you. Sheba can go with us and care for Anna, but if she decides she doesn't want to leave her family, I'll understand and get someone else. Whatever else happens or whoever else goes with us, Anna and I are going." The look on his face was one that did not brook any argument on the matter.

"If we decide to make Thomasville our home, we won't be that far away. It is less than a twelve-hour journey by rail and one of the most popular resorts in the south, hardly the wilderness. When we get settled your parents can come for a visit."

Ben shrugged his shoulders in surrender. "When do we leave?"

* * *

Joseph never knew what Ben said to the Earls during the weeks they prepared to leave Savannah, but neither Beth's mother nor father tried to interfere with his plans. He realized their grief was intense as they watched the preparations that would take their only grandchild away from them. They were good kind people and he did not like being responsible for bringing more grief into their lives.

Margaret Earl was a petite, rather frail appearing, southern gentlewoman. During the days of preparation she frequently took Anna to Three Oaks to spend a few days. Her son-in-law was taking Beth's baby away from her and to compound her grief, her only living child was going with them. She spent many hours in prayer as the day approached when they would leave.

Beth's father, Hamilton Earl, broad shouldered and tall—several inches over six feet with gently graying hair, was the personification of a southern gentleman. He never raised his deep voice, but then there was no need—he was accustomed to having his wishes carried out quickly and efficiently. After much cajoling on Ben's part, Hamilton arranged for his son to represent his business interests in Thomas County. Hamilton fervently hoped that Ben would mature under Joseph's influence and with his new responsibilities—the good Lord knew that he had not been able to accomplish the task, but not for want of trying.

* * *

As the final preparations were being made, Margaret Earl came to the house and helped Sheba prepare and pack the garments and accessories they would need to take with them. Margaret brought many new soft cotton garments; most she had made herself in graduated sizes, to make sure that Anna would have new clothes to grow into. There were long white cotton cloaks, batiste robes with layers of lace and ribbons, snowy white dresses made from the finest cotton, grown and woven on Three Oaks, petticoats, bibs with delicate embroidery and dozens of the very essential flannel diaper drawers.

She came early one day before they were to leave and did not leave the nursery until the following morning. Sheba hovered over them packing last minute items, but Margaret Earl would not leave the side of her small granddaughter.

* * *

Hamilton Earl arrived the next morning to take his wife home. With tears streaming silently down Margaret's cheeks, she tucked carefully wrapped pictures into the large horsehair chest. One picture was a daguerreotype of the Earls, when Benjamin was a robust three years old and Elizabeth was about Anna's age. There was a picture of Elizabeth in a lovely long dress, embroidered with beads and trimmed with lace and ruffles; her coming out gown. Another was of Elizabeth and Joseph on their wedding day. Joseph, seated in a throne-like chair, was remarkably handsome in a dark suit with a stiff white collar. His unruly blond hair was slicked back for the momentous occasion. Elizabeth stood at his side, one hand rested lightly on his shoulder. She was a vision of loveliness in her beautiful gown covered in lace and ribbons.

It was painful for Margaret to part with the precious pictures, but she was determined her granddaughter would have something to remind her of her mother and loving family back in Savannah. She added several mementos: a dried oak leaf from Three Oaks, a bit of lacy gray Spanish moss and a dried magnolia blossom for a hint of fragrance.

Excitement permeated the house, as the adventure drew near. The commotion was contagious and Anna became restless. Instead of sitting in the middle of the floor playing with her wooden animals or chewing on her stuffed dolls, she crawled from one trunk to another. She was always underfoot, no matter how hard Sheba tried to keep her confined to the safety of the nursery.

Chapter Four
August 31, 1886

The day finally arrived. It was time for the
wonderful journey to commence and they were eager to
board the Savannah and Gulf Railroad car for Thomasville.
Seventeen-year-old Sheba was beside herself with
excitement. She knew there was a whole other world outside
Chatham County, but she never expected to see any of it.
The prospect of a train ride half way across the state to
Thomasville was enough to make her ill with anticipation.
Ben had told her that Thomasville was a city full of
rich Yankees. The civil war had only ended thirty years
before and stories of how the Yankee carpetbaggers had
taken everything that the soldiers had not looted were still
genuine concerns in the Deep South. Sheba was accustomed
to hear Yankee used as the surname for those northerners
who found themselves south of the Mason-Dixon Line.
"Anna, I wonder what they'll be like?" She held the
baby to her and danced around in circles, narrowly missing
some of the boxes. Years later she would confide to Anna
that she would have still started out on the long journey if

she had been able to foresee all that lay ahead of them in their travels and travails. The adventure was worth it all.

Margaret Earl kissed Anna's rosy round cheeks one last time before she allowed Hamilton to lead her away. Their carriage, kept on the mainland for their use in Savannah, waited to take her to the boat. It would carry her back to Three Oaks. Hamilton and the groom assisted her into the closed carriage and settled her comfortably on the plush cushion.

After delivering his wife to the dock and assisting her into the boat, Hamilton accompanied the carriage back to the Townhouse to transport the travelers to the train station.

* * *

When she arrived home, Sheba's mother Ruth met her at the plantation dock. "Ruth, I may never see our baby again." Her face was contorted with despair at loosing her only granddaughter. Travel was difficult and there was no telling where Joseph's final destination would take him.

Ruth had her own grief to contend with, as well as supporting her employer and longtime friend. A large woman, round of belly and ample of bosom, a smile or a scold came equally swift to appear on Ruth's full lips; she was wholeheartedly devoted to her family and that included all of the Earls. Her daughter and the tiny Anna, who was so dear to the heart of the entire household, would probably be gone a long time—if not forever. After settling Margaret Earl in her room, Ruth asked to be taken to Savannah.

* * *

"Anna, what will we do if something happens to keep us from going?" Sheba cried, holding the baby snuggly against her. She moved about the room making sure all the trunks were tagged right, so the ones that were going with them would get to the baggage car on the train. Others would be sent later after they were settled.

Sheba grew pale, nearly fainting with dread when her mother appeared and asked to see Doctor Joseph in his library—alone. Ruth had looked so somber that her daughter had stared at the closed door, trembling with apprehension after Ruth and Doctor Joseph had gone into the library and closed everyone else out. Finally, Sheba's legs failed her completely and she collapsed to the floor. Her full-skirted gray muslin traveling dress billowed around her. She still clutched the squirming baby, but her arms felt as numb as her legs and her hold loosened on her charge.

Wiggling free, Anna crawled among the trunks and furniture, unimpeded by the usual restraint of her ever-diligent nursemaid. Sheba remained on the floor—her charge forgotten, her head buried in her arms and her body limp.

* * *

Ben came in to join the travelers and found Sheba huddled on the floor her head in her hands and Anna asleep on a pile of discarded muslin in a corner of the wide entrance hall. Ruth and Joseph were still talking in the sitting room.

"Sheba!" Ben thundered. "What do you think you're doing? Anna's filthy and sleeping on a pile of rags. If you can't take care of her properly Joseph will find someone else to go with us and tend to her needs."

The tone of the rebuke and stated threat were enough to break through her stupor. She jumped to her feet and rushed to the sleeping infant. Sheba scooped Anna up in her arms and quickly bathed her with one of the cleaner bits of muslin—hastily retrieved from Anna's impromptu bed. To complicate the situation even more, the sweet natured baby began to whimper.

It was at that moment the sitting room door opened. A scowling Joseph emerged and retrieved his crying daughter. He comforted her gently before handing her back to Sheba. "Is everything ready? It's time for us to leave for the train."

Sheba, obviously relieved to discover she was still to go, quickly assured Joseph that all was ready. She hugged her mother and hastily bid her goodbye—before Ruth could interrupt the great adventure.

Joseph picked up his handgrip and walked out the door without looking back. After helping Sheba and Anna into the waiting carriage, he silently said goodbye forever to Beth's beloved Savannah.

* * *

The Central of Georgia Railroad station, a long, narrow, two story, red brick building; was a welcome sight to Sheba. The large station had been part of the Savannah landscape all of Sheba's life, but until this moment had held no particular significance for her. She had never dreamed she would enter it one day to climb aboard one of the huge black trains.

She contemplated the eighteen high windows in the front of the station, as the carriage proceeded up Liberty to Broad Street. In her mind, they resembled huge curious eyes—maintaining vigilance over approaching carriages that bore excited passengers to the waiting trains.

Ben was talking nonstop, his green eyes flashed with excitement over the journey that lay ahead. He was sure Thomasville was only the beginning of this great journey. There was no telling where they might finally end up, or how many places they would pass through on the journey. He marked the date well—August 31, 1886. It was the beginning of the rest of his life.

Joseph was pensive. He spoke only when asked a direct question or to give instructions to someone. He appeared to be lost in thought, a scowl furrowed his brow and a faraway contemplative look clouded his eyes.

Isaiah and his family would join them after the town house had been properly cleaned and prepared for the new occupants. A young lawyer form Charleston who was moving to Savannah had purchased it. He would be arriving with his wife and children in a couple weeks to take possession.

Sheba whispered excitedly to Anna, who responded with bubbling laughter. It was almost as if she understood they were embarking on a new and exciting journey. Anna smiled at each stranger they encountered, but hid her face against Sheba whenever she heard a loud noise.

They alighted from the carriage and Joseph and Ben hurried Sheba and Anna through the terminal to the waiting black giant, while Hamilton visited with some business associates. The immense black engine—polished to a glistening shine—stood puffing and belching on the track that led toward their destiny. The engine seemed impatient to embark upon the illustrious pilgrimage, as the men assisted Sheba and Anna into their private coach.

Hamilton Earl was joining them on the first part of the trip. He had business in Jessup, sixty miles down the line with a local cotton planter. He insisted on paying for a private car for the trip to Thomasville, so they could relax and enjoy the trip in comfort.

Sheba did not want to miss a moment of the most exciting thing that had ever happened to her. She chose a seat close to the window and pushed back the plush mauve drapes for an unobstructed view. Holding tightly to the squirming Anna, she watched the train back out of the station. Anna cried at the sudden noise and Sheba was momentarily distracted as she comforted her charge.

Ben and Joseph opened several windows so the car would not seem as stifling. In spite of their efforts, the travelers' clothes were soon drenched with perspiration from the muggy August weather and coated with soot from the engine.

Feigning indifference to the passing scenery, Ben joined his father and Joseph in a game of cards to while away the time. He was actually as excited, as Sheba and dignity permitting would have plastered his face against a window right alongside Sheba's, in order to devour the glorious sights rushing past.

"Ben!" Hamilton Earl snapped at his son, after he had again played his cards foolishly. "Keep your head in the game or get out. The disgust was obvious in the elder Earl's voice, as he scowled at his son.

"Oh! Sorry sir. I guess my mind is elsewhere today." Ben excused himself from the table and sheepishly settled into a chair beside Sheba, trying to ignore his father's displeasure.

"Come here, Savannah." He reached for his niece and poised her on his knee. "Ride the horsy." Up and down, he bounced Anna on his knee until she was laughing excitedly.

"Not so hard," Sheba softly admonished. "You'll scramble her brains."

"She loves it," Ben insisted, laughing along with his niece, who reached out in an attempt to capture the bugs that flew in the windows and through the coach.

"Yes, I can see that. But then not all that we love is necessarily good for us, is it?" The sarcastic undertone of her words was not missed on Ben, but he refused to think about anything that might mar this wonderful adventure.

"Party pooper. She's such and old party pooper, isn't she Savannah?" He continued to jostle Anna, using her full name instead of the nickname--Anna that everyone but her grandmother and uncle used. He did change to a less energetic bouncing than he had been doing.

When she tired of the game, he placed her on the floor so she could explore. She pulled herself up on the furniture and made her way joyfully, but cautiously around the strange moving room.

Sheba maintained her vigil at the window and called out each town they passed: Ways Station, Flamingo, and McIntosh. They occasionally caught sight of small weatherboard houses with homemade rockers prominently displayed on the front porches. Now and then grizzled old men or women waved languidly from their rockers. Children waved also as they ran alongside the tracks when the big train flew past their homes or fields. Dogs of uncertain parentage could be seen running alongside the children.

The palms and gray clay of Savannah were beginning to be replaced by swampy areas of Cyprus, cattails and willows. Moss festooned live oaks and green palmettos, with their wide fan-shaped leaves, remained a prominent aspect of the landscape. Cabins were scarce in this area and rarely did they see anyone taking note of the trains passing.

"Sheba," Ben teased. "You know what Spanish moss really is don't you?"

"What?" she questioned warily, unable to control her curiosity.

"Each one of those patches of gray moss represents the ghost of a dead soldier fallen defending the south-land," Ben replied seriously. "Do you realize how many wars have been fought on our fair land? Our brave forefathers could not stand tyranny of any fashion and many a patriotic young man gave up his life, thus giving us the opportunity to enjoy our freedom. Our Heavenly Father has honored their memory, by decorating the most worthy trees in the world— the mighty live oaks—with the ghosts of those fine brave fighting men."

Sheba's eyes opened wide with wonder and her light bronze complexion grew pale. She could not help becoming caught up in the fanciful tale.

"Ben!" admonished his father disdainfully. "Don't put such ridiculous thoughts into Sheba's head. Great Caesar's ghost!" he exclaimed in disgust. He turned back to Joseph, his displeasure with his son evident in his expression. "I declare, I don't believe that boy will ever grow up!"

"Now Hamilton, let them have their fun," Joseph entreated. "You know you are as proud of that boy as you are your old hound." He grinned wickedly at Ben over his father-in-law's shoulder.

"Thanks a lot," Ben mouthed. He shrugged his shoulders and smiled mischievously, settling back to enjoy the scenery that seemed to fly past the train window. He furtively slipped Sheba's warm hand into his and squeezed it gently then winked conspiratorially before returning his attention to the passing scenery.

She felt her face grow scarlet and in an attempt to cover her discomfort withdrew her hand and picked up Anna, who had grown sleepy with the rocking motion of the train. Anna began rubbing her eyes and sucking her thumb, a sure sign she was about to nod off. Sheba gently rocked her to sleep in her arms, and then tenderly and securely tucked her into a large travel basket.

Sheba had prepared the wicker basket to use as a traveling bed for Anna while they were on the train. She had carefully padded it with soft cotton bunting and feather pillows. After bracing the basket and its precious contents securely under the bolted down desk, Sheba settled back to watch the scenery as they sped through the barren countryside. She was moving faster than she had ever traveled before in her life and was enchanted with all that she saw flowing by the window.

After Waltourville and Johnston's station, they pulled alongside the Jessup depot where Hamilton Earl disembarked. They bid him goodbye with promises to write often and keep him informed about their progress. Joseph entreated his father-in-law to bring 'mother Earl' to Thomasville for a visit after they settled. He knew she would be concerned, unless she could see for herself that her granddaughter was safe in a civilized community.

Jessup was a bustling town filled with horses and carriages. As they pulled away from the Jessup depot, Sheba noticed the women who were walking in the dusty roadways wore sturdy dark cotton frocks. She was rather shocked to observe their shoes peeking out from under the hems of the practical everyday dresses. These women were so unlike the fashionable ladies she was accustomed to seeing in

Savannah. Savannah maidens, in their long straight skirts, would not consider venturing out into the hot sun without a parasol to protect their delicate complexions, but these women seemed oblivious to the way the sun had tanned their skin to a golden hue.

The women of Jessup were dressed more like the nursemaids and ladies maids who were prominent in Savannah--airing children or shopping in the markets along the river front. Upon reflection, Sheba realized these women would have to wear their skirts shorter in order to keep them out of the dirt. The streets of Jessup were not paved with cobblestones or shells from the ocean like those in Savannah.

"We've left the city for certain." She shook her head in amazement at the sight of wells beside the houses along the tracks. Sheba was accustomed to having the convenience of water inside the house, along with paved streets and walkways in which to roam. She loved Savannah's enchanting public squares; abundant with flowers, live oaks, beautiful statues and well trimmed green hedges. The squares had provided the perfect haven for her and Anna to meet with other nursemaids and their charges.

Joseph lay down on the divan built into the side of the railroad car. He was tired after all the excitement and preparation preceding their departure. Sleeping fitfully, his companions heard him occasionally call for Beth or Anna.

The train stopped at Screven to discharge a family who had been to Savannah for a visit with relatives. Sheba recalled having seen them in church a couple pews behind the Earls and the Warrens the previous Sunday and nodded to them as they passed her window.

They passed Steam Mill and were approaching the Blackshear depot. Ben decided this stop provided an excellent opportunity to stretch his legs. Many of the passengers disembarked to take advantage of the necessary houses located behind the depot. There was a small space partitioned off at one end of the private car for a water closet, but Sheba found it awkward and a little embarrassing to utilize it with only the partition between her and the gentlemen.

Checking to make sure Anna was still asleep in her basket, Sheba disembarked and followed the women to the long narrow building. When it was her turn to enter with the other nursemaids and ladies maids who were in line, she was surprised to discover all six of them were to use the facility at the same time. To Sheba, who was accustomed to the luxuries of the town house and Three Oaks Plantation, a six-seater water closet was a most unusual form of togetherness. *Guess it is necessary to prevent delays. Long lines at the necessary houses could certainly raise havoc with the train schedule,* she mused.

Everyone quickly reboarded and the train continued toward Waycross. They looked forward to obtaining a sumptuous meal at the bustling town, where two train tracks crossed. There would be a couple hours of leisure before the trip resumed and they planned to spend the time walking through a nearby park.

"Oh!" Ben exclaimed excitedly. They had been passing an area dominated by swampland. "We're almost at the border of the Land of the Trembling Earth."

"What's trembling?" Sheba's eyes grew large as she looked around at the ground beside the tracks.

"The swampland. There's over six hundred square miles of swamp south of here occupied by Indians who will never be found or surrender to the authorities." Ben was thoroughly enjoying the effect his tale was having on the unsophisticated girl. "It is probably the only area in our great country where white men won't try to move the Indians out. Who would want it?" The distasteful look on his face emphasized his words.

"You think so Ben? Are they friendly?" Her expression was grave and fearful.

"Well! I've heard they're just waiting for a chance to bring the Seminole's up out of the Florida wilderness, massacre all of the inhabitants in South Georgia and reclaim not only the swamp ridden Florida but Georgia as well for their tribes."

Sheba stared out the window. In spite of knowing how much Ben loved to tease and exaggerate, she was frightened.

"Ben!" Joseph had caught most of the grizzly story and knew that Sheba was probably frightened. "Let's play a game of chess."

Ben grinned at Sheba and shrugged. "Guess you'll have to get along without the travelogue for now." He started to join Joseph, but not before whispering in Sheba's ear. "You'll have to watch for the Indians by yourself." He ambled over to the table where Joseph was setting up the chess pieces and slid into a chair at the table.

Sheba checked on Anna, who was still sleeping peacefully, before settling back in her seat to watch the scenery—a little more apprehensively than she had before.

Chapter Five

"Look at the birds!" Sheba cried, as the sky was suddenly filled with birds in frenzied flight.

The two men glanced up from their game. Suddenly the air was split with the terrifying sound of crashing metal. They leaped to their feet. The car began to roll onto its side. Both the men were propelled forcefully against the furniture. The sound of the cars crashing into one another was deafening. When the train finally stopped its chaotic motion and came to rest, it was reduced to a jumbled heap along the embankment.

Passengers, frightened and injured, began to crawl from any opening they could find. The only sounds that penetrated from the depths of the great wounded giant were the cries of the injured and scrapping of metal as it settled along the tracks.

Ben was the first in the private car to recover. The coach was lying on its side with the roof resting against the sandy embankment. The windows on one side were completely blocked and on the other were too high above them to reach. He began to search frantically for his companions. He scrambled over the mass of furniture calling their names and throwing debris out of his way. Finally he located Joseph and was appalled to see blood streaming down his brother-in-law's face. He had a large jagged gash above his left eye.

"Joseph!" The grotesque sights surrounding him and the eerie sounds emerging from the crippled train were almost more than Ben's mind could accept. For a moment, the thought crossed his mind that the Lord had returned and he was the only one of his companions that remained. After one of his numerous youthful escapades, Reverend Johnson had predicted that would eventually be his fate. Realizing that Joseph was injured but very much alive erased that speculation and even given the chaos surrounding him he felt relief.

"Anna! Where is Anna?" Joseph's voice was weak and he was unable to sit up. When he tried he discovered his leg was pinned by the table. His head was spinning and the pain when he attempted to move was excruciating, but he knew he had to find his daughter.

Ben was activated by the sound of Joseph's voice and lifted the heavy table aside, freeing his brother-in-law.

Joseph groaned and attempted to move when the pressure against his legs was released. The room was spinning and he felt faint. He fell back against the debris.

"Lay still! I'll find Anna." Ben's tone demonstrated more confidence than he felt. He suddenly realized one of the sounds he had been hearing was Anna's muffled whimpering. He located the desk, which was still bolted to the floor. Unfortunately, the floor was not where it should have been. It was perched at a precarious angle.

Ben carefully moved the furniture away from the desk where Sheba had so carefully wedged Anna's basket. The basket had moved further up into the opening, but Anna was still snugly encased among the pillows. She did not appear to be injured, only frightened. He picked her up and soothed her as he wiped the tears from her cheeks. Ben cuddled Anna carefully in his arms and made his way cautiously across the rubble to Joseph.

Joseph was still calling out for Anna. His hand groped upward to his aching head; he was surprised to find it crimson with his own blood when he withdrew it. Quickly he clamped his hand over the gash above his eye and strained to see through the rubble and billowing dust at what remained of the once fashionable and luxurious private car.

"I have her Joseph. She doesn't seem to be hurt only frightened." Ben placed the squirming Anna in her father's lap. "What do I need to do for your head? It looks terrible," he added with a grimace.

Reassured that Anna was not injured after a perfunctory examination, Joseph told Ben to find his black bag and something that could be used for bandages.

Joseph searched through the debris, until he located Joseph's black bag and a piece of linen then made his way cautiously back to Joseph over the rubble.

Joseph had been holding one hand over his wound in an effort to stanch the blood flow, as well as attempting to comfort Anna. He instructed Ben how to put a temporary bandage on his head and eventually the scraggly wrap was in place. Anna played contentedly with the left over material, oblivious to the chaos, which surrounded them; once she knew she was back in her father's lap.

"Where's Sheba?" Joseph asked beginning to take stock. His head still ached and he felt like someone had been swinging him around in circles for hours the vertigo was so bad, but he managed to struggle to a sitting position.

"Thunderation! I totally forgot about her. If you can hold onto Anna for a while longer, I'll search for her. Don't let Anna down. There's a lot of broken glass around where you're sitting. We're resting on the windows actually." Ben moved away and began to carefully search through the debris. He finally located Sheba. She was unconscious and her legs seemed to extend from her body at an unusual angle.

"Sheba! Sheba!" He gently patted her face until he heard her groan. She moved her hands upward toward her face. A trickle of blood oozed from a laceration across her cheek and her upper lip was beginning to swell noticeably. He would have had a difficult time identifying her if there had been others in the car.

"Joseph, she seems to be grievously injured." Ben had never been around anyone severely maimed before and had been quite overwhelmed by Joseph's wound. Sheba's impairment was certainly beyond him.

A frantic call reached them from the end of the car, the door was opened from the outside and curious faces appeared in the opening. "Anyone in here?" A man called to them as he tried to see into the dark interior of the toppled coach. He barely could see the shadowy silhouettes of the occupants.

"There are four of us; a baby, two gravely injured adults and myself," Ben responded. He was relieved to find someone to take over the responsibility of ministering to his family.

"Are you the doctor?" The question was filled with hope, as the man pulled himself up into the car. "We were told there's a doctor on the train and we're looking for him. He is sorely needed out here to care for the injured."

"No! My brother-in-law is, but he is injured himself."

"Here man," Joseph called, as he made his slow painful way across the debris to the doorway. "Take my daughter." He extended the protesting Anna toward the arms of the stranger. "I have to check on one of our companions and then I'll be out to help you with the others." The stench of coal oil filled his nostrils. "You must get all the injured as far back from the train as you can. There's likely to be a fire from the coal oil. It's all right Anna. Papa will be along right away. I just have to check on Sheba and see what I can do for her."

He made his way cautiously over to Ben and Sheba, ignoring Anna's outraged wails. Sheba's eyes opened slightly and she moaned softly during Joseph's efficient and cautious examination. Ben looked stricken as he watched helplessly. When Joseph finished his careful exploration of Sheba's trunk and limbs he shook his head sadly.

"Ben, I'm afraid her back is broken. We need to get her out of here before there is a fire and we all get trapped inside."

Sheba began to cry out in her agony as her conscious level grew. She tried to move, but the fierce pain she experienced forced and ear piercing scream from her throat. The sound brought more faces quickly to the doorway.

"We'll have to carry her out on something flat." Joseph looked around the damaged car for something that would work.

"How about this door, doc?" One of the men in the doorway immediately began removing the door. With the help of others, they soon had it off.

"That is just the thing we need," Joseph agreed as the men made their way to them through the rubble. Joseph instructed them how to lift her and place her on the door then he assisted them in tying her snuggly to it with strips from the sheet, so she would be stable while they carried it. Cautiously they made their way to the end of the car over the scattered rubble. Other hands were waiting to lift her through the opening. They had to tilt the door to get it through the opening, but because she had been fixed so snuggly in place, she did not move. When she was safely through the hole and willing volunteers were carrying the door away from the train, others helped the men from the car.

Chapter Six

Joseph surveyed the damage as he climbed out of the wrecked train. He observed that many of the injured had already been carried a safe distance from the tracks. After being reassured that Anna was adequately cared for, Joseph went to see about those still needing his attention. Fires were springing up sporadically throughout the wreckage and this was a grave concern for the rescuers as they frantically searched for trapped passengers.

Joseph worked feverishly, going from one injured person to another. Many of the ladies aboard the train, those who had managed to escape injury, volunteered to assist him. There were broken arms and legs, as well as many cuts and abrasions sustained by the passengers. The fireman had been killed when he was pitched from the engine and the wood car had rolled on top of him. Several people had concussions, caused by being thrown against heavy objects or having flying missiles strike them.

There were others like Ben, who had come away unscathed. As soon as the injured could be freed from the debris, those who where able, carried or assisted them away from the train.

"Joseph, the tracks are separated," Ben informed him. He wiped perspiration from his brow with a once snowy white handkerchief that now looked like it had been used to pick up coal. His appearance was that of a laborer more than the dandy he tried to personify. "Nobody knows how it happened. One of the crew members left to dispatch a telegraph message for help."

"We'll have to find some homes nearby where we can care for the injured until another train arrives from Waycross." Joseph surveyed the field beside the tracks where the injured lay waiting his attention. It was an overwhelming task. It looked much like the battlefields his professors had described in medical school; only this battlefield included women and children as well as men.

He carried out what makeshift arrangements he could for the injured, while instructing the ladies assisting him how to correctly place bandages fashioned from linens found in the wreckage. The older children helped tear them into usable strips. Everyone who was able pitched in and helped in the rescue effort. Men and women from the surrounding area had also began to arrive at the scene and offered their assistance.

"I don't know how I'm going to get all these broken bones set." Joseph shook his head, as he moved from one injured person to another. "I need something to strap the broken limbs to that won't move."

Ben pondered the problem, studying the materials available to them. "I know what you need. Leave it to me." Ben commandeered some stout young men standing nearby to accompany him.

When Ben returned he, along with his helpers, had dozens of wooden staves torn from the damaged cars. They stacked them up in neat piles, assorted by size.

"That's perfect Gater." Joseph went to work setting the numerous broken bones using the staves and makeshift bandages. A middle-aged woman, Joseph guessed to be in her mid-fifties, named Bernice Harrington aided him. She informed Joseph that she had been a nurse during the war. Her assistance proved invaluable to Joseph in his overwhelming task. Bernice seemed to know what he needed done, before he asked her to do it.

The devastation caused by the train wreck brought back loathsome memories to Bernice, but she quickly organized the able bodied women and instructed them in simple emergency procedures. She was able to evaluate the patients and bring the more serious cases to Joseph's attention quickly.

Bernice was a large woman, broad of hip, with a voluminous bosom and a large brown mole perched precariously on her chin. But her most striking feature, when Joseph first saw her was her left arm, which dangled crookedly at her side. She did not allow the broken arm to deter her efforts. She efficiently continued to assist the other injured passengers, in spite of severe pain.

Joseph insisted she let him set her arm before she assisted any more patients. He instructed one of the women how to fasten it securely into Bernice's dress front, where it would be suspended over her heart. Joseph admired the nurse's courage and strength; with barely a grimace she returned to the task at hand. A less stalwart soul would have surrendered to the pain and let others carry the burden of attending to the injured passengers.

"Bernice, I couldn't have managed without you. Truly you are one of God's angels." He paused for a moment to wipe his brow, between patients. His bandage, which Bernice had insisted on changing as soon as she saw it, was crimson underneath the layer of soot from the train.

She smiled and continued moving from one group to another in her quite, no nonsense way.

Ben managed to secure wagons from surrounding farms to transport the injured. All of the families nearby willingly opened their homes to the injured passengers. The women of the homes administered to their immediate needs, made them comfortable in beds or pallets and cooked huge pots of thick soup to feed them. The more seriously injured were shuttled to the nearest home, about a quarter mile north of the tracks. Joseph set up a makeshift clinic in that home, so he could more easily watch over those who were more critically injured.

It was not until later that they learned the cause of the derailment was an earthquake. The epicenter, located near Charleston, South Carolina had devastated that coastal city. The tremor was felt as far as a thousand miles distant. The train had not been far from the center of the large quake when the shifting earth had separated the rails and caused the disaster.

Dishcs had smashed to the floor in many a Georgian cabin, even in Savannah a few houses were shifted from their foundations. But by far, the most extensive damage in all of Georgia was sustained by the derailment of the train headed for Thomasville.

* * *

News of the derailment went up and down the track quickly. Hamilton Earl was at the livery stable arranging for transportation home when the great quake had hit. He joined a group of men who were standing around discussing the unusual phenomenon.

Jessup had sustained minor damage, but no one had been injured. Old-timers were bragging about quakes and storms they had lived through, when the news reached them of the train wreck. Mr. Jenson, the stationmaster, had picked up the message for assistance over the wire and had sent a passing boy to alert the townsmen.

"Paw! Paw!" He yelled, as he raced into the livery stable. "Mr. Jenson says to get all your horses and wagons down past Blackshear as fast as you can. The train has done jumped the tracks. Half the passengers been killed. The other half is dying. They need water, food, linens and bandages."

"Boy!" Hamilton commanded, as he reached out a large hand and grabbed the boy's shirt. "What're you blubbering about?" He grew pale and fearful as the boy repeated his startling story.

"Now George, what did Mr. Jenson really say?" He looked sternly at his son, who was known to tell fish stories when he had not been near the creek.

"I swear Paw." His blue eyes grew wide and he looked the picture of innocence. He stood proudly before the men, enjoying having an audience for his important announcement. Numerous freckles stood out on his nose and his red hair was aflame in the afternoon sun. He embellished and enhanced his tale with each telling, for the attentive spectators.

"He said for you to hitch up all your horses and pick up the men and supplies in the square."

Just then the fire bell began to ring, tolling the news of disaster and summoning all able-bodied men. Hamilton Earl thrust some money at Mr. Browning, George's father.

"I want your fastest horse. My family is on that train." He headed for the stables with Mr. Browning right behind him.

A large black stallion was quickly saddled and Hamilton headed out of town at a gallop. He passed the town square where the people were beginning to gather. He followed the tracks southwest from Jessup, the thought uppermost in his mind was checking on his family and getting the correct account back to Savannah before Margaret heard the sorry tale he had just heard. She would be devastated if she thought anything had happened to their loved ones. He was sure the disaster could not be as bad as the boy's story. Stories of disasters usually became magnified in the telling. He could only hope this one had been blown all out of proportion to the true facts. In any case, he found himself fighting back tears on much of the thirty-four mile ride.

He quickly realized that if he did not slow his pace; he would kill his mount and find himself a foot in the sparsely populated area he was passing through. He changed horses twice at small towns along the tracks. The tale of carnage grew each time he stopped; giving him renewed impetus to hurry the new mount along. The heat was oppressive and the horses lathered quickly, even at a fast trot. As darkness descended, he was forced to walk the horse, but pressed on because he only had to follow the tracks and the moon shone off them—lighting his way.

It was daybreak, fourteen and a half hours; from the time he had first heard the report of the disaster, before he rode in sight of the crumpled black monster. The scene was alight with fires, which seemed to be burning uncontrollably. He could hear shouts and groans, as well as another steam engine further down the track.

Hamilton saw people milling about through the debris, which reassured him somewhat. The reports he had been hearing along the way of numerous deaths were obviously exaggerated, but no one could dispute the fact that the wreck had been devastating.

He dismounted unsteadily. His legs felt like they were made of rubber, after so many hours in the saddle. Apprehensively he began searching for his family.

"Hey there!" he shouted at a man carrying a trunk from the wreckage. "My family was on the train. Who's in charge of the rescue operation?"

"Man up yonder by that wagon," the stranger replied. He gestured toward a wagon about a hundred yards from the wreckage.

"Much obliged," Hamilton called. He led his horse cautiously through the scattered rubble.

"My name's Hamilton Earl of Savannah," he introduced himself to the man who seemed to be in authority.

"What can I do for you Mr. Earl," the man responded wearily.

"My family was aboard this train--in a private car," he added. "I have come to locate them and make arrangements for their return and any care they might need."

"Well, I'm afraid you will just have to look around. As you can see, there were a lot of folk on the train and we have many injured."

"My granddaughter, an infant of only seven months was with her father and my son," Hamilton pressed. "Surely someone can tell me something. My son-in-law is a physician. He is no doubt attending to the casualties."

"The doc huh," the man responded in a more courteous manner. "Yes sir, he's taking care of the injured passengers. There was a small child killed when a heavy trunk fell on her, but I don't think she was the doctor's baby. You might try up that way." He pointed toward wagons lined up on a dirt farm road, a short way across a field.

Hamilton grew more apprehensive as he made his way through the crowd to the road, leading his horse behind him. Some of the passengers appeared dazed; they sat on the ground or on the scattered trunks—their expressions desolate.

One woman was crooning softly to a cornhusk doll. She gently rocked it back and forth in her blood streaked arms. Her dress was torn and liberally splattered with crimson stains. Hamilton helped the grief stricken woman to her feet and led her to one of the wagons, as his horse nuzzled her shoulder. A large motherly woman settled her onto the clean straw. The woman spoke to her softly and comfortingly.

"Do you know where the doctor is?" He looked at the woman hopefully.

"Sure do," she responded. "He's at my brother's house tending to the worst of the injured."

"Where's that?" Hamilton asked eagerly. "Can you take me there, or show me the way?"

"We're headed that way. Tie your horse to the back of the wagon and climb aboard. We can use some more muscle handling all these folk".

Hamilton quickly tied his horse to the wagon and climbed up in the wagon bed alongside the injured passengers being transported to one of the houses. He questioned the woman about the rest of his family and learned that Anna was being taken care of by her niece. She was quite sure the toddler was all right, but did not know about Ben or Sheba.

"Although, I did hear tell of an injured nursemaid at my brother's house." She laughed softly as she confided to Hamilton. "Someone told the doc that he would have to take her down to one of those cabins." She gestured to a row of small cabins at the edge of a field obviously inhabited by the black sharecroppers.

"The doc told them that if she went down there so did he. That put an end to that foolishness. I am afraid that she is the most seriously injured of all the passengers; the ones still alive anyway."

Chapter Seven

Hamilton caught sight of his tall son when the wagon pulled up to the gate in front of a smallish unpainted farmhouse. Ben's clothes were streaked with dirt and dried blood, as he trudged across the yard carrying a water pail in each of his large hands. Hamilton reflected that he could not remember the last time he had seen his son performing manual labor--of any kind.

"Ben!" Hamilton yelled, as he jumped nimbly from the moving wagon. His fatigue was forgotten in his delight at having found at least one member of his family. He ran to his son and grabbed him in a crushing bear hug. The contents of the buckets splashed haphazardly over their legs and into their boots.

"You're alright! You're really alright!" Hamilton brushed away tears of relief. He looked Ben up and down; assuring himself his son was unscathed.

"Of course I am." Ben was embarrassed by this unaccustomed show of affection from his father. "You know only the good die young. I'll probably live forever."

Hamilton immediately began pumping Ben with questions about the others. "How is Joseph, someone said he was injured. Is Anna all right? What about Sheba?"

"Joseph is injured, rather severely I believe. But he won't stop patching people up long enough to receive any care himself." Retrieving the buckets, he refilled them and headed back toward the house. "He's going to be looking for this water and will have my head if I delay getting it to him."

The two men entered the small, cramped, room, which was never meant to hold so much humanity. The heat was stifling. The injured lay on pallets in the two rooms on each side of a central hallway. There was hardly room to move, even the kitchen-contained pallets of groaning men, women and children.

Joseph barely glanced up from his patient, a smallish man who moaned feebly while Joseph's deft hands explored his injuries. The house was full of the sounds of people in pain and the smell of hot sweaty bodies. Joseph had dispensed all of the medications containing morphine, opium, or codeine he had brought with him. His limited supply was not enough to begin to stifle the suffering that surrounded him.

Those who were patched and able to travel were being carried by wagons to the waiting train. Others, too badly injured for transporting, would have to be cared for in nearby homes until they were able to travel. Hamilton's attention was quickly centered on a young girl. She looked to be about nine and was making her way cautiously through the pallets, carrying Anna.

"Anna!" Hamilton said so softly it was almost a prayer. Relief flooded over him on a wave of joy, his granddaughter was not injured. "Your grandmother will certainly be happy to hear you are all right young lady." He took the smiling baby into his arms. "Happy to see your old granddad are you?" His tears flowed openly down his cheeks, as he held his granddaughter close to his sweat stained shirt.

"Sir," called a girl who looked to be in her mid teens. "Sir, could we step outside a moment."

"Who are you?" Hamilton inspected the girl who stood before him. She was petite—only a little over five feet tall—with a waist stylishly slender. Although he mused, it was unlikely she was aware of current fashion trends in her blood stained gingham dress.

"My name is Hannah Brown," she replied politely. Her blue eyes were flashing, but there was only a hint of exasperation in her voice. "I'm the eldest daughter of this house. Please sir, will you step outside with me?"

The girl's longish, plain, blue gingham dress, which reached the top of her serviceable, well worn brown boots, was splattered with dried blood and dirt. Her long blond hair had been pulled away from the round curve of her cheeks. It was held in place by a large handkerchief, made from the same material as her dress, but the handkerchief was askew and her hair was crawling from beneath it. The freckles sprinkled across her nose gave her an even more childlike appearance. The manner in which she conducted herself however, vouched for her adeptness and maturity.

"Yes, yes, of course," Hamilton said impatient to get his family and make arrangements for their return to Savannah. He hugged Anna snugly to his side and followed the girl out the door.

As he followed her into the yard, he was mindful of the state of his own clothes. A fastidious dresser, he was acutely aware his clothes were filthy and reeked of the horses he had been riding and his own perspiration. He was sure he smelled somewhere between an erupting skunk and week-old chicken innards.

The girl, wisps of escaping hair plastered to her face from the heat and humidity, studied the city man in his expensive suit. She perceived that he was a man accustomed to giving orders.

"Sir," she addressed him respectfully. "Doctor Warren has been ministering to others continuously since the accident. Several times I thought he might fall on top of one of his patients. He has lost considerable blood from his head wound and is exceedingly weak. He absolutely must be made to lie down and rest before he collapses. Miz Bernice has expressed her concern that if he does not rest, he will be in a bad way."

"Young lady," Hamilton addressed her. "I'm sure you are quite correct, but I am unclear what you want me to do about the situation."

"You must insist that he lay down." Her tone was respectful but firm. "Word has just come that another doctor has arrived on the train from Waycross. He can take care of the remaining injured. If you could get Doctor Warren on the train and down to the City, he'd have a chance to recover. There's a hotel across from the depot and just down apiece. You should be able to find comfortable accommodations there for your party. I've visited Waycross myself and my parents personally are acquainted with the proprietor."

"You think I can make him go, do you?" he asked, with a twinkle in his eye. "I'll see what I can do young lady, to assure your confidence in my abilities. By the way, do you know where Anna's nursemaid is? I'm sure she's assisting the injured, but her first responsibility is to my granddaughter."

Hamilton realized he did not sound very charitable and maybe he came off as a little pompous, but he was deeply concerned about Anna's welfare. It seemed obvious to him that she had been passed from one child to another. Joseph had probably pressed Sheba into duties for the injured, but she must take over her responsibility for Anna. He was determined to see that a responsible person was taking care of her.

"Then you don't know about her impairment? I'm afraid your granddaughter's nursemaid is quite seriously afflicted and like Doctor Warren, requires expert care and rest." She had caught the condescending tone in his voice and manner. Rising to her full five feet one and a half inches, she remained respectful but firm.

"I'm quite capable of taking care of an infant, sir. I have been looking after my eight brothers and sisters all of their lives."

He realized he had offended her and attempted to make amends, but before he could utter an apology their attention was drawn back to the house.

"Father, I need your help with Joseph!" Ben was calling him frantically from the doorway.

Joseph's loss of blood, the stifling heat and incredible pace he had been working non-stop for over fifteen hours had finally taken their toll. Joseph had collapsed in the middle of the floor. His head barely missed the edge of a stool, due to the quick thrust of an injured man's good arm— extended to divert Joseph's forward pitch.

Hamilton Earl was in his element. He procured a wagon without delay to transport Sheba, who had been placed in the only bed on the ground floor and the unconscious Joseph to the waiting train. Bernice Harrington agreed to accompany them and minister to the invalids, when she was assured that trained nurses had also arrived on the train. Hannah Brown eagerly agreed, with the reluctant permission of her parents, to temporarily assume Sheba's nursemaid responsibilities. Ben reluctantly went with them; he found he really enjoyed doing something useful for a change. He could not escape the fact his father would need him; with three of the party injured, a baby to care for and a young inexperienced girl the only other able bodied person in attendance.

After arriving in Waycross and settling everyone in the rooms at the hotel, Hamilton telegraphed his wife. He wanted to assure her that Anna and Ben were safe and uninjured. He cautiously concealed the seriousness of Joseph and Sheba's injuries by simply not mentioning them. That news could wait until he returned to Savannah. Joseph should be well on the way to recovery and they would know more about the extent of Sheba's injuries by that time. He did not want to needlessly distress Margaret, she had been upset enough just by their leaving. He was not sure how he would face Ruth with the news Sheba might never again walk. He decided to ford that river when he came to it.

Their trip was delayed several months; while Joseph regained his strength; Bernice's arm mended; and Sheba was well enough to travel. Hamilton rented a house, so they would be more comfortable during their convalescence and arranged for a local physician to look in on them periodically.

After sleeping for thirty-six hours, Joseph began to rouse. Hannah was kept busy supplying Joseph and Sheba with soup and beverages and looking after Anna. Bernice had managed to acquire enough laudanum to help Sheba through her weeks of pain, but refused to take anything herself.

"I'm afraid I might not be able to respond quickly enough, if someone needs assistance," Bernice confided to Hannah. She continued to bare her own intense pain with fortitude, as she looked after her patients.

Anna was learning to walk and enjoyed her occasional excursions outside. She had the natural inquisitiveness of all toddlers and kept the adults busy picking things up and putting them out of her reach, or plucking her off the latest piece of furniture she attempted to scale.

The tracks had been repaired and trains were again running between Waycross and Savannah. Hamilton stayed as long as he felt he was needed, but finally bid them farewell. He was torn between staying to help and returning to Margaret. He paid in advance for their room and board and left instructions with Ben to notify him at once if they needed anything.

Ben was restless during the convalescence of his companions and welcomed the opportunity to hunt with local gentlemen that he met on strolls through the town. Quail were plentiful. Thanksgiving they feasted on quail that Ben had bagged in the grassy pine covered fields. Hannah requested permission to fix their dinner in the hotel kitchen. She prepared the quail with fluffy white dumplings, greens and glazed sweet potatoes. They found her to be an excellent cook and although the food at the hotel was very good, the travelers were delighted to enjoy the home cooked meal.

Early in December, Joseph finally regained his strength and Sheba was stable enough to allow them to continue their journey. Bernice and Hannah were asked to accompany them on to Thomasville. Bernice's arm had mended with only a slight stiffness. She was able to care for Sheba and run the household. Hannah's main responsibility was to take care of Anna. This was to be a temporary arrangement until Joseph could hire a nanny in Thomasville, thus the Brown's agreed to allow Hannah to continue her employment a little longer.

Ben arranged for a bed to be set up for Sheba in the private car, attempting to make her as comfortable as possible for the trip. He placed her bed near the windows so she could enjoy the passing scenery, knowing how much that would mean to her.

Sheba was noticeably apprehensive at the prospect of another train ride, but everyone made such a fuss over her that she was soon caught up in the spirit of the adventure. She had begged to be taken along to remain near Anna. As much as she would have hated being parted from Anna, she dreaded even more the prospect of being banished to Savannah. She kept that and other reasons for wishing to continue—to herself.

Joseph had significant doubts about the wisdom of taking her with him, but decided to go along with her wishes for now. She did seem to be recovering some feeling in her legs, so her injuries might not be as serious as they had once feared. He allowed her to accompany them. Arrangements could be made later to return Sheba to the care of her mother, he reasoned. Joseph was confident that she would eventually realize Savannah was the best place for her.

The train took them through the communities of Glenmore, Homerville—with its beautiful courthouse—and Dupont. At Valdosta, they caught glimpses of multistoried southern homes. The women were especially enthralled with the sight of the large sumptuous homes and beautiful sprawling green lawns that could be seen from the train windows. Ancient live oaks dripped lacy gray moss from wide spreading limbs, some of which reached nearly to the ground.

Ben got off the train when they pulled up to the impressive red brick station and purchased refreshments for all of them. When he handed Sheba her food, he pressed a dollar bill into her hand.

"This is counterfeit! It has a woman's picture on it!" She accused, as she examined the paper money Ben had handed her. Sheba had not possessed many dollar bills, but she knew men's faces were supposed to appear on the crisp paper money.

"Martha Washington," Ben announced quite pleased with himself. "It is good money. They put Martha on the dollar instead of Father George in this series. Just what do you think of that?" He had a smug look on his face as he grinned at Sheba.

"Well it's something all right." Sheba tried to hand it back, but he shook his head.

"No, you keep it. It will make you a good souvenir to show your grandchildren some day." He smiled at her reassuringly, as he saw the tears glistening in her eyes.

They resumed their journey, as a sudden thunderclap rumbled in the distance. Anna hid her face and clapped her small hands over her ears. She did not remember the train wreck, but the noise was a terrifying memory to her. The tumult reverberated off the passing forests and the lightening flashed across the sky in great furious streaks. It was a great display of heavenly fireworks. The deluge washed the dust from the buildings and trees. Suddenly the sun shone with a brilliance that illuminated the tops of the trees they passed. The train passengers caught their breath in awe, as they glimpsed a magnificent double rainbow that stretched across the sky kissing the tops of the tall southern pines. It was like an omen heralding good fortune and blessings, to the small group who really needed a special promise after the devastation wrought by the earthquake.

"And God said, 'This is the sign of the covenant which I am making between Me and you and every living creature that is with you, for all successive generations; I set My bow in the cloud, and it shall be for a sign of a covenant between Me and the earth.' Genesis 9:12-13." Sheba repeated the Scripture in an attitude of prayer and the others said Amen.

* * *

The train swept by Quitman, with its scattered stately mansions. They were at long last approaching Thomasville. This would be a new beginning for all of them. Each of them contemplated what the new life which was about to dawn might have in store for them personally.

Joseph looked forward to replacing the old pain with new experiences. He hoped to make a new home for himself and Anna. He would make sure he told her about her mother; it was not that he wanted to forget Beth; he just wanted to be able to remember the happy times without the overwhelming grief.

Ben was eager to make new friends and experience challenging adventures. This was his first time to be on his own. He felt like he had finally been set free of the restraints of his parents and being hampered by being known by everyone he would meet, as Hamilton Earl's son.

Bernice longed to replace the appalling memories of war, which she hadn't been able to banish over the past thirty years—she had been so young and the war had been so frightful. She wanted new pleasant experiences with this interesting group of people. *They have so much faith in the future and the goodness of the Lord, even Sheba with her serious disability. If they can, so can I.* Maybe at long last she could actually move on with her life.

It was escape for Hannah. She had one precious infant to attend to instead of eight brothers and sisters, all younger than her. They had seemed to need her attention from the moment she awoke until she slid into the bed at night—and sometimes even during the night. She was actually to be paid for this unique opportunity to build a new life. She willed it to continue forever. It was hard for her to comprehend her good fortune, at having attained this position and she thanked the Lord daily for this blessing. As she glanced at Sheba, she felt a twinge of guilt. She was prospering at another person's ill luck and that realization served to somewhat dampen her enthusiasm. She vowed she would make it up to Sheba, in every way she could.

Sheba was elated with the passing scenery. The stately pines and strange red clay were so different from Savannah's palm trees and gray soil, but they were exciting and captivating all the same. They passed large green camellia bushes with beautiful ivory buds and waxy green leaves shimmering in the winter coolness and tall pale beech trees that reached upward toward the gorgeous blue sky with its dotting of fluffy white clouds.

The pain, eased by Bernice's cautious administration of laudanum was bearable as long as she could stay with the two people she loved most in the world. She would be content as long as she could remain near the man she loved and the precious baby—called Anna.

Chapter Eight

The train's path took them through virgin southern pines, so tall they seemed to stretch into the clouds and sprawling live oaks that gave the appearance of reaching out toward the train as it sped past. The oaks were lavishly draped with garlands of the familiar gray Spanish moss that hung in densely matted clusters.

The travelers continued their silent reverie as the train slowed for its approach to the Thomasville station.

"Oh look! Isn't that a charming hotel?" Hannah was entranced with every thing she saw, but the Piney Woods Hotel especially grabbed her attention.

The scene was like an enchanting dream for Hannah. Ladies and gentlemen promenaded in front of the magnificent hotel and stood on the stately verandahs in clothes straight out of Harper's Bazaar. *I have never seen anything to compare with it, not even in Waycross.* She stared unabashedly as the train moved slowly toward the station.

Sheba soaked up the picturesque scene spread before her as if it was a magical dream, while the train wove its way slowly through Thomasville. She was sure there would be an element of refinement and culture here, similar to that of Savannah. *Even if the streets are dirt instead of paved with oyster shells*, she mused. A gentle smile temporarily replaced the deep pain furrows that had become her most dominant feature. She knew in her heart that this place held something special for her—whether or not she was able to ever walk again.

The serene view, slow pace, stately trees and captivating fragrance wafting from the flowers, filled Bernice with an unaccustomed sense of peace. She would have enough tasks to keep her occupied, but she hoped the tranquil atmosphere might provide a calming influence, after the years of turmoil and pain she had been unable to put behind her. *I sense peace here,* she thought to herself.

Ben saw Thomasville as a place of unlimited adventure. There was an ample supply of young ladies to court with the attractive southern bells, visiting Yankee debutantes and students attending Young's Female College.

"Joseph, you have to go hunting with me. Everyone hunts here. They say it's a sportsmen's paradise. There's quail, deer, wild turkey and ducks in such abundance we'll be eating like kings. The gentlemen I met in Waycross gave me the names of some of the plantation managers and I plan to call on them as soon as we get settled."

Joseph smiled at Ben's exuberance, but did not commit himself to be a partner in Ben's plans. He expected to keep busy with his patients and the special project of gathering and recording folk remedies that he planned to begin here. *This will be a new start,* he contemplated. *I feel a tranquility here that I have not felt in a long time.*

Ben continued to dwell on his good fortune. *If Joseph doesn't go with me, I'll still have plenty of companions. Thomasville will be full of visitors seeking respite from the cold northern winters.* He had been told that the influx of visitors and winter residents swelled the area to more than double its summer population. Like birds they flocked to the south for warmth when the snow fell in the north. *Snowbirds that's what they are,* he mused. The many locations up north that the winter residents came from, would supply both versatility and an abundance of companionship.

They put aside their musings and began collecting their belongings, as the train pulled alongside the depot. Joseph had telegraphed ahead to notify Mr. Joiner of the time they anticipated arriving. He was pleased to see a wagon and carriage pulled by magnificent matched teams hitched alongside the entrance. A pair of matched sorrel mules was hitched to the wagon, while a splendid team of midnight black carriage horses pulled the carriage.

"It seems that we will be transported in a grand manner to our new home." A smile brightened Joseph's face, as he too looked forward to this change and the adventures that awaited them.

Bernice insisted on accompanying Sheba in the wagon that had been supplied so Sheba could lie down, in deference to her condition.

"I should be the one to ride with Sheba," Hannah protested. Miz Bernice, you ought to ride in the carriage, with Doctor Joseph and Mr. Ben."

Anna had enough of the foolishness and began crying her protests. She refused to be comforted until she was placed in Sheba's arms. They all laughed, as Hannah and Bernice were both assisted into the wagon, to snuggle down on the thick layer of hay that had been spread in the wagon bed for a more comfortable ride. The two women laughed together as they prepared to look after their respective charges and enjoy the beautiful picturesque scenery.

Joseph and Ben climbed into the carriage, after the women and Anna were made as comfortable as possible. Riding through the town, they passed a multitude of shops. It was the apothecaries shop that caught Joseph's attention.

"I'll have a good supply of medicines to treat my patients." He was pleased to discover what appeared to be a modern apothecary available in Thomasville.

"Joseph," Ben said nudging his brother-in-law. "Look over there. That appears to be a gentleman's club. It will be a perfect place for meeting the local gentry and the visiting Yankees."

Joseph laughed at Ben's enthusiasm. "Probably so, but I am sure we will also meet many of them at Church or in someone's parlor."

Ben grinned mischievously. "I'm, sure you're correct, but I had planned on meeting the young ladies of the town at church and in parlors. I wouldn't want father to get the idea that I was not out drumming up business for him."

"This is like a hay ride through paradise," Hannah uttered, enthralled with each new sight. "Did you see that library? I think that was a bookstore just down the street from it. Just imagine all those books," she said wistfully.

"Smell those pines," Bernice said breathing in the refreshing aroma. Intermingled with the wonderful bouquet of the abundant flowers and the fresh hay in the wagon, the fragrance was balm to her soul. If anything could remove the stench of war from her nostrils, this town full of aromatic flowers certainly should. She enjoyed Hannah's exuberance. It enhanced her own sense of optimism and expectation.

The only sights Sheba could see were the tall trees they passed. The sides of the wagons rose too high for her to see over, but she enjoyed listening to the enthusiastic descriptions of each marvelous sight by her new friends. She contentedly cuddled Anna, who slept snugly in her arms, lulled by the slow rocking motion of the wagon.

Before long, the drivers turned the horses eastward out of the city. The afternoon sun while warming them comfortably was not in their eyes as they faced toward their future. It seemed to the women that even the elements of nature were cooperating to welcome them to this delightful place.

Sheba occasionally caught a glimpse of the two men seated on the tall back seat of the carriage. She could see Ben gesture expansively, as they passed the various plantations her companions mentioned. He seemed to be as intrigued with the town and its surrounding area as the two women.

Sheba was content for now to look upward at the blue sky, fluffy white clouds and the towering pines. As they passed under a giant live oak, the sun glistened off strands of gray moss hanging low over the road and the branches seemed to wave a welcome to the adventurers. She could not resist saying a silent prayer for an unknown soldier, one from Ben's fanciful tale who had shed his blood for his country and home.

The trip from the train station took nearly two hours. The groomsman, with the reigns clasped lightly in his strong hands, held the mules to a slow deliberate pace in deference to the injured Sheba. In spite of her determination to bare the trip in stoical silence, Sheba cried out occasionally at an unexpected jolt. Anna would awaken briefly, but quickly snuggle back contentedly in Sheba's arms. The movement of the gently swaying wagon and the rhythm of the mules' hooves on the hard red-clay road were as tranquil as a rocking chair and warm milk.

When they reached Dogwood Plantation, Hannah maintained a running dialogue. She described everything they passed in great detail, so Sheba would not feel left out.

"Look at the wonderful gate house with the climbing roses. Oh! I can hardly wait until they bloom and I can see what shade they are. And look over there! That door has such unique carving." Her enthusiasm was bubbling over as she discovered each new sight. "The main house is enormous. Why, it would hold everyone in my whole county with half of it still empty! The porch is bigger than any house I have ever seen up close, but it looks real inviting with the rockers and swing and all the flowers. Sheba, smell those flowers. They're absolutely heavenly." Hannah could not be still she was so excited to finally be here and see such an enchanting place. Her experience had been confined to simple country homes, sharecropper one-room dwellings and occasional trips to Waycross—the largest city she had ever visited.

Sheba was able to vicariously enjoy this magic world they entered through Hannah's enthusiastic prattle. She had lived most of her life on the spacious grounds of Three Oaks, so Hannah's descriptions made Sheba feel as if she was coming home.

But the vast plantation was like dropping into a dream world for the callow unsophisticated country girl. Hannah's family was not poor. Her father farmed over a hundred acres of cotton. His land supported not only his family, but also the families of numerous sharecroppers. Their house was large in comparison to the usual two rooms that were typical of their neighbors.

Hollis Brown, Hannah's father had constructed beds with rope springs for each room, instead of the pallets that were rolled out at night for children in most of the surrounding homes. Caroline Brown had painstakingly fashioned mattresses of feathers and cornhusks and covered them with homemade muslin. Hannah was aware that her family enjoyed luxuries the majority of their neighbors did not possess, but nothing in her young life had prepared her for what she was observing from the bed of the wagon.

Hollis Brown had wooed and won a Savannah girl and had determined she would have the best he was able to provide for her and their children. Six days a week, he worked hard from sun up to sundown. But he always had time for his children and they never missed attending the local church services. When the visiting minister was unable to make it to their humble country church, Hollis often led the congregation in prayer and devotion. A God fearing man, he read God's Word to his family each night and from Hannah's earliest memories they had prayed together as a family. Hannah knew that even though she was far from them, they would pray for her, just as she prayed for each of them.

Bernice smiled at Hannah's youthful enthusiasm, while she absorbed the peacefulness and serenity of the plantation grounds. Birds sang joyfully in the trees, a dog leisurely scratched a troublesome flea and clouds drifted slowly overhead.

"Protected," she whispered. "This place is protected; a safe harbor. What more could I possibly want?"

"What did you say Miz Bernice?" inquired Sheba.

"Nothing dear," Bernice smiled and solicitously rearranged Sheba's position. *We are going to have to be real careful about pressure sores, with her limited mobility.*

"We'll all love it here. It is a lovely place and seems so peaceful."

Hannah beamed "I am sure we will." Anna had awakened and was struggling to free herself from the constraint of Sheba's arms. Hannah retrieved the squirming toddler and held her up so she could see over the side of the wagon.

"Look Anna!" Hannah had spotted a small building with a large iron bell prominently displayed beside the door. "A school house, Sheba there's a school house." She turned her head quickly from side to side, not wanting to miss anything.

She spotted several horses in the pasture they were passing. "Horses," Hannah said breathlessly. "They have horses for riding not just plowing." Two children approached them on well-groomed saddle horses.

Sheba and Bernice smiled at Hannah's enthusiasm. Her exuberance was infectious and they were all excited as they pulled alongside a two story red brick house. It was larger than any house that Hannah had seen outside of Waycross. This was the guest cottage where they were to stay.

"A cottage," Hannah said in amazement. "Imagine calling this mansion a cottage." Her eyes were wide with wonder as she took in every detail of what would be their temporary home.

"Yes, it is lovely," Bernice, agreed. She looked with awe at the beautiful house and the surrounding lawns and outbuildings. This place reminded her of the plantation she had grown up on, so long ago. It did not exist anymore. The Yankees had burned it to the ground. The thought brought sadness to her eyes that took some of the joy out of arriving at their destination.

Chapter Nine

Joseph and Ben were having a discussion with the carriage driver apparently over the accommodations. The women in the wagon could not hear what was being said, but could tell it in someway involved them. The groom occasionally gestured toward the cabins, barely visible on the other side of some out buildings—a short distance to the north of the cottage. They could only hear a few words that Dr. Joseph and Ben said.

"Injured…must have care." They assumed the discussion-involved Sheba.

"Then we'll all leave," Joseph stated firmly. "She will stay with us, if not here then somewhere else." He turned toward the wagon.

Hannah was becoming apprehensive at the possibility her dream was about to be shattered. She did not think she could bear it if instead of this marvelous new adventure she found herself back home in the girls room, five to a bed. But she knew she was not willing to compromise where Sheba was concerned. They had all grown very close and the three women, in spite of their diversities looked upon one another as family.

The man called Joseph back and they discussed the situation further. Finally they walked to the wagon. Apparently they had reached an agreement. Joseph had the trace of a smile dancing in his eyes, even though it was obvious he was trying not to let it show.

"We are home ladies." Joseph reached for Anna as he approached the side of the wagon.

"Did you see the horses sweetheart? Aren't they beauties?" Anna tried to wiggle down. She had been constrained long enough.

Ben held his arms up to assist Hannah. Placing one hand on each side of her narrow waist, he lifted her effortlessly to the ground. Then as gallantly, he turned to assist Bernice from the wagon.

Hannah took the toddler from Joseph and entered the spacious cottage. She located a large double doorway in the parlor and hurried to tell Joseph it would be easier to bring Sheba in through the side entrance.

They discussed the best way to move Sheba and decided it would be less painful for her if Ben picked her up and carried her instead of both of them trying to do it. He carried her into the parlor and placed her on the settee, before going back to the double glass doors and staring out over the plantation grounds. Joseph and Bernice toured the cottage after making sure Sheba was as comfortable as she could be under the circumstances. They discussed which rooms would accommodate each person's needs most suitably.

In addition to the parlor on the first floor there was a dining room, kitchen, pantry and two bedrooms. A water closet was between the two bedrooms with a door opening into each room. It was decided the downstairs bedrooms would be ideal accommodations for Sheba and Bernice.

"Look at these bedrooms!" Hannah enthused as she carried Anna through the house. She had discovered the four spacious bedrooms upstairs. "Water closets and bathing rooms," she said in awe, as she wondered through the rooms.

"Bernice look! Each bedroom has a dressing room with a place to hang clothes. Did you ever see such luxury? Imagine six bedrooms and all these water closets! I wish my mother could see this house. She would love it as much as I do." Hannah danced Anna around from one room to another in her enthusiasm."

This guest-cottage was the most luxurious home Hannah had ever entered. Her eyes were glowing as she prattled on to the baby. Anna squealed with joy joining in with Hannah's enthusiasm.

The trunks were brought in from the wagon and the women set about directing their placement. The arduous task of putting every thing away and settling into their new home had begun.

Ben pushed Sheba's bed close to the window, so she could look out on the gardens. "Look at those Camellia's? They're beautiful." Sheba was propped up so she would have a good view of the flowers out her window. "Don't you know the other flowers will be gorgeous in the spring with all the colors and fragrances?" I see a lot of rose bushes, just imagine what they will be like in several months!" She sighed deeply, as she took in the beauty from her window and imagined what it would be like with the coming of spring.

"Yes! The view from your window is great." Hannah stood beside Sheba's bed admiring the view with her. "Look, you can even watch the horses over there in the pasture." Hannah gestured to where they could see a couple of thoroughbred colts frolicking in the thick green pasture.

"Doctor Joseph promised to make me a special chair with wheels. Then I'll be able to get about the cottage and grounds with you and Anna. I won't be such a burden then and maybe Doctor Joseph will forget about sending me back to mama. Hannah it would be awful going back as an invalid, living at home for the rest of my life. The most exciting thing I would have to look forward to each day would be mealtime. I want to continue this journey, wherever we're going. I'm sorry I'm such a burden now on everyone." She began to cry softly, the tears glistening on her cheeks as they slid down to wet her gown. It was hard for her to accept being totally dependent on someone else for the most mundane tasks. She was accustomed to taking care of others, not having someone wait on her.

"Sheba," Hannah enthused, popping down on the bed beside her. "Everyone loves having you with us. I'm sure Doctor Joseph won't send you back. We'll have lots of good times here. You'll see. I'll push you everywhere in your new chair and you can hold Anna. The three of us will explore this whole plantation." She gestured expansively, as her eyes danced with excitement.

Anna had crawled up beside Sheba and took her head in her small pudgy hands. She leaned down and kissed Sheba's wet cheek and jabbered something that sounded very close to "wuv eba" while liberally sprinkling slobbery kisses across Sheba's face.

Sheba hugged Anna and the two girls plotted and planned while Anna sat between them. They anticipated many exciting adventures while they resided at Dogwood Plantation.

Bernice busied herself with settling in; she was content to be here with her newly acquired family. The plantation and interesting companions were a welcome interlude for the former army nurse. It stirred memories from the past which she felt were better left buried, but her soul craved the seductive peace of these surroundings.

She glanced through the window and saw a magnificent ginger colored thoroughbred galloping across the pasture. Bernice sighed deeply at the sight of the superb beast. Tears filled her eyes as she recalled her own exquisite Faxon. *No one would believe I was once a noteworthy equestrian, she thought ruefully. Poor beast that attempted to haul me around now*, she considered, patting her rotund hips. She had become what the dressmakers described as full-figured, but at one time had been considered a svelte beauty. Sighing deeply, she reminded herself to forget the past and enjoy this newfound peacefulness.

There was a well-stocked medical clinic on the plantation. The doctor who had preceded Joseph had been an elderly retired physician from Chicago, who accompanied the owners during the winter months, until he had become too old to make the trip. Joseph insisted on treating the plantation household and staff without charge. He hoped in this way to partially repay Mr. Joiner for allowing them the use of the cottage. He saw patients regularly in the plantation clinic on Wednesday afternoon, but was available to those who lived within the grounds of the plantation at any time.

He readily located office space in a vacant house on Dawson Street for his general practice and hung his shingle out. Soon a steady stream of patients thronged to his door, they were mostly northerners vacationing in Thomasville. One of his first acts upon opening his practice was to plant a young live oak directly in front of the office, as a symbol of his renewed life.

Bernice assisted in the office, as well as taking care of Sheba. She manipulated Sheba's flaccid legs and assisted her with bathing and dressing before leaving for the office each morning. Arthritis had begun to bother her in the arm she had broken, but other than becoming a good weather barometer it did not give her much trouble. She hardly gave it a thought unless the normally mild temperature suddenly dropped or the air became damp.

As he had promised, Joseph designed a chair on wheels for Sheba. The plantation carpenter and blacksmith constructed it in the small carpenter shop across from the dispensary. Bernice assisted Sheba with her toilette each morning then lifted her into the remarkable chair. She pushed her into the parlor or out into the garden if the day was clear, before leaving for her other obligations. When Bernice was off the plantation, Sheba's care became Hannah's responsibility.

When Isaiah and Esther arrived to assume the household chores, they moved into a white cabin in a row of small houses. The neighboring cabins accommodated the plantation household staff. They were soon completely at home in the new community. Isaiah and Esther helped out in the main house whenever a large soiree was held. They began to feel very much at home on this plantation, which was more like a small town in itself. It reminded them of life on Three Oaks. Isaiah thought the Yankees did talk a little funny though; rather harsh and a little twangy to ears accustomed to the slow drawl of southern speech. Hannah was freed from cooking and baking responsibilities as well as the care of the house, with their arrival.

Ben spent most of his time in town mingling with the winter people, rarely making the contacts his father had sent him there to pursue. Occasionally, he arranged a meeting with one of the plantation owners or a local farmer. He would then discuss the prospect of his father's firm handling the marketing of their cotton. If he was successful in acquiring a new account, he immediately telegraphed his father. Ben knew it would not do for Hamilton to suspect his son was spending more time pursuing frivolous endeavors than he was his father's business interest.

Anna was growing rapidly as toddlers are want to do, with each day being a new and wonderful adventure for her. She loved excursions to the flower garden with Sheba and Hannah and was delighted when more flowers began to appear in the carefully nurtured garden. The lavender and yellow crocus peaking up through the pine straw brought squeals of pleasure from the toddler as she delighted in clutching the tiny flowers in her small hand. Hannah had to watch her closely to prevent her pulling up the flowers-- bulbs and all.

* * *

The days passed swiftly. Soon the woods were abloom with patches of white from the dogwood blossoms. Purple wisteria intermingled with festoons of gray moss to decorate majestic live oaks with a festive touch of color. The azaleas and roses added a rainbow hue and finally all the spring flowers were in bloom. Their scent filled the air with fragrant perfume.

Early in March, the children of Thomasville gathered to watch the train back up to the Piney Woods Hotel. The Yankees were leaving for their homes back up north.

Passenger cars would be filled to capacity with the inhabitants from the hotels in town; therefore the most reasonable and by far the most sensible thing to do was to bring the train to the passengers. Watching this great parade was one of the highlights for the year-round residents of Thomasville.

Joseph had arranged for a wagon to transport Sheba and her chair, along with Hannah and Anna, into town for the spectacle. He knew they would consider it a treat to see all the ladies parade along the walkways—displaying the latest fashions in dress and accessories.

"Look at their traveling gowns!" Hannah gaped at the women coming out of the hotel to board the train. "They're wearing one layer on top of another. Even with all that material they have such tiny waists."

"Corsets," Sheba said knowingly. "They are all cinched tightly into corsets. It's a wonder they can breath."

"Look at their backsides," Hannah giggled. "What's all that behind them?"

"Bustles! They make their waists look pencil thin and then make their backsides look bigger. It's a mystery, isn't it? And look, you can see their shoes beneath their skirts. I never thought I would see the day that fashionable ladies wore their skirts so short."

"Yes and look how straight their skirts are in front, but they billow beneath their bustles in back. How awkward they look. But I guess they do look a little glamorous too, if you don't mind being that uncomfortable." Hannah was not really sure if she was repulsed by their dress or envied it.

Most of the ladies carried parasols of lace and satins and wore elaborate hats of straw; they were trimmed with bright ribbons and tulle. Many had lightweight traveling cloaks over their dresses, to guard against the soot and grime from the train. The travelers were in a festive mood, which generated a carnival like atmosphere. The girls loved the show from their perch in the wagon next to the hotel.

After the winter people had departed, Joseph had more free time. He began accepting a few of the many invitations he received from local families. Everyone had been anxious to entertain the handsome new doctor and his equally good-looking brother-in-law. Hostesses especially sought them to fill in as extra-unattached males, to complement a dinner party or soiree. Ben was only too happy to accept the many petitions that came his way, but Joseph had declined most overtures since their arrival. His heavy work schedule during the winter kept him much to busy to socialize. When the word spread across Thomas County that the handsome blond widower was now available for supers and dinner parties, he was flooded with invitations.

Bernice was seldom needed at the office after the winter people returned to their homes; Isaiah was happy to fill in when extra hands were needed. He enjoyed helping with the 'doctoring' and was only too happy to be back assisting Joseph. Bernice spent more time with Sheba or roaming around the plantation grounds on her own. She had made special friends with one or two of the horses and they watched for her and the treats she always had hidden in a pocket.

With the young Yankee ladies and gentlemen gone, Ben began paying more attention to his assigned tasks. He even showed up at the family dinner table occasionally.

Several times during the warm nights, Bernice thought she heard a stir in Sheba's room. After rising to check on her a few times and finding her presumably asleep, she finally concluded the noise was caused by domestic animals outside the window. The windows were always opened at twilight and sound floated in on the night air. It was difficult to distinguish from which direction the sounds originated.

One night Bernice grew hungry after everyone else retired. Not wanting to wake Sheba, she slipped out to the pantry without lighting her lamp. Sheba seemed to be experiencing reoccurring pain from her injury and she did not want to disturb her. It had become necessary for Bernice to give her small quantities of laudanum some nights, just so she could get to sleep; the pain was so severe. As Bernice was returning to her room, she noticed a dark figure steal furtively through the kitchen door. She started to call out, but suppressed the words. She made her way quietly back to her room and did not speak of her suspicions to anyone. A decision she later regretted.

Chapter Ten

With the exodus of the snowbirds, Joseph was finally able to begin his project. It had been his dream for many years to chronicle the history and uses of folk medicine. He knew that most *new discoveries* in medicine had some basis in folk or granny medicine: herbs and poultices that had been used for ages, passed down from one healer to another. He was concerned that the history of these old time cures would be lost. It was his ambition to keep a journal of all the folk cures that he could discover and not only preserve them, but provide their modern uses, with Bernice's assistance. He planned to make this his life long work and eventually publish his findings.

Bernice enjoyed working with the residents of the sprawling plantation. She assisted Joseph with gathering and keeping records of the home remedies used by many of them.

One of the most interesting persons they encountered was Aunt Maude. Maude was an ancient diminutive granny whose ancestors came from Africa on one of the notorious slave ships. She attributed her long life to her practice of eating a raw onion each day followed by chewing bits of parsley. Maude could not give an accurate account of her age, but she knew she was somewhere around one hundred. She swore by her onions and claimed they prevented apoplexy and kept a body's mind sharp. Bernice and Joseph agreed she was irrefutable proof of the worth of her prescription. Maude also made a confection from cocoa that was dark and just a tad bitter, although she mixed a bit of fresh honey with it. She explained that she ate a tablespoon of the mixture daily. Joseph tended to dismiss the benefit of the dark chocolate confection as being nothing more than an unusual dessert.

Rauka, a stable hand, smeared the ugly gray mold from old bread on the fresh wounds of the animals he cared for. He vowed it healed even the most gruesome tear without festering. Rauka maintained he had learned the trick from a foreigner—a shepherd, he thought. The stranger had visited the plantation where he had lived when he was but a boy.

Others claimed to have remedies for curing or preventing everything from a stuffy nose to colic. Some of the favorite recipes for a cough or congestion were made from such common ingredients as violets, coughwort, mint and Indian sage. The latter was also good for dyspepsia, according to many of the grannies and aunties Joseph encountered. It could also be used to diminish the after affects of intemperance, one wise elderly man had confided. Bernice painstakingly recorded each ingredient and the recipe for concocting the tonic or potion.

There were so many cures found on the shelves in the humble cabins Joseph visited, that he sometimes wondered why he ever had any patients. He never turned down herb tea and listened intently as the virtue of each herb was extolled. Woundwort was guaranteed to stop bleeding, as were leaches for some mystical reason. Elf Dock was a superior tonic and a cure-all for lung ailments—including consumption. Wild lettuce was as soothing to the spirit as a glass of homemade wine.

A sure cure for the pain of rheumatism could be made from Red Cedar shavings; also the berries from this tree were reputed to be an excellent diaphoresis. This was a claim Joseph discovered in a southern medical book that had been published in 1867.

In the **U.S. Dispensatory** of 1885, Dr. Korab wrote of some experiments he was doing with Elecampane, better known as Elf Dock. He claimed it was a powerful antiseptic and bactericide. Elf Dock was considered particularly destructive to the tubercle bacillus.

All of these interesting observations were carefully chronicled in the ledgers kept in Joseph's tall secretary. Joseph was eager to learn all he could of folk medicine, as well as any new scientific medical discoveries.

* * *

The bright greens of summer began to fade subtly into the oranges, yellows, crimsons and browns of fall, heralding the return of the winter staff to the plantation. This increased the number of patients Joseph saw on a weekly basis dramatically. There was no longer time to spend hours in the cabins or leaning on fence posts and chewing wild mint. Joseph had enjoyed this time of listening, while remedies handed down orally from one generation to another were shared with him. He regretted this delay in his research, but it was time to tend to his other obligations.

As the nights became longer, he enjoyed reading bits of news from the Thomasville Dispatch and some of the northern papers to what had become his extended family. The girls especially enjoyed items about celebrities. They wept over the report of Jenny Lind's passing at her home in Malvern Hills, England; Hannah had secretly longed to one-day see the famous singer on stage.

"Did I ever tell you that my name was almost Jenny?" Joseph asked when he finished reading the article.

"You are kidding us," Hannah said. She looked at him wide-eyed and eager to hear such and outlandish story.

"No, my father swore it to be the truth." His eyes twinkled with the laughter he was trying to suppress, as he enthralled his audience. "I was born the year the Swedish nightingale was married in Boston. It was at the close of her United States tour. My father frequently teased my mother about naming her first-born Jenny. He swore I would have been saddled with the feminine name if he had not put his foot down. Mother always just smiled her angelic smile and said, 'she was an angel wasn't she Joe.' So you see, if my father had not been master of his home and possessed a strong will, I would probably have been named Jenny."

* * *

There were other spectacular events in 1887, including Queen Victoria's fiftieth anniversary. It was celebrated in England with a special Jubilee Service and caught the fancy of the United States populace. The girls were eager to hear every detail and Sheba frequently encouraged Hannah to confiscate the paper before supper so they could pour over the exciting events recorded within the pages. Hannah always surreptitiously returned it beside Joseph's chair and they listened as intently as always to Joseph's recitation after supper.

* * *

Mr. Joiner and his family returned for the winter. The influx of the rich Yankees seeking the sunshine and the healing reputation of the pines caused Thomasville's population to double. Bernice and Isaiah were pressed into full time service in Joseph's town office, to handle the additional patients.

Sheba was finally able to care for herself with only minimal assistance. Bernice laid her clothes out across the bed and brought her breakfast before leaving for town. Hannah assisted her with her toilette and then pushed the wheeled chair outdoors, while Sheba held Anna in her arms. Anna loved riding in the wheeled chair with Sheba and it was about the only time, except when she was asleep, that she was still.

Hannah was able to devote all of her time to Sheba and Anna. The girls loved exploring, as much as Sheba's chair would allow. The hard packed dirt and red clay roads on the plantation offered a good surface for the wheeled chair to travel, except for immediately following a rain—when it was often impassable.

While Hannah manipulated Sheba's limbs little Anna worked her cornhusk doll's cloth covered legs. Sheba's limbs did not seem to be as flaccid as they had been and this encouraged Hannah to work with her even more.

Anna celebrated her second birthday with many well-wishers stopping by the cottage. The visitors marveled at the extensive vocabulary she had already acquired, for one so young.

The Joiner children, as well as the children of the household staff, enjoyed spending their free time in the garden or out in the pasture admiring the horses with the two young women and little Anna. Sheba and Hannah took turns reading to them from the Bible and the various children's books they had brought with them or Doctor Joseph had purchased. Tom Sawyer, Huckleberry Finn, Daniel and the Lions and David and Goliath were favorites. The children eagerly gathered to hear the next exciting adventure from the current book.

The reading sessions turned into teaching sessions with Hannah tutoring the younger children in reading, writing and arithmetic skills. They used Noah Webster's books and the informative McGuffey's Readers.

The children were fascinated with Sheba's needlework and that was added to the impromptu classes. The girls each began a sampler under Sheba's patient tutelage.

The Joiner's were impressed by the progress their children were making with the additional flower-garden-instruction. They were especially awed to discover the children eagerly sought the additional education.

An afternoon shower kept the girls indoors one afternoon, so Hannah was catching up on some much needed mending while Anna played with her toys on the parlor floor. She was surprised by a knock at the front door. People usually just opened the door and called to them before stepping in to the house. Their surprise callers were Mr. and Mrs. Joiner themselves.

"Oh! Do come in. I am afraid you have missed Doctor Joseph, he's at his clinic in town." Hannah ushered their visitors into the parlor where Anna quickly walked up to them and held out her hand.

"How d'you do," she said shaking first Mrs. Joiner's hand and than her husband's.

Hannah smiled at the precocious two-year-old and picked her up as she turned to the Joiners and invited them to sit down.

"Actually, it is you and Miss Sheba we have come to see," said Mr. Joiner politely. "I am sure you are aware that we brought Miss Emily Webster with us from Pennsylvania, to teach the children. Unfortunately she has become indisposed with a bout of influenza. The children seem so found of both of you and seem to learn so quickly from your tutelage, that we wondered if you could see your way clear to continue the children's studies while their teacher is recuperating.

"Oh, I would love to and I am sure Sheba would find it a delight also, but Anna is our responsibility and I would not want to turn her over to any one else."

"Yes, we quite understand. We certainly would not have any objections to Anna staying in the schoolroom with you. If you don't think Dr Joseph would object, of course."

"I'll discuss it with Sheba and then we can discuss it with Doctor Joseph when he gets home. I am sure he won't mind, but I would want to clear it with him before I commit to helping you out. Your children are such a joy; we have all enjoyed being with them."

"Thank you for saying so, but I fear you are being overly kind. They can be a handful at times. Please let us know after you have all discussed it. That is all we can ask. If you can let us know something tomorrow, that would be very helpful." The Joiners moved toward the door.

"Yes, I am sure I will know something to tell you by then." Hannah walked them to the door, but before she closed it, she smiled her most beguiling smile at the couple. "Of course, the lessons we have been teaching have been for **all** the children on the plantation. The children seem to learn so much faster when they are **all** together. I am sure you would want to include **all** the children in the instruction."

The Joiners looked at each other in consternation. This was certainly not something they had considered. Mrs. Joiner smiled and nodded to her husband.

"Yes, of course. I am sure that can be arranged." He bowed to the girls and taking his wife's elbow, escorted her off the porch and down the steps.

Hannah barely got the door closed behind her when she picked Anna up and began swinging her around in circles. "I'm going to be a teacher. I'm going to be a teacher, a real teacher.

"Sheba, did you hear what they said."

Sheba wheeled her chair out of her bedroom and her smile matched Hannah's. "Yes, I heard. And they want both of us. Maybe there are things I can still do, even in this chair." There was a lilt to her voice that had been long absent and the smile that lit her face and made her dark eyes shine put a tear of joy in Hannah's eye. "Thank you for making sure the workers children were included. So many people act as if they don't even know they exist and have needs like anyone else. They will love having classes in the schoolhouse. It will be a real treat for them."

Joseph readily agreed that it was an ideal solution in the absence of the teacher. He had no qualms about Anna joining them in the classroom. As bright as she was, he felt sure she would pick up on some of what was taught to the older children.

The plantation carpenter constructed a small desk for Anna that matched the others in the one room school. Hannah prepared a pallet in the corner for her naps and quiet play times. Anna loved going to school with the big kids and felt very important sitting in her very own desk that had been constructed to fit her perfectly. When she sat down, her feet touched the floor and she could draw on her slate just like the older children. Frequently when they were reviewing lessons, Anna's small hand was the first one raised with the correct answer.

Sheba and Hannah were enjoying their temporary responsibilities. It was a constant challenge, thinking up new and interesting ways to present the lessons. The children's ages ranged from six to fifteen and they had to have something to keep each of them interested and challenged. Sheba was good at arithmetic and Hannah was best in penmanship and grammar. They both taught reading with Sheba working with the younger children and Hannah the older students. They pulled current events from the paper and poured over history books in the plantation library, so they would have a well-rounded curriculum. Doctor Joseph agreed to teach a science class before his office hours started on the plantation on Wednesday mornings.

The task they had taken on acted as a stimulus for Sheba. She was tired and her body ached at the close of the day; but after a warm bath in the hip tub, a bowl of hot pot prickly lettuce and a cup of warm milk, she slept like a baby. She was always ready to go the next morning with a big smile on her face.

"Sheba, I love working with the children," Hannah confided one afternoon. She was pushing Sheba's chair back to the cottage after lessons were over for the day.

"I know. It has been a real joy working with them and they seem so eager to learn." The smile and look of contentment on her face was testament to how much these days in the classroom meant to her.

Anna ran beside Sheba's chair chattering about everything she saw. She stopped frequently to pick wild flowers or pick up a pretty stone and present them to Sheba or Hannah.

"I wish I could get more education. You know—go on to college. The older children frequently ask questions that I just don't know the answers to and I want to know the same answers." Hannah sighed deeply lost in her own thoughts and oblivious to the beauty around her. "If we could both go to college and become real teachers, wouldn't that just be something?"

"Yes that would be something all right." They continued on to the cottage, both with wistful looks on their faces as they dreamed of the things that could open up to them if they could get more education.

Hannah and Sheba read whenever they were given a chance. Hannah borrowed books from Doctor Joseph's library and later, after obtaining permission, from the extensive library at the main house as well. **Ben Hur: A Tale of the Christ**, by General Lew Wallace kept her enthralled for days. She also enjoyed the works of Sidney Lanier, a fellow Georgian.

Bernice liked to join them in having access to the libraries whenever she had a moment of solitude and wasn't totally exhausted from a hard day at the clinic. She had always loved to read and had devoured books in her father's library when she was young. One morning after arranging Sheba's breakfast tray, she retired to her own room to read and meditate before going to the clinic.

Bernice was reading from her beloved Psalms, when she thought she heard Sheba choking and quickly ran into her room. She found her retching and surrounded by a pool of vomitus.

"You poor dear, I hope you aren't coming down with influenza." She ran to the bed, scooped her up and placed her in a chair. She poured water on a clean cloth and bathed Sheba's face, before giving her a cup of water to rinse her mouth. "Do you feel better dear?"

"Yes. I don't know what happened." There were tears in Sheba's eyes and she looked like she felt miserable.

"Don't you worry about it." Bernice quickly stripped the soiled linens from the bed and after assuring herself that Sheba was all right sitting in the chair, she retrieved clean linens and efficiently remade the bed and settled Sheba back under the covers. She sponged her face again and laid a cool cloth to her throat, laying her hand gently on her forehead. She was concerned about the abrupt onset of Sheba's illness.

"I tried to miss the covers," Sheba wailed sorrowfully. "I'm sorry Miz Bernice. It came so quick. I tried to not make a mess."

"Don't you worry about it sweetheart," Bernice soothed her. She brushed Sheba's hair back from her face. When Sheba calmed and seemed to doze off again, Bernice cleaned up the rest of the room and then settled in a chair beside Sheba's bed. When she was sure that Sheba had slipped into a restful sleep, she left the room to find Joseph.

"Joseph, I won't be able to go into the office today. Sheba woke up sick to her stomach this morning and I feel that I need to stay with her."

"I'll look in on her. Do you think it's something serious?" Joseph's eyes searched Bernice's face to gauge the depth of her concern. Contagious illnesses could quickly move from one to another until the entire area was devastated.

"No. I'm sure it's nothing to be real concerned about. If she gets worse I'll send for you. Hannah hovered in the background, concerned for her friend. "Hannah, it looks like you and Anna will have to handle the school today. Don't worry about Sheba. I'll make sure she gets the best of care."

Sheba appeared much better when she aroused from her nap. But because of the possibility that she was coming down with influenza, she was not allowed to return to school. Miss Webster had recuperated sufficiently to join Hannah for part of the day and soon was able to resume her duties completely. The girls missed the schoolhouse, but continued the extra lessons in the garden, whenever the weather permitted.

Sheba had several more episodes of vomiting when she first aroused in the morning. She seemed to do better if allowed to sleep a bit longer, so everyone was as quiet as possible in order not to disturb her. After several weeks, the strange ailment left as quickly as it had come and Sheba seemed as perky as usual.

The household was a bustle with excitement and activity. Anna's grandparents were planning a trip to Thomasville for a visit. Everyone was pressed into service to make the Earl's visit extra special. The day before their scheduled arrival, a telegram was delivered informing Ben that his mother had been put to bed with a sudden onset of consumption. He was summoned home.

Joseph planned to follow in a few days with Anna, but before he could make arrangements to leave, they received word she had succumbed shortly after Ben arrived. She was to be buried immediately. Ben sent a telegram to Joseph explaining there was no time for him to get there; so there would be no need for him to leave his patients and make the hurried trip. There was nothing Joseph could do and Ben knew the funeral would just rekindle sad memories of Beth's passing for his brother-in-law.

Chapter Eleven

March arrived with a profuse display of multicolored spring flowers. It was almost as if the red, pink and yellow blooms of the abundant roses were a signal to the winter population that it was time for them to migrate north. Joseph was becoming restless. As the Yankees prepared to make their exodus, he felt it was time to resume their journey. With Anna's grandmother's passing, there was little to hold them in Georgia. He had enjoyed being in this beautiful southern town, but he still had a lot to learn and the western states continued to beckon him.

New discoveries were being announced in medicine regularly and he felt somehow left out. He loved his research, the delving into the properties of medicines, some of which had been used for centuries, but had never really been studied.

"Listen to this." Joseph sat in the parlor surrounded by family and friends. He was reading an article to Bernice from the latest medical journal, which had arrived that afternoon. "Dr. Fitz of Boston advocates removing the vermiform appendix in certain disorders of the intestine. Dr. Fitz performed hundreds of postmortem operations before publishing his conclusions. His advice is being followed successfully by many American surgeons."

"Are you considering learning the technique?" Bernice was working on some personal mending as she sat and rocked, enjoying a bit of leisure after the busy winter months.

"Maybe I should. It's important to keep up with the latest procedures. Actually, it appears that the operation has been performed for years in Europe. We have to keep up or loose patients needlessly."

Joseph thought about Sheba's recent stomach disorder and contemplated the possibility of a link between her illness and this newly recommended procedure.

When Ben returned, Joseph informed him he planned to resume the journey. "I have explored the possibilities and think that Arkansas would be the ideal place for us to build a new life. From what I can learn, it is a civilized place, around the capital anyway and it is the last state before Indian Territory. I believe the state will provide us with enough adventure, yet afford a mode of comfortable living. There is a train running from Thomasville to Atlanta, from there we can head west.

"We will make an adventure of it. Take our time and explore as we go. I discussed the pros and cons of various locations with Mr. Joiner prior to his return to Pennsylvania and while he expressed his personal regrets concerning our departure, he concurred that Arkansas held abundant opportunity for all of us."

Mr. Joiner had actually expressed his regret that he could not just pull up stakes and go with them. He claimed there were no new discoveries to be made in the East. "Son," he had insisted. "The only adventure left in America is to be found west of the Mississippi River. The East is turning out nothing but gadgets. Take the telephone. It is the pinnacle of modern sophistication as well as the bane of mankind. There is just no hiding from the blamed thing. Why I predict it won't be long before every town has one."

Since Bell's invention of the telephone in 1876, phones were becoming a common convenience in the homes of the wealthy. They were even beginning to appear in middle class homes throughout the northeast and Middle Western states. Mr. Joiner insisted Joseph was wise to seek his fortune in the West, which only served to reinforce Joseph's own conviction that he was doing the right thing.

Mr. Joiner wanted to make a contribution to their trip, so he had a sturdy covered wagon, constructed by the plantation carpenters. Joseph and his family would use it when they reached their destination, to explore the surrounding area.

Joseph had heard some exciting things about Arkansas, which was considered one of the frontier states. He was anxious to check out the area for himself. The wagon would enable them to travel throughout the land and continue Joseph's important research. It was to be transported to their future home by train.

Joseph called the family together in the parlor for an important discussion. Joseph was aware that everyone had become quite fond of Thomasville in the past year. It had been a peaceful refuge for all of them after the storms of life they had gone through. Each person would have to decide for his or herself whether to stay at Dogwood Plantation, return to their homes in Savannah, or continue on the long journey to an unknown future.

Ben, to enable her to participate in the discussion, wheeled Sheba's chair into the circle. Sheba held the sleepy Anna on her lap, cuddling her in her arms and smoothing her dark straight hair back from her face with gentle strokes of her hand.

When Joseph informed them of his plans, Sheba grew pale with apprehension. She dreaded the thought that this exodus might mean she would be sent home. She was dismayed by the prospect of being separated from her circle of friends. They were dearer to her than anyone else in the world. She would be sad to never be able to see Mama Ruth again, or her beautiful Savannah, but it would be much worse not to be able to continue the journey and watch Anna grow from year to year and, be with the others. Her hands began to tremble and she hid them in the folds of her wide skirt.

The discussion continued with many questions being asked. Everyone agreed that whatever lay ahead, they all wanted to be included.

"Hannah, I am aware that you have been offered free schooling in Pennsylvania, if you accompany the Joiners when they return home. That is a wonderful opportunity for you and I know you will have to think carefully about your decision. As much as I want you to continue on with us, I want you to make the decision that will be best for you."

It was obvious it was hard for Joseph to get the words out. He had become fond of this young woman who had joined them after the train wreck; she seemed so good for Anna. Her intelligence was obvious and he knew she would make a wonderful teacher. There was no way he could duplicate the offer the Joiners had made to her. Her hunger for education was apparent in the way she almost devoured his books and the vast library the Joiners had made available to them. She also asked intelligent questions when she did not fully understand something she read.

"Yes, it would be wonderful to go to college and become a real teacher, but I don't have to think about my decision. I want to go with you and Anna and whoever else decides to go on this journey. Someday I might want to go up north, but right now I am content to continue westward through the south.

"Besides, I am not at all sure I would make a very good Yankee." She teased as she grinned up at Joseph. "I can be ready to go whenever you are ready." Smiling she sat up straighter in her chair, her determination to continue the journey obvious by her demeanor.

"Well," Joseph said, laughing at her exuberance. "You should go home first and discuss it with your family. They only agreed to let you come as far as Thomasville. I have already talked with Ben and he will be going back to Savannah to speak with his father, before continuing on with us. He can see you to Waycross. I will wire your father to meet you there. You will have a return ticket, so all your father will have to do is put you back on the train for Thomasville."

"I do not have any living family, except you'll right in this room," Bernice declared. "I will stay here and see to the packing and help with Sheba and Anna while they are saying their goodbyes."

"There is a train going straight to Atlanta from Savannah. I can meet all of you there after I have taken care of things in Savannah." Ben could not contain his excitement as the discussion continued.

When all the plans were completed, they realized Sheba had not said anything. Joseph glanced around the room at his companions and caught the apprehension in Sheba's expression.

"Sheba. Don't be alarmed. Ben can take you back to Savannah with him." Joseph completely misunderstood her anguish. "No one is going to make you go on the long trip."

"Oh no, Doctor Joseph, please don't send me back. I can pull my weight, honest I can. I won't be any trouble." Tears were streaming down her face. "I'm learning to walk, aren't I Ben." She turned her tear-streaked face to Ben and reached for his hand. "Tell them. I can do it." She almost dropped Anna when Ben took a step away from her. She flung her trembling hands to her face and burst out in anguished sobs.

Hannah rescued the sleeping child and carried her to bed, while Bernice moved quickly to Sheba's side to comfort her.

"It will be all right Sheba." Bernice squatted in front of Sheba's chair and soothed her in a gentle voice. "Don't upset yourself. It will be all right." She looked questioningly at Ben who had backed up toward the wall in obvious retreat.

"I… I have been helping Sheba try to walk. Her legs really are getting stronger. She has been practicing at night with me holding her up. We didn't hurt anything. She just wants to walk so much. I did not think it would hurt anything to help her."

"I am sure that Sheba wasn't hurt and probably was helped by your assistance, Ben. Right now, would you go to the kitchen and ask Esther to heat some milk. Wait for it and bring it back, if you would." Joseph retrieved some medicine from his bag and insisted that Sheba shallow the bitter potion, while Bernice cradled Sheba's head in her hands and crooned to her softly.

When Ben returned with the milk, Bernice held the cup to the girl's trembling lips. She encouraged her to sip the soothing liquid.

"Sheba, you are one of our family." Joseph sat on a chair opposite Sheba; close enough to gently hold her hand. "No one is sending you away. I told you after the accident," he reminded her. "You will always have a home with us." Tenderly, he cupped her chin in his large hand.

Tears continued to stream down her face and hiccup's jerked her body, but the hysteria had passed.

"I thought you might be frightened about the prospect of the long trip. That's why I suggested you could return to Savannah with Ben. If you want to come with us, there will certainly be a place for you. I have no intention of sending you away. Actually I am relieved that you want to continue on this journey. Another pair of hands is always welcomed."

"Hannah, if Anna is asleep, would you mind helping to get Sheba into bed? It would be good if you could stay with her for awhile, if you don't mind."

Bernice and Hannah assisted Sheba into her nightgown and then helped her into bed. Hannah retrieved the Bible from the parlor and settled into a chair beside the bed and began to read to her from the Psalms. "I will lift up mine eyes unto the hills, from whence cometh my help. My help cometh from the Lord, which made heaven and earth…" Her musical voice, combined with the praises and comforting words, enhanced the calming effect of the medicine and warm milk. Sheba was soon peacefully asleep.

Ben had slipped out to hunt up friends he would soon be bidding goodbye, probably for ever. Joseph and Bernice stayed in the parlor to discuss what had just taken place and been revealed.

"Did you know about Ben and Sheba working on her walking?"

"No, but I did hear someone a time or two, or thought I had anyway. Her leg muscles do seem to be getting a little more tone to them, so I am sure whatever they did has helped and not hurt her progress—although I doubt if she can actually walk." Bernice studied her hands thoughtfully as she considered her words. "It is hard to imagine Ben playing nursemaid, though."

"Yes, I wondered about that myself. She has done remarkably well for her fragile condition. I do wonder if there is not more happening then we are aware of. We probably need to keep a closer eye on the situation. I love Ben, but of all of his many good attributes, I never counted excessive compassion among them.

Chapter Twelve

Roses bloomed in abundance throughout Thomasville, filling the air with their fragrant aroma. The City of Roses was aglow with the beautiful blossoms. It was the middle of May 1888.

Hannah returned from her parent's home, but she did not come alone. Daniel, her fifteen-year-old brother, had pleaded to be allowed to join the adventurers. Hollis and Caroline Brown were reluctant to allow either of their children to go so far away, but ultimately the two young people prevailed. The Browns had decided that if Hannah was determined to accompany the doctor and his family, it would be better to have Daniel along to watch out for her. Seven children remained at home to feed, cloth and help with the farm work.

After much discussion and prayer, they decided this was too good of an opportunity for their older children and they should not prohibit them from accepting. It would be a once in a lifetime chance for them to see more of the country.

When it was time for Hannah's visit to end, the brother and sister packed up their worldly goods and left together. They parted from their family amid tears and hugs, but with their parents' blessing. Hannah was able to pay for Daniel's train ticket with some of the money Joseph had paid her each month for taking care of Anna. Daniel promised to reimburse her, as soon as he found employment.

Joseph was surprised, but pleased to have Daniel join them. He had met the young man briefly while taking care of patients in their home and had found him to be a hard and willing worker. He was especially gratified to learn that Daniel was experienced at working with horses. Daniel had followed behind a plow and hay wagon since he was five years old.

Concerned about his own ability to choose good riding horses and the mules that would be needed to pull the wagon—when they reached Arkansas and were ready to begin exploring the area, Joseph was delighted he would be able to delegate that task to Daniel.

Joseph and Bernice were sitting in the living room in deep discussion about the trip. They had many last minute arrangements to talk over. The living room of the cottage was nearly empty of their things.

"Well, Bernice!" Joseph deposited some coins in his leather pouch, as he spoke. "More money for the trip; that is the last of what furniture belongs to us. I loathed selling it, but it would be cumbersome having to transport it halfway across the country. The money will help with the cost of the trip expenses."

"If you were not so quick to give away your services there would be more coins in that bag," Bernice chided him gently.

"I'm always paid," he said with a sheepish grin. "I just sometimes receive goods or prayers in lieu of coin."

"And sometimes the "goods" amounts to a baby being named after you. If I were a wagering person, I would bet there were more Joseph's born in the last year and a half in Thomas County than in the past ten years." Bernice smiled and patted his arm. "You are a good man Joseph Warren."

"But you are forgetting the little girl named Bernice by her parents last month. As I recall you spent a couple days and nights looking after the mother and her other children, while the father was away on a logging expedition and little Bernice decided to make a premature arrival in joining her family."

"Yes! You're right. We frequently receive immortality for our services." She chuckled to herself as she thought about the beautiful baby girl, who had fought with such tenacity and who was doing splendidly. "What more could anyone want?"

Bernice fished for a card in her pocket. "Not to change the subject, but I picked this advertisement up at the apothecary. I thought you might be interested." Bernice handed the card to Joseph and smiled as she watched him read it.

"Amputation of hip $1.00, thigh $ .50, common labor costs $ .50, placenta only $ .12. Coloreds half price." Joseph read out loud. "Well there we are. That is my problem. I don't advertise."

"I do not know what you would do with more patients," Bernice laughed as she moved about the room tiding things, as best she could anyway with crates stacked around and most of the furniture gone. "During the winters the Yankees kept us both hopping, not to mention all the ailments, cuts and broken limbs of the plantation folk year round, of course you have never charged them at all."

"Now wait a minute. You are forgetting those fine chickens and the slab of bacon we were given after I sewed up Brother Jacob. That was mighty good eating and besides I never aspired to be a rich man."

His jovial mood changed, as he glanced around the room at the empty spaces where the furniture he had brought with them from Savannah had sat the week before. He had not brought much with him, but Beth and he had picked out each piece together. It had been hard to part with this part of his past.

"I do regret having to sell the furniture," he said pensively. His gaze rested on his magnificent secretary. He had set it aside to go with them. A gift from his beloved Beth on their first anniversary, he just could not bear to part with it. "Well I did not get rid of everything."

"No! And I thank you for agreeing to take the rocking chair and Anna's small chair and desk that the plantation carpenters made for her. One day these things will be very precious to Anna. And perhaps one day she will have siblings who will also enjoy them." Joseph stared straight ahead and totally ignored her last statement.

The cheerful two year old was well loved by the plantation staff. Her large hazel eyes, framed by long dark eyelashes and her inquisitive nature, endeared her to the hearts of all who came in contact with her. She was well loved and protected on the plantation, much as she had been at Three Oaks.

Someone was always presenting her with a handmade toy or dress. Joseph hoped and prayed that he was not making a mistake by moving his diverse family group away from this place they had grown to love.

Hannah had returned with a couple of surprises. In addition to Daniel, she appeared with a large, ornately carved Marriage Bed. It was a bulky piece of furniture about two feet by five feet—when folded into a piece of standing furniture.

"I'm sorry Doctor Joseph," Hannah apologized on the verge of tears. "I did not mean to burden you with another large parcel of furniture. I know you are trying to reduce our paraphernalia to the bare essentials, but my parents insisted that I take the bed.

"Mama brought it to her home as a young bride," she explained. "It was a wedding gift from her parents. She always meant to buy one for me when I married and she's been setting coins aside for years. But with me leaving and moving so far away, she said she knew that she had little chance of being with me when I marry. She wanted me to have something of my own when that time comes; something that would remind me of home, so I would know their thoughts were with me, even if they couldn't be there themselves."

Joseph's eyes grew large as he stared at the compact bed. "You, you took their bed? What are they using?" It was all he could think to say as he stared at the huge piece perplexed by this added item he would be responsible for freighting and storing.

"It is a lovely piece." Bernice walked around the large, very heavy, contrivance.

"Daddy said he would build mama a bed. I know it is an imposition." Tears began to slide out of the corner of her eyes and trickle down her cheeks. "I tried to talk mama out of it. I told her there probably would not be room for it and that you were trying to get rid of everything we did not absolutely have to have before we left Thomasville."

Joseph silently stroked his chin as he stared in consternation at the newest addition to their 'essential' household furnishings.

"Sir," Daniel interrupted Joseph's reverie. "I realize this adds to your burden, but it really meant a lot to my folks to be able to do this for Hannah, especially mama. It was most painful for them to let Hannah go off so far. My mother's been making plans for Hannah's wedding for years. She has been sewing linens and putting money aside. Her being the oldest of all of us and having to care for all the little ones and having extra responsibilities about the house and garden, well sir, they just couldn't send her off empty handed."

"You are absolutely right, Daniel. It will be a stately addition to the household." Having settled that situation, Joseph headed for the door.

"Daniel, I am going out to check on the wagon. Would you like to accompany me?"

"Yes sir!" The grin on Daniel's face made it plain that he was happy the issue was settled amicably. He did not know what they would have done if the doctor had refused to be burdened with the bed in addition to him going along. He winked at his sister, as if to say—I told you it would be all right. Daniel followed Joseph from the room whistling cheerfully as he went.

When Bernice and Hannah were alone, Hannah pulled the bed open to reveal a treasure of linens inside.

"Mama packed quilts and her hand sewn muslins in here for me." The pride she felt in this gift was evident in her tone and the glow on her face. "See the borders?" The borders of the muslin sheets and pillowcases were embroidered with dainty pink and lavender flowers intertwined with delicate olive green leaves.

"This represents a real labor of love. Mama has been working on these ever since I was real young. She had to do her sewing by lantern at night after all the chores were finished and the little ones were tucked in bed.

"She made things for all of us girls of course, but there is only the one marriage bed. I hated to add more to Doctor Joseph's problems, but I just could not refuse to accept these lovely things. It meant so much to them. It was hard for them to let Daniel and me leave. But they have never really been anywhere and did not want to prevent us from having this adventure."

"Of course you could not refuse their gifts. Joseph understands that and we will mange just fine. I imagine they are out there right now deciding how best to carry it with us."

"This was my folk's bed. I didn't want them to be without. I tried to make her promise to use the set-aside money to buy them a bed, but daddy insisted he had wanted to make them one for a while now. You know, I have never really owned anything of my own before. All of us kids just always shared everything. It really is grand, isn't it?" Her eyes sparkled as she gazed at the treasure, as if she really did not believe it was actually hers.

"Yes! It really is grand." Bernice smiled at the girl, who had transformed into a lovely young woman since she had joined them.

"Bernice, do you really think I will meet someone who will want to marry me someday?"

"I am sure you will and when you do, you will have this wonderful piece of furniture and the lovely linens made with your mama's own hands, as a dowry to bring to the marriage. Even though she isn't with you in the flesh, you will be reminded that her thoughts and prayers are there every minute."

"It is really mine and Doctor Joseph is going to let me keep it!" Hannah did a little dance around the bed in her enthusiasm. "And Bernice, someday I will share it with my husband." The thought brought a rush of color to her cheeks and set her mind awhirl with mental images of what her future mate might look like, would he be tall like Ben or medium height like Doctor Joseph. He might be a large muscular man or slender and wiry. Dreams flitted through her head, as different visions of sizes, shapes, hair colors and dispositions came to mind. "I know one thing, Bernice. The man I marry will be a good Christian and loving father to our children." This was said with a resoluteness that left no room for compromise.

Their speculation was interrupted by sounds, which heralded Anna and Sheba waking from their naps. Hannah had another appreciative audience to show all the wondrous gifts she had brought from her mother.

Anna enjoyed climbing over the bed, while the women examined each item Caroline had so lovingly packed for her daughter. It was like having a bridal shower, for the girl entering womanhood, now all she needed was the groom.

Chapter Thirteen

They were finally ready to board the East Tennessee, Virginia and Georgia train for the trip to Atlanta. This time they would ride in a Pullman car and would be able to sleep in a Pullman berth—a bed of sorts for each of them. This was more than even the private cars they had ridden in previously had boasted. During the day they would have seats to enjoy the scenery flying past, but as night approached their seats would be converted to berths.

Hannah carried two small plants with her, one a yellow rose bush and the other a camellia, plants from Thomasville that they would replant in Arkansas once they were settled.

"There is even a dining car," Hannah pointed out excitedly. "Daniel did you ever think in your wildest dreams we would be traveling around in such luxurious accommodations?"

"It is terrific all right and I am sure proud we are going to get to eat." Daniel's number one thought from morning to night was with what was he going to fill his stomach. At fifteen it was hard to fill him up, no sooner would he finished one meal before he would be looking for something to snack on until the next meal.

"We are going to be on this train a day and a night, according to the schedule. That would sure be a long time to go without eating, or only subsisting on sandwiches from stops along the way."

"Yes! I am afraid it does stop at every little town between here and Atlanta." Joseph looked over the printed schedule he had been given when he bought the tickets. "Of course it beats going by horse back. You have to expect some inconveniences to go along with these modern contrivances."

"The stops will just allow us to see more of our beautiful state." It was Bernice's habit to look for the good in any situation. She considered each a blessing from God.

At mealtime they made their way through the train to the dinning car. Sheba's chair had been placed in the baggage car, so Daniel carried the slight young woman in his strong arms.

Many curious passengers followed their progress through the train. The procession was led by a distinguished looking gentleman, followed by an attractive young woman carrying a small child, who gaily called out greetings and waved to the other passengers. Next was a stately middle-aged matron, who carried herself as the refined southern lady, she was. A husky farm lad carrying a strikingly attractive woman of color followed her. It was quite a spectacle indeed and kept the passengers engrossed. They speculated among themselves on the origin and possible destination of such a group.

The family was not unmindful of the stir they caused, but simply smiled politely as they proceeded to their seats.

* * *

"Look at this menu! Have you ever heard of such food?" Daniel was awed by the elegance surrounding him. White linen cloths covered the tables and large white linen napkins lay in napkin rings beside each plate. The silverware was of the finest quality and matching silver salt and pepper canisters adorned each table.

"Roast duck, Parisian potatoes." Hannah read from the menu. "Sounds wonderful, doesn't it?"

"Yes, it does appear to be posh cuisine all right." Bernice smiled affectionately at the Brown's enthusiasm.

Joseph ordered for them and they ate with relish each new dish that was placed before them. They spent the better part of an hour consuming the various delights and speculating about what new adventures awaited them in Atlanta.

When they returned to their seats, they were delighted to discover water closets were available for the travelers at the end of each car. They would not need to disembark and share the community necessary houses behind the depots during the various stops. The travelers felt they truly had all the comforts of home and were riding in the lap of luxury, even if they were not in a private car this time.

Their train did indeed stop at every small town they passed, prolonging the trip, but they were quite comfortable and enjoyed the freedom of moving around as they wished. When the train stopped, they were able to step out on the platform for a few minutes and get some welcomed fresh air, albeit hot and muggy. The twenty-four hours spent on the train passed quickly. There were new towns to see and beautiful forests and farmlands to admire. The train twined its way north through Albany, Americus, Fort Valley, and Macon before turning northeast toward Atlanta.

When they finally arrived in the State Capital, they were surprised by the size of the city. The exploding population had nearly reached sixty-five thousand and even Sheba was impressed by the burgeoning city. The city fathers had rebuilt what had been destroyed during the war and Atlanta was sprouting new growth at an escalated pace.

"Look!" Hannah called excitedly, pointing to the clock on top of the temporary capitol. It's three o'clock. Imagine having a clock on top of a building to give us the time. What will they think of next?"

The train continued its slow progress to the center of town. The giant smoke stack looked like the bowl of a pipe, with the deep gray smoke belching up from the round black cavity. The fireman stood ready to throw more wood in the firebox, if the train should begin to lose its momentum.

"Oh, Joseph!" Hannah was almost jumping up and down in her excitement and did not even realize that she had just used his Christian name, instead of addressing him as Doctor Joseph. "How long will we be here?" Her eyes sparkled with delight and her face shown with the anticipation of exploring the large city.

"We'll be here a while." He smiled at Hannah's exuberance. He did not want to commit himself to a timetable, but he suddenly realized that he wanted very much to encourage Hannah's enthusiasm. He enjoyed seeing her happy; she worked hard everyday and never complained. Anna loved her and was growing physically, spiritually and more knowledgeable under her tutelage. They were lucky to have her. He did not know what they would have done if her parents had refused to allow her to accompany them.

It suddenly occurred to Joseph that he had not noticed before that Hannah had grown into a young lady while she had been with them. Her innocence and joy lifted his spirits more than anything had in a long time. He continued to study her radiant face, glowing with excitement, as she hugged Anna and pointed out many of the sights to his daughter. It was quite evident that this was all a great adventure for her, one of which she was enjoying every minute.

Hannah still wore her long blond hair straight and hanging loose down her back, which made her appear younger than she actually was. Joseph mused that her hair looked like spun gold when the sunlight caught the strands as she turned her head back and forth, in her eagerness to see everything. It reminded him of Beth's lustrous hair.

He grew pensive as he remembered how much he had loved to watch as Sheba brushed the long dark tresses for her each night, before he and Beth retired. Thinking about his loss brought a lump to his throat and tears to his eyes. The joy of a moment ago forgotten in his sudden grief. Abruptly he returned to the present when he realized Hannah was calling his name.

Hannah was regarding him curiously, concerned about the sad and preoccupied look on his somber face. She had not missed the glimmer of tears in his eyes. "Doctor Joseph! Is everything all right? The other passengers are disembarking and Daniel has gone to fetch Sheba's chair. I believe I glimpsed Mr. Ben waiting for us on the platform." She gestured out the window, where a moment ago she thought she had caught a glimpse of Ben, but when she turned back around she could no longer see him.

"Yes!" Joseph tried to put some enthusiasm back into his voice. "Here we are at last! The first stop on our journey to Arkansas." He took Anna from Hannah and hoisted her to the ceiling of the passenger car, causing her to squeal with delight. Feeling some of the heaviness lift from his heart, Joseph smiled at his daughter's enthusiasm. "I pray God will continue to bless this journey of ours."

Ben and Daniel joined the women to assist them through the crowds that lined the train platform. Daniel lifted Sheba effortlessly in his strong arms and carried her to her chair, which he had left sitting on the platform. Ben assisted Hannah and Bernice as they gathered the items they had kept with them on the train.

Joseph had already departed in order to make arrangements for collecting the trunks they would need while in Atlanta. He had arranged before they boarded the train to have the furniture, wagon and the rest of the trunks sent on to Memphis. It would be waiting for them in storage when they arrived in that city, which resided on the banks of the great Mississippi River.

Ben escorted Hannah and Bernice to the waiting carriages. He had already obtained their accommodations at the luxurious Aragon Hotel.

There were several horse drawn carriages secured to the hitching posts along the sidewalk. The horses waited impatiently in the dusty street, stomping restless hoofs and swishing flies off their broad backs with long graceful tails.

"I can hardly wait to get to the hotel and unpack, so we can begin our sightseeing." Hannah was so excited she could barely sit still when she climbed into the carriage with Ben's assistance.

"Me too!" her brother echoed as he picked Sheba up out of her chair and handed her up to Ben. Daniel and the coachman tied the chair to the back of the coach and then Daniel joined the coachman on the tall seat in the front. He was sure he would be able to see more from that advantage point and the driver had assured him it would be all right for him to ride beside him.

"It sounds good to me." Sheba laughed, as she was settled in beside Hannah. "I think a little rest on an actual bed, might not be amiss first though." In spite of her laughter, her eyes had the dullness of someone who was very tired or in pain and both were true for Sheba. The trip had been exciting, but she was in dire need of rest and was thankful they would spend some time in Atlanta before continuing their journey.

"You must be tired dear after that trip." Bernice studied Sheba's wan countenance, as she settled across from her. She took in the girl's dark eyes and noted that they had lost their sparkle during the long trip. The trip had been difficult and exhausting for her, but she had never once complained. "We all need to relax a little before we begin exploring.

"I not s'eepy," Anna insisted, as she snuggled her head onto her father's shoulder.

"If you don't get a nap pretty soon Savannah, we will have to prop your eyes open." Ben grinned down at his niece and coaxed a smile from her. He took her from her father and passed her up to Hannah, before hopping nimbly to the ground. Ben instructed the coachman where to take them and then joined Joseph in the other carriage.

Everyone laughed in happy companionship. The coachmen lifted the reins and made a barely audible sound to signal the horses. The team immediately pulled into a trot with puffs of dust scattered behind them. The carriages pulled away from Union Station. A new adventure had begun.

Chapter Fourteen

"Would you look at that building Hannah?" He turned around and pointed out the tall structure to his sister. "I didn't know they made buildings so tall. It looks like they might fall right over and squash everyone." The young man's frank astonishment brought smiles to the faces of his companions.

Hannah had also been surprised at the sight of the numerous three and four story buildings they passed as they entered the Capital. The seven story Centennial building was beyond her comprehension.

The brother and sister, reared on a cotton farm in South Georgia, had never before been in a city half the size of Atlanta. They marveled at each new delightful sight.

When they arrived at their destination, the happy group alighted from the carriages with great enthusiasm.

"Look at that! There are brick sidewalks just everywhere!" Hannah's zeal bubbled up and seemed to spill out over all of them. Inadvertently, she grabbed Joseph's sleeve in her excitement. The delight she felt caused her face to glow like a bright candle as she smiled up at him with elation. Hannah thanked him exuberantly for bringing them to this marvelous city.

Joseph enjoyed the intensity and zeal she expressed in her innocence with each new discovery. For a short time, the heaviness—always near and threatening to consume him—lightened a little, as he let Hannah's enthusiasm lift him out of the gloom he had sunk in after Beth died and could not seem to crawl out of, even though he knew God was in control.

* * *

The next couple weeks the adventurers spent hours each day exploring Atlanta. Daniel pushed Sheba's chair, while Anna walked between Hannah and Bernice. When she grew tired, she crawled into Sheba's arms or was hoisted onto Daniel's broad shoulders. Passers-by frequently stopped to stare at the strange procession; the young bronze skinned woman—in the unusual wheeled chair—being pushed by the muscular young man, who although he wore country clothes was quite ruggedly handsome, or one of the fair complected women. One of the women was an older lady with the carriage and dress of a southern lady and the other was a young pretty girl in her late teens, dressed in calico with the long gait of a country girl. Occasionally strangers approached the curious band and asked about Sheba's chair, or where they were from, they seemed so diverse a group, many took them for Yankees until they heard them speak.

"Ma'am," asked a curious six year old, his large brown eyes staring up inquisitively out of his dark brown complexion. "How did you get hurt?"

"Don't be pesky, Josiah," his sister admonished, tugging her brother away from the white folks, before he got them in trouble.

"It's all right," Sheba answered good-naturedly. "I was in a train wreck and my back was injured. These are my friends." And she introduced them.

"A train wreck, wow!" Josiah's eyes grew large, as he stared at Sheba in astonishment and awe. Hearing about the train wreck was even more surprising than the fact that the lady in the chair, although lighter complected than he was, introduced the white folks as her friends.

The young people took turns telling about the 'Great Earthquake' that had caused the train to derail. As they spoke of the events after the great train had been tossed over on its side and related stories about the many injured passengers, they collected a large audience of enthusiastic listeners.

Sheba became quite a celebrity in the capitol city as word spread about her adventure and subsequent injury when the train had derailed during the quake. Before long passersby began calling out greetings to them as they walked along, instead of just staring at them curiously. Children ran alongside Sheba's chair begging to be allowed the honor of pushing her along the board sidewalks.

Joseph spent his days conferring with doctors and apothecaries in Atlanta. One afternoon while visiting the hospital, he received an invitation to bring all of his family to Sunday dinner at the stately home of Dr. Dorian Ranch, after worship service on the following Sunday.

They were all excited about the visit to one of Atlanta's most beautiful homes, especially the women. After the service they walked up Whitehall Street dressed in their

Sunday best. As usual, Daniel pushed Sheba's chair, while Joseph carried Anna and Ben escorted Bernice and Hannah.

Dr. Ranch and his wife Lillian greeted them at the door. Ben and Daniel carried Sheba's chair up the stairs to the wide wrap-around porch. There was an awkward moment when Dr. Ranch suggested Sheba might be more comfortable eating in the kitchen with his servants. The group looked at one another stunned. Sheba was family. If she was not welcomed at their table, none of the rest of them would feel welcomed in this home.

The good doctor's wife saved the day. "But of course Sheba will eat with us in the dinning room. I have heard so much about her and I'm eager to hear from her own lips of the harrowing accident that put her in that unique chair. Do all come in and sit down. Dinner is ready. I will show the ladies around after dinner if you would like a tour of the house." Graciously she took Bernice's arm and swept the entire entourage into the dinning room.

After the meal, Sheba took one look at the curved staircase flowing gracefully up to the second floor and politely excused herself from the tour. "I'll just sit out on the porch with Anna and your children and take a bit of fresh air, if you don't mind. Your flowers are so lovely and the spring air will be most welcome."

The children entertained Sheba, who they had heard was quite the celebrity in Atlanta, encouraging her to tell them more about the train wreck and asking her pointed questions about her infirmity, as children are want to do.

Lillian Ranch proudly showed Hannah and Bernice through two floors of the large three-story structure, while the men retreated to the library. The top floor contained the nursery and servants quarters and was relegated to a brief mention. Daniel would have much rather toured with his sister, he had never been in such a fascinating private home, or even chatted with the children and Sheba on the porch, but one stern look from Ben and he joined the men folk.

* * *

On the way back to the hotel, Hannah entertained Sheba and Daniel with a running commentary of the spacious rooms and beautiful decorations throughout the house.

"There was the most beautiful arabesque ornamentation and rose tinted lace curtains in the sitting room upstairs," she said dreamily. "Of course I did not know what it was until Bernice told me. And there were silk screens painted with butterflies and birds in the brightest colors, sun yellow, brilliant blues and royal purple, sitting on meandering twisted branches. I have never seen anything so beautiful. Mrs. Ranch said they came all the way from the orient. Can you imagine?"

"It does sound wonderful," Sheba said a bit wistfully, as Hannah continued her description of the beautiful home.

Onc afternoon several days later, after the adventurers had returned to the hotel to rest, Hannah put Anna down for her nap with Sheba. Then she went to her room and removed her dress to make herself more comfortable on the sultry afternoon. She laid her dress over a chair to prevent further wrinkles and was about to lie across her bed in her petticoat for a short rest when she heard an unexpected knock on her door. Thinking that Bernice had forgotten to tell her something, or Sheba needed help with Anna, she jumped up and hurried to the door. Modestly she opened the door and peered around it, only to discover it was not Bernice summoning her.

"Oh! Dr. Joseph! I thought it was Bernice," she stammered. Her face blazed crimson, as she peered around the door.

"Sorry," he said backing up. "I have come at a bad time. I should not have disturbed you during your rest. You must be very tired from your excursion this morning. Please accept my apology for interrupting your rest. I—I was on my way to visit an apothecary and had thought you might wish to accompany me." He turned to leave.

"Again, my apologies for disturbing your rest," he spoke rapidly as he moved away from the door. "I am afraid I have caused you discomfort in addition to disturbing your rest, perhaps another time." His smile was replaced by his customary solemn expression and his shoulders drooped dejectedly as he turned away.

"No wait! Give me a few minutes to get dressed. I would love to go," she assured him. "I will meet you in the lobby," she called, as she disappeared behind the closed door without giving him time to protest.

Quickly slipping her dress back over her head, she splashed refreshing rose water on her neck and forehead. *That might not make up for a missed nap, but at least I feel a bit fresher.* She pulled her comb rapidly through her long hair and deftly twisted it into a knot at the back of her head, before clamping a pink straw hat on top. She would be cooler with her hair up and the hat would shade her face from the hot sun. Glancing in the small mirror over the washstand, she shrugged in dismay at the image that stared back at her. She was hopeless. Her nose was dotted with freckles, her eyes were too large and her nose turned up.

Hannah sought Joseph in the lobby, after informing Bernice she was going out for a walk and asking her to look in on Anna and Sheba.

"I really am sorry for disturbing you," Joseph proclaimed, as he took her arm and they strolled along the brick walk and crossed the dusty streets.

"Well I certainly am not," she assured him. "I'm pleased that you asked me to join you. This is a perfect way to spend a sunny afternoon and you really spend too much time alone." She was just echoing what the others had said many times.

"It is good to have your company." The smile was back on his face as he glanced down at his companion. "By the way, that is a very attractive hat you are wearing, but I wonder if this little fellow is really meant to flitter around on the flowers attached to it." As he was talking, he gingerly plucked a June bug out of the collection of flowers on the brim.

"Oh drat. Wouldn't you know, I'd wear a hat that would attract bugs?" She laughed gaily, obviously not in the least concerned about her hitchhiker.

He studied the hat for any more offending critters and decided he did not like her hat at all, because it covered her beautiful hair. He was surprised at how disappointed he felt, just because the silly hat hid her golden tresses.

"It was a gift from Bernice," she explained. "Everyone in Atlanta seems to wear a hat everywhere."

Joseph smiled at her a little wistfully. He perceived again that she really was not the child he had considered her to be, but had grown into quite a young lady over the past couple of years. *Was she eighteen or nineteen now?* She looked more mature with her hair pinned up and with the quaint straw hat perched on top of her head. For some reason, this was a consideration, which made him somewhat uneasy. *Others will be seeing her for the young woman she has become. Someone will be stealing her away from us,* the thought was disquieting.

They stopped at Jacob's pharmacy, located on the corner of Peachtree and Marietta streets. The rich dark beverage, created by John S. Pemberton was dispensed at the soda fountain in the charming apothecary.

"I want you to try Dr. Pemberton's special drink," Joseph said as he led her to one of the small, round, spindly-legged, white stools and assisted her up on it.

She had sampled many of the concoctions Doctor Joseph had made from his formulas. *He just asked me here to try another one of his medicines,* she thought with dismay. The disappointment she felt at this realization, surprised her somewhat. *You silly goose,* she chided herself. *Why else would he be seeking my company?* She did not even consider why that hurt so much.

Joseph bought one of the deep amber drinks for each of them. The drink was surprisingly refreshing. Hannah noticed she no longer felt as tired and her slight headache seemed to have disappeared.

"It's very nice," she replied politely to Joseph's inquiry. "As a matter of fact, it is very good." This was said with a little more spirit. "What is it called?"

"It is called, Coca-Cola. I am not sure what Dr. Pemberton named it after, maybe some of the ingredients. He won't tell what it contains, but maybe it has cocoa beans in it."

As they walked back to the hotel, Hannah felt quite refreshed, even though she had not rested as she usually did at mid-day. *I will have to bring the others here on one of our outings,* she considered. She made a mental note of the landmarks around Norcross corner, so it would be easier to find her way back to the apothecary again. It was not unusual for her to get lost, when left to her own devices.

Hannah was not invited to accompany Joseph on any more of his frequent exploration around Atlanta, but she visited many Atlanta establishments with her brother and friends.

One of the places they enjoyed going to was the construction site of the new State Capital building. They watched the engineers and masons diligently labor on the large building that was being constructed on Washington Street. Another of their favorite haunts was the Hart Brothers' Five and Ten Cent store on Whitehall Street. They spent hours looking at the many trinkets for sale in the store and chatting with the sales girls. The girls long white aprons, which covered their gray shop dresses, reminded Bernice of the uniform she had worn as a nurse during the war. Because of that, the place was a bit depressing for her.

Hannah, Bernice and Sheba enjoyed visiting the park with Anna. Daniel usually accompanied them and occasionally Ben joined them. It was especially entertaining for the women to observe the fashionably dressed young women who strolled through the park with their various escorts. Most wore elaborately adorned hats and almost appeared deformed, to the young people, with their tiny corseted waists and enormous bustles. Hannah and Daniel considered the style outrageously funny. They could not understand why anyone would want to cinch their waist so tight that breathing would be a struggle and then make their backside stick out so far that sitting was hazardous.

One strikingly lovely young maiden that they frequently encountered and had nicknamed Canary was quite often attired in a walking dress of bold bright yellow and black plaid. She always acknowledged their smiles and timid greetings, whenever they happened to meet. Several young well-dressed gentlemen usually flanked the young woman. Ben was frequently among her suitors, but appeared aloof and unaware of their presence when their paths crossed. Hannah and Daniel thought it humorous and teased him about being ashamed of his 'country cousins' over dinner after such an encounter, but Sheba became more withdrawn and melancholy.

One afternoon when they noticed Canary across the street, Daniel inquired of Sheba, the group's style expert, what the young lady was wearing on her head.

"It's a panache and those are ostrich tips and wings covering it." Having been raised in the Earl home and watching the myriad of fashionable young ladies who visited Beth, Sheba had been introduced at an early age to the world of fashion.

Hannah and Sheba especially enjoyed the opportunity to observe the latest fashions; even if most of the time they did consider them ridiculous. Some of the ladies they encountered appeared to step right out of the pages of Harper's Bazaar.

Sporting costumes they observed on country excursions or on the tennis court were less elaborate, but none the less cumbersome. Most of them were heavy, hot and uncomfortable; the most athletic young female was apt to swoon during a lively game of tennis or even a game of spirited croquet.

After observing Canary faint during a vigorous game of tennis with Ben, Hannah vowed she would never wear such restrictive clothes. "I am glad I am a country bumpkin if being a fashionable city girl means layers of trappings, your waist squeezed tight enough to strangle a body, plus putting up with all that baggage behind. I would sure like to see one of them plow in such foolishness.”

Her companions laughed at her unaccustomed vehemence and teased her about becoming a grand lady of fashion.

“I can see her now,” declared Daniel. “A devotee of Harper’s Bazaar, well corseted and bedecked with a bustle extending two feet out behind. Her entourage of suitors followed her everywhere and seemed to bow to her every wish.”

They all laughed, including the butt of the joke, Hannah.

One beautiful Saturday afternoon, Ben, in an expansive mood, organized an outing to Vinnings. Located in a beautiful wooded area about eleven miles from Atlanta, Vinnings was an immensely popular recreation area with Atlanta’s elite society. The trees and surrounding foliage were a lush cool green and provided a refreshing shaded respite from the hot sun.

The group picnicked in the shade, atop the flat surface of a large boulder. It was a wonderful carefree day of laughter and relaxation for all of them. Sheba and Anna napped on a quilt while the others walked along the trails, picked berries and sang cheerful songs throughout the afternoon.

They all agreed it was one of their favorite spots, until upon returning to the hotel they found themselves itching unmercifully from tiny red bugs that had burrowed beneath their skin, especially around their waists.

Joseph had acquired a new salve that was made in Atlanta. It was a yellow lubricant reputedly made of wool fat and bee’s wax. The apothecary claimed it would heal any sore on man or beast. Joseph gave them each a can of it to daub liberally on their bites.

Although the salve did seem to ease their distress, they decided one trip to Vinnings was quite enough for a lifetime.

The country raised Browns were introduced to many exciting adventures in the big city. They were naturally drawn to anything concerning horses, for both of them were placed on horses at a young age and learned to love the large animals. The Atlanta police, who patrolled on their exquisite mounts, were dignified but friendly. They wore pith helmets and white gloves and were quite dashing on their high-spirited horses. Another group of horsemen the group frequently encountered were the Governor's Horse Guard.

Occasionally they were spectators to the breath-taking spectacle of the speedy dash of the Atlanta Fire Department through the city streets. The horse drawn hook and ladder vehicle, one of the four steamers, or two-horse reels would race down the streets frantically warning everyone out of their way with the loud fire bell clanging. Pedestrians rushed to the sidewalks whenever they heard the fire bell. Spectators watched as the wagons rushed past, horses galloping and firemen clinging precariously to the sides and backs of the fire wagons.

It was an exciting time of progress and new inventions in America and the capital city enjoyed the fruits of these new discoveries. The small group of adventurers was caught up in the excitement of the time. They had mixed emotions when Joseph announced one Friday evening in late June that it was time to continue their journey. Although they looked forward to even more adventures, they felt a certain amount of loss over leaving Georgia behind. Every one of them had been born and raised in Georgia and there was a sense of loss associated with leaving the state of their birth.

"We will be leaving Monday morning. As a farewell treat, I have arranged an excursion to Grant Park after the church service tomorrow. We can go boating in Lake Aban. We will take a picnic lunch and make a day of it. How does that sound?" He smiled at them, as they cheered their approval.

Hannah and Daniel hugged each other and danced around the room in their exuberance. Daniel grabbed Anna up and swung her in a big circle, as she squealed her delight at being included in their high jinks. Ben laughed uproariously, partially at the young people, but mostly from the joy he felt at the prospect of their journey resuming. Sheba smiled and clapped her hands in delight. They all agreed they had enjoyed Atlanta immensely, but they were ready to continue their adventure.

Chapter Fifteen

In late June 1888 the adventurers boarded the Savannah and Western train for the trip to Birmingham, Alabama. The trip would take them nearly one hundred and fifty miles along winding tracks through the sparsely populated area of west Georgia. The train made brief stops at Lithia Springs, Douglasville, Temple and Waco before entering the Tallapoosa River Valley. Eventually they began the ascent leading to the Piedmont Plateau Watershed with its high rolling emerald green hills, speckled with a carpet of wildflowers in various colors and hues.

"Look at the mountain." Hannah was enthralled with the splendor before her. Having lived all her life in the flat sandy coastal area of southern Georgia, the mountains they were entering held her spellbound.

"These are the foothills of the Appalachian Mountains," Joseph explained, as he enjoyed watching her enthusiasm in the discovery of new sights. *This must be how the first explorers felt as they crossed this land and came upon each change in topography and spotted new animal species,* he considered as he watched Hannah's excitement.

It is a pity we can't all keep such an innocence of discovery, as we go through life.

"It is lovely," Bernice agreed, almost reverently as she gazed through the train window at the passing scenery. "I believe this is some of the most beautiful scenery we have seen. But then, I have always been partial to mountains."

Sheba had been propped up so she could look out the window and enjoy the view with her companions. "Just look at the colors. The red clay and the trees in all their different coats of green that cover the mountainside are really beautiful. Oh, I wish I could paint it!"

"There are sure a lot of different species of trees." Daniel leaned over his sister's shoulder to get a better view of the passing scenery. "I see pine, oak, beach, yellow poplar and those real tall ones are hickory nut."

The trees were thick and lush with their summer growth. Mountain laurel with its beautiful pink blossoms bloomed near the many shimmering streams that wound throughout the hills alongside the tracks. Honeysuckle seemed to be blooming everywhere, spreading its rich sweet fragrance over the picturesque scene. It wafted through the open windows and tantalized the travelers with its delightful aroma.

Joseph sat back and quietly enjoyed his companions' enthusiasm. He glanced at his daughter sleeping peacefully in Hannah's arms. Hannah tenderly stroked Anna's hair and occasionally bent her head to kiss the sleeping child, as she continued to stare in fascination at the passing scenery.

They look like they belong together, Joseph mused as he watched them inconspicuously. *We all belong together.* He looked at each of his companions and felt immense satisfaction and a rekindled peace that was beginning to settle over him on this journey with this diverse group of people. Each of them had become quite close to him during this journey. They had become his family, as sure as if they were genetically linked. God had closed a door in Savannah, but seemed to be opening up a new door for him now, if he only had the courage to walk through it. *We belong together. We are a family.*

"This has turned into a marvelous adventure, hasn't it?" His eyes shown with delight as he looked to the others.

There was a chorus of agreement from his companions.

As they crossed the Alabama line, they passed a small town. A profusion of vines intertwined in the brush adjacent to the tracks.

"Look at those muscadines!" Daniel gazed excitedly out the window. "Imagine the jelly just waiting to be cooked up, that's hiding under those broad green leaves."

"Just like you to be thinking of your sweet tooth, instead of enjoying the scenery." His sister teased. Anna had awakened and Hannah was busy taking care of her needs.

"I am looking at the scenery. That's how I saw the muscadines." His expression revealed that he thought he was being unnecessarily criticized because he enjoyed eating.

"Did you see that deer!" Ben shouted as a white tailed deer bounded for cover in the thicket. "I had heard Alabama had a lot of game, but I am surprised to see them so close to the train. Will we be stopping over?" This was addressed to his brother-in-law with an almost pleading wistfulness to the question.

"I don't think so Ben, but I am sure there is a lot of game in Arkansas." Joseph smiled at Ben's enthusiasm. "You will get plenty of hunting when we get there. I'll expect meat on the table every night," Joseph teased him. Ben had been fairly quite on most of the journey, preferring to act the sophisticated southern gentleman rather than join into the enthusiastic discourse of his companions. Joseph knew it must be hard for Ben to temper his youthful enthusiasm, as they saw land they had never visited before.

Edwardsville was the first stop in Alabama, only one passenger joined those heading west and no one disembarked.

"Oh my, look up there at all those deserted houses and buildings." Bernice motioned toward a cluster of buildings on a rise above the tracks. "They look like they are in really bad shape."

"I would say they are on the verge of collapse," agreed Ben, as he glanced at the buildings. "They appear to be long neglected. I doubt if anyone has lived in them for quite some time."

Their conversation stilled as the new passenger entered the coach. He paused beside the brass cuspidor that sat beside the door and spit some vile looking stuff into it before making his way slowly along the aisle.

He was a small-wizened man, bent with age. His hair was unkempt and appeared to be a dirty ashen gray. As he drew closer they could see that his mouth was stained a muddy yellowish brown color. He shuffled past Joseph and his entourage and Daniel and Hannah could not help staring in fascination, their good manners temporarily forgotten. They were mesmerized by the appearance of the gnome-like man.

* * *

As night began to fall, the passengers settled down for the night while the train continued to maneuver along the winding tracks deeper into Alabama.

The next morning while they were eating breakfast, the strange little man who had gotten on in Edwardsville entered the crowded dining car. As he passed, many of the ladies pulled their traveling cloaks snugly around their shoulders, as though afraid of being soiled by his presence. Many of the passengers turned their backs toward the aisle as he passed, seemingly to discourage him from asking to share their tables.

Hannah nudged Daniel's foot with her boot. He glanced up questioningly, having missed the display behind him.

"Ask him to join us," she whispered.

"Who?" Daniel turned to glance over his shoulder and up the aisle behind him. He found himself staring into a pair of faded grayish-blue eyes, which immediately looked down at the floor. The old prospector, dirty, sweat-stained hat in hand, moved quickly to pass their table, rather than encounter another rebuff.

There was little room at their table, but Joseph and Ben were seated alone at the next table and had adequate room for another person to join them. Joseph overheard the exchange between the brother and sister and rising from his seat, motioned for the odd little man to take the seat beside his own.

The newcomer looked startled at the overture, but gratefully accepted. When his food was delivered, he ate heartily without comment, even though Joseph attempted to draw him into the conversation. Except for a few grunts to acknowledge Joseph's overtures, the man kept his head bent intently over his food. Upon finishing his meal, he wiped his mouth on his grungy shirtsleeve and turned to leave, but not before thanking Joseph for his hospitality.

"Do you have to go? I thought you might tell us something about the country we are passing through." Joseph paused a moment, before gesturing toward the window. "The scenery is so beautiful and we are interested in anything we can learn about the area." He smiled encouragingly at the newcomer.

"Sure and I ken tell ya the tales bout Bama aw right," he replied, winking conspiratorially. "I reckon I know more 'bout this country than any man alive."

"Wonderful! You are just the man we have been looking for to enlighten us on the area." Joseph settled back in this chair and tilted his head toward the man. "Were you born around here?"

"No, but I've been in these parts since the gold rush in the thirties. Edwardsville were really somethin' in those days." He got a dreamy look in his eyes, as he spoke in a heavy brogue.

Joseph nodded encouragement, as the newcomer began his tale.

"They were new saloons and gambling halls built ere week. People poured in to strike it rich and as many came to relieve them of their finds. Edwardsville were a reg'lar den of iniquity. Not like the sorry sight you saw yesterday."

"Sounds exciting all right," Ben intoned, as he became caught up with the old prospector's story.

"Let me introduce myself and my companions. I am Joseph Warren, doctor of medicine. This is my brother-in-law, Benjamin Earl." Overhearing the anxious whispers at the next table, Joseph turned to introduce the rest of his companions. Nodding toward each one, he introduced them to the prospector.

"Sure and aren't I as pleased as punch to meet each of ya, name's Donald O'Malley." He nodded to the ladies, before he resumed his travelogue. "I've got to say now, that you missed a most interestin' place while ya slept. We stopped at Anniston—'twere Annie's Town when twas first settled. 'Twere named for Miz Annie Scott Tyler and 'tis still a beauty of a place, as was Miz Annie herself. The rugged peaks of Choceolocco Ridge, Coldwater Mount'n and Blue Mount'n hedge it in on three sides. The sandstone cliffs jut from the side of the mount'n and ya never seen such thick forestland; 'tis a place of healthy lungs and cool breezes."

Joseph was intrigued by the newcomer's picturesque speech. He decided Donald O'Malley might prove to be a most interesting enigma to explore.

"Old Samuel Noble had Annie's Town laid out with wide streets and lots of parks, not like some minin' towns 'round here. The main roads have water oaks leanin' right over the streets, to shade passersby from the hot Baba sun. It's a boomin' minin' town. The place has grown by nearly ten thousand folks this ten y'ars past." Donald grew more animated as he sensed the interest in his audience, his voice rose and lowered for more dramatic effect and he gestured widely with his gnarled hands.

Joseph noticed that Ben was eagerly leaning forward; enthralled either with Donald or his stories and Daniel and Hannah had eagerly turned their chairs so they would not miss anything. Even Bernice sat with a smile on her face and appeared to be attentive to what the old man had to say.

"Now right now, we're goin' thru the Cross Valley. We're bout to cross the spurs of Beaver Creek Mount'ns and then we'll be getting' on to the hills at Birmin'ham; now that's an iner'estin' place to explore." He winked up at his audience and added enticingly, "If you've got the time of course."

"And what is so special about Birmingham to cause a delay in our journey," Joseph added with a smile, to encourage the old prospector to continue his stories.

Their newfound friend did not require much urging to continue sharing with them. Donald seemed to be as charmed with his audience as they were with him. "Why it's just the purdiest place on God's green earth, is all," Donald, declared vehemently. "That's of course if you can see it for the fog and smoke," he added with a twinkle in his eyes.

"A bit hazy, is it?" Joseph inquired with a smile. He was enjoying the old man's stories.

Hannah was allowing her curiosity to overrule her good manners. She leaned toward the other table eagerly in an effort to catch the fascinating newcomer's tales. Joseph was acutely aware of her head tilted toward them. He furtively contemplated Hannah's delicate profile and silky blond hair, while endeavoring to concentrate on Mr. O'Malley's stories.

"The fog is from being nestled in Jones Valley. When the fog mixes with the smoke from the stacks, the whole town stays kevered with the grayish-yellow haze, but when God clears it away with a gentle breeze and gives you a peak of the real Birmin'ham; 'tis truly a sight to delight any eye."

The tables were being cleared and theirs was the only party remaining in the dinning car, so Joseph decided he had better move his group back to the Pullman car. He encouraged Mr. O'Malley to join them and continue his recitation about Alabama. The old prospector regaled them with his stories until the conductor came to make up the berths. The time seemed to fly by for the travelers.

Chapter Sixteen

It was late afternoon when they entered the valley town. Mills dotted the area with their tall chimneystacks rising toward heaven and belching dark curling smoke from their furnaces. Haze from the furnaces covered the valley and reached up into the surrounding mountains. Gray factories were also abundant with their rows of windows smeared with soot, which prevented the inhabitants from seeing out and the sun from penetrating into the depths of the dark interior.

Birmingham appeared to be hemmed in by a tangled web of railroad tracks and mountains. The Savannah and Western pulled into the Birmingham station and the tired passengers gratefully disembarked.

Joseph carried a squirming Anna struggled in his arms to climb down--having had quite enough of being confined to a small space. He spent a few minutes in earnest conversation with Mr. O'Malley, all the while trying to sooth Anna and reassure her she could soon be able to run and play, prior to rejoining his traveling companions.

In the meantime, Ben escorted Bernice and Hannah through the train. He assisted them down the aisle and after they had stepped through the door, he held it open for Daniel, who carried Sheba. He preceded the ladies down the steps and then assisted each of them down before turning to help Daniel and Sheba. When they were settled on a bench inside the station, Daniel went to the baggage car to retrieve Sheba's chair. Ben paced up and down, anxious to join Joseph, but attentive to his responsibility to stay with the women until Daniel returned. They knew there would be a short layover in Birmingham and they were anxious to explore the city during whatever time they were given.

Joseph rejoined them, looking like the cat that had just caught an elusive mouse. "How would you like to spend a week here? Mr. O'Malley has agreed to act as your guide. He has assured me that he can introduce you to all the interesting sights in the area." Joseph watched their expressions change from weary travelers to the excitement of eager explorers.

"Wonderful!" Hannah's eyes were alight with excitement, "Another big city to explore."

"This is very nice Joseph." Bernice was a little more sedate in her excitement, but her smile indicated she was just as happy about the opportunity to explore Birmingham. "Won't we have to do something about the trunks? We will all need more clothes if we are to stop-over for a week."

"Yes, I will take care of that right now."   Daniel arrived with Sheba's chair and quickly scooped her off the bench and gently deposited her in the chair. "Daniel, if you and Mr. O'Malley will stay here with the ladies; Ben and I will go see about the trunks." He handed Anna over to Hannah after placing a gentle kiss on his daughter's round rosy cheek. She quickly held her arms up to go with her papa, but he waved and assured her he would be right back.

Anna had been cooped up long enough; she immediately tried to climb down from Hannah's lap.

"Been still long enough, have you?" Hannah laughed and standing, she took the small hand in hers. "Maybe Daniel will help us take a walk." They each took one of the child's small hands and walked around the station exploring each nook and cranny. After the long train ride, it felt good to walk around on a stationary floor and they each enjoyed the bit of exercise.

When the men returned with the porter and a cart piled high with their trunks, they were ready to be on their way. Sheba was quite pale and her face was drawn even though she attempted a weak smile. The first order of business would be to find rooms and get her into a bed for a good rest.

"The Morris hotel is close enough to walk to and is said to be quite comfortable," their guide assured them. "Just one thing, before I go, you must start calling me Donald. You will have me thinkin' I'm an old man if you keep calling me Mr. O'Malley." The twinkle in his eye belied the seriousness of his tone. He gave them directions to the hotel, which was actually very close and then upon agreeing to meet them after breakfast the next day in the hotel lobby he was off to take care of his own business.

On the way to the hotel, Bernice expressed concern about the wagon and furniture that had been sent on ahead to Memphis. At the mention of furniture, Hannah's attention also went to Joseph.

"Everything will be fine. I arranged for all of it to stay in storage until we arrive, so it will be waiting for us whenever we get there. I decided it would be a shame to pass through without giving you adventurers at least a chance to explore Birmingham. Sometimes we just get in so much of a hurry to get to our destination that we miss all the treasures on the way there. Our time is our own and we had best take advantage of as many opportunities that come our way. We may never come this way again."

None of them had ever been to a large industrial city before and the smoke stacks reaching skyward fascinated them as much as Atlanta's tall buildings had. They learned that Birmingham had been laid out in carefully planned squares, with the streets running north and south and the avenues east and west. This would make it easier for the newcomers to find their way around without getting lost.

Anna was delighted with being able to run again. The train ride had been very restrictive to the active two year old and as soon as she was able to free her hands, she took off down the boardwalk as fast as her short legs would take her. Daniel pushed Sheba's chair, while Hannah and Ben— setting all traces of dignity aside—unwound by running alongside Anna.

Bernice and Joseph followed at a more sedate pace. Although Joseph reflected, *a nice long run after the long confinement would feel pretty good.* While in Thomasville, he had picked up the habit of either walking or running along the plantation roads after a long day at the clinic. He found it helped him unwind and he seemed to sleep better after a long run. The happy explorers took pleasure in studying and discussing the architecture of the buildings they passed.

"Look at those enormous ornate columns and those exquisite spindled porch railings." Bernice was entranced with the lovely homes they passed. "And what a marvelous wraparound balcony, would you look at that beautiful curved stairway leading to that entryway."

"Yes, but I like that carved door with the beveled glass in it. It makes the entryway look special. A good home for a promising young doctor," he said laughing heartedly.

"Why doctor! You aren't planning on staying in Birmingham are you?"

"No, just enjoying imagining what sort of home we will have in Arkansas, when we finally settle down to one place. I am afraid we won't be able to travel around much longer without doing some additional harm to Sheba."

"She has been looking more peeked since we left Thomasville," agreed Bernice, a frown on her face. They both glanced toward the chair Sheba was riding in and noted the slump to her shoulders and droop to her head.

The party of adventurers meandered through the city away from the station. There was a pleasant breeze, but they were still hot and a little tired when they reached the hotel. But they all agreed that they had enjoyed the stroll after being cooped up on the train.

The following morning, Sheba felt indisposed and declined to join her companions. Hannah and Bernice each volunteered to keep her company, but Sheba entreated them to leave her to rest in bed. She promised to join them later that evening. After bringing her breakfast and making sure her water pitcher was filled, they reluctantly agreed to go without her. Joseph left instructions at the desk for someone to look in on her occasionally—while they were out. To assure she would be well cared for, he tipped the chambermaid to stop by and check on her every hour. He was concerned that she seemed to be losing ground; she no longer attempted to stand or walk even though each of them had tried to assist her. He did not know how he would explain to Ruth if anything else happened to her daughter.

Donald proposed a walking tour for the morning, with a stop at lunch for teacakes and ices. He had shown up bright and early wearing clean clothes and obviously having bathed, as he both looked and smelled better than he had on the train. They started out walking north on Nineteenth Street, pausing to admire each beautiful building along the way.

Anna was like a bird let out of a cage. She chattered a mile a minute and did not miss a thing. When a grasshopper caught her eye, she chased after it with Hannah and Daniel running along beside her. Passersby took notice of the three and smiled at their exuberance. No one appeared to take offense at their gaiety and high spirits, although more than one person commented they were envious of their energy.

They were in the city's most fashionable residential section when Donald called their attention to a three story, red brick, house, which faced Eighth Avenue.

"Isn't that romantic," Hannah commented dreamily. She gestured toward the exquisite second floor balcony that extended across the front, with its ornate columns and intricate scrollwork.

Joseph smiled at her fondly. He contemplated how she so easily swung from youthful companion to Anna to whimsical young lady. She was a precious jewel and he did not know quite what he would do if she was not around to brighten up each day.

Ben had begun to become a bit cantankerous for the past few days and when he brusquely excused himself to go off on his own, no one objected strenuously. They continued their stroll until they came to a sidewalk café. They were happy for the shady respite and the treat of blackberry ice and spiced teacakes that they enjoyed at the small white tables under the striped awning.

Hannah and Bernice were becoming uncomfortably warm in their layers of undergarments and long dresses. Even though they wore their clothes more loosely than what the current fashion called for, modesty dictated certain attire as being essential when out in public.

Hannah, with her country girl background, was accustomed to rolling her long sleeves up to her elbows in the summer, not having her arms covered to her wrists with the buttons buttoned all the way down. She could feel the perspiration rolling down her body under its tight confinement and unbuttoned the top couple buttons of her high-necked dress. That would at least allow a bit of the lovely breeze that wafted through the valley to help cool her heated skin.

They returned to the hotel to rest during the hot afternoon. Sheba was still not ready to get out of bed and Bernice brought her a plate of sandwiches and fruit along with a tall glass of chilled lemonade, before retiring to her own room to rest. The group planned to resume their exploration later, after it had cooled off a little and Anna had taken a much-needed nap.

When Bernice went to Sheba's room to assist her to dress for the afternoon, she still insisted that she was not up to joining them. She did submit to Bernice's urging and agreed to sit in her chair for a while. She had been in her bed since the evening before and that was quite unusual for the fun-loving Sheba.

"Sheba, you have barely touched your lunch," Bernice scolded. "I will leave it right here, where you can reach it easily." She arranged it on a table beside Sheba's chair. Bernice pulled the drapes back and opened the window a bit to allow the afternoon breeze to cool the room. Sheba's room was on the east side of the hotel, so the sun would not shine in and further heat the room.

"I'm not hungry right now. Maybe I will eat a bit later. I will sit here and read for a while and just watch out the window. You run along and have a good time and I will expect to hear about everything at supper." Sheba managed a small smile and picked up the book tucked into her chair.

Bernice smiled back, but as she turned to leave her face changed into a picture of concern.

When Ben rejoined his companions, he was in better spirits and ready to continue exploring Birmingham. Joseph made his apologies, stating he had writing he could not put off and would not be able to join them.

"Bernice would you mind accompanying me, I want to look in on Sheba." When they had moved away from the others toward the stairs that would take them up to Sheba's second floor room, he confided to Bernice. "Earlier, I checked with the chambermaid on how Sheba was while we were away. She informed me that Sheba had company the last time she went to check on her and the door was locked. I am afraid something is going on that we are going to have to get to the bottom of before the situation gets worse."

When they reached Sheba's room, Joseph knocked lightly on the door. "Come in," Sheba called and they quickly entered and glanced around. Joseph walked to her side and inquired about her indisposition.

"Oh! I am just tired from the trip. Nothing to worry about, you'll go on and enjoy yourself. I'll probably feel like joining you later on." Tell tale tears were pooling in her eyes and she did not look directly at her companions.

"Sheba, I am afraid your problem is more than just being tired." *How could I be so stupid?* He berated himself as the reason for her odd bouts of sickness and sudden weight gain dawned on him. Joseph confronted her about the tiny life growing within her body. The roundness of her middle would soon be so noticeable that they would not be able to keep the fact that Sheba was expecting a little one from the others much longer. Even sitting in her chair with her full dress draped carefully, her condition would soon be obvious. Anna had even complained that Sheba was, "in the way of her w'ap" on several occasions. Sheba turned away from Joseph and stared out the window sullenly.

"Sheba," he said gently. "No one is condemning you. If someone has hurt you, we need to know, so something can be done about it. We are also concerned about you going without food and spending so much time in bed. This is not good for you or the baby."

Bernice stood behind Sheba's chair with tears streaming down her cheeks. She felt she had failed her charge, by allowing someone to harm her.

"I am married good and proper Doctor Joseph. Don't you think I would be letting someone fool around without God's blessing. Brother Jeremiah married us in Thomasville."

"But who did you marry, Sheba?" The question fairly jumped from Bernice's lips. "Who is the father of your baby?"

Sheba continued to glance out the window with tears trickling unobstructed down her cheeks. She wore such a look of despair that Bernice had to turn away and busy herself straightening the room in order to hide her own tears.

"Sheba, we need to know so we can help you and if you don't eat your baby will suffer. I know you don't want to hurt your baby. You're one of our family. We love you and when you are hurting then we hurt also. There is no doubt that life has dealt you a hard blow, confined to this chair, but you are still one of the adventurers and we are all headed west to a new life." He looked down on her, smiling comfortingly as he took her hand into his and gently patted it. "If you were getting married, why didn't you tell us? We're your family; we would have wanted to be with you. Who did you marry? Why didn't you stay with your husband instead of traveling with us? I know this has been doubly hard for you with a baby on the way."

"I am married!" She looked up at them fiercely. "I know you don't believe me, but we were married proper by that preacher that lives with the workers at the plantation. We had witnesses too; his wife and daughter were there when he married us."

"Sheba, it isn't that we don't believe you. It is just that we need to know whom you married. Who is the father of your baby?"

"I am sorry Doctor Joseph, but I can't tell you. Please don't send me back." She buried her head in her hands and cried in earnest. Great wracking sobs shook her body as the pent up sorrow emerged.

"No one is sending you anywhere, Sheba. Just get that thought out of your head. We love you and when you are hurting we hurt. No one will send you where you do not want to go. I have to be honest with you though, it is going to be difficult for you to deliver the baby, Sheba." Joseph looked at her with compassion. "You are going to need expert medical attention in a hospital. I am concerned about you making the trip with us for that reason. You could go into labor on the train or in some small town that doesn't even have an infirmary."

"Doctor Joseph, I don't want anyone taking care of me but you," Sheba was crying fearfully now. "Don't make me go to a hospital, Doctor Joseph. Please don't. I don't want to die." She broke down into spasms of wailing.

Joseph and Bernice both tried to comfort her. They realized that her apprehension stemmed from early memories of people being carried to hospitals as a last resort. The unfortunates usually did not survive. It was especially true among the people of color.

Joseph tried to calm her fears by talking about the tremendous advances in medical knowledge and the remarkable equipment that had been developed in recent years. Her fear was so ingrained in her thinking it blocked her ability to comprehend what he was trying to tell her.

"Joseph, would you mind asking the others to go on without me? I'm a bit tired from this morning and I think I'll just sit here with Sheba for awhile." Bernice pulled a chair up beside her and slipped her hand into Sheba's. She began speaking to her in a reassuring tone. "Don't you worry about anything right now; just let us work out the details. You just need to take care of yourself and the baby."

"I'll tell them," Joseph said softly as he slipped out the door. He knew that in her present state, she was incapable of discussing the situation rationally. Bernice would be able to calm her down and later they could approach the subject of the father of the baby. *What was this about a marriage in Thomasville?* Joseph left to find the others with a lot of questions floating around in his head.

Chapter Seventeen

Donald had arranged a carriage to take the sightseers to some of the outlying areas of Birmingham. They visited several beautiful Ante Bellum homes on the west side of the city. The stately Smith Place, located on a hill overlooking the city was one of their favorites.

"Isn't this lovely!" Hannah was almost drooling as they walked up to the mansion. "Look at those gigantic trees; they are probably hundreds of years old. And those gardens! They absolutely surround the house with beauty. Wouldn't it be great to tour the inside?"

"Look over there sis!" Daniel pointed at a small family cemetery snuggled in a grove of trees west of the house. Both of them walked closer, so they could see the names prominently displayed on the granite markers.

Another home they especially liked was the stately Georgian Colonial house, which had been built by William Mudd in 1842. Like the Smith Place, the Mudd home was perched on a hill overlooking Birmingham. Giant Live Oak trees festooned with layers of Spanish moss invitingly shaded the spacious green lawns and gardens.

The next day the entire group toured together. Donald took them to the construction site of Howard College, a Baptist institution. They had visited many construction sites in Atlanta, but this one was special because it would be a place for young men called to the ministry to study.

They continued their tour. "Sure and if you'll look over there to your right," Donald swept his short arm expansively to where he wanted their attention focused. "You'll see the Jefferson County Courthouse."

Donald had proven himself the perfect tour guide and they considered it most fortunate that they had encountered him on the train and Joseph had engaged his services. He had been entertaining as well as informative and the travelers were delighted with the prospector.

"Sure and you can see that it is built of Birmin'ham's own red brick. But look at the decoration; it has that braw reddish-brown terra cotta trim."

"Look at that clock tower!" Hannah seemed to have taken an especial liking to all clock towers. "Isn't it lovely? Look how graceful it is; the way it raises from the center of the courthouse."

"You are much to preoccupied with time, young lady," Ben teased. "Are you perhaps concerned that time might be passing you by and you'll end up an old maid?"

Hannah's eyes briefly met Ben's, before she turned scarlet and glanced away from the handsome young man who grinned down at her. "I—I just think it is pretty that's all," she stammered.

Other members of the group, some of whom grew pensive as they considered the exchange while continuing the tour, did not miss the subtle flirting on Ben's part, or Hannah's reaction. She was a young, unsophisticated girl from the country. *Ben's attention was probably pretty heady for one of her limited experience,* considered Bernice and Joseph.

They took a short rest in one of the many parks and Sheba was delighted when they encountered A.H. Parker, the son of a freed slave, and Donald introduced them. After they had visited for a short time and Joseph had explained their journey, Mr. Parker began to tell them some things about himself.

"I passed the exam for school teacher last summer and I will be teaching in a local grade school in the fall. One day, I hope to see a high school in Birmingham for young people of color. That is my dream," he told his audience wistfully. "Then when I dream really big, I visualize a time when all children will go to school together."

"Amen, to that, Brother Parker." Sheba had been educated with Beth on Three Oaks, but knew that many others on other plantations were not even taught to read or write and most could not sign their own names. *I want a better life for my baby.* Sheba was especially attentive and interested in his accomplishments under what could be considered insurmountable odds. It gave her a lot to consider as they continued their tour.

The group all enjoyed the encounter with the bright young man and they talked about the things he had said as they walked back to the hotel. Each of them had very different experiences growing up and came from different perspectives. They were all in agreement that they looked forward to the day when all children would receive the same kind of educations together with the same opportunities of higher education and employment.

When they returned to the hotel, Donald promised to take them up on Red Mountain, which overlooked all of Birmingham. "Sure and you'll be able to enjoy the real splendor of Birmin'ham from that vantage point."

They were all excited at the prospect of the excursion up the mountain. It was early evening when they gathered in the lobby to await Donald and the two carriages that Joseph had hired to transport them. Since they would not be able to utilize Sheba's special chair, Daniel had carried her down to wait with the others. Bernice hovered nearby to assist with anything that might be needed by her charge, while being careful not to dampen her excitement in the up coming trip up the mountain. Hannah played with Anna and speculated about what they might see.

When the carriage arrived, the three women and Anna were assisted into one of the carriages before, Ben, Joseph, Daniel and Donald climbed nimbly into the other. The temperature was mild and the scenery beautiful with the abundant pines and hardwoods dressed in their various shades of summer green. The night air was scented with the delicate aroma of honeysuckle and pine, which added to the romantic atmosphere of the outing.

They made frequent stops on their way up the mountain in order to rest the horses and view the city from different angles. At each stop, Donald would nimbly climb down and stand between the carriages to explain what they were seeing below. He pointed out the many places they had visited and they were treated to a birds eye view of the same places where they had strolled in the past couple days. They were all in a festive and carefree mood; even Sheba seemed to come out of her shell and laughed gaily with Hannah and Anna.

Joseph found himself relaxing, as he perceived the enjoyment of his newly expanded family. He was content that he had made the right decision in tearing up his roots in Savannah and heading west. His only real concern right now was Sheba's dilemma. *I can't imagine whom she could have married. Why had her husband not come forward before they had left? She seemed anxious to come with us; not at all reluctant to leave Thomasville. If she was married and knew she was carrying a child, it seems more likely that she would have asked to be left behind, not begged to continue with us on what has to be an arduous journey for her. I feel that I have failed her and Ruth.*

Joseph's countenance had become troubled as these thoughts flitted through his mind, but his resolve grew to get to the bottom of this problem and see that Sheba was taken care of to the best of his ability and any unnecessary hardship was eliminated.

They were all resting on rocks during one of their stops and Donald was spinning one of his marvelous tales about Alabama. Suddenly Sheba split the air with a shriek.

"Snake," she screamed. Her terrified eyes were glued to a serpent slithering through the grass toward the rock where she sat.

"Oh little darlen! Sure and don't be frightened of the little creature." Donald spoke in his soothing Irish brogue. He squatted beside her and patted her hand comfortingly, calming her with his musical voice. "That wee creature is only a harmless blue racer. He's probably much more frightened of you than you are of him."

Sheba's eyes still appeared as big as saucers, but she was not trembling as much as when she had first spied the reptile slithering across the grass toward her slippers. Tears still slid down her cheeks, but her sobs had grown quieter. She felt helpless; unable to even remove herself from danger creeping up beside her.

"Sure and did you know that the conjure doctors have a cure for snakebite?" He quickly began another story while Daniel ushered the snake back to the woods and away from the ladies. "They take a black chicken and split it, then bind it over the snake bite. When the chicken's skin turns green, all the poison has gone into the chicken and they remove the chicken and bury it twelve inches in the ground facing north."

"If you are still alive," Joseph muttered, shaking his head at Donald's tall tale.

Bernice chuckled as she observed Joseph's grimace and she gestured as if she were writing on a tablet. He grinned back at her and shook his head no.

Donald's audience loved his stories, even though some made them a bit squeamish. Hannah was sitting next to Ben on a large flat rock during the telling of the chicken tale. She unconsciously pressed closer to Ben during the narrative and he casually placed his arm protectively around her shoulder.

Bernice was sitting slightly to the side of the others holding Anna. She was more engrossed in studying Donald's audience than his grizzly story. She noticed the proprietorship towards Hannah displayed by Ben and the half confused half angry expression that crossed Joseph's face when he glanced at them. The other rather startling observation she made was the crestfallen look on Sheba's face, when she glanced up at the couple sitting across from her on the rock.

I'm afraid that our happy group is in for some rocky times ahead, she thought pensively as she studied each of them closely. *I wonder how Daniel fits into all this.* She turned slightly so she could catch a glimpse of the stocky young man, who had shown himself to be most protective of his sister and had become Sheba's defender since joining them. She noted that Daniel wore his usual good-natured smile. *I guess he missed the exchange between the reckless, rather worldly Ben and his unsophisticated sister.*

When they reached the top of the mountain, the only two who were able to enjoy the beautiful view were Ben and Hannah. Anna had fallen asleep and Sheba insisted on remaining in the carriage with her. Bernice was deeply concerned about the implications and undercurrents troubling their close little group. Joseph looked stormy.

Ben and Hannah were standing on a boulder that jutted out from the mountain and overlooked the panorama of the valley below. Ben casually slipped his arm around Hannah.

"Can't have you falling off this rock," he said as he smiled down at her.

"Isn't it beautiful!" She caught her breath at the spectacular scene spread out before them. In her excitement, she was not even aware of Ben's close proximity or that his arm was holding her close to his side.

"It is beautiful. Almost as beautiful as you are." Ben whispered close to her ear.

Bernice vowed to have a talk with Hannah about Ben when they returned. She felt guilty about not intervening when she knew someone was visiting Sheba on the sly and now she claimed to be married without a husband in sight and a baby on the way. Bernice was determined the same fate would not mar Hannah's life. She could not help looking over at Joseph. *Joseph Warren, you are a fool,* she thought vehemently.

"Ben," Joseph called sharply. "Let's take a walk up that trail over there. I think I saw some deer tracks." He motioned toward a path leading into the woods.

The tall pines kept undergrowth down and the area was quite clear of bushes and brambles. The women were accustomed to the men sauntering off and were not concerned about them wondering off into the moonlit night. Hannah was so engrossed in the spectacular view from Red Mountain that she had missed the sharp edge in Joseph's voice when he called to Ben.

Ben, with a mischievous smile on his face, turned to follow Joseph; but not before kissing Hannah lightly on the cheek. She glanced up at him startled by the unaccustomed show of affection. She watched them walk into the wood with a quizzical expression on her face. She was even more surprised when she glanced at Bernice and noticed that she was watching them depart with a look of concern on her face.

Bernice, although she was glad that Joseph finally planned to do something about the situation before it got out of hand, was concerned about Joseph. *Ben is much taller and has grown stouter, in the past year and a half. Joseph hasn't done any manual labor—other than running whenever he gets a chance. He's been much too busy with his practice and working on the journal.* She watched apprehensively as the two men disappeared around a bend in the road. No one noticed Daniel slip nonchalantly in behind Joseph and Ben.

The women were surprised when a few minutes later they saw Joseph hurry back along the trail alone.

"What happened? How did Anna get hurt?" Joseph was calling to them as he rushed toward the women. "When I left I thought she was asleep in the carriage."

"Well she was until you woke her," Sheba called, a little crossly from the carriage. Anna's soft cries were muffled against Sheba's shoulder. Her father's shouts had awakened her. She began crying in earnest, as the confused adults only frightened her more in their frantic haste to find out what had happened.

"But Daniel said that Anna fell out of the carriage and I was needed to take care of her." Joseph explained his actions as perplexed as the woman. He was out of breath from his mad dash back to the carriage in his fear at not knowing what had happened to his daughter.

"Anna was asleep until you came back," Hannah replied looking as perplexed as Joseph. "Why would Daniel have said such a thing?"

They heard some shouting in the distance followed by a muffled thud. Bernice could not help smiling, as she reconsidered her appraisal of the easy going Daniel. Obviously, he was mindful of Ben's actions and took some action of his own.

Daniel reappeared with some scratches and a few tears in his clothes. He walked nonchalantly up to the others grouped around the carriage.

"Daniel! What ever happened to you? You look like you had a run in with a bear and what were you thinking scaring Doctor Joseph like that?" Hannah was beside herself with concern over her brother's appearance and him lying to Joseph. "I just don't understand why you would do such a thing."

"It's all right Hannah," Joseph said gently. "I must have misunderstood what Daniel said." It was not hard to put two and two together and come up with what had taken place. Joseph chuckled to himself as he assisted the women back into the carriage. *I wonder if he was protecting the old man or his sister's virtue,* he considered.

"Will Ben be along?" Joseph turned to Daniel and inquired. Unable to keep the smile off his face, he made sure he was turned away from the carriage where the women waited.

"Actually, he said it was such a fine night, with the moonlight and all that he wanted to walk back down the mountain; said he would see us in the morning and not to worry about him." Daniel related this quite solemnly, as he made his way to the other carriage and gingerly leaped into the seat.

Joseph rubbed his chin, where the stubble of golden hair—the beginning of a beard, was growing. He concealed a grin behind his hand and motioned for a grinning Donald to climb into the carriage before he settled himself in the seat opposite Daniel.

Bernice watched for a reaction from Daniel, but all she saw was a trace of satisfaction on the boy's face. Hannah appeared to still be confused by the unexpected events that interrupted the perfect night they had been experiencing. Sheba looked stricken and kept glancing back over her shoulder, as the horses twined their way down the mountain back toward their hotel.

The next morning Joseph had a message waiting for him at the hotel front desk. The note read;

I plan to strike out alone for a while, maybe do a little exploring and hunting in Alabama and Mississippi before continuing on to Arkansas. I will catch up with you later. Ben.

"The man who left the note must have been in a fight because he had a beauty of a shiner," the man behind the desk volunteered. "It was plain to see even with his hat pulled down like it was."

Joseph thanked him for the message without further comment. He joined the others for breakfast to find that Sheba had remained in bed.

"She said she was tired from the excursion up the mountain," Bernice explained. "She does look a bit peaked." Actually she looked more than peaked. Bernice was concerned that she might be in a lot of pain, because her eyes were red and her face was swollen from what had obviously been an extended period of crying.

When Joseph announced that he had gotten a note from Ben stating that he was starting out on his own for a while to do some hunting, Bernice glanced up at him knowingly. Inadvertently they both looked at Daniel, who was concentrating earnestly on making his ham and eggs disappear into his mouth.

"Sounds like a great idea," Daniel said, between mouthfuls, as he glanced at them casually. "Ben loves to hunt and this country is full of game. There is supposed to be a lot of panther and lynx in the mountains, along with beaver, coon, deer and squirrels. He should really enjoy himself."

No one would suspect his part in Ben's decision to leave, from his demeanor. He was the picture of innocence. But Hannah gave him a sideways glare that he returned with a shrug of his wide shoulders, as if to say, "I've no idea what your problem is."

Donald arrived promptly at eight for another escorted tour. They wanted to get an early start, so they could see as much as possible before the day grew too hot. As they were leaving for their day of sightseeing, Bernice overheard Hannah whisper to her brother.

"Was that really necessary? Do you think I'm a complete fool?"

He grinned up at her, his big boyish face revealing the depth of affection he had for his sister. Bernice knew she would not have to worry about Hannah. She had underestimated both of the young people.

Chapter Eighteen

It was time for them to reboard the train and continue their journey. Donald agreed to accompany them as far as Memphis, but had informed them emphatically that he would have to leave them before they crossed the Mississippi. It was at Memphis that they would cross the great river to the shores of Arkansas—their long awaited destination.

Donald continued to regale them with his fanciful stories as the train clicked off the miles. When Anna began to cough, he told them of an old folk cure he had heard of for whooping cough, the scourge of young children.

"Sure and first you have to find a wee frog. The frog must have a smooth belly. Now this is important. Then ya hold his mouth open while all the wee bairns in the home spit in it. After that, you write the sick bairn's name on the frog's smooth belly, before stringing the frog up to a limber tree limb by his left hind leg. T'is important it's the left leg and not the right, ya know. Leave him there. When you go back within the hour, the wee frog will be coughing having taken the whooping cough onto himself from the wee bairn." Donald winked at the wide-eyed Anna, who had been listening intently to each word. "Then of course the wee bairn will get well. Sure and then ya turn the wee frog loose, no worse off than he was before."

"Doctor Joseph, would you like me to document that cure for your journal?" Bernice asked Joseph facetiously, an impish grin lighting up her face.

"I don't believe so Bernice. I think I can recall that one if I ever have a need for it." Joseph smiled contentedly as he looked over his companions. At that moment, he felt more relaxed and content than he had in a very long time.

Since Ben was no longer with them, Joseph asked Hannah if she and Anna would join him at his table in the dining car. He rationalized his choice of including them because he had not been spending enough time with his daughter. And of course, he had to include her nursemaid.

Anna adored Donald, as much as he did the 'wee bairn' as he called her. He frequently joined them and sat with Anna, across from Joseph and Hannah. He delighted in amusing Anna by telling her stories and playing games with her throughout the meal, leaving Hannah and Joseph to speak of other things. It was during this brief time together that they grew to know each other better. They shared stories about their lives before the train wreck brought them together. Joseph learned more about her longing for more education, which had not been available to her on the farm with only a one room school house nearby that taught grades one to eight. Hannah received additional insight into Joseph's hunger to learn and record the folk cures that had been passed down orally, but most had never been recorded.

Over a brief stop at Jasper station, Donald began regaling his audience with some of the history. "Sure and Jasper's the county seat of Walker County. There's a grandfether oak tree in Jasper that folks 'round here call the Gallows Tree. Close to forty yars ago, a man, name of Lot

Franklin, was convicted of first-degree murder on the word of his son. The sheriff stood old Lot on his own coffin. The coffin was sittin' in a wagon hitched to a team of horses. They took an old black kerchief and put it over old Lot's eyes, while the entire time he was declarin' his innocence.

"Sure and I want ya to know that a crowd had gathered the like this county had never seen before. The sheriff, he was just a preenin'. A rider from the Governor's office raced up with a stay of execution. Sure and tha sheriff was enjoyin' all the adulation from the crowd. He weren't really a very good sheriff and it weren't often he heard kind words from the people he served. Sure and he didn't want to have a rowdy crowd on his hands if he had to stop tha show. He decided the stay weren't legal and he hanged Lot anyway."

Donald added emphasis by snapping his fingers. Anna did not follow the grisly tale, but she was intrigued with the noise made by his snapping fingers. She tried and tried to make the wonderful sound with her small fingers, until she fell asleep in the old prospectors lap.

Hannah was relieved when Anna went to sleep. Every time Anna attempted to snap her fingers, she was reminded of the hapless Lot, dangling on the end of a rope with the crowd cheering the show. She was happy they would not have time to visit the 'infamous' oak tree. She did not need that visual reminder of the poor man who had died at the hands of the dishonest glory-seeking sheriff.

Their journey continued and before long Donald announced that they were passing the hamlet of Hilliard. "Sure and the first court house of Walker County was built in Hilliard in 1835."

Further down the tracks, Donald announced they were passing through Townley. "Townley is a mining and lumber town, don't ya know.

"Sure and we'll pass through Chisca before we reach the station at Carbon Hill. Ya have to get off there and see the Pisqah Tavern and Post office. The train will lie over long enough while they take on more fuel. Sure and it's the sort of place the ladies have been liken to see you know."

The adventurers looked forward toward another sight seeing trip with their picturesque guide. The ladies whispered to one another that they hoped this place did not sport any famous hanging trees or bring to mind anything to do with dead chickens.

When the train pulled up to Carbon Hill station, the travelers disembarked, grateful for the opportunity to stretch their legs on a non-moving surface. Joseph again rented two carriages for the ride up the hill. It seemed everything in the land they passed through was either up a hill or down into a valley. They were anxious to see the unique building that Donald had told them about.

"Sure and Squire Hogan built it on this lovely hill," Donald informed them when they arrived and the women were assisted out of their carriage. "That way, he had a good view of his vast holdin'. T'was a stagecoach and express relay post along the Jasper-Pikeview Road. The Squire built it to serve all his and his family's needs, home, post office and tavern."

"See them logs, would ya? Sure and those different colors are from the trees he used. There's mulberry, cedar and cypress in there. Sure and you won't see colors like that in many buildings."

"You are right. It is most unique." Bernice walked slowly in front of the building studying the unusual design and shades of the wood.

They all agreed the building had certainly been worth visiting, with its unusual architecture and the magnificent view from the bluff.

"Camp Springs is a beauty of a place too," Donald, informed them when they were settled back in their seats on the train. "Sure and an Indian Village used to stand there. The overhangen rocks make perfect shelter for hunters--and old prospectors." The later was added with a big wink.

It was dark by the time the train pulled into Winfield. Bernice and Hannah took advantage of the brief stop to settle Sheba and Anna into their sleepers. It had been a big day and everyone was ready to relax.

"I think I will go along and write some letters to friends," Bernice said as she excused herself. They had made many new friends on their journey and Bernice tried to correspond with as many as possible, to let them know how they were doing as they continued their great adventure.

Donald and Daniel moved to the end of the car to get some air and to allow Donald to chew his tobacco without offending the ladies.

Joseph asked Hannah to accompany him to one of the seating coaches. He looked forward to visiting awhile and unwinding before they went their separate ways and retired for the night. He had begun to anticipate these rare visits between just the two of them.

"This has been a wonderful trip," Hannah said, her eyes dancing with delight. "It just does not seem possible that it has actually been two years since the Great Earthquake which brought us all together."

"Yes, the time has flown by. So much has happened and it seems we have been involved in so many different things. It has been good—all of us being together like a family."

Suddenly their pleasant conversation was interrupted by the terrified cries of a child, as the door to the car opened. Hannah whirled around in her seat, startled to see the conductor carrying Anna. The two year old was crying hysterically and trying to climb over the conductor's shoulder to get to someone behind him.

"Don'ld! Don'ld!" She cried over and over.

Hannah and Joseph rushed up the aisle. Hannah whisked the frightened child into her arms, while an incensed Donald yelled at the harried conductor.

"Ya confounded Englishman. Sure and if you don't give me back that wee bairn I'll rip out your gizzard." Donald turned to Joseph most distraught. "This lunatic, wouldn't give the little darlen to me and she was crying most fierce." Donald's face was scarlet as he stomped up and down angrily.

Joseph attempted to calm Donald. The prospector continued to jump up and down and berate the beleaguered conductor. Joseph decided that Donald looked somewhat like an elf throwing a fit. At the same time he questioned the conductor about how he happened to come into possession of his daughter. Anna was still sobbing with her face buried in Hannah's shoulder. They were drawing a considerable crowd with the noise and Donald's antics.

"I'll take Anna back to her bed while you sort this out," she said softly to Joseph, as she continued to sooth the crying child and moved to leave the car. Hannah patted Anna's back gently and held her close while murmuring soothing words into her ear on the way back to the Pullman.

When she reached the sleeper where she had left Sheba and Anna sleeping earlier, she found Daniel attempting to console the weeping Sheba.

Sheba had been in a frenzy when Daniel had reached her. She had awakened and on discovering Anna missing had started calling for help. People had gathered around her berth in their nightclothes, but were unable to understand her in her hysterical state.

Finally she had lunged out of the bunk and tried to drag herself down the aisle of the train. The passengers who had gathered agreed among themselves that she was quite demented and everyone kept their distance in fear of what the crazy woman might do next.

Daniel had found her crawling up the aisle of the train sobbing hysterically. He quickly scooped her up and carried her back to her berth, while speaking to her soothingly.

"Anna's all right Sheba," he reassured the sobbing woman. "The conductor found her and is taking her to Hannah and Joseph. Donald went with him. Everything is going to be all right. You just settle down now, or you're going to make yourself sick."

"These legs, these useless legs, and my big belly," she derided herself between sobs.

"She might have been killed. It would have been my fault. She was left with me. I promised Beth I would take care of her and I let her get lost. Oh God! Just let me die. I'm no good for anything."

Daniel held her in his arms and spoke quietly to her, as the crowd exchanged curious and disapproving glances.

"He's obviously one of those Yankees," one young woman was heard to utter, in a deep southern drawl.

"It is probably his bye-blow she is carrying," another passenger whispered to a companion, as he ushered his family back to their berths.

"Don't you pay any attention to them Sheba," Daniel soothed, while flashing a glare at the passengers who were making disparaging remarks. "You are all right and so is Anna. You need to just relax." He patted her arm and continued to speak low and soothingly to her. Sheba's sobs grew quieter and her body began to relax under Daniel's soothing administration.

Hannah arrived with Anna and placed the child in Sheba's arms, so she could see for herself that Anna was not injured. Anna wrapped her small arms around Sheba's neck and buried her head in her bosom. Both of them were still sobbing, but no longer in a hysterical fashion. Hannah crawled into the tight space—made for one person not the three it now held--clothes and all. She whispered comforting words as they quieted.

When Joseph and Daniel joined the group at Sheba's sleeper and everyone had calmed down, they were able to piece together what they suspected had happened. After Sheba had fallen asleep, Anna must have awakened and either crawled from or fell out of the berth. Likely she had wondered around the car and half asleep followed someone out of the Pullman into the passageway. The door to the next car probably closed before she was able to go through to that car and then she could not get back through the door she had just come through and could not get back into the Pullman. What they did know was what the conductor had related to Joseph. He had found her cowering behind the door, crying uncontrollably.

As he was attempting to find whom she belonged to, he had encountered Daniel and Donald walking back to the

Pullman car. The conductor had explained to Joseph that he had been reluctant to hand the child over to the old prospector, or the young farmer. Daniel had told him where to find his sister and Anna's father and had left to check on Sheba while Donald went with the conductor.

As soon as Anna had spied Donald, she had tried to get to him, but the conductor had held onto her firmly. The more Anna cried, the madder Donald became and shouted abuse upon the hapless conductor. His actions only made the conductor more determined not to relinquish the frightened child, until he had located her parent.

After Joseph was finally able to calm Donald down, Donald had continued to heap abuse upon the head of the conductor for not relinquishing the little darlen to him, he thanked the conductor and tipped him generously.

Later when Joseph, Daniel and Donald sought Bernice out to explain what had happened, Donald began ranting again. "The tyrant wouldn't let me have the wee bairn. She was frightened somethin' fierce and he wouldn't give her to me." His face was bright red and he stomped his tiny feet in his anger.

"I know Donald. And we all appreciate you staying with her and looking after her."

"But the dunderhead...."

"Yes, but you stayed with her anyway," Joseph continued in a soothing voice. "If you had not stayed with her like you did, Daniel could not have gone to see about Sheba and no telling what would have happened to her." He shuddered as he thought of all that had taken place. Daniel had told him of the response of the other passengers. He knew it could have ended much worse for Anna and the injured expectant mother. *God certainly sent his angels to look after all of them on this night*, he reflected.

When Donald had calmed Joseph left him with Daniel; then he and Bernice went back to check on Sheba and Anna. They found them asleep with Hannah wrapped protectively around both of them. He reached over to kiss his daughter. As he withdrew, he brushed his lips across Hannah's cheek and whispered thank you in her ear.

"I'll sleep in Hannah's birth tonight. It's right above them and I can make sure everything stays calm," Bernice offered. She felt partially responsible for what had happened, because she had retired to another car to write her correspondence instead of being close by when Anna had awakened.

"No, that's ok. I'll sleep there tonight," he said softly. "I don't know how they are all wedged into that one bunk, but I'll just climb up there." He indicated the bunk above Sheba's where Hannah was to have slept. "It will be easier for me to climb up there than it will be you." He knew it was an excuse, but he could not explain even to himself why he insisted on sleeping in Hannah's berth.

"I should stay close by, in case there is any further trouble." After everything had quieted down, he fell asleep listening to the even breathing from the occupants below him. He slept peacefully the rest of the night, savoring Hannah's scent, which lingered on the pillow.

Hannah took a long time getting to sleep with the memory of the warm glow she had felt at the touch of his lips on her cheek and the whispered words in her ear. She had not slipped into sleep at the time. She hugged her charges closely and soothed Anna back to sleep when she stirred and whimpered softly. Several times during the night Anna cried out in her sleep, but Hannah patted her small back and sang lullabies quietly until she again fell into a peaceful sleep.

For weeks afterward, Anna would wake in the middle of the night screaming in terror if someone was not there to hold and comfort her. The episodes became less frequent, but someone was always nearby whenever she was put to bed. Sheba felt responsible and became withdrawn and hollow eyed. When Anna slept with her, she remained awake and hovered over her or held her close all night. If one of the others insisted on Anna sleeping with them so Sheba could get some sleep, Sheba accused them of not trusting her to take care of Anna anymore. It was a difficult time for all of them.

Chapter Nineteen

It was the first day of July in the year of our Lord 1888, a hot sweltering day without cloud or rain dropping from the sky to block the sun, when the travelers arrived in Memphis. Arkansas, the state of their destination, lay directly across the river. There was no bridge spanning the great width of the winding muddy river at Memphis. They would have to cross by ferry and resume their train trip on the other side.

As they pulled into the station and were gathering up their belongings, Hannah picked Anna up just as the child's breakfast decided to make a return trip. Hannah, Anna and the surrounding area were covered with the previous contents of Anna's stomach. Hannah stood in the aisle looking stricken and holding Anna gingerly in her arms with regurgitated oatmeal and milk running down her arms and traveling gown. Everyone but Daniel looked as shocked as Hannah and he was trying to hide the laughter bubbling up at the site before him. At the sound of Daniel snickering, Anna began to cry and hid her face in Hannah's very damp shoulder.

Joseph was the first to react. "Here let me take Anna," he said as he scooped his daughter out of Hannah's arms, regurgitated food and all. Bernice grabbed up some muslin and began wiping Hannah's dress and Anna's face and dress.

"There will be water inside," Bernice remarked, failing to make much headway on the mess. "Let's get both of you inside and see what we can do, while Joseph locates a carriage to take us to a hotel."

"That sounds like an excellent idea," Joseph agreed. He instructed Daniel to bring Sheba. "I'll take some of this." He picked up some of their bundles, while still holding a rather smelly and very soiled Anna in his arms. "Donald if you can grab the rest of this paraphernalia, we can meet them at the carriages." He led the way from the train carrying a still sobbing Anna.

Bernice assisted Hannah, Daniel carried Sheba and Donald followed with the rest of their things. People up and down the train and platform stared at them curiously.

"Well one day I know we will all laugh at this," Daniel insisted, excusing his laughter at the mishap. Sheba looked up at him with a censuring look, while Donald glared at Daniel and looked stricken at his wee bairn's mishap.

When they reached the platform, Joseph hesitantly handed Anna over to Hannah. She insisted on carrying her to prevent anyone else becoming covered in the mess, which already adorned her, Joseph and Anna.

After the ladies had repaired Hannah and Anna's clothes as best they could with the basin of water, they joined the others on the station platform. They had teased Anna into a better mood by splashing water at one another; after all they figured they could not do more damage than what had already happened.

Donald was busy telling Daniel and Sheba about Memphis when Bernice, Hannah and Anna walked up to them.

"Memphis isn't an incorporated city, ya know. Sure and 'twas all of nine yar ago, yellow fever hit the town o'r and o'r, the town weren't able to get out of debt afterward. The fever took all the town's resources. They're workin' on fixin' everythin' up though. There're lots of things happenin' 'round here. The town fathers are puttin' in a new sewage system hopin' to banish forever the dreadful pestilence. They're also diggin' the largest artesian water works in the whole world. They'll be back big as ever. Sure and ya mind my word." The last was said with a big wink for his audience.

By the time Joseph found a hotel--where they could all stay together, Hannah and Anna's dresses were dry from the hot sun, but their bodies were covered by a fine sheen of perspiration. The temperature was not hotter than what they were used to, but there was dampness in the air that made it seem hotter. It was almost as if you could feel the wetness in the air as it collected beneath the bulky clothes that fashion and custom dictated. The women were ready to settle down, get out of their traveling clothes and rest.

When they arrived at the hotel, Joseph left Daniel to see about the women, while he and Donald left to check on the household goods and wagon that had been sent ahead and placed in storage. It would soon be time to make arrangements for crossing the Mississippi and continuing their journey.

The bustling river port was crowded with merchants and river men, in addition to the construction crews working on the many building projects the city had in place. Joseph felt fortunate to have Donald along to guide him through the city. The old prospector had visited Memphis often during his travels and moved along the streets with ease.

Locating their belongings, they found everything in good order. Joseph paid the storage fees, plus an additional week to give them time to decide how to proceed. He was concerned about Sheba continuing the trip in her condition and he needed to make sure that Anna's upset stomach was not anything that might turn into something serious. He felt most uncertain about how long they should remain in Memphis.

On the surface, Sheba did not appear to have any physical aftereffects from her fall on the train, but her emotional condition had deteriorated after Anna's frightening experience. The baby that resided in her womb seemed active enough, when he had examined her. Joseph had been unable to detect any medical complications other than Sheba's disability. Her paralysis would definitely hamper the delivery and he was anxious to avoid any additional problems. He had never dreamed that she could get pregnant in her condition, nor did he consider that the possibility would ever arise.

He smiled as he thought of little Anna placing her small hand on Sheba's ample girth to 'feel the baby kick'. He had explained to her that Sheba was carrying a baby inside of her and when it was ready to be born he or she would live with them. Anna was very excited about the anticipated event and looked forward to having another child to play with.

The hotel was crowded so Bernice and Sheba were sharing one room, while Hannah and Anna were in the adjoining room. They left the door open between them and all lay down for a rest, after Hannah and Anna climbed out of their soiled clothes and Hannah finished washing them off with the pitcher of water provided.

"One day soon you will have someone to play with," Hannah told Anna, as they lay together with the child's head pillowed on her arm. "Won't that be fun? We will take the baby wherever we go."

"Anna hold baby?"

"Of course dear, you will need some help though. Sheba's baby will be larger and heavier than your doll and real babies are very wiggly."

"Why'd Sheba eat it?" Anna looked up at Hannah with a puzzled look on her face.

Bernice and Sheba were listening in the other room and had to smother their laughter in pillows. Hannah was at a loss as to the best way to answer the child's question and was thankful when Bernice appeared at the door.

"Sheba didn't eat the baby honey." She moved to the bed and took Anna from Hannah's arms. Cuddling her close, she attempted to explain why the baby was snugly nestled in his mother's womb, in a way that a two year old might understand.

"God placed the baby there, right under Sheba's heart." She placed the small hand over her own heart, to illustrate her words. "He put the little one there so Sheba can nourish him and care for him until he is big enough to live here with the rest of us." She smiled at Anna before glancing over her head at Sheba, who sat in her chair in the doorway.

"Thank you Miz Bernice," Sheba said softly, her eyes brimming with tears. Her spirits seemed to improve after that and she began talking more about the baby. But she continued to refuse to divulge the name of the father.

Chapter Twenty

Joseph considered remaining in Memphis until after the infant's birth. He had heard conflicting stories about the land west of the Mississippi River. Some people described it as if it were still an undeveloped frontier land, while others told of modern cities boasting all the comforts of the late nineteenth century. Joseph was reluctant to take his assorted company into this new land without more information. He discussed it with Donald as they walked around Memphis.

"Perhaps I should go on alone and come back for them." His brow was furrowed in concern, as he pondered the best way to proceed.

"Well now, Joseph," he replied. "I've not been to this land you're about to enter, but one day I'm a goin'. Sure and I've heard tell there's no place like it on earth. I've heard with my own ears, old prospectors that have been there claim that when they die they want to go to Ar-kan-saw. Claimed it's the closest they'll get to heaven. Sure and ya know it's in the Bible?"

"The Bible?" Joseph looked at his new friend, with his half grin and eyes twinkling.

"Noah looked across the ark-an-saw. Sure and even if the words aren't there," he said mischievously. "I'm most positive it happened."

"You are probably right Donald and I imagine it is very beautiful." Joseph grinned at Donald's enthusiasm. "But I'm afraid the ladies might not enjoy living out under the stars, even while surrounded by such beauty."

They continued to discuss the pros and cons of crossing over the river into Arkansas right away, or remaining for an extended period in Memphis. Joseph was still not sure it would not be better to wait, at least until after Sheba's baby was born.

After their rest and Joseph and Donald had returned to the hotel, Joseph called them all together to discuss what they should do. He had about decided to stay for several months in Memphis, before crossing over into the unknown. He proposed doing just that and was surprised to find they strongly opposed such a plan.

"But Joseph! We have waited so long to get this far. We are anxious to cross the Mississippi and reach our new home." Hannah's countenance beseeched Joseph to reconsider.

There was a chorus of objections to the long delay. Hannah appeared crestfallen, but seemed to realize how disrespectful and ungrateful she had sounded, after all that Joseph had done for them.

"I'm sorry Doctor Joseph. We will do whatever you think is best." She looked sharply at her brother, who was loudly objecting to the delay. Daniel quieted under his sister's scrutiny, but his posture still proclaimed his dissatisfaction with Joseph's proposal.

Joseph smiled at the drastic change in Hannah's demeanor. She had shown such spirit and had looked so beautiful while expressing her true feelings. The somber, subservient role really did not fit the spunky young woman. He could see that she struggled with her emotions, as she attempted to resume the role of nanny to his daughter and therefore his employee.

"Well, we don't have to make a decision today. Let's enjoy the Memphis sights and make inquiries about Arkansas from people who have recently been there. That way we will have more information to make a decision on, plus have time to enjoy this town and rest a bit before continuing. In a few days, we can sit down and decide what will be best for everyone. We can all go together, or maybe a couple of us go on ahead and prepare a place before the others follow." Joseph smiled at them. He considered how fond he had grown of each of them and how they had become a real family even with their diversities.

"Ar-kan-saw," Anna parroted, practicing the new word she had heard Donald mention. She crawled into her father's lap and snuggled close. Joseph brushed the hair back from her face and tenderly placed a kiss on top of her head.

"Yes, Anna. We are going to Arkansas."

The following days were filled with the sights and sounds of the bustling river city. They visited the museum and were enthralled with the many interesting exhibits.

"Would you look at all these modern contraptions?" Daniel gazed with awe at the shelves containing some of the latest inventions. "It is surely a miracle. Imagine all the time saving conveniences that have been invented in only the past ten years." He pointed at first one thing and then another. "Electricity has made most of these things possible. Look at those circulating fans. Why you would never need to be hot again with the air stirring like that." He stood close to the fan and reveled in the feel of the air blowing in his face.

"And the flatirons," said Hannah. "You don't even have to heat them on the stove." Her voice revealed the awe she felt at all they were being introduced to in the museum.

"And the fountain pens," chimed in Sheba. From her position in her chair she stared into the glass cases and could easily read the plaques that explained each exhibit. "They hold ink right in the pen and you don't have to continually dunk them into an inkwell, what a wonder."

"Look at this," Daniel called as he moved down the aisle. "Linotype has revolutionized the printing industry. Maybe I'll edit a paper some day. What do you think Hannah? Would I make a good editor? I'll bet you could even put out a paper more than once a week with something like this."

"These dictating machines have saved countless hours for businesses," Bernice added, as she became caught up in the excitement of all the modern inventions displayed before them. They were standing in front of a cubicle made to appear like a modern office with a wax mannequin representing a secretary transcribing from a Dictaphone.

"Doesn't she look lifelike?" Hannah studied the mannequin. Her attention was quickly diverted when she heard Anna's squeal.

"Wheels!" She had spied an exhibit featuring wax figure children wearing roller skates. "Anna want wheels."

They all laughed as they coaxed Anna on to another exhibit.

"This is my favorite," Daniel said enthusiastically. He was examining the new box camera invented by George Eastman. "I'll bet I could take great pictures with one of these and that new roll of film." He pointed to where the film for the camera was displayed. "When I save up enough money, I'll get one and keep a pictorial record of our adventures in Arkansas. Maybe that is what I will be a photographer."

There were many more exhibits and they marveled at each one. Joseph took his pleasure in studying the faces of his companions as they discovered items they never knew existed and were introduced to new uses for some things they were familiar with.

Donald left them to go on his own. He had business to take care of and wanted to visit with old friends. He was able to learn a lot about the land across the river from men who had actually lived in different parts of Arkansas.

Joseph visited with doctors in Memphis and spent some time at the hospital. He learned that there was a medical school as well as a quality hospital run by the Catholic Church, located right in Little Rock—where he hoped to set up practice. This information made him less apprehensive about Sheba. He decided it would be safe to press on if the others were still anxious to leave.

The others chatted with people they met in the parks and shops, always seeking information about the state they could glimpse across the river. They enjoyed an Independence Day celebration on the river, with fireworks displayed over Mud Island. After three days of questioning people and seeing the sights of Memphis, they gathered in Joseph's sitting room to share what they had learned.

"There are thousands of miles of railroad tracks," Daniel shared enthusiastically. "We can get anywhere we want to go by rail." He was very excited about all he had heard from others. "The Indians call it Down Stream People and there are arrowheads, pottery and other treasures all over the place. The whole state is divided cattycorner in half by the Arkansas River. There are giant caves in the mountains to the north just waiting to be explored and more streams to fish and woods to hunt than anywhere in the world, so I've been told," he added, attempting to modify his excitement somewhat.

"I think we all know how Daniel feels about Arkansas," Joseph said with a chuckle as he beamed at the young man. "Bernice," he said turning to the oldest member of their party. "What have you learned?"

He expected Bernice to give a well thought out, reasonable account. If anyone voiced any reservations or called their attention to circumstances that would indicate they should delay continuing their journey, he was confident it would be the levelheaded Bernice. He had learned to trust her judgment in many things and frequently looked to her for advice if he could not puzzle something out himself.

"From what I have heard," she said looking around the room at each of her friends. "I believe we will find quite adequate medical facilities in Little Rock." Her countenance was serious and thoughtful as she continued. "It is the capital of the state and located right in the center of Arkansas. As Daniel has already pointed out, there is a very good rail system throughout the state. Transportation does not seem to be an issue." She paused briefly before continuing. "It sounds like a most healthy environment with both fresh air and water." She glanced up at Joseph with a twinkle in her eye. "I am not sure if that is good or bad news from your point of view Joseph."

The others burst out laughing, which helped to relieve some of the intense atmosphere, while they attempted to convince Joseph to proceed with all due haste to continue their journey.

"You have a point," Joseph replied with his own very special crooked grin. "After all we do have to make a living."

"We have heard of many healing springs in the state," Bernice confided. "Especially in the area called Hot Springs. Apparently this has been a most popular resort area for many years. I believe we will be able to find a generous reservoir of information to add to your journals."

"Donald," Joseph asked turning to their new friend and guide. "What have you learned?" He had come to depend heavily upon the old prospector's advice concerning the areas they had passed through. His knowledge of the territory had proved to be most valuable and enlightening, if one disregarded the tall tales he loved to throw into the mix.

"Sure and I believe the stories I've heard to be true, but I'm afeard I speak not from personal experience, only what I've been told by others." He doffed his old hat and his hands were busy walking their way around the brim as he related his information. "Sure but it does sound like a piece of heaven, fallen from the sky. Ar-kan-saw seems to be a prospector's dream. Sure and I wish I could join ya right now. But I tell ya for sure, I'll be a followin' yea for certain sure as soon as I'm able."

"Doctor Joseph," Hannah said turning to look at the man who had become so important to all of them. "I have heard the beauty is unsurpassed by any place in the world. If only half the stories I have heard are true it is certainly a wondrous place. The skies are reputed to be a deeper blue than anywhere else, the mountains higher, although I tend to question that claim, the water purer and more abundant, the clouds fluffier and the grass greener than anywhere in the world."

"Sure and wait a minute thar. T'iss no greener grass that grows on God's good earth than what grows in my Ireland," Donald disputed the claim hotly, throwing his hat to the ground and stomping on it with his short legs. The others laughed at his antiques and quick defense of his homeland.

"Oh Donald, I am just repeating what we have all been told. I am sure they are mistaken about the green grass," she said to mollify their friend. "But I must tell you, from all I have heard, I am ready to leave today," she declared passionately. "The educational opportunities for Anna appear to be limitless. We have heard about the large University in the northern mountains, a Female College a little north of Little Rock and a Baptist College in the western mountains, to name only a few of the institutions of higher learning. There are common schools scattered abundantly throughout the state. It would seem a person could do whatever they set their mind to make of themselves in such a place."

It was the longest speech he had ever heard from Hannah and he was tempted to dismiss all other considerations and tell them to pack. He was amused to hear the bit of brogue that she used in her speech, obviously picked up subconsciously from Donald. Over the past months it had become very important to him to make this delightful young woman happy, something that he had not taken the time to puzzle over. *There are other considerations that I must take into account.* His gaze automatically swung from Hannah to Sheba. She had been sitting quietly in her chair listening to the recitals of the others.

"I know why you are afraid to move on." Her look was accusing as she stared hard at Joseph. "It's because of me and this baby I carry under my heart." She picked up the words from Bernice's description to Anna. "Well let me just tell you something," she declared forcefully. Joseph perceived that she looked just like a miniature version of her mother Ruth, as she straightened her back and looked around the room. "This baby and me, we can do anything the rest of you can. We are ready to go to Arkansas, so just pack your belongings and push my chair to the ferry."

Cheers went up around the room as she finished and Joseph realized that he would be quite outnumbered if he persisted in delaying the trip. The consensus of the group was to forge ahead. He felt reassured by their unity and released from any further reservations.

"Westward-Ho!" he shouted. His only regrets were in leaving their new companion, guide and friend behind and they had yet to see any sign of the missing Ben. "Well my friend," he said turning to Donald and placing his right hand on the small man's shoulder. "It looks like we leave for Arkansas tomorrow. Would you accompany me while I arrange our passage on the ferry and railroad? It appears we will soon be saying goodbye."

The two men departed to make the necessary arrangements for the continuation of the marvelous adventure. The excited women packed all of their paraphernalia and Daniel moved the trunks about for them.

The next morning at dawn they were ready for the crossing. They bid Donald a sad farewell. He had proven himself to be a good friend and valuable guide and his stories had kept them amused as they traveled from place to place. They parted with him reluctantly and all fervently hoped they would see him soon again.

" We…we will miss you Donald," Hannah stammered as she gave him a big hug. Tears streamed down her cheeks and wet them both.

Donald turned his head to the side, so his new friends would not see him wipe the tears from his own eyes. He had grown to love this makeshift family and felt honored to be considered one of them. He had not felt so close to anyone in many years and he wished each of them God's speed on their journey.

Anna cried when he did not join them on the ferry. He could hear her little voice calling to him, "Don'ld, Don'ld, don't weave us."

"Sure and I'll ketch up to you, little darlin'," he called, as the ferry pulled away. He stood on the riverbank waving a brand new hat that Joseph had presented to him as a parting gift. Salty tears trickled down his cheeks, but he was oblivious to the curious stares from those around him.

Chapter Twenty-One

The ferry ride was exciting. They enjoyed the adventure in spite of their sadness at saying goodbye to Donald. The mighty Mississippi held Hannah and Daniel spellbound, they had never seen anything comparable. Sheba grew a little homesick for the spacious ocean waters of the Atlantic and the beautiful winding Savannah River.

Daniel stood at the rail and watched as fish jumped in the muddy water. When he thought he saw an alligator enter the river from an island they were passing, he became so excited that he nearly toppled into the murky waters. He had leaned out over the rail for a better view. Hannah grabbed his shirt, narrowly adverting disaster.

"Watch what you are doing!" She scolded him and wrinkled her nose at the fishy smell permeating the air.

Joseph and Daniel had lifted Sheba onto the ferry in her chair and small children gathered around her to study the unique contrivance better. She was a big hit with them, especially when they learned she had been injured during a great earthquake. They clamored to hear the details of the earthquake and resulting train wreck.

The trip seemed very short and before long they landed at Hopefield, which was little more than a small cluster of simple houses along the banks of the river. *I hope the name of this first town in Arkansas proves prophetic,* Joseph considered wistfully.

They quickly moved from the ferry landing to the train station. Before long they had boarded the Memphis and Little Rock Railroad for the last leg of their journey. As they settled once again on a train there was a collective sigh of relief that soon their journey would be over.

During the first few hours they began to question some of what they had been told. The land was beautiful to be sure, but most of what they were passing was swampland, laced with streams. They constantly had to swat at the numerous mosquitoes and other bugs that flew into the open windows. It was much to hot and stuffy in the train car to close them, but they found the bugs to be a great nuisance, buzzing around their heads and diving in for a quick strike.

Cypress trees were plentiful in the area and Daniel speculated that the land was no doubt inhabited by all manner of game. They occasionally caught glimpses of waterfowl in flight and deer running for cover as the rushing train frightened them from their feeding areas. He had never had time for sport hunting like Ben liked to engage in, but had learned at an early age how to put meat on the table.

Their first stop was at Forrest City. They were eager to catch a glimpse of their first Arkansas town, but were none too impressed with the view from the train. The next stop was Brinkley and after that DeValls Bluff. They crossed two sizeable rivers, the St. Francis and the White. The White River, although low in the summer heat, appeared to wander through marshland. In the areas not as swampy, they passed huge cotton fields.

"This land looks like home, a little anyway," Sheba said in surprise.

"Doesn't miss it by much, does it?" Joseph gazed out the window at the swampy area they were passing. "I believe the mosquitoes are as big as or maybe even bigger than Savannah's and I didn't think that was possible." He swatted yet another of the little dive-bombers as it landed on his neck.

"I would say it is as hot as Savannah also," he said wiping his brow with what had been a snowy white handkerchief, but was now covered with the soot from the coal engine blowing in through the open windows and his own perspiration.

"I'm sure of that," Hannah added. "I believe I melt a little each time we stop." She held Anna, who slept fitfully in the oppressive heat. Hair, shiny with perspiration, was plastered to her face and neck.

Sheba appeared to be miserable with her clothes clinging to her body and perspiration standing on her upper lip. She was much more uncomfortable now than she had been when they left Thomasville. It felt like the baby was manufacturing heat from the inside and with the hot summer weather, she felt like a wilted, bloated blob.

They were happy to see a porter make his way down the aisle distributing fans and pillows. He informed them they would be able to purchase refreshment from the news-Butch. The weary travelers made themselves as comfortable as possible. Joseph purchased lemonade and sandwiches from the news-Butch, when he came through the car.

"We only have two more stops before we arrive," Joseph announced, as he passed out the cool beverages and slightly mushy sandwiches.

The women accepted the refreshing drinks and news gratefully. They were enjoying the breeze, which blew through the open windows that was created by the speeding train. But whenever they stopped, the hot humid weather seemed oppressive. The porter assured them the weather changed frequently and the next day would probably be more pleasant.

The train stopped briefly at the quaint farming town of Lonoke and just as dusk wrapped them in a dusky haze they pulled into the community of Argenta, right across the river from the capital city nestled along the Arkansas River. They were delayed in Argenta longer than at the other stops, but finally crossed over the Arkansas River on the Baring Cross bridge. They eagerly peered out the windows and saw street lamps reflecting off the river in a wavering ghostly dance.

"It is so beautiful," breathed Hannah. Tears of joy filled her eyes, as she took in the breathtaking sight of the city they were going to call home.

Joseph reached for her hand and squeezed it lightly. His heart raced as Hannah glanced up at him through her tears. *She is so beautiful,* he mused, his thoughts tumultuous as he looked down at the beautiful young woman. *I am nearly twice her age. She probably thinks of me as a substitute father, being so far away from her folks. I will have to be careful that she never sees how much she has come to mean to me,* he vowed.

Hannah, overwhelmed with finally arriving in Little Rock after the long journey, placed her hand on Joseph's arm. She was bewildered and a little embarrassed when he pulled away and abruptly left his seat and moved to the back of the train. She was confused by the intense emotion and turmoil she felt and stung by Joseph's obvious rebuff.

Bernice had not missed the exchange. She had noted how he had looked at Hannah earlier, when she was looking out the window and could only see his refection in the window. She felt both anger and compassion for the suffering Joseph, as well as sympathy for the confused young woman. To help smooth over the incident and give Hannah time to regain her composure, she began gathering their belongings.

"Hannah, if you will carry Anna, I believe Daniel and I can mange with Sheba. Doctor Joseph has gone to make arrangements for us to detrain."

Bernice was relieved to see Hannah quickly gather Anna's toys, pick her up and head for the end of the car. She noticed Hannah again held her head high, as she helped Anna from the train.

When they exited at Union Depot, they quickly found Joseph and the hired carriage. He had arranged for them to stay at the Capitol Hotel, located twelve blocks east of the large wooden train depot and overlooking the beautiful tree lined river.

The next day while Joseph sought a house for them to rent, Hannah, Daniel and Anna explored their new surroundings. Sheba was exhausted from the trip and remained in bed, with Bernice staying nearby in case the expectant mother might need anything.

The young people were surprised in the daylight to discover the river so close to the hotel. The riverbank bustled with exciting activity. They were cautioned not to venture out into the water. They had been warned at the hotel of the treacherous currents that flowed briskly past Little Rock. All they had to do to enjoy the magnificent view was stroll along the craggy bluffs. Hannah was careful to hold firmly to the exuberant Anna's hand.

Across the river and slightly upstream, cliffs rose majestically. Hannah was sure there could not be a more beautiful place in the world than this spot to which Joseph had brought them. "Thank you, Jesus," she murmured. "Thank you for leading us to this heavenly place."

"Amen, to that," Daniel whispered, smiling down at his sister.

"Isn't this wonderful, Daniel?" She grabbed Anna up and whirled around taking in the city that flowed back from the river. "Just look at this beautiful modern city, right here on the banks of this picturesque river." She gestured expansively as she looked around them.

The three spent the morning walking along the bluffs overlooking the river. As they approached the docks, they noticed a large steamboat making its way down stream.

"Would you look at that boat?" Daniel stared in awe at the large boat. "Some day, I'm going to take a trip on one of those."

The brother and sister, with Anna firmly anchored between them, watched the imposing craft draw near. It was laden with cotton bales, which had been loaded upstream and would eventually make their way to northern textile factories along the great river road.

"Used to be boats all up and down the river," came a gruff voice beside them.

They turned startled to see a wrinkled old-timer in tattered clothes sitting against a large cotton bale. The giant bale of cotton made him appear even smaller than he actually was.

"How do you do?" greeted Hannah smiling at him politely. "We are new here and were just admiring the wonderful view. It is unbelievably beautiful."

"It's purty aw right," the old man acknowledged. "Nothin' like it were ten yar ago though," he replied forcefully.

"Were you a boatman?" Daniel inquired politely.

"Of course, I were a boatman." His reply was most emphatic, as he moved toward them in an odd swaying gate. Every other step he took, made a clunking sound against the wooden dock. "Fit the Yankees duren the war, an' crewed on most every paddle wheel up and down the Miss'ssippi and Arkansas." His tone demonstrated his pride in these accomplishments, as he advanced closer to the three awe struck newcomers.

"You…You must have really loved the river." Hannah peered down at the small man who reminded her of their friend Donald.

Anna had been examining the stranger from the safety of Hannah's wide skirt. Suddenly she darted out from her cover and ran toward him, her eyes gleaming with recognition.

"Don'ld's buba?" she asked, confronting the stranger.

"No Anna," Hannah said hurrying to reclaim her hand. "He isn't Donald's brother."

The man looked surprised, as he squatted beside the friendly child and studied her pixie-like face peering at him eagerly from under the wide brim of her sunbonnet. "Well little miss, aren't you somethin'. Who's this here Don'ld? Don't recollect haven a brother by that name, but then I have been gone a spell." This last was said with a big wink at Hannah and Daniel. He spoke in a thick Irish brogue; similar to Donald's, so it was easy to see why Anna thought they must be related. Although when he stood they could tell he was several inches taller than the diminutive Donald.

Hannah's face turned a rosy hue while Daniel explained.

"Donald is a friend of ours. He stayed in Memphis while we came on to Little Rock. Anna misses him. She was real partial to the old prospector."

"Oh! Weg's hurt," Anna said sorrowfully, as she pointed at the stranger's left leg. She was studying the man curiously, not at all afraid of him although she was usually shy around strangers.

"Anna, that is not polite," corrected Hannah gently. She pulled the toddler to her side and again had a good hold on her small hand.

"Why?" Anna asked looking from the newcomer to Hannah quizzically.   Her large eyes were wide with innocent curiosity.

The old man grinned at the child. His toothless mouth made him appear quite comical, as he pulled up his pant leg to display a wooden peg leg.

"Gater ate it," he informed Anna. "Gater ate it in '58, but this here peg gets me wherever I need to go." Winking at Anna, he leaped into the air and demonstrated his dexterity on his one good leg and the wooden peg.

"I can even dance a jig." He quickly demonstrated his agility while playing the Irish Washerwoman on his French harp.

Anna laughed and slipping her hand from Hannah's, gaily clapped her hands together and jumped up and down in an imitation of the man's dance. Hannah was too stricken by the man's announcement of how he had lost his leg to enjoy the performance.

"You were actually attacked by an alligator?" Daniel inquired, curiosity lighting his face, as he leaned closer to the newcomer.

"Sure an' I was boy," he replied with another big wink. "An you better watch where you walk along the river or you'll lose both of yern."

Hannah turned quite pale and began furtively looking around. "Are their alligators here? Right here in town?" she asked incredulously, her eyes large with apprehension.

"Well-l-l-l, not like there are along the Bayou," he acknowledged. "I've seen them 'round though," he added brazenly.

"We must be getting back to the hotel," she stated firmly. The hot Arkansas sun was directly overhead. "Our friends will be waiting for us to return for lunch," she explained to their new acquaintance, softening her tone.

"We are very glad to meet you," said Daniel. "My name is Daniel Brown and this is my sister Hannah.

"Me Anna," Anna piped up pointing to herself, before Daniel had a chance to include her in his introductions.

"I am pleased to be meeten you miss Anna," he said bowing to the child. "And I'm called Peg. Just call me Peg," he added cockily. "It's what ere one calls me here abouts."

"Well, Mr. Peg, we must be going now," Hannah said with a warm smile. "We're very happy to have made your acquaintance. Perhaps we will run into you again."

"It's nice to meet you," Daniel agreed extending his hand to shake hands with Peg. "Maybe you could tell me about the river sometime?" he asked eagerly.

"Sure boy." Peg winked conspiratorially, as he turned to move down the dock in the opposite direction. "Anyone kin till yea where old Peg's at. Just ask around," he called after them.

They hurried back to the hotel holding firmly to both of Anna's hands. Tales of alligators nearby had made them uneasy in their new surroundings.

They picked up a message from Joseph at the front desk. He would not be returning for lunch, but would join them for dinner. Sheba was still not feeling well and remained in bed. The others ate in the dining room, sharing with one another their first impressions of Little Rock. Anna, tired from their busy morning dawdled over her food, while Hannah and Daniel told Bernice about the interesting character they had met on the docks.

After lunch and a tray had been carried to Sheba, Hannah put Anna to bed. Then joined Bernice in the sitting room to write a letter to her parents and catch up on her reading. It was slightly cooler than the day before, but hot enough to keep the ladies confined to quiet activities while the sun was overhead.

Daniel excused himself to explore along the cliffs, which rose abruptly from the river. He looked with longing at the high bluff upstream on the north bank. "What a grand place to explore," he said wistfully.

"A gran' place it is," came a voice beside him.

Daniel whirled around, embarrassed at being caught talking to himself. "Oh! It's you Peg." He was relieved to find the slightly eccentric Peg standing beside him and not a complete stranger that might think him a bit addled.

"Have you been over there?" Daniel motioned to the mountain upstream and across the wide river.

"Aye," Peg responded. "I've been up on yonder hill. Ye can see forever up thar. Ye ken even hear the ghosts of the Injens what was driven from this land, from the top of Big Rock, on a clear moonlit night. If you listen close enough, of course."

Daniel did not quite know how to respond, so he changed the subject. "Hannah and I are going to walk around town to sort of get our bearings and explore a little. Would you like to join us, if you aren't busy, of course?" The latter was added to give Peg and out if he did not want to waste his time traipsing around town with them.

"An' wouldn't it be a pleasure to keep comp'ny with you now. 'Tis always nice to escort such green newcomers 'round about," he replied with a flourish. "'Tis hot out for the lady and little Miss though," he added thoughtfully.

"We won't venture far, just along the water front and maybe a few blocks into the town. There is a nice breeze coming off the river," he added licking his finger and holding it up to test the strength of the breeze.

Daniel arranged to meet Peg at the front of the hotel in about an hour, before hurrying off to clean up form his exploring.

Hannah was standing in the lobby gazing out the front window when Daniel walked in covered with mud. She greeted her brother warmly before catching a glimpse of the state of his clothing.

"What have you been doing?" she scolded in her big sister manner.

He greeted her with a kiss on the cheek, as he tried to slip past. Hannah was quicker and grabbed hold of his arm, looking him over closely.

"It was nothing. I took an impromptu slide down the river bank, while I was walking along the side." Hannah's eyes automatically went to his boots. "I stopped before I actually went in, but I got my pants a bit muddy," he admitted mischievously.

Hannah laughed and turned him loose. "A bit, huh. It looks more than a bit to me. I may never get those pants clean again," she said shaking her head, but smiling at her brother good-naturedly.

"We're going for a walk with Peg, as soon as Anna gets up," he called as he made for the stairs. Several sedate hotel guests in the lobby watched his progress with frowns, as he leaped up the wide staircase, taking the steps several at a time.

Chapter Twenty-Two

Joseph had returned, looked in on Sheba and then joined Bernice. Joseph and Bernice appeared on the landing and Hannah smiled up at them. Her eyes met Joseph's and for a moment Joseph's face seemed to brighten and he returned her smile.

She makes her simple dress look like an expensive gown, he mused. *Hannah has no need of the fashionable corsets that society dictates*, he reflected as his eyes sought her tiny waist and than moved to her lovely sun-kissed face, cheeks glowing a rosy hue. He continued to study her. Suddenly his look of admiration turned to a scowl as he chastised himself. *I'm a fool to be thinking she might be interested in me, as more than a friend.* Abruptly he turned on his heel and moved swiftly back down the hall to his room, which was located over the German National Bank.

Bewildered by Joseph's abrupt change in demeanor, Hannah moved to a settee beside one of the large pillars in the spacious lobby. She sat in the corner of the seat and turned her face to lean on the cool pillar. She was totally confused; he was smiling at her and suddenly he looked like he was angry with her. She could not think of anything she had done to cause such a startling change.

Bernice quickly took in the scene and moved down the stairs toward Hannah. When she reached the young woman, she sat beside her and took her hand in a comforting gesture. Hannah threw herself into Bernice's arms and let the dammed up tears flow freely. She was totally oblivious to the inquisitive stares of the other hotel guests sitting or passing through the lobby.

"Why does he hate me so Bernice? We have had such good times together. While we were traveling we were a close family, but now I hardly know if it is safe to speak to him."

"It is not you honey," she soothed. "The problem is inside of him. He will come around," she promised, wiping at the tears flowing down Hannah's cheeks with a dainty white linen handkerchief. Bernice wished she felt as confident about that as she sounded speaking to Hannah.

Hannah finished drying her face by rubbing her sleeve across her face and excused herself to check on Anna. She had left her lying on a trundle bed in Sheba's room.

Anna was awake when Hannah entered. She had climbed onto the bed with Sheba, who was telling her stories about Three Oaks.

"Feeling better, Sheba?" she asked, walking to the bed and holding out her arms for the rambunctious youngster. Anna jumped to her feet prepared to sail off the high bed. Hannah rushed to the edge of the bed before Anna could launch herself into the air. She caught her and settled her on her hip.

"A little, I had a nice nap, but I am ready for this little one to make his appearance." She was pale and still appeared extremely tired.

"Would you like me to read to you?" Hannah moved to the table beside the bed and picked up Sheba's Bible.

"No thank you, but you are welcome to take this whirlwind out of here and I will lie down and rest some more. This baby is getting mighty restless is all and with the heat…." Her voice trailed off, as if she did not have the strength to even complete the sentence.

"You rest," Hannah, entreated, as she wet a cloth from the cool water in the pitcher on the washstand. She laid the cloth gently on Sheba's warm forehead, and then sponged her face and arms.

"Thank you, that feels so much better," Sheba murmured.

Hannah scooped Anna up, dressed her in a lightweight gingham dress, but discarded her petticoats in deference to the heat. They left Sheba to rest and joined a much cleaner Daniel in the lobby.

Peg seemed to materialize out of nowhere, as they stepped out of the hotel onto the sidewalk. Carriages were rushing past on the busy street. The hooves of the horses pulling them clicked on the newly paved street. The coachmen guided them to the side of the road as the streetcar conductor clanged the bell and the big car moved down the tracks in the center of the street.

"How modern Little Rock is," Hannah marveled, as they faced south on Main Street. "The street car tracks seem to go forever. Someday we will have to ride it to the end of the line, just to see where it ends up." She was in awe of all the activity. For a country girl the hustle and bustle of the capital city left her astounded. "Imagine people thinking of this as a backwoods place. The way some people talked along the way, once we crossed the Mississippi we would have totally departed from all visages of civilization."

"Oh, Hannah girl, but don't yea know that tis the people here that spread such rumors," confided Peg. "Sure if heaven gets to crowded, it no longer seems so heavenly. Does it now?"

"I believe you have something there, Peg." Daniel laughed and slapped his leg in high spirits. A fun loving young man, he thoroughly enjoyed Peg's humorous statements and lilting speech.

Hannah glanced at Anna who had been craning her neck upward, at the windows above the bank building. She was waving and trying to get someone's attention.

"What is it Anna?" Hannah followed her gaze up to the window. She could not see anyone, but noticed a curtain fluttering behind an open window. Assuming it was Joseph behind the curtain, she determined to not let him or anyone else spoil their beautiful day of exploring.

She took Anna's hand and began strolling briskly down the walkway. Daniel gazed at his sister furtively and then back toward the window where Hannah and Anna had been looking. He thought he caught someone stepping hurriedly behind the curtain. He was sure someone had been standing in the window watching as they left the hotel. His protective instincts were on alert. He would make sure no one was out to harm his sister or their small charge and he moved closer to Hannah and Anna.

They stopped to admire the State House with its spacious lawns, ornamental fountain and the four grand white columns that stood as sentries across the front.

"Who would ever guess this wonderful place is here?" Hannah gazed up at the imposing structure, marveling at the beauty of it.

"Anyone coming down the river would." Peg laughed and slapped his wooden leg with his hat. "It has two fronts. Ta other one faces the river."

Daniel teased his sister about being a country bumpkin, as they turned south at Center Street. Although he did have to admit to himself that he was surprised to find this modern city where he had expected a wild frontier town. *They are even putting in electricity*, he considered in amazement.

The four explorers spent the next couple hours strolling along the streets, admiring the beautiful homes and many churches. "Every existing denomination," Daniel said with awe, as they noted the variety of worship houses available to them. *Well, everyone I have ever heard of anyway.*

They passed a variety of thriving commercial enterprises in the flourishing community. Hannah especially enjoyed browsing in Ottenheimer's Emporium and Quinn's Dry Goods. Daniel was fascinated with the streetcar and was anxious to ride the line to its end.

Anna loved everything she saw, but was very partial to the animals they met. Horses were tied along the sidewalk, flicking their ears and switching their tails to ward off pesky flies. Dogs wandered down the street, in and out of the shops, or patiently waited at the door for their masters to emerge. There were cats of all descriptions: huge long-haired gray cats that watched the parade of people and animals from windowsills; sleek yellow cats strolled down the sidewalks, ignoring the bustle around them and hissing at an occasional dog that drew near; and nondescript alley cats that slunk between the buildings to catch unwary mice. Anna adored them all and begged with each encounter to be allowed to take that particular cat home with her.

"Not yet sweetheart." Hannah smiled down at Anna fondly. "I hope we will be in a house soon. Then you will be able to have some pets to care for. Won't that be fun?"

Anna clapped her hands and danced in circles at the prospect of pets of her very own. She missed the animals that were always around on the plantation in Thomasville.

"Anna have a dog?" Her eyes were alight with the anticipation of having a wiggly puppy of her very own.

"You probably can," Hannah agreed, laughing at the excited Anna.

"Kitty too? Anna's Kitty."

"We will have to see about that." Hannah was beginning to regret making a rash promise to Anna without first consulting Joseph. She knew she should have discussed it with Joseph before saying anything to Anna. "Of course, first we will have to ask your father."

"Papa woves puppies and kitties," Anna assured her unhesitatingly. "Orsey?" Anna put both of her small hands across her heart and declared, " Wov orseys."

"Now wait a minute, little bit," Daniel said affectionately, as he swung her up on his shoulders. "There has to be room for us you know."

Anna giggled as Daniel jogged down the street like a trotting horse. She gripped his curly blond hair tightly and squealed with delight as she bounced up and down on his shoulders. Daniel whirled around just as a young lady emerging from the store they were passing. They hit with a crash. Parcels went flying. Daniel barely managed to escape toppling over on the unsuspecting girl, while managing to maintain his hold on Anna.

Daniel quickly slipped Anna off his shoulders and steadied the attractive young woman, chagrined at nearly having sent her sprawling into the street. "I'm sorry miss."

Daniel's face was flushed with embarrassment. He quickly bent down to retrieve the parcels that had flown from her arms onto the board sidewalk.

"Oh!" She straightened her straw hat and bent to help retrieve her parcels. "I'm afraid I wasn't looking where I was going. "I'm just as much to blame," she assured him.

"I'm Daniel Brown, at your service ma'am." Daniel doffed his hat with a flourish and bowed low before the startled young woman, as he presented her fallen parcels to her. She was dressed all in blue, the shade of a clear summer sky and her smoky blond hair hung down her back to her waist. *I've run into an angel and she will think me the worst kind of oaf.* "This wiggle wart is Anna Warren. I take full responsibility for the mishap and offer my most profound apologies."

"I am pleased to meet you both. My name is Louise…Louise Michaels." She smiled at his antics. "Perhaps next time we won't meet with quite so much force," she teased, causing Daniel's face to turn even a deeper red as he grinned sheepishly at the lovely young woman.

"Are you all right?" Hannah called anxiously as she ran up to them with Peg close behind.

"Yes! We are quite all right." Louise turned toward the duo hurrying up beside them.

"This is Louise—Louise Michaels," Daniel introduced the young woman. "And this is my sister, Hannah and our friend Peg."

"Well, just one Louise." She extended her gloved hand first to Hannah and then to Peg.

"I am so happy to meet you, Louise. We are new to Little Rock and have not met many people yet." She noted that the packages were a bit dirty and bent, but Louise did not appear to have been harmed by the collision. Hannah was relieved that Daniel's reckless prancing down the sidewalk had not injured anyone.

"Sometimes my brother forgets he is no longer on the spaciousness of the farm." She gave Daniel a firm censorious sisterly look before turning back to Louise with a big smile.

Peg remained a little behind Hannah, but nodded his head politely to the young woman when he shook hands with her.

"Is this your darling little girl?" Louise smiled warmly at Anna, before glancing up inquiringly at Hannah.

"No," Hannah replied somewhat reluctantly. "I guess you would call me her nursemaid or nanny." She leaned down to give Anna a hug. "We all love her like she belongs to each of us though."

"That is easy to see." She glanced up at Daniel through her long thick eyelashes, a coquettish smile on her face.

This made Daniel turn red again. He stammered so much when he tried to make polite conversation that Hannah decided she had better rescue him. "We really must be on our way if we are going to see more of the town today, but I hope we will see you again, Louise."

"Will you be staying in Little Rock long?"

"We plan to make this our home," Hannah replied, taking Anna's hand when she started to move toward a dog up ahead. "We will probably travel around quite a bit though. We really must be going. It was very nice to meet you and I hope we'll see you again soon." She could not help adding. "Perhaps we can do it a little less spectacularly next time."

Daniel picked Anna up in his arms and she continued to wave goodbye over his shoulder as they moved down the sidewalk, giving Daniel an excuse to turn and smile at Louise.

Chapter Twenty-Three

After viewing more of the sights they bid Peg goodbye just before dusk and headed back to the hotel. They were surprised to discover their companions were not in their rooms. Daniel went down to the desk to inquire if they had a message.

"Yes, there is one here for Miss Hannah Brown from Dr. Joseph Warren." The desk clerk handed him the message. "Your friends left in somewhat of a hurry, after inquiring where the hospital was located." Daniel tore into the message as he ran up the stairs to Hannah's room.

"They have taken Sheba to the Sisters of Charity Hospital," he yelled as he raced into her room, not even thinking to knock on the door. "He wants us to stay here and take care of Anna."

Hannah took the note and quickly read it. "He asks us not to try to find the hospital until tomorrow and promises to send word of Sheba's condition as soon as possible. Joseph and Bernice expect to spend the night at the hospital with Sheba." Hannah sat down heavily on a chair beside the bed. "Oh Daniel, the baby is not ready to be born. It is still too early. Maybe we were wrong to insist on leaving Memphis. I am afraid the trip was just too much for her." Tears began to trickle from her eyes and Anna ran to her and buried her head in Hannah's lap. She did not know what was happening, but the concern in Hannah's voice alerted her that all was not right with her world. Anna began to cry along with Hannah.

Daniel put his arm around his sister in an effort to comfort her, while patting Anna's small back.

"It's all right honey." Hannah picked Anna up on her lap and dried both of their tears with her skirt. "Everything will be all right. Your papa and Bernice are taking care of Sheba. We will go check on them tomorrow if they aren't home." *I only wish I was that confident;* she could not help thinking.

Joseph returned the next morning disheveled and tired. Hesitating beside Hannah's door, he continued on to his own room when he decided it was too early to disturb her. He turned the key in the door and wearily pushed it open. Surprised to catch a glimpse of someone in his bed through the open door, he quickly retreated and double-checked that he had the right room. Assuring himself he was in the right room, he reentered to find Hannah sitting up on the edge of the bed drawing her wrapper over her light cotton nightgown.

"Doctor Joseph how is Sheba?" She kept her voice low, so she would not disturb Anna. She was so concerned for the welfare of her friend that she did not consider the impropriety of being in Joseph's room in her nightdress.

Joseph studied her uncertainly. His astonishment at finding Hannah in his room was quickly replaced by a feeling of the rightness in coming home to have her greet him after an exhausting night at the hospital. He smiled at her longingly and glanced to where his daughter was still curled up in innocent sleep. It was not hard to put two and two together and come up with Anna insisting on sleeping in her father's bed during his absence.

"Anna was fretful with you and Sheba both gone and wanted to sleep in her papa's bed. I tried to dissuade her, but when she sets her mind to something…"

"No explanation necessary. I had already surmised that for myself."

"I should not have yielded to her, but we were all so worried about Sheba and…" Her explanation was abruptly cut off when she saw his smile turn to a look of pain. "What has happened? Is she worse? Did she loose the baby?" Hannah felt her insides wrench with despair. For a moment, he had seemed happy and content.

"No nothing like that." His expression quickly changed to professional detachment, from the look of dejection when he chided himself for thinking that Hannah could be his. "She is doing better, but we thought it would be best to keep her in the hospital until after the baby is born." He busied himself removing things from his pockets with his back to Hannah.

"She's quite frightened about being in the hospital, so it will help if you and Bernice take turns staying with her, for awhile anyway. Maybe Daniel can take over more of Anna's care while you two are busy with Sheba. I know Daniel would not mind staying with her, but it is a woman's ward and they do not allow men to stay." He turned back to look at Hannah, but he was careful to make sure he wore a neutral look on his face. It would not do to let Hannah know how much he longed for a deeper relationship with her.

"Of course, I'll go speak to him now. You need to get some rest." Anna had awakened upon hearing her father's voice and was sitting up in the bed rubbing her eyes. Hannah moved to the bed and picked her up, but she struggled to get to her father.

"Papa, papa where's baby?"

Joseph took his daughter from her, being extra careful not to come in contact with Hannah in the exchange. "The baby is not ready to come live with us yet sweetheart." He was reluctant to make any promises with the precariousness of the situation. Anna flung her arms around him and gave him a big hug.

"Papa, we're so gwad your home."

"Me too sweetheart, but papa needs some rest. You go along with Hannah now and I will see you later." He kissed her on the head, before handing her back to Hannah.

"Hannah…" Joseph began haltingly. "I…" he fumbled for the right words, but could not say what was in his heart. She looked so very young and innocent.

"Yes, Doctor Joseph?" Hannah kept her voice quite formal. She knew she must not let him know how she really felt or he might send her back home. She just could not stand it if he sent her away from him and Anna.

"Thank you, for taking care of Anna," he said brusquely. He turned away from them and walked to the window. He did not turn around to see the hurt in Hannah's eyes or her bewildered expression.

Later that day, Daniel got his wish about riding the streetcar. He and Anna accompanied Hannah to the end of the trolley line and then they walked the rest of the way to the hospital. Daniel played with Anna in the yard behind the attractive white picket fence, while Hannah entered to relieve Bernice.

Several days later, Joseph was able to rent a house near the hospital. He became well acquainted with the other physicians in town during Sheba's lengthy hospitalization. When the head of the Medical School learned of his vast studies in pharmacology and his interesting work with folk medicine, he was eager to hire Joseph as an instructor for the fall term at the medical school.

Joseph was also asked to assist in the private practice of Dr. Phillip Kramer, who was getting on in years and was looking forward to relinquishing his practice to a younger man. Once more money was coming into the household instead of only flowing out in a one-way stream.

Bernice took a temporary nursing position at the hospital. She decided if she was going to be there all the time anyway, she might as well help by contributing to the family's resources. The only drawback was that she had to sign a contract, agreeing to stay for six months, so she would be obligated to work there until the middle of January.

Hannah visited with Sheba every day, but with Bernice able to drop in and out and Sheba becoming more comfortable with the situation, it was not necessary for her to stay with her. Most of her time was spent with Anna and the household chores. She stayed too busy with her responsibilities too do much of anything else.

Daniel found work plentiful with all the buildings being constructed in Little Rock, so everyone was able to contribute to the well-being and economy of the family.

Chapter Twenty-Four

The weeks passed quickly for the family with all the activity. Everyone was busy but Sheba; the mother-to-be grew restless and melancholy being confined to a hospital bed. The nurses were thoughtful and attentive and soon she became less apprehensive about being there. Each of the family members did their part to help relieve her boredom, but it was the first time since the accident that Sheba truly felt useless. There had always been some function she could serve within the family, but now she was relegated to a bed—that was not her own, in a room full of strangers.

She became acquainted with some of her roommates, but most were so sick they were not interested in visiting. Few mothers were admitted to the hospital to deliver babies and the ward was mostly made up of women who were very sick or dying with various illnesses.

Hannah painstakingly fashioned a hand puppet from one of Daniel's old socks for Sheba's amusement. She embroidered comical features on the puppet's face after dyeing it brown with walnut hulls. Regrettably, walnuts being what they are, she dyed her fingers as well. Daniel was the best puppeteer and frequently made the trip to the hospital after a long day at work. With Bernice and Joseph popping in throughout the day and Hannah coming to see her whenever there was someone to leave Anna with, her days were bearable.

The big day finally arrived. Sheba's labor began in earnest. Joseph and Bernice stayed with her during the long twelve hours. Unfortunately, her labor was not proving to be fruitful and Joseph had to take drastic measures.

Daniel had tried to work, but after hitting the same thumb with a hammer three times he put his tools up and told the foreman he was needed at home. Hannah and Daniel with Anna excitedly skipping between them made the trip back and forth to the hospital many times throughout the day.

A small but robust baby boy was finally delivered with the aid of a new procedure called caesarean section that Joseph had been studying in case it was needed for this delivery. Daniel thought the newcomer resembled an Indian papoose, with his reddish skin and very black hair that curled delightfully over his head. He teased Sheba about giving birth to a small warrior.

She was still weak from her long ordeal, but not too weak to have a quick comeback. "When did you ever see an Indian with curls like that," she flashed back. "But I am going to name him after a famous warrior. I'm going to name him Joshua after God's warrior in the Bible." She lay back on the pillow with the small bundle nestled in her arms. It was obvious from her countenance that she already adored her small son. "You'll see, he'll be a great warrior like his name sake one of these days."

"You bet he will!" Daniel was obviously delighted with the new arrival from the large smile spread across his face.

"Oh Sheba, he's so beautiful!" Hannah just stood and gazed dreamily at the tiny bundle. "He sure has good lungs." She laughed with delight as she studied the baby. "I can hardly wait to get him home."

"Doctor Joseph said we have to stay at least two more weeks. I don't know if I can stand being here another two weeks. I want to get home and begin taking care of my son." Tears were filling her eyes and began to run in rivulets down her cheeks and onto little Joshua's head.

"I know you are anxious to come home and we are certainly ready for both of you to get home. I can hardly wait to get my hands on Joshua myself. I am sure that Joseph just wants to make sure you don't have any complications. This has been so hard on you." Hannah fluttered around Sheba's bed straightening everything and fluffing pillows.

She did not hear Joseph enter behind her until he was standing beside Sheba's bed. His arm brushed against hers and she inadvertently stepped aside as the warm flush flowed through her body and made her face glow. If Joseph was aware of the electricity between them or even that she had pulled away, he did not respond.

"Physician heal thyself," Bernice muttered, as she entered the room from the hall and observed the reaction between Joseph and Hannah. They had both grown so very dear to her, but sometimes she just wanted to shake some sense into them. *I'll have a little talk with you later Doctor Joseph. This has gone on long enough.*

"Sheba, Joshua is doing very well and appears to be strong and healthy." He had thoroughly examined the infant earlier. "He appears to be a real fighter." Joseph smiled down at the proud mother and infant. "Have you had any problems nursing him?"

"Not at all, he's a good eater." She was anxious to assure Joseph that they were well enough to go home. "Don't you think he would do even better if we were at home, Doctor Joseph?" Her expression was of such hope and pleading, it was hard for Joseph to deny her request.

"Maybe in a couple weeks," he hedged. "We'll see how things go." He barely acknowledged Hannah's presence, but stopped to confer with Bernice before strolling from the room.

The ward for women of color, where Sheba was confined was crowded with women. There were mostly elderly women with apoplexy or the very sick. The ward was noisy and stifling and not really conducive to getting much rest. That night at the dinner table Bernice broached the subject of Sheba coming home. Everyone was home at the same time, which was rare in itself since Sheba's confinement.

"Doctor the hospital is crowded. I was wondering if Sheba and the baby would not be better off here at the house, where they would not be exposed to so many kinds of illnesses."

"I know Bernice. I have considered the consequences of leaving them there versus bringing them home, but Hannah has her hands full now. I am hesitant to put additional work on her." He carefully kept from glancing at Hannah, where she sat with her mouth open. "Sheba requires so much care, more now then before, plus all the care of little Joshua. She already is responsible for the entire household plus Anna; it is not fair to Hannah to put these additional burdens on her."

"But you know that I don't mind," she jumped to her feet. "Let them come home." Hannah pleaded, as she paced up and down the kitchen. "Sheba has been gone so long and she hasn't even seen our house. It will be wonderful having the baby in the house and Sheba back where she belongs."

"You just don't realize the amount of care required." Joseph still avoided looking directly at Hannah. "The baby is small and must eat every two to three hours around-the-clock and Sheba has had additional trauma to her back plus the incision for the delivery. It may be months before she regains the abilities and strength she had before Joshua's birth…if she ever does." This was added softly, as he seemed to study the food on his plate.

"There would be all the additional laundry and carrying things back and forth. It would be impossible for you to keep up with everything. The rest of us have jobs away from home that will prevent us from assisting you." He related the latter statement with obvious regret and dejection. He felt someway he was failing his family.

"I realize it will mostly fall on Hannah, but I can help her. Perhaps I can take off a week when they first come home then when I go back to work I will help more when I get home." Bernice looked from Joseph to Hannah. He wore a determined look that was clear he had studied the matter and made up his mind, but Hannah had her hands on her hips and was fairly sputtering with indignation.

"I cannot get out of my contract at the hospital right now, but as soon as it runs out I will be back home to help even more." Bernice looked from Joseph to Hannah, both of whom had that 'don't trifle with me' look on their faces.

"I'll help after work," Daniel offered. "I can do the heavy things like scrub the floors and help with the wash."

"Daniel, be realistic. You are working all the time now. You leave before sunup and have not gotten home before dark all month." Joseph looked at them helplessly. "You are all doing so much; I cannot ask you to do more than you already are. Sheba will understand."

"You have not asked us to do anything." Hannah's voice was low and controlled. "We want to do it for Sheba and Joshua. The only question to be considered is where they will be better off, at home or in the hospital."

"When you have her room ready let me know and I will arrange for her to come home." He pushed back from the table abruptly, his supper half-eaten. "God help us all," he growled, as he strode toward the outside door.

"I could cheerfully strangle him with my bare hands," he muttered before slamming the door and walking out into the night.

"What was that all about?" Hannah, still standing, watched in astonishment as Joseph disappeared down the porch steps.

"He is not mad at us." Bernice began gathering the dishes to wash. "He is proud of the way we love and want to help each other. He has told me many times and I have heard him bragging about each of you at the hospital; how hard everyone works and how we have become a real family." She went to Hannah and placed her arm around her shoulders. "He knows how hard this will be on you. No matter how much the rest of us do, reality is that you are going to have the bulk of the responsibility for an invalid, a small infant, a toddler and the household chores. That is a lot of responsibility and will be exhausting, especially at first with the baby needing to be fed so often.

"He is mad at himself and the baby's father. He feels responsible for what happened to Sheba." Bernice took a deep breath before continuing. "Ruth warned him before he left Savannah. Joshua is not Sheba's first baby." The brother and sister looked at her with astonishment. "Sheba lost her first baby when he was only a few weeks old. He was born a couple months before Anna. Joseph suspects that the babies had the same father. Sheba was quite young and like Joshua her first baby came early.

"When Joseph's wife died, Sheba became Anna's wet nurse. She was like a sister to Beth; they grew up together." She paused and looked at Hannah and Daniel, who sat at the table and looked stunned by what she was revealing to them. "I do not mean to be carrying tales, but I thought you had a right to know some of what is tormenting Joseph, since it affects all of us."

Hannah was crying softly, as she thought of Sheba's pain and the anguish Joseph must be feeling in all this. "But who is the baby's father? Why isn't he here?"

"Joseph checked with the preacher that Sheba said married her and she is married. Joseph put the father's name on Joshua's birth certificate." Having revealed so much, Bernice did not feel that she had the right to reveal the name of the father. Sheba or Joseph would have to tell them that. "I don't feel it is my place to tell you who he is and I have no idea why he is not here."

Daniel's expression grew hard with anger, as the sorry tale unfolded. He had become very close to Sheba since joining the group in Thomasville. He felt as close to her as one of his sisters. *I'd like to get my hands on the sorry devil.*

"There are other things also that are bothering Joseph, but he will have to work those difficulties out himself. I did not want either of you thinking you had done anything to cause Joseph's bad disposition. Because you have not," she said with strong emphasis. "Be patient with him; eventually he will forgive himself. When he is able to work out his other problems, he will once again become the person we all remember and love."

"Thank you Bernice for sharing this." Hannah wiped her tears with her apron. "It helps to know some of what is troubling him. Poor Sheba, she has been through so much."

That night Hannah could not sleep and sat by her window looking out into the moonless night. She felt like that inside, she decided, dark and foreboding. "Oh God, why?" she cried softly into the still night. She felt her soul was tormented, as she considered her feelings for Joseph, his aloofness to her and the pain that Sheba had experienced in her life. "I want to help him, Lord. He is carrying so many burdens, but he won't let me." She disregarded the tears trickling down her cheeks. "I do know something of what Sheba feels. I love someone who disregards my love too."

The next few days were busy, as they rearranged the house. Daniel stayed home a couple days to do the heavy moving, as Hannah and Bernice planned the easiest arrangement to care for Sheba and the baby. Daniel had been sleeping in a room off the kitchen, at the back of the house and they decided that would be the best room for Sheba and the baby. They cleaned up the enclosed porch, so Hannah could sleep there close enough to hear the baby when he awoke at night, or if Sheba needed anything. She had been sleeping in an upstairs room in the marriage bed with Anna.

"Bernice if you don't mind sleeping with a wiggle wart, it would probably be best for you to take my bed. It is too large to put on the porch and I am afraid the baby will wake Anna up if she has to sleep on the cot downstairs with me. Then Daniel can take your bed, if that is all right.

"I am the one who should sleep on the porch and care for them at night," Bernice insisted. "You will have all the responsibility during the day, the least I can do is relieve you at night."

"No, you will need your sleep in order to go to work and besides," Hannah added with a dreamy smile. "I am looking forward to rocking the baby. I can catch a nap sometime during the day when they are asleep. If the housework has to be neglected a bit that won't be a big thing. If anyone gets upset over something that is not done, well they can just do it themselves," she said lightly.

After much discussion, Hannah's plan was finally accepted as the best arrangement. Daniel placed Sheba's bed up on blocks of wood, so Hannah would not have to bend over to care for her and the baby. The baby's cradle was placed beside Sheba's bed. A cot was made as comfortable for Hannah as possible and by leaving the door open to the kitchen she would be able to hear Sheba and the baby easily.

Chapter Twenty-Five

True to Joseph's prediction, Hannah had her hands full with Sheba's care, Joshua's around-the-clock feedings, plus seeing to Anna, the house, laundry and meals. The washing itself was a gigantic task, with dirty clothes and linens for four adults, a toddler and an infant. Sheba had been wearing makeshift diapers since the accident and now there were also the baby's diapers and gowns added to the regular wash of an active household.

It became necessary for Hannah to fill and heat the washtub twice a week instead of only on Monday to even begin to keep up with the mounting laundry and the diapers had to be boiled before they were washed. Washing was a full day, out in the back yard, chore, with running in to see about Sheba and the baby periodically.

Little Anna helped, by running back and forth to keep Hannah informed if she was needed while she worked out in the yard. She took this responsibility quite seriously and watched over Sheba and the baby like a little mother. It was not unusual for her to appear on the back porch with a squalling Joshua clutched around the middle, yelling at the top of her lungs that he had, "messed his diaper" and needed Hannah's immediate attention.

No amount of scolding or cajoling could dissuade her from 'helping' with the baby. And to be honest, Hannah did have to admit that it helped her a lot when Anna scooped the baby out of the cradle and handed him up to his mother to feed, instead of fetching her from a task out in the yard. It seemed to be much more sensible to teach her the proper way to carry Joshua and caution her to be extra careful of the top of his head, than it was to forbid her to pick the baby up at all.

One evening after work, Daniel came home with a stray puppy that had mysteriously found its way under a house where Daniel was working. He had asked around, but none of the neighbors knew where it had come from.

"Anna, I have brought you something." He took the small brown ball of fur out of his shirt and handed it to her. "Now you will be totally responsible for his care. You will have to make sure he gets fed and has water every day. The yard is fenced so he can play out there, but on washdays, you must keep him away from the fire. Puppies are curious and he won't know of the danger. Everyone else is very busy, so you will have to take care of him. Do you think you can do that?" He looked down at her, a serious expression on his face, so she would know he meant every word of it.

Anna's eyes shown with delight, as she cradled the wiggling puppy in her arms and cheerfully accepted wet puppy kisses. "Anna take care him," she promised. Her face glowed with happiness. She had prayed every night for a pet of her very own and God had finally answered her prayers.

"What will you name him?" Joseph stood to the side, smiling at his daughter's rapture with the puppy. They had discussed her desire to have a pet and he had agreed they would need to find one for her. Perhaps taking care of a pet would keep her so busy she would not be so drawn to Joshua's cradle.

"Don'ld," she said without hesitation. "My Don'ld." She buried her face in the fussy wiggling bundle in her arms. The others looked at one another surprised that she still remembered their friend Donald after all these months.

Don'ld occupied much of Anna's time and when she wasn't helping to 'run and fetch' for Joshua and Sheba, she played with the puppy.

The weather had begun to turn cool. They enjoyed the refreshing breeze and marveled at the beautiful colors of autumn. Anna loved to gather the brightly colored leaves and brought bouquets of them to show Sheba and the baby. Don'ld loved to run through the leaves and jump at them as the wind carried them spiraling up in the air.

Relations between Joseph and Hannah remained strained. With the additional work added to the emotional tension, Hannah began to loose weight at an alarming rate. She had not been very big to begin with and was beginning to take on a skeletal appearance. Bernice finally took matters into her own hands and confronted Joseph with his 'gross stupidity' when they found themselves alone, as they walked home from the hospital one evening.

"Joseph Warren, I used to think you were the most intelligent man I knew." She stood before him her hands on her hips and a look of outrage on her face as she castigated him for his shortcomings. "I have always prided myself on being an excellent judge of people, but I certainly was mistaken about you." She stopped and glowered at him. "When are you going to come to your senses?" Her face was flushed with anger, as she faced him with all the furry she could no longer suppress.

"Bernice, whatever are you talking about?" He looked at her with an incredulous openmouthed stare. He was totally bewildered by her unexpected outburst. The one person he would have sworn would never turn on him was the motherly loving Bernice.

"You have to do something about Hannah."

"Yes, I have noticed how exhausted she is. But it is exactly why I did not want to add the burden of Sheba and Joshua to her already demanding tasks. I have checked on a laundress to do all the laundry. That should help a little. I don't know what else I can do to help. Do you have any suggestions?"

"Yes, I certainly do. You can ask her to marry you. The girl is so much in love with you she isn't eating enough to keep a bird alive and she is doing the work of five people."

"In love with me, Bernice you don't know what you're saying? Hannah's a child. It would not be fair to her to be saddled with…"

"Oh, wake up Joseph!" She interrupted him before he could even finish his sentence. "She has not been a child for a long time. She is a woman and she does love you. She loves you as much as you love her and you are both afraid to let the other one know how you feel."

He rubbed his hand through his golden hair and contemplated her words. "I don't know, Bernice. I will have to think this through. I will however arrange for the laundress and maybe I can hire someone to come in and clean once a week. That should give her a little respite from the total burden of carrying for the family."

Nothing more was said about Bernice's revelation about Hannah, but Joseph made it a priority in his prayers. Bernice continued to pray for both of them and called upon the Lord to reveal to Joseph what was so obviously in his heart. Joseph made arrangements for the laundress to come twice a week to do the laundry and for a cleaning lady to come in and clean once a week.

At first Hannah did not know what to do with herself. She had been going night and day since Sheba and Joshua came home from the hospital. Now she actually had time to sit down in Sheba's room and do some of the mending that had gotten so far behind. They both enjoyed the time to visit and watch Joshua and Anna. Most days, Sheba felt well enough to sit up in her chair for extended periods during the day and they could sit on the porch and enjoy the cooler weather, while they mended, snapped beans, or pealed potatoes. Any task that could be completed sitting down, they tried to relegate to the porch so they could enjoy the sights and smells of autumn.

Chapter Twenty-Six

Friday night at the supper table, Joseph announced he was going to hike out south of town and camp along one of the streams. He planned to spend the weekend fishing and hunting. The others looked at him in astonishment. They could not recall Joseph doing anything just for his own pleasure, since the journey had begun. He invited Daniel to join him on the excursion.

"Winter is coming and we can get some meat put up. You must have cured meat on the farm?"

"Sure we did. Sounds like a great idea, but what about the work? I was going to build some more shelves for the vegetables Hannah and Sheba have been putting up."

The weather was brisk and cool and the invitation was very welcome to a young man who would rather go hunting or fishing than almost anything else in the world. Daniel was reluctant to leave the women with all the work though. Hannah still was much to thin and even though she no longer had the laundry or heavy cleaning, she had a heavy load with the extra canning and Joshua still took a lot of her time.

Bernice and Hannah both urged him to go; Bernice was off for the weekend and would be there to help Hannah. Daniel excitedly agreed to go with Joseph, when he was assured he was not leaving his sister in the lurch. He promised to build the shelves when he returned.

Hannah went about her tasks with her usual patience and attention to detail, but it broke Bernice's heart to see her looking so sad. Anna asked repeatedly where her papa and Daniel were and when they would return.

"Why?" She asked plaintively with every explanation given to her.

"Why don't you and Anna take a walk?" Bernice suggested to Hannah Sunday afternoon. Bernice had gone to church that morning and Hannah had stayed home with Sheba and the baby. They had been taking turns staying with Sheba and Joshua since they came home from the hospital. Anna had asked the same question for what seemed the hundredth time and she reasoned a walk might get her mind off her father and uncle being away.

"Oh, I don't know, Bernice. There is still so much to get done before Monday. I have clothes to sort and put away and meals to plan."

"I'll take care of that. You need to get out a bit. Sheba has just fed Joshua and they will take a nap pretty soon. This is a good time for you to get out in the fresh air."

"P'ease," cried Anna. She ran to where her coat hung on the hook by the door and tried to tug it down. Hannah agreed as she smiled at Anna's attempts to jump up and dislodge her coat from the hook.

"All right," Hannah walked over and lifted the coat down for her. She slipped into her own cape after helping Anna with her coat, "Just a short walk."

"Take Josh. Josh go too?" Anna was jumping up and down in excitement. Everyone had been so busy since the birth of the baby, that the long walks they had become accustomed to taking had been sidelined. A neighbor had leant them a carriage for Joshua and Sheba readily agreed to let him accompany them.

They bundled him in the carriage and Anna, Joshua, Don'ld and Hannah went out for a stroll in the crisp autumn air.

A number of beautiful two story homes had been built in the area, along with a few smaller houses. There were no sidewalks in this area, but the roadway was hard and firm and it was not difficult to push the carriage.

The trees were beautifully dressed for autumn with their red, yellow and orange leaves swaying seductively in the breeze. Anna scampered along gathering leaves and chattering about everything she saw. Lizards scooted through the grass and Anna and Don'ld gave chase. She caught a small green chameleon and Anna and the small creature became fast friends. He rode along on her sleeve, occasionally running up her arm to become tangled in her long hair or to rest on the brim of her straw hat.

"You have a decoration," Hannah teased her when she spotted the chameleon perched on Anna's hat as if it was his new home. "Maybe we had better let him go back to his mama. If we get too far from his home he may not be able to find his way back."

Anna carefully removed her hat and held it down to the ground so her little green friend could crawl back into the grass. "Bye bye baby wizard," she called, reluctantly agreeing to let him go back to his mama. She watched him rustle through the leaves followed by Don'ld's encouraging barks.

The cool air and beauty along with their light hearted spirits added to the pleasure of the outing. Before Hannah realized it, she found that they were in a much more sparsely populated area of large sprawling lawns and outbuildings.

They came to a quaint two-story house that appeared abandoned. The grass had grown tall in the yard and boards were missing in the unpainted picket fence. There were several outbuildings visible at the side and behind the house, in various states of disrepair.

"Swing!" Anna spied a swing hanging from a tree in the front yard that absolutely beckoned to her. "Swing? P-- e—a—s—e," she begged, pulling on Hannah's skirt.

"Oh Anna, I don't think we should go in." Hannah laughed at her antics in spite of herself.

Anna was holding onto the fence, her face pressed to the slats for a better view of the coveted swing. Joseph and Daniel both had promised to put one up for her, but had not gotten around to doing it yet.

Hannah saw a 'For Sale' sign tacked to a post on the porch; the house was obviously empted, so she yielded to Anna's pleas. Opening the gate, she pushed Joshua's carriage into the overgrown yard.

"I guess we can say we are prospective buyers desiring a closer look at the house," she said laughing spontaneously. Hannah parked the carriage in a sunny spot and helped Anna into the swing. "I hope the rope doesn't break." She gave Anna a tentative push, while gazing upward to gage the strength of the old rope.

"Wuv to swing," Anna chirped happily. Hannah pushed her gently, while they sang the alphabet song. She had sadly neglected Anna's schooling with all of her other responsibilities.

"You are so smart." Anna already knew most of the alphabet with very little coaxing. Hannah made a mental note to somehow spend more time with her. She would soon be three and there was so much she was capable of learning.

Joshua began to fret and Hannah's attention turned to him. Picking him up, she began walking about the yard to comfort him. She glanced in the uncurtained front window of the big house and saw a lovely chandelier made of crystal and brass. Hannah studied it for a while, watching how the sunlight danced off the crystal. It sent flashes of multicolored lights dancing throughout the room. She ventured closer until she finally made her way up the wide front steps to the wrap-around porch.

A large window provided a wonderful view of the parlor. The room was quite dusty and full of cobwebs, but the hardwood floors seemed to be in good shape, from what she could discern through the dirty window. The fireplace, against one wall, sported a beautifully decorated mantel and delicately figured wallpaper covered the walls. The ceiling was high with a lovely chandelier hanging in the center of the large room. She could not make out the wallpaper pattern, but it appeared to be some sort of a floral design.

"Me swing," Anna called, as she ran back to the swing.

Hannah turned to watch her; a big smile replaced the tired lines that seemed permanently etched in her face, since the birth of little Joshua. Anna was not looking at her, but was facing the other direction. She saw Anna waving and knew someone must have discovered them. Trying to think of a good excuse for their trespassing without telling an outright lie, she turned toward the gate. She found herself looking into the low afternoon sun and had to shade her eyes with her hand before she realized the man striding through the gate was Joseph.

"I suppose I should turn you both over to the authorities for trespassing." His tone was quite serious as he walked toward Anna and lifted her up in his arms where she plastered his face with slobbery kisses.

"I…we…that is…" Hannah stammered. Suddenly she laughed. "Guilty as charged." She was determined that no one, not even Joseph, would spoil this beautiful day for either her or Anna.

"Guilty," Anna echoed, "Guilty, guilty."

Joseph hoisted Anna to his shoulders and walked around to the back of the house. He casually inspected the various outbuildings and cistern.

Hannah snuggled Joshua into his carriage and pushed him to the gate, to wait for Joseph and Anna to return. She was the very picture of the dutiful nanny waiting until the gentleman of the house was ready for her to resume the care of his offspring.

"What a wonderful beautiful day this has been." Hannah looked around at the autumn colors that were spread before her like an artist's palate and hugged her arms across her chest. When Joshua stirred she patted him and sang softly as she moved the carriage back and forth until he drifted back to sleep. She thought about Joseph and their relationship, *or non-relationship, to be more specific,* she mused. She simply did not know how to respond to him anymore and it seemed safer to pretend it did not matter.

"Did you have a nice day?" Joseph asked Anna, as they joined Hannah and Joshua and started for home.

"Yes, papa. Found baby wizard. He was teeny and green. Wif one eye. He whispered to me," she confided. "Wode on my hat." She skipped along holding her papa's hand, as she related the adventures of their walk. "Let him go back to his mama." The last brought a sad look to her face, but was soon replaced with her usual merriment.

She delivered so much information, so quickly it was hard for Joseph to keep up with her prattle and he looked to Hannah for clarification.

"She found a chameleon, he rode on her hat, but we let him go so he could return to his home," she related laughing, in spite of her resolution to remain aloof. It was hard to stick to her resolve in order to avoid becoming vulnerable to one of his quick mood changes, when he smiled at her. *He didn't use to be like this. He was so patient, loving and kind to all of us while we were in Georgia and now he is so unpredictable. One minute looking at me with a loving look and the next as if he is mad at me.*

Joseph interrupted her reverie with an observation about the house they had looked at. "It does seem to be a nice place doesn't it?"

"Yes, very nice," Hannah echoed without emotion. She reminded herself that she could not be hurt, if she did not allow herself to want what she could not have.

Chapter Twenty-Seven

Several weeks later Hannah and Anna had occasion to pass by the house again. Anna tore through the gate and headed toward the swing.

"Wait Anna. It looks like someone has painted the swing. Someone must live here now." She could not have explained, if someone had asked, just why the thought of someone buying the house made her feel a deep sense of personal loss.

Anna stopped and looked at the swing curiously. It had been painted a gleaming white and was hung with new ropes.

"Anna, you know it isn't your swing. We just borrowed it the other day." She looked toward the house. It also bore a fresh coat of paint, as did the outbuildings and even the fence they had come through. "Someone must have bought the house," she explained to Anna. "See the sign is gone." Hannah motioned to where the 'for sale' sign had stood on their earlier visit.

"Anna swing?" She looked up at Hannah with pleading in her eyes as she inched closer to the inviting swing.

"I'm afraid not Anna. The house belongs to someone else." Unbidden tears formed in her eyes at the thought that someone else would live here and they would not be able to visit it anymore. "Maybe we can ask Daniel to put a swing up for you in our backyard. Wouldn't you like that?"

The next Sunday they were all able to attend worship service together. Even Sheba was feeling up to making the trip in her special chair. They sat together in back, placing Sheba's chair in the aisle beside their pew. Although they received some curious stares from the congregation, no one said anything adverse to them, even though Sheba was the only woman of color in the congregation, who was not seated in the balcony.

That afternoon, after Anna had been put to bed for a nap and the dishes were cleared away, Joseph asked Hannah if she would like to take a walk. She looked so tired and frail, he almost ordered her to rest instead of asking her to accompany him.

"Anna won't be up for awhile," she replied misinterpreting his invitation.

"I asked you to go, not Anna." He looked at her with a smile and a soft glance that she was not able to interpret.

She began telling him of all she had to get done that afternoon, not even considering the rare invitation from him. One day had become much the same as the next for her. She got up in the night to change the baby and give him to Sheba to nurse, then up at dawn to fix breakfast and help Sheba with the baby again. Then until nighttime, there were always chores that needed doing, or Sheba, Joshua or Anna needed tending. It seemed that all the spare time, which she appeared to have after the laundress and housekeeper were hired, was quickly consumed by other responsibilities.

Her main escape times were walks with Anna, rocking Joshua, reading her devotional from the Bible and praying before she crawled into bed exhausted, or sitting in church during the Sunday or Prayer meetings. She really did not know how to just relax anymore because there was always something that needed doing.

Bernice and Daniel assured her they could take care of what needed to be done. They both insisted that a walk in the cool autumn air would do her a world of good. She finally relented, when Sheba added her voice to the others and Joseph looked at her and said, "Please."

Sheba was able to spend more of her time in her chair during the day and could see to many of Joshua's needs herself. She had asked Daniel to remove the blocks so she was able to reach baby Joshua's crib and lighten some of Hannah's load. He was beginning to sleep through the night some, so all three of them were getting more sleep.

Hannah followed Joseph listlessly, not really noting where they were headed. She was surprised to discover that they had stopped at the white picket fence she and Anna had visited. Joseph opened the gate and taking Hannah's arm led her up the stone walk to the newly painted porch. She noted the grass had been cut and the yard cleared of debris.

"It's beautiful, isn't it?" She gazed around her with longing. *What would it be like to have such a beautiful place?* She wondered. "Should we be in here? I believe someone has bought it." She looked around furtively as if expecting someone to toss them out the gate any minute.

"It will be all right." Joseph self-confidently strolled up the steps, still holding Hannah's arm in a firm grip. "I know the new owner. Would you like to go inside?" Not waiting for an answer, he took a key from his pocket and opened the front door.

Hannah did not think to question how he came by the key, as they stepped through the door and she took in the view before her. A curved staircase toward the end of the hall rose gracefully to the upper floor. Four rooms opened up off the wide front hall and they walked through each of them. It was not ostentatious, but quite pleasant and attractive. *Homey! It is homey.* Hannah thought as they looked around.

She noticed a water closet and bathing-room had been added downstairs off a back bedroom. *What a marvelous idea.* She found herself gawking in openmouthed fascination as they went from room to room. After their careful perusal of the parlor, kitchen, library and downstairs bedroom they made their way to the stairs. It was while they climbed the stairs to the upper floor that Hannah again questioned their right to be there.

"Are you sure it is permissible for us to go through this house? It looks like the people who bought it have already begun moving furniture in; won't they feel that we are intruding on their privacy?

"Are you ready to leave?" Joseph looked down at her with a twinkle in his eye that told her he was teasing. He noted that as they had walked through the house, some of her old spirit was returning.

"Not really." She laughed blithely, as she continued on up the stairs. This time she was pulling on his arm. "Since we are already trespassing we may as well look at the rest of the house." Her fatigue seemed to have lifted as they moved slowly through the large house.

They entered the upstairs hall with two bedrooms on each side and a bathing-room, containing a large metal tub, directly over the one below. There was also a water closet at the end of the upstairs hall.

"This house is so modern!" Hannah looked around dreamily. "Are those electric lights?" Her voice demonstrated the awe she felt by all the conveniences available in this house, which they did not have in the rented house where they lived. "Can you just imagine having two bathing-rooms, one upstairs and one down? And there is water right here in the house." She walked to the tub and turned the faucet on just to watch it run into the tub and then circle it before running down the drain in the bottom.

Joseph guided her to the large front bedroom. "I thought we could put your marriage bed in this room."

A door leading out of the bedroom opened onto an upstairs balcony that extended over the side porch. "I think this will make a nice summer sleeping porch. Of course we will probably spend most of the summer traveling in the wagon." He was watching her closely, so far she had not commented on anything he had said. Her back was to him, so he could not see her expression but she held her shoulders stiffly and her back was rigid.

"This smaller room back here should be a good place for Anna." He walked across the floor and opened the door to the smaller bedroom. "I thought Bernice and Daniel could have the rooms across the hall. Sheba and Joshua can share the large back bedroom downstairs with the new nursemaid.

"I think I forgot to tell you that I hired a nursemaid for the children. Her name is Rose Jennings. Sheba's room is right beside the stairs. If they should need us during the night, we will be able to hear them readily." He purposely rushed on to prevent any objections she might raise.

Hannah stood in the middle of the room. All of her carefully preserved defenses collapsing. She began crying in spite of a heroic effort to hold back the tears. "What are you saying Joseph?"

"Hannah." The word was barely above a whisper. "Will you do me the honor of becoming my wife?" He fell to one knee and looked at her beseechingly.

"Oh Joseph! Why did you wait so long to ask me?" She just blurted out unable to stop the question from escaping. "I thought you were mad at me about something. It almost seemed as if you hated me." It was said with so much pain that he quickly got to his feet and moved to close the gap between them, enfolding her in his arms.

"I love you so much." Joseph whispered in her ear and kissed her hair as he held her close to him. "I just did not think you could be interested in me. You are so young and have your entire life ahead of you, why would you want to saddle yourself with a widower with a small child?"

"But I have loved you both for so long. I didn't think you cared. It tore me apart." She cried softly against his rough wool coat.

"Is that a yes?" He put a finger under her chin and raised it so he could gaze into her blue eyes, still swimming with tears.

"Yes, yes, yes," she almost yelled, as she threw her arms around him.

"I guess you will want time to make a dress and do some planning," he said reluctantly.

"I can wear my Sunday dress," she assured him. "Would tomorrow be too soon?" She gazed lovingly into his eyes, able at last to reveal her true feelings. It seemed she had to hide how she really felt about him for such a long time.

Joseph picked her up and swung her around the empty room, hugging her tightly to him, causing her to squeal in delight.

"I believe you just cannot wait to get me in that marriage bed," he teased her. She blushed a beautifully becoming scarlet.

"Oh Joseph!" she repeated, hiding her face in his coat.

"I'm sorry, Hannah. I should not have said such a thing to you." He was genuinely sorry for carrying his teasing much too far.

"It is true," she murmured, glancing up at him. "Is that awful of me? I am looking forward to every aspect of being your wife." She did not want him to think her brazen, but she decided she was not going to hide her true feelings from him ever again.

"Not at all, it is a wonderful thing for you to acknowledge." He smiled at her tenderly.

"What will the others say?"

"Well, Daniel has given us his blessing. Your father was not available, so I asked Daniel for your hand in marriage while we were on our weekend trip. He is looking forward to giving you away, glad to get rid of you I imagine," he teased. "He probably thought you would be an old maid and he would have to support you the rest of his life." She cuffed him on the shoulder, as she laughed at the teasing.

"I thought I would have to threaten him with bodily harm, if he so much as gave you a hint. I wanted to have the house ready before I asked you. Haven't you wondered what he has been whistling about and why he has been wearing a grin from ear to ear for the past month?"

"I just thought he had a new girl friend." Hannah laughed as she recalled that Daniel had been acting strangely and was rarely at home.

"Well I kept him out of the house as much as possible. He did most of the work on the house and outbuildings, with Peg's help. Peg as it turned out is quite a good carpenter himself. I wanted it to be perfect for you." His voice was thick with emotion as he held Hannah close. "Bernice thinks I am crazy because I did not ask you a year ago. Sheba wants to help with the wedding. I asked Anna how she would like you to be her mama, just before I tucked her in for her nap. She began to cry…"

"Oh dear!" Hannah's face was filled with alarm at the thought Anna might not want her for her mama.

"Let me finish." He gently soothed her by rubbing his hand up and down her arm. "When I got her quieted down I was able to get the reason out of her, she told me she though she was going to loose her Hannah. I explained that you would have even more time to spend with her, because I had hired someone to help with Joshua and Sheba. She was so excited then that I was afraid I would never calm her enough to get her too sleep."

"Everything is just so perfect. When did you tell the others? I cannot believe everyone knew and no one said anything to me."

"It was difficult enough keeping Daniel quiet. I did not say anything to the others until right before we left. As much as I am all for your suggestion about tomorrow, I do think we should at least wait until next Sunday afternoon. That way we can get some things moved over here before hand.

"I could move over here and over see everything, that way it will be easier to make the transition. What do you think?" She nodded a smiling approval and he continued.

"We won't be able to go on a trip until Christmas. I thought we might go to Hot Springs, unless you would rather go some place else?"

"I would love to go to Hot Springs. I have heard how lovely it is, but anywhere will be all right as long as we are together."

"You can be sure of that." He swept her up in his arms and carried her through the rest of the rooms upstairs. He was finally able to acknowledge the love he felt for this lovely young woman.

Hannah and Joseph planned to be married quietly in the parlor of their new home the Sunday following their engagement. They looked forward to sharing their happiness with their family and closest friends, but their plans were soon altered. Joseph had made many new friends at the hospital and the entire family had become part of the Christian fellowship at the Main Street Fellowship Church where they regularly attended services. When the news of their engagement spread so many of their new friends wished to be included, that they reluctantly relented and postponed the wedding for a month. Hannah was adamant about the location though. The event would be held in their new home.

The suggestion was made after prayer meeting following their betrothal announcement—by several of the more outspoken good ladies of the church—that spring weddings were the loveliest. The inference being, they should wait until then. There was concern among some of the matrons that the young woman might be rushing into this marriage too hastily, with such a short engagement and her mother not available to advise her.

Upon seeing the stricken look on Hannah's face at the suggestion of postponing the wedding, Opal Carpenter, a motherly widow, interceded in the discussion. She had loved her late husband dearly and missed him as much after the twenty years of his passing as she had on the day of his funeral.

"Oh but ladies," she interjected. "Autumn weddings are so very much more practical. Having your man in your bed during the cold winter to snuggle up to is ever so much more comfortable and satisfying than hot bricks." She winked conspiratorially at Hannah, as she turned on her cane and made her way slowly down the aisle of the church and out the door.

Several of the good ladies gasped, but no further attempts were made to convince Hannah and Joseph to postpone their wedding until spring.

Chapter Twenty-Eight

The plans for the wedding progressed with much excitement and tears. Joseph moved to the new house the day he asked Hannah to become his wife. He wanted to be nearby to supervise, while the work on the house and grounds was being completed. As much as Joseph and Hannah regretted the separation, it would not have been proper for the betrothed couple to continue occupying the same house.

Anna, who was to be the flower girl, was excited about being a participant in the wedding. She pranced around the yard—with Don'ld at her heels, scattering brightly colored leaves as pretend flower pedals. Don'ld chased after her--wagging his tale and circling his enthusiastic mistress. He tried to catch the falling leaves in his mouth and sent them swirling into the air as he ran though them.

Daniel was to assume the responsibility of his absent father. He would escort Hannah from the base of the stairs, through the assembled friends and neighbors.

Joseph had sent a telegram to Caroline and Hollis Brown, as well as Hamilton Earl, informing them of the upcoming wedding. A letter arrived from Hannah's parents a few days before the wedding. Hannah read it to the family.

Dearest Daughter Hannah and our soon-to-be-son,
We received your wire of the approaching wedding and are happy for both of you. We wish we could be there to help you celebrate the beginning of your life together. Hannah we want you to know that our love and prayers are with you, even though we are unable to be there in person.

Joseph we pray that you will be good to our daughter and love and care for her the rest of your life. We bid you to read together the text from God's Holy Word found in Ephesians, chapter five, verses twenty-two though thirty-three, and the book of Colossians, chapter three, verses eighteen through twenty-five. You will find in these verses much of God's direction for husbands and wives. They are good verses to begin each day together—both for reading and meditating—but do not neglect the rest of the Holy Bible in your devotional time together.

Our family is well and prospering. Your brothers and sisters bid you their good wishes. Little Minnie has started school and Clara is helping with her lessons. George and Lilly are both getting top marks, but Jacob's mischievous nature keeps him in the corner much too often. Our Elsie has an eye for the boys and they for her. Alexander is stretching at the bit to follow you and Daniel to Arkansas, so do not be surprised if he shows up on your doorstep one day. Your brothers and sisters miss you and keep you in their prayers, as do your loving parents.

We love you girl. Be a good wife to the doctor and a kind and loving mother to his small daughter.

Give our love to Daniel and greetings to the rest of your household. Merry Christmas to all of you and we bid you the happiest New Year of all.

Your loving parents

When Hannah finished reading the letter she wept with a wave of homesickness. She realized she would probably never return to her South Georgia home and she missed seeing her family. Even so, she would not leave what she had here for anything in the world. She only wished her parents and the rest of her siblings could be with her to share this special time. She looked through her tears into the troubled eyes of Joseph.

"Don't look so troubled." She went to him and laid her hand on his arm, using the other hand to wipe at the tears running down her cheeks. "I am just happy. Besides, I have a wonderful family with me." She smiled at her adopted family, who lovingly surrounded and supported her.

"Bernice will you stand up with me?" she asked going to the older woman, who was trying to hide tears of her own.

"No," she said surprising them all. "I am going to represent the mother-of-the-bride. That is by far the most exalted position at any wedding, after the bride and groom of course. And besides," she added. "The mother-of-the-bride is allowed to both sit and cry during the ceremony."

"Oh, Bernice, I love you so much." Hannah flung herself into Bernice's arms and hugged her tightly, then quickly turned to Sheba and with great enthusiasm announced. "You shall be my attendant."

"But how can I? I can't walk. Besides Hannah, it would not be proper."

"Not appropriate for my dearest friend to attend me," Hannah retorted. "Daniel can place your chair to the side of the fireplace. Bernice can hold Joshua and if he becomes fussy, Rose can carry him out. Everyone will have a part in our wedding."

The wedding participants were decided; each of them had a responsibility. Daniel was pressed into double service; Joseph's groomsman as well as substitute father of the bride.

Hannah, Bernice, Sheba and Anna rode the streetcar to Gus Blass Dry Goods to purchase ready-made dresses for the wedding. Rose stayed home with Joshua, but they were to have new clothes also. Daniel accompanied them, to assist with Sheba's chair and lift her on and off the streetcar. He did however decline their invitation to go inside. Daniel joined some other young men of his acquaintance, who also waited on the sidewalk for wives, mothers or sisters.

It would be the first time anyone of them except Bernice had ever owned 'store-bought' dresses. Joseph had arranged credit at the store and they were told to get whatever they needed for the auspicious occasion. They carefully inspected every dress in their various sizes, selecting Anna's first because they knew she would soon become tired and restless with shopping. By the time they were ready to leave with their bundles, Anna was sound asleep snuggled comfortably in Sheba's arms.

As soon as they returned home with their bundles, they untied them and modeled the new finery. Hannah's dress was a deep blue, the color of bluebells in the summer that enhanced her sparkling blue eyes. The white collar and cuffs, made of delicate Irish lace, gave the simple dress a touch of elegance. It would be a beautiful and practical dress to wear to Sunday service.

Sheba's dress was soft brown muslin with a full skirt that draped attractively over her wasted legs. The beige collar and cuffs were edged with lace. Bernice could not help wondering if Sheba realized how very attractive and bewitching she was, with her winsome light brown complexion, lovely brown eyes and high cheekbones. *If she could walk, she would have to outrun half the males in the county.*

Rose had been trying to pacify a fretting Joshua, so Bernice assisted Sheba back into her everyday cotton dress. While Sheba nursed the baby, Hannah helped Anna into her new dress. The white cotton dress was decorated with layers of satin ribbons and lace down the front of the skirt. While they were at the store, Hannah purchased new boots for her as an early birthday present. She would need them for winter, which they had been told could get cold at times and even snow occasionally. Anna loved them and pranced around, as if she were modeling for "Harper's Bazaar" with Don'ld racing behind her. The adults laughed and clapped as she displayed her new dress and boots.

Hannah and Joseph planned to leave for Hot Springs a couple days after Anna's third birthday, which was only a week away. They would spend a few days in the new house before Anna joined them, but planned to take her with them to Hot Springs. Hannah insisted Anna must be made to feel an important part of the new family union. The others would move into the new house while they were gone.

The day of the wedding they awoke to a downpour. It was a real Arkansas gully washer. It had been cloudy and damp with numerous brief showers for several days, but nothing compared with the deluge falling outside as Hannah and Joseph's wedding day dawned. The rain slacked off a little by noon. Joseph, concerned about the women, sent an enclosed carriage for them.

It would be difficult to transport Sheba's chair in the rain. An emerald green velvet chair, which had been purchased for the new house, was placed in the parlor where she would sit in a place of honor beside the bride and groom during the ceremony. Unfortunately this would severely limit Sheba's mobility. She would have to be carried everywhere, an unavoidable embarrassment.

Since she might have to nurse Joshua, she could not be placed in the chair until the service was about ready to begin. She was afraid he might fret and ruin Hannah's beautiful wedding. Bernice and Rose both assured her they were quite capable of taking care of Joshua. Bernice concealed a treat in her pocket in case the baby began to fret at an inopportune time.

Hannah sat on the floor in the large bedroom that now contained the treasured marriage bed. It was spread with the beautiful handmade linens and Log Cabin quilt her mother had given her when she left home. Tears streamed unbidden down her cheeks as she feasted her eyes on the lovely items and recalled watching her mother sewing by lantern light late into the night. She missed her family and wished they could be here for this special day, but she was content in the knowledge that she had their love and blessing.

Daniel had carried Sheba upstairs because she insisted no one else could dress Hannah's hair. She sat in a chair with Hannah at her feet and with her skillful hands lovingly arranged her hair. She reminisced to herself about all the times she had fixed Beth's hair for parties and balls and even for her wedding to Joseph. Of course, Hannah's fine blond hair was nothing like Beth's jet-black tresses. *Beth had always outshone anyone at a gathering,* she mused.

Deftly Sheba framed Hannah's face with tiny curls and then pulled a nest of curls to the crown of her head with a long trail of ringlets cascading down her back. The blond curls falling on the deep blue gown were charming. Feeling almost disloyal to her childhood friend, she conceded to her self that Hannah's blond good looks might have actually outshone her Beth.

When Hannah's hair was ready, Bernice presented Hannah with a wreath of delicate white flowers and lace to be tucked into the elaborate hairdo.

"You are a vision." Bernice looked at Hannah with a mother's love. She was very fond of the young woman and had certainly become a surrogate mother to her. "You look like a fairy princess. Sheba you did a wonderful job." She turned to Sheba and noted her pride in the part she was able to play in the wedding.

The guests were arriving and mingling with one another downstairs, while the women finished their preparations in the master-bed-room upstairs. A keg of fresh apple cider and pitchers of lemonade were set up on tables in the backyard and many guests had wandered out there to refresh themselves. The downstairs furniture had not been moved over from the rent house and the newly purchased furnishings were placed upstairs or shoved against the wall, to make room for the well-wishers. The only exceptions being, the chair Sheba would sit in and two chairs near the front for Bernice and Rose. Several elderly guests would be able to sit in the chairs against the wall. Everyone else would stand during the brief ceremony.

Daniel was carrying Sheba down the stairs, preparing to place her in her chair before the ceremony began. Joseph was already standing beside the minister, his back to the fireplace with its warm flickering glow. It had begun to rain harder so the guests had quickly made their way into the house.

A tremendous clap of thunder resounded throughout the house. It rattled the windows and startled the guests, as a late arrival entered through the front door. The newcomer was drenched and came in shaking his wide cloak, spraying water across the polished entryway. He removed his dripping hat with a flourish and tossed it on the hat rack in the hall.

"Ben," Sheba breathed softly, her eyes growing wide.

Daniel could feel her body begin to tremble, as he held her in his arms. Benjamin Earl, always the one for the dramatic entrance, strode across the floor and bounded up the stairs to where Sheba and Daniel had paused transfixed by his unexpected appearance. Quickly he swept Sheba into his arms and carried her effortlessly down the stairs, straight to the green chair, as if he had been rehearsing it for a month.

Joseph stared at him a moment before assuring himself this was not an apparition, but actually was Ben standing in his parlor.

"Gator!" Ben quickly strode to him and clasped his hand firmly. "Where did you materialize from?" He looked his brother-in-law over, as if to reassure himself that it really was Ben. "You even have the heavens accenting your entrances now, I see."

"That was merely a trifling clap of thunder. Wait until you see what I do for an encore." The minister looked from one man to the other, not sure by their tones if this was a pleasant meeting or not, as the two men regarded one another cautiously.

Joseph shook his head and laughed in spite of himself. He had to admit he was glad to see his scalawag brother-in-law and pleased to have him present to help them celebrate his wedding day. Recovering from the shock of Ben's unexpected appearance, he remembered his manners and introduced Ben to the minister.

"You are a friend of Dr. Warren's from Georgia?" The man of the cloth looked up at the newcomer and smiled.

"Yes sir. I have come all the way from Savannah by train and ferry to be his groomsman." Turning to Joseph, he raised a dark eyebrow and regarded him with a look half way between a dare and pleading. "We couldn't expect Daniel to fill in for his father and your best friend, now could we?"

Daniel had followed Ben into the room and stood beside Sheba in a protective manner. He was quite prepared to throw the rascal out, if he got out of line in the least. Ben was larger than he was by several inches, but the construction work that Daniel had been doing had made his muscles strong and he was sure he could take Ben without much struggle. He was aware that Sheba had not taken her eyes off Ben since his spectacular entrance. Her chair was placed at such an angle that she could easily see both Ben and Joseph without turning her body.

Bernice handed Joshua to Rose and quickly moved to Daniel's side. "It will be all right," she whispered in his ear, lightly touching his sleeve. "Hannah is waiting for you." When he did not move and continued to glower at Ben, she tugged gently on his sleeve. "You need to go to Hannah— now," she added quietly but firmly.

Joseph glanced at them. He saw Daniel's rigid posture and the scowl on his face as he glared at Ben and nodded toward the hall. Finally Daniel yielded to Joseph's firm glance and Bernice's touch. He turned and strode from the room.

Bernice leaned over and whispered something to Sheba. She quickly patted her shoulder, squeezing it slightly, before turning and walking from the room. She hurried up the stairs to where Hannah was waiting, but paused on the landing to glance back over her shoulder to assure herself that Sheba was all right. Bernice could see her through the doorway into the parlor and her face was still turned to where Ben stood beside Joseph.

"What a conundrum," she murmured as she entered the bedroom. Daniel was silently pacing up and down the room still wearing a scowl and Hannah was staring at him in apprehension not knowing what had caused her easygoing brother to be in such a black mood on her wedding day.

"Tell me, what has happened!"

Bernice quickly filled her in on Ben's appearance, assuring her that Joseph had everything under control. She assisted the nervous Hannah to the head of the stairs. She turned back to Daniel. "Get yourself under control and get ready to escort Hannah down to her groom." She gave him a sharp, 'I am not putting up with any nonsense from you look' and walked down the stairs to take her place beside Rose. She gave Joseph and Sheba a smile of assurance before taking a squirming Joshua from Rose and looking toward the minister as if everything was as it should be and it was time to begin.

The piano had been moved from the church and placed strategically at the front of the room for the ceremony and the minister's wife began to play. The guests quieted. Hannah, Daniel and Anna came slowly down the stairs. When they reached the foyer, Anna proudly strode into the parlor tossing camellia petals, mixed with brightly colored leaves at her insistence, along the aisle made by the parting of the guests. Everyone smiled at the enthusiastic child, who made her way so prettily toward her papa. She eyed the strange man who stood beside him with curiosity, but did not hesitate in her mission.

The strains of "Here Comes The Bride" began and Bernice stood to watch as Hannah entered the room on Daniel's arm. Murmurs drifted through the room of, "How beautiful," and "Isn't she lovely?" as she walked toward Joseph.

Ben leaned over and whispered something to Joseph, which caused a momentary frown to replace his adoring look as he followed Hannah's progress toward him. He willed himself to ignore everything but the vision gliding nearer. Tears filled his eyes as he was overcome with emotion. *How can one man be so blessed by God?* He considered the depth of his love for this beautiful young woman. *When will I awaken from this marvelous dream? I can't believe she really agreed to become my wife.*

Hannah, so nervous she had almost stumbled on the stairs, grew calm as she gazed into Joseph's eyes. One look at him, reassured her of his love.

They repeated the words of the minister were polite to their guests, made appropriate responses as they unwrapped gifts, but their thoughts were wholly for one another.

When the last guest departed and the other members of their family had returned to the rent house, Hannah and Joseph stood for a moment in their new home gazing at one another and basking in their love.

Eventually they drifted into a peaceful sleep, snuggly embraced in each other's arms. Beautiful dreams floated through their subconscious, as they looked forward to their future together.

Chapter Twenty-Nine

A resounding explosion disturbed the peaceful night, waking the newlyweds with a start. Hannah huddled under the quilt, while Joseph snatched his trousers from the chair and flew to the upstairs porch. He opened the door to find his yard filled with lanterns and merrymakers, shooting guns into the air.

"Chivaree, chivaree," echoed up from the yard below.

Joseph shook his head in disbelief and returned to his frightened bride. Sitting beside her, he explained that their friends had returned to celebrate their wedding.

"In the middle of the night?" Hannah stared at him with wide-eyed astonishment.

"I am afraid so. It's called a chivaree and I am sure Ben put them up to it. I'll have to go down before they wake up all of our neighbors and we have the sheriff at our door. I will send them home as soon as possible. There is usually strong drink involved and when I tell them we don't approve of such I am sure they will go elsewhere for their revelry." He bent over to pull the covers around her shoulders and kissed her briefly. "You stay in bed." He sighed deeply when he reluctantly turned to join the merrymakers below and hopefully discourage them.

Joseph was surprised to find Daniel and Peg in the group, whooping it up with the rest of the merrymakers. He was happy to discover that their only beverages were the fresh apple cider and slightly tart lemonade. Their enthusiasm was coming from the excitement of the event and had nothing to do with hard liquor.

He visited with the men and asked them to tone down the noise, so his neighbors would not run him out of the neighborhood or call the law on him. They complied with his request with the exception of celebratory outbursts when someone scored a ringer at moonlight horseshoe, or sent someone's ball off into the bushes during a wild crochet game, that did not seem to conform to any set rules. It turned out that it was all right, because his new neighbors had joined the merrymakers. Daniel and Ben had hung lanterns throughout the yard, but the full moon was their main light for the revelry.

There was a lot of good-natured teasing of Joseph by the participants, which he accepted in as good humor as possible, given his lack of sleep and desire to be upstairs snuggled in a warm bed with his bride. *It's my wedding night and here I am outside in the cold in the middle of the night with a bunch of rowdy men,* he thought disgustedly.

He did have time to think over the past couple years and the progress he had made both in his personal well-being and the journal he had begun on the trip. He thought of the horrible train wreck and Sheba's impairment. That had been devastating, but God had provided Hannah out of that disaster. He could not imagine his life without her. *It is true that God can work something good out of the most devastating happening.*

They had acquired good friends and family along the way; like Bernice, who had also come to them from the train wreck and their good friend and Alabama guide, Donald. They all missed Donald and hoped he would join them again, especially Anna, who still remembered her special friend.

Anna was growing daily into a precious little girl. She had been only an infant when they started out. *Thank you Jesus,* he whispered, as he thought about how close Hannah and Anna had become since Hannah had joined them. When he looked at her with her little pixy face and mischievous ways, he wondered how she would turn out. *What lays ahead for you my little charmer?* For some reason the thought disturbed him. *Oh Lord,* he prayed. *Watch over my precious Anna, for some reason I feel uneasy about what is ahead for her and I feel she is going to need your special protection. Please, Lord, send your angels to surround her and watch over her. Whatever comes dear Lord be with her through it all and give us the strength to endure, Amen.* It would be years before he would have occasion to think back on this particular night and the prayer he had prayed on his wedding night in behalf of his precious Anna.

It was nearly dawn when the last of their unexpected guests wandered home and Joseph finally was able to return to his sleeping bride. In her sleep, she snuggled closer to Joseph as he slipped into bed with her. They were not disturbed the rest of the day.

When Bernice discovered what Ben and Daniel with the help of Peg had done the night before, she parked herself on the front porch of the new house and forbid entrance to anyone who came near. When well meaning friends and neighbors showed up with gifts of food, plants and linens for the newly weds, she thanked them profusely, but refused them entrance. She took the offering from them and promised to relay to Hannah and Joseph that they had stopped by and what they had brought with them. Painstakingly she listed each person who called and whatever gift they had presented, so the newlyweds could later thank the gift bearers in person.

The following day, Joseph decided he must locate Ben and discover what had actually brought him to Little Rock. He was reluctant to leave for Hot Springs with Ben hanging around to cause mischief. He stopped by the rent house first to check on everyone. Joseph was surprised to find Ben sitting before the fire, bouncing Joshua on his knee and laughing at the baby's cute expressions.

"Greetings Joseph," Ben called as Joseph entered the room. "You must have an urgent errand to pull you away from your beautiful bride."

"Ben," Joseph acknowledged, apprehension replacing his smile. He thought he might find out where Ben was staying from Sheba or Daniel, but he had not expected to find him sitting before the fire playing with the baby.

"He is a fine boy. Isn't he Joseph?" Ben held up the cooing baby to show him off. He wore a mixture of pride and defiance on his handsome face.

"Yes Ben," Joseph replied. "Joshua is a wonderful baby. He favors his father, but none of us hold that against him. We are all hoping he inherited his mother's brains, to make up for it."

"Touché" He tilted his head in Joseph's direction and snuggled Joshua on his lap. "I assume you are here to determine my intentions." He looked at Joseph with some of his old arrogance, but also there was a touch of uncertainty in his voice.

"You were never one to beat around the bush Ben." A look of concern distorted his handsome face as he settled

into a chair across from his friend. "I want you to know that
I will not allow you to hurt Sheba or Joshua further. Why
have you come?" he asked abruptly. "Your presence can
only make things harder for Sheba, if you don't plan to stay."

The mixture of concern, compassion and firmness in
Joseph's face was more than Ben could stand. The
expression of devil-may-care, man about town, crumbled as
Ben gazed at the baby in his arms. Joshua resembled a
lightly tanned version of his father; the main difference being
his tightly curled hair, where Ben's black hair while wavy
could not be called curly.

"I can't change what has already happened, Joseph. I
went back to Thomasville and learned that our marriage is
legal then I went to Savannah because I felt I had to tell my
father in person. I expected to be disinherited, but instead he
said I was not good enough for Sheba and he would change
his will to make provisions for both of them." He looked
chagrined as he relayed that information to Joseph.

"You aren't." came the caustic reply.

"Well, Ruth put in her two cents also; actually I
thought she might bash me over the head with her iron
skillet. I will support them, but I just don't think I can stay
here. I have business interests up north now and I have to
see about them. I understand you have hired someone to
take care of them and I insist on paying her wages and for
anything else they need.

"I offered to buy her a house, but she wants to stay
with you and Hannah. It would be hard on her to be
separated from Anna. If you allow them to stay, I will gladly
pay for all their expenses and send Sheba an allowance each
month. They will have everything they need."

"You know that Sheba will always be welcomed to
stay with us Ben, but it is not your money that she needs."

The two men looked at each other over the head of the baby, neither of them speaking for a few minutes.

Finally Ben began to speak again. "Joseph I have made some changes in my life, but I still have more to go before I can come back and set up a home for the three of us." He looked down at the floor. Ben was ashamed of the way he was treating his family, but was unwilling to change. He had always put himself and his own needs first and could not bring himself to give up his life style. As quickly as he had become serious, his mood changed and he began to communicate news from Savannah.

"Katherine was married this summer. She and her mother finally hooked a poor unsuspecting dentist from Charlotte. The poor man came to town for a convention and did not have sense enough to go home.

They both laughed as they thought of the last time the three of them had been together. Becoming solemn again, Ben shared some of the hardships of the past few months.

"The grippe is getting bad along the coast, many people have gotten sick and there have already been some deaths. Ruth was ill when I left, or I think she would have attempted to make the trip with me. She was anxious to see Sheba and her new grandson." He went on to tell Joseph about Hamilton Earl and his cotton business, other family members and mutual acquaintances.

"Ben, I am glad you are acknowledging your responsibility to your wife and son," Joseph said bringing the conversation back to the present situation. "I wish you were willing to settle down and take care of them, be a part of their lives. They are of course welcome to stay with us as long as they want. They are our family and we love them very much."

He looked Ben straight in the eye. "But Ben, I want you to know that Sheba nearly died delivering your son and if I could have gotten my hands on you that night, I would have probably throttled you within an inch of your life without a flicker of remorse."

Ben did not as much as blink while Joseph spoke, he held his gaze steadily, while Joseph continued.

"If you ever get her with child again and go off and leave her, I will contact your father and tell him just what kind of heel his son is and when I get through I will make sure he disinherits you."

"I see. Of course, that would be advantageous to you and Anna wouldn't it?" Ben added sarcastically.

Joseph jumped to his feet in a fury, but regained control of his emotions before he spoke. He looked at Ben solemnly.

"Think what you want to, Ben. Just be assured that I am not making an idle threat." He enunciated each word slowly and deliberately. "I will tell Hamilton and I will make sure that your wife and child gets your inheritance and you will never get your hands on it. Sheba almost died giving birth to Joshua and I will not have her going though that again, especially not without her husband by her side.

"I will continue to pray for you Ben. Maybe the good Lord can get though to you." He quickly left the house, before saying something he would regret and never be able to take back. He walked for several miles, lifting Ben up in prayer, before returning to his waiting bride.

Ben left before Anna's birthday. Joseph saw him to the station himself and watched the train cross the Baring Cross bridge. He felt great sorrow that they were parting with so much unresolved hostility between them.

Anna's birthday party was held in the new house and she was excited about opening her gifts. All the furniture from the other house and the rest of the family had completely moved in, so they were all under one roof. Peg had come by to join the merriment and brought Anna several seashells from the Gulf. Daniel had made her several wooden animals. Sheba had fashioned a button necklace and Bernice had knitted a new scarf to keep her warm. Hannah gave her a pair of mittens that she had crocheted, to match the scarf. Anna insisted on wearing both of them and her new boots outside even though the temperature had grown quite warm for December. Peg had proclaimed it tornado weather.

Her Uncle Ben had left behind a package containing a doll with a real china head. He had also brought a dollhouse and furniture from her grandfather, all the way from Savannah. Her favorite gifts were her new mama, the new house and her very own swing. It was the swing that held her spellbound throughout the afternoon.

The adventures were about to continue. After the trip to Hot Springs, Joseph was looking forward to taking them all on exploratory trips around the state during the warm weather. They were a family and the adventurous journey had just begun.

Part Two: The Abduction

Matthew 18:10 See that you do not despise one of these little ones; for I say to you, That their angels in heaven continually behold the face of my Father who is in heaven.

Hebrews 1: 14 Are they not all ministering spirits, sent out to render service for the sake of those who will inherit salvation?

Chapter Thirty
December 1888

The newlyweds boarded the St. Louis, Iron Mountain and Great Southern Railroad for Hot Springs, two days before Christmas for their honeymoon. The weather had turned cool, but the sky was a wonderful cerulean blue that reminded Hannah of bluebells. The morning they left Little Rock, there was only a hint of fluffy white cumulus clouds dotting the western sky. Joseph's three-year-old daughter Anna accompanied them, but the rest of their accumulated family and friends were left behind on this trip, with promises of a lot of exciting travels to come.

Benjamin had already left for his business interests in the north, leaving behind his three-month-old son Joshua and invalid wife Sheba. Bernice was left in charge of the household while Joseph and Hannah were on their honeymoon.

Daniel stayed to help Bernice and continue his work in construction in the growing river city. In his spare time, he was busy courting Louise Michaels, who Daniel had literally run into soon after their arrival in Arkansas. An attractive young lady with smoky blond hair, which flowed in waves down to her waist, she enjoyed the attention showered on her from the friendly young man from Georgia .

Rose Jennings completed their household. She had been hired to care for Sheba and Joshua, to lesson Hannah's workload. Peg was at the house almost daily helping out. Missing was Donald, the prospector they had met in Alabama, who had become an important member of their diverse group.

Anna was excited about riding the train and chattered constantly about everything she saw, until the rhythmic clicking of the train lulled her into a deep peaceful sleep.

"You are going to be sorry; you talked me into bringing Anna with us." Joseph smiled at Hannah. The love he felt for his bride was evident in his eyes, as he wondered how he had been lucky enough to win the lovely young woman for his bride.

"Never," she laughed as she stroked Anna's dark hair. "This is the beginning of our becoming a family and she needs to be a part of it." She looked from the child in her arms to the man seated across from her. *He is so handsome and such a wonderful person. And he is my husband.* She was choked up, just thinking about it. Hannah smiled at Joseph letting her eyes and smile convey the deep love she felt for him.

* * *

At Malvern they changed trains, to the small, narrow-gauge railroad that Diamond Joe of Chicago had built. When they were settled on the train, Joseph eagerly related the history of the railroad to his bride.

"Diamond Joe liked to visit Hot Springs and he insisted on doing it in comfort. He financed the construction of this narrow-gauge railroad, after he had made many uncomfortable trips to Hot Springs, in a very bumpy stage. According to what I have read about him, he really loved coming to Hot Springs, so instead of changing his destination, he contracted to have this railroad built."

"Well, I for one am glad he did," Hannah declared. "Isn't this the most beautiful scenery? I can just imagine what it is like in the autumn when the leaves are all multicolored splendor, or in the spring when the wild flowers are blooming. Can't you just visualize the dogwoods and redbuds glowing in the woods?"

"You realize that you have said that about every place we have visited, don't you?" Joseph teased her. He smiled lovingly at his bride, as he thought about their adventures after the train wreck changed their lives: the beautiful mountains of north Georgia and Alabama; meeting Donald, the old prospector who made their journey so interesting with his descriptions and tall tales; the visit to Atlanta, Birmingham and Memphis; and then boarding the ferry to cross into Arkansas.

"I know," Hannah laughed. "But it really is wonderful. Look at the mountains; even without the leaves on the trees the scenery is beautiful."

"We are in the Ouachita mountains here. There are two or three mountain ranges in Arkansas, depending on who is doing the telling.   The Ouachita Mountains are unique in that they run east and west instead of north and south like most mountain ranges. The Ozark Mountains are in the north leading into Missouri. One day we will explore them also. The Boston Mountains are in the northwest, but are generally conceded to be part of the Ozarks. Then of course there is Crowley's Ridge in the eastern part of the state. As far as I have been able to make out, no one knows what it is." He laughed, as he completed his state topography lesson.

"It all sounds wonderful to me and I look forward to seeing every bit of it."

The terrain was seldom level and they soon found themselves going up and down steep slopes. The train wound through thick forests of southern pines interspersed with tall, bare, hard woods, whose branches reached out like ghostly arms and intertwined with the green boughs of the pines. Missing was the gray lacy Spanish moss they were used to seeing in southern Georgia.

"Joseph, look! What river is that?" The sun shimmering on the flowing water had her entranced, as she leaned closer to the window to study the dancing light sparkling on the swiftly flowing river.

"It's the Ouachita River." Joseph had read up on the geography of the area they would be going through. He knew that Anna would ask a million questions, but he was delighted by Hannah's interest in their surroundings.

"It looks like tiny fairies dancing across the water." Hannah was enchanted with the scene.

"Where fairies?" Anna eagerly pressed her nose against the window to get a better view.

"Just pretend," Hannah assured her. "But see how the sun glistens on the water?"

"I'll bet Donald would have had a story to tell about it." Joseph laughed as he thought of some of the wild tales that Donald had entertained them with that involved dead chickens and frogs.

Before long they passed the Cove Creek Station. "Look at that beautiful depot, Joseph. I wish we could come back and get a closer look on one of our wagon explorations. With the sun shinning on it, the station looks like it is made of diamonds." Anna patted the window, as Hannah gazed at the unusual building in awe.

"Well it is in a way. Those are called Hot Springs diamonds. They are really native crystal. I agree that it would be an interesting place to visit." Joseph looked at the area they were passing through with some interest. "How would you like to come back in the summer?" He looked at Hannah to gauge her interest. "If the springs really have the healing powers that are claimed, we could bring Sheba over to take the baths while the rest of us explore the area." His voice was filled with excitement. It was obvious he was eager to resume his research into folk healing.

"You sound like a small boy talking about the circus coming to town." Hannah laughed gaily and gazed lovingly at her husband. Her eyes sparkled with happiness and her love for Joseph was clearly exhibited for the rest of the world to view.

"I suppose I do." Joseph looked at his bride sheepishly. "I love you so much Hannah Warren. You have given me a new enthusiasm for my work on the journals. I guess I tend to forget that others may not be as excited as I am about packing up the wagon and seeking out folk cures in remote areas." He chuckled, but glanced at his bride wistfully, willing her to share his enthusiasm and desire to travel throughout this wonderland.

Hannah could hardly suppress her laughter when she looked into his eyes. His expression pleaded with her to want this great adventure as much as he did.

"You're absolutely right." She tried to keep her face and voice as serious as possible, but the twinkle in her eyes could not be suppressed. "Not everyone enjoys traveling around in a wagon like a pack of gypsies." She watched his expression change from wistful to grave and decided she had teased him enough. "Of course, Anna and I are exceptions to that. We love being gypsies, don't we Anna?" She hugged her stepdaughter close and smiled mischievously at Joseph.

"'Ceptions," Anna murmured snuggling closer to Hannah and smiling at her father.

The train pulled into Lawrence Station, which was located near Sulphur Springs. Ten of the passengers disembarked before the train continued on toward the Hot Springs Depot. They were startled to see a large assemblage of hawkers pushing and shoving to be the first to inform the travelers of the benefits of the various business enterprises that they represented.

Joseph was slightly taken aback by some of the slogans and vowed to investigate many of the so-called cures when they returned. One of the signs proclaimed, "Ladies, Right this way to Doc Springer's Cure for Women's Diseases and Rheumatism." *If they have a medicine that can cure those things, it should be in every medical journal available.* He just shook his head and continued to look around.

A squat little man, wearing a sandwich sign, hawked "Doctor Wart's curative waters and tonic." Hannah blushed when he turned around and she read the other side of the sign. "Sleep and play at Mrs. Busts Room, Board & More."

Anna appeared to love the commotion and she danced around and clapped her hands. As far as she was concerned, the hawkers simply added to the excitement and adventure of the holiday trip.

The newly arrived travelers boarded the hotel carriage-bus and soon found themselves craning their necks to see out the windows and admire the beautiful wonderland they had entered. The town was situated on the banks of the snaking Hot Springs Creek and nestled in the narrow valley between Hot Springs Mountain and West Mountain. They saw sightseeing boats and boat-taxis traveling up and down the meandering river between buildings that were built right along the riverbanks.

Joseph had to agree with Hannah that the view was breathtaking. Their carriage took them up Valley Street and deposited them at the door of the Arlington Hotel.

"Isn't this elegant?" Hannah sighed as they strode up to the hotel. "It's so beautiful, almost regal."

"It is nice," Joseph agreed. "We are right on the river here. It is practically at the door. The hotel is edged against the mountain at the back. Hmm! Wonder what happens when they get a heavy rain?"

"Everyone moves to the roof." An elderly woman with the most beautiful snowy white hair that Hannah had ever seen was leaning on a gnarled walking stick, as she made her way leisurely past them. She responded to

Joseph's statement without missing a beat and continued her slow pace across the room.

Hannah laughed gaily and Joseph chuckled as they watched the woman make her way across the lobby. "Do we have to wait until summer to return? This place is so serene."

Joseph smiled at the rapt look on his brides face. "Perhaps we should wait until after the spring rains," he teased. "Anyway, we just arrived. Let's enjoy the time we have here now and then we will have the rest of the winter and spring to anticipate our return. After all, I will have to work several months in order to afford our summer travels, or we will find ourselves eating weeds and tree bark like the deer do in the winter." He shifted the sleeping Anna on his shoulder and took Hannah's arm as he escorted her across the lobby to check into the charming hotel.

* * *

They would have been content anywhere, but the two weeks they spent lounging in the baths and on long hikes with Anna were pure magic. They sought information continually about the unusual city, during their short visit.

Many claims were made for the healing properties of the fifty-six springs that could be found throughout Hot Springs. People flocked to the resort from across the country and even from foreign lands to bathe in the hot water purported to have healing powers. The temperature of the mineral enriched water was so hot it actually had to be cooled before anyone could enter. Health seekers drank the mineral water, carried off gallons for later use or to present to less fortunate individuals, unable to make the trip. Others soaked their weary or arthritic feet in the outdoor springs.

The water was reputed to cure everything from inflammation of the brain to corns and bunions. There were disciples eager to testify to the validity of each cure.

"Isn't it marvelous what God has put on his earth? All of this and so much yet undiscovered, all for us? Sometimes His love just overwhelms me!" Hannah looked around her in amazement as they walked up a path to yet another spring.

Hannah and Joseph found most of the springs, which were set aside for drinking, to have quite a pleasant taste. The baths relaxed them after a day of exploring the park and surrounding mountainous area. They were certainly willing to testify to the beneficial properties of not only the springs, but also the entire valley. Anna enjoyed herself immensely. She loved exploring with her father and Hannah, but also enjoyed being left with the hotel nanny to play with the other children.

They were all three reluctant to see their retreat come to a close, but were also eager to be reunited with the rest of the family and tell them all the wonders they had seen. Hannah felt as if a giant load had been lifted from her shoulders.

She felt so rested after the long months of so much work and responsibility that had weighted her down after little Joshua's birth. She had been responsible for not only the new baby, but also most of the care of Sheba and Anna, along with the vast amount of laundry and cooking for seven people and of course all the cleaning and shopping for all of them. Hannah had become accustomed to working from the time she got up until she fell into bed at night. One day had run into another since Sheba and Joshua had come home from the hospital.

After Joseph hired someone to do the laundry and Rose to look after Sheba and the children, things were easier for her, but still she could imagine heaven being a little like this marvelous city, with the mountains and trails that exuded peace—and no housework at all.

"It is really rather odd, Joseph. I am legally less free than I have ever been, yet I feel totally released for the first time in my life."

Joseph's heart seemed to swell and his throat grew dry with emotion, as he considered his tremendous love for his bride. He was so choked up he was unable to respond to her for several moments.

"You will always be free to be yourself, Hannah. If there is anything you want to do, you have but to tell me and some way we will manage it." He gazed at her with adoration glowing in his eyes.

"You are so beautiful and my love for you is so very great. Sometimes, I just cannot believe I was so lucky to have you agree to be my wife." Tears of joy filled his eyes as he contemplated his enormous good fortune. Hannah actually returned the love that had absolutely overwhelmed him for the past six or seven months. He had not thought it would be possible after he lost Beth, to ever love again like this. God had been so good to him and Anna to bring Hannah into their lives.

"Well they say that beauty is in the eyes of the beholder. And I am afraid you are a might prejudiced," she teased, smiling up at him as she cuddled more snuggly into his arms.

They clung to one another, vowing never to allow anything to destroy their love. In such a peaceful surrounding, they could not imagine the horror and anguish that would arise in their future.

Chapter Thirty-One

They were delighted with the lovely valley and the beautiful Ouachita Mountains and on their return home they could talk of little else for weeks. The others looked forward eagerly to the summer, when the wagon would be packed and the new adventures would begin. They had long family meetings when they mapped out their plans for the upcoming summer.

They would all make the journey on the train as far as Malvern. Rose, Sheba and Joshua would then board the train to Hot Springs. Sheba would take the course of baths under the direction of one of the resident physicians Joseph had met on their honeymoon trip. She would take a bath each day for three weeks, then would rest one week before beginning the course again.

This regime would continue throughout the summer, if she was able to tolerate it and if she seemed to be deriving any benefit from the treatment.

Rose had their planned itinerary, so if something came up that demanded their presence she could simply post a letter to one of the post-offices in a town they were scheduled to visit.

Although Sheba was reluctant to be parted from the rest of the family, she was hopeful that after the treatments she would be able to participate more in family activities.

The rest of the family would start out in the wagon. They would explore as much of the countryside, in the western mountains surrounding Hot Springs as possible; learning all they could about the people, history and especially from Joseph's point of view their folk cures.

In February, Bernice finally completed her contractual obligation to the hospital, taken on while Sheba was hospitalized prior to Joshua's birth the September before.

Joseph resumed his practice of reading news from the paper to the family after dinner each night.

In March, while their plans progressed, the newspapers brought disquieting news of a tremendously powerful hurricane hitting Samoa. A United States Naval Squadron cruiser was in the harbor and seven American navy men had lost their lives during the violent storm.

The family agonized over the loss of the sailors to the terrible storm and prayed for their families.

Another frightening piece of news, which affected them personally, was the worsening epidemic of grippe, or influenza that raged along the Atlantic Coast.

Thousands of inhabitants of the coastal area fell victim and many lost the battle to its ravages.

Word came from Savannah that Sheba's mother, Ruth, had succumbed to the dreaded illness and even Hamilton Earl had been afflicted.

Sheba grieved for her mother and regretted that she had been unable to return for a visit. Ruth had died without ever having seen her grandson.

Joseph conducted a memorial service for her in their parlor and that seemed to ease Sheba's pain somewhat, allowing her the opportunity to say goodbye until she joined her in heaven. Sheba had the peace that comes from knowing that a departed loved one was a Christian and had served the Lord diligently and that one day they would be reunited.

April's biggest story was the Oklahoma Run, which opened up for homesteading the Unassigned Lands of Central Oklahoma. Joseph was incensed by what he considered a deplorable, dastardly exploitation of the Indian Nation.

"What do those idiot politicians think they are doing in Washington? Don't they realize that we are the intruders here? The Indians are the Native Americans. We have got to learn to live in peace with them. It can't be done by continually shoving them off treaty lands." His voice had risen drastically and his face was fiery red.

Anna went about telling everyone for weeks about the poor Indians run off their lands by the "das'turd buro'cats hurten poor Engines. Idiot pool'icians!" she exclaimed loudly to anyone who would listen.

Hannah overheard her repeating her interpretation of what her father had said, to the preacher's four-year-old daughter, who had come to play for the afternoon.

That put an end to the discussions concerning the Indian Lands, at home or anywhere else in front of Anna. Hannah was on pins and needles for days afterward. She half expected to be called on by an irate parent, informing her to leave the church or at the very least tell them that Anna could not play with their daughter again.

Joseph laughed at her uneasiness, but from that time forth he was more careful about what he muttered in his daughter's presence.

* * *

The spring seemed destined to bring nothing but tragic events. They read the paper with horror when the news arrived on the first of June of the tragic Johnstown flood. The Susquehanna River had overflowed into the Connemaugh valley and the reservoir dam burst at Johnstown drowning more than six thousand people.

"If that wasn't bad enough, driftwood and other debris caught up against the stone railroad bridge." Joseph's countenance was sorrowful as he continued the poignant newspaper article. "The whole thing caught fire and the inferno burned to death another fifteen hundred people. What a tragedy!" They bowed their heads and prayed for the survivors and the loved ones of the deceased.

"Joseph, I certainly will not miss the newspaper this summer. It seems like it has brought nothing but tragedy the entire first half of 1889." Hannah confided to Joseph a few days later as they packed for their summer trip.

"There certainly have been a lot of sad news stories since our return from the springs," Joseph agreed. "It will be wonderful to sleep out under the stars observing nature and enjoying its tranquility, instead of reading about tragedies around the world; I can't dispute that."

Everyone was busy getting ready for the trip. Daniel left early in the week to buy a team of mules for the wagon and a couple riding horses, along with the tack they would need.

The women were busy sewing. They fashioned loose britches to be worn by Hannah, Anna and Bernice to wear when they rode the horses or walked in rugged areas. Of course, they would not consider wearing them in inhabited areas, but Joseph thought it best they have them available, so they could move about more freely when they found areas they wanted to explore.

Their adventure would take them through stretches of isolated rugged countryside. When the britches were finished they modeled them in Sheba's bedroom, while Joseph was at the hospital visiting a patient and Daniel was working on a house.

Anna loved the freedom the pants gave her and practiced climbing on everything in the room. She pretended she was riding a horse by straddling the bed rail. When it was time to take them off, she cried so hard, Hannah relented and let her keep them on—but only as long as there were no guests in the house.

Hannah was very self-conscious of her round bottom being outlined by the strange, scratchy pants. She was not sure she would ever be able to put them on an actually wear them outside the confines of the wagon. Even on the farm as a child, the girls had always worn dresses—her mother had seen to that.

They were not such foreign apparel to Bernice, who had grown up with horses and had been quite the hoyden in her youth. She had frequently slipped out of the house in a pair of her brothers riding pants, cinched around the waist with a length of rope. She had loved riding like the wind across the meadows, unencumbered by a riding dress and the innocuous, but uncomfortable sidesaddle.

When all the necessities had been securely packed in the wagon, it was loaded aboard the train. At Malvern, they bid Sheba, little Joshua, who was not so little anymore, and Rose a tearful goodbye. Hannah hugged Sheba with tears streaming down her cheeks.

"How shall I ever manage without you and Joshua," she sniffed. "You get well this summer. I promise we will never leave you behind again."

"You just make lots of notes of everything you see, because I will expect to hear about all of it. Every single detail," she added with tears shining in her dark brown eyes.

Ben had provided the expense money for his family. True to his word, money arrived by post regularly once each month to meet Sheba's expenses and pay for her and Joshua's room and board. Joseph opened an account for her in the bank to draw on, as she required funds. Rose received a handsome salary, which she certainly earned by the excellent and conscientious care she gave her charges.

The others were not concerned that Sheba and Joshua would be neglected while they were apart; they knew that Rose would attend to their every need with loving care.

Sheba was a bit ambiguous about the summer; although she looked forward to the treatments in Hot Springs and hoped they would help her infirmity, she was sad about missing the first real adventure in the wagon. The only times she had ever been away from Anna since the day she was born was during Hannah and Joseph's honeymoon trip and Sheba's stay in the hospital before Joshua's birth. She would miss her dearly.

She had grown to love Hannah like a sister. Joseph could not have done better if he had scoured the world over than the quiet, lovely young woman he had chosen for his bride and mother for little Anna.

Bernice mothered them all, adults and children alike. She had become grandmother to Anna and Joshua, the only one either of them had known or could remember. Sheba would miss the family.

* * *

Joseph rode one of the large, sturdy horses and the other riding horse was tethered to the back of the wagon, while Daniel drove the team of matching gray mules. They would switch off, so no one got too tired or bored with any activity.

Anna was beside herself with excitement as they began the trip. She had to be restrained so she would not fall off the wagon; she was bouncing around so much. They planned to follow alongside the Ouachita River southward toward Arkadelphia.

The first night, they camped along the river near Social Hill and the next night just north of Midway, a small settlement halfway between Little Rock and Hot Springs. It was a great adventure. They cooked over a campfire, washed the dishes in the stream and slept under the stars.

Everyone shared in the work and everyone stopped to rest or play at the same time. At night they told stories and although they had been together for nearly three years, they learned more about each other during their visits around the campfire; stories shared about their individual childhood experiences seemed to meld them into an even closer family unit.

* * *

They arrived at Friendship mid-day of the third day and bought provisions at a small country store. It provided Joseph an opportunity to visit with some local men. He had come upon them as they swapped stories outside the store and they had invited him to 'sit a spell.'

He shared some of the recent events, which had taken place in the Capital and they communicated information about the roads and trails ahead.

* * *

All of the adults took turns riding the horses, driving the team, although Hannah had a bit of difficulty mastering that skill and walking behind the wagon. Joseph wanted to make sure that in the event of any emergency, everyone would be well trained in handling both the horses and the mules.

Anna loved riding with her father on the big horse and 'helping' Daniel or Papa with the mules.

Chapter Thirty-Two

They arrived at the city of Arkadelphia a week after they had started out. Joseph, after conferring with the others, decided to spend several days at the rather large city, located southwest of Little Rock.

The first night, Hannah shared with the others what she had learned from one of the early Pennsylvania Dutch settlers of the community. "Arkadelphia means 'Arc of Brotherly Love' or 'Arc of Fellowship.' Isn't that beautiful?" Her face was radiant as she enthusiastically talked about the city. "There is a thriving Baptist College here. They are going to graduate their first senior class in 1890."

The next day they wondered over the campus and were surprised to learn that the state had plans to build another college in Arkadelphia. Hannah could not get over the fact that there would be two colleges in this one town. It was certainly one of the highlights of the trip for her. She loved exploring the charming city with its beautiful college campus. The emphasis placed on education captivated her;

the attainment of knowledge was something very dear to her heart.

Joseph was able to add to his file of folk cures in a most unexpected way, Bernice came down with dysentery. One of the many friendly inhabitants they had met in Arkadelphia introduced them to the medicinal properties of the red hawthorn.

They were instructed to crush the ripe fruit and boil it with an equal amount of water, about as long as cooking a hardboiled egg. After straining the juice, they were told to add a few drops of bee honey to make it 'more tasty' and drink a swallow after each run.

The imparter of this wisdom assured Joseph this was also an excellent remedy for curing sore throats. Bernice testified that it had indeed seemed to help with her problem and Joseph added it to his journal.

Their travels took them northwest toward Amity. It was growing dark when they reached Terre Noire Creek, so they stopped and set up camp. Anna and Don'ld wandered down to the enticing stream while the others were busy building a fire, cooking the evening meal and preparing pallets for their beds.

Anna, with Don'ld at her heels, meandered beside the peacefully flowing water. She picked bright yellow brown-eyed Susan's and wild Iris and searched for pretty stones along the bank, while the adults set up camp. Daniel and Joseph tended the horses and mules, while Hannah and Bernice gathered kindling and began preparations for the evening meal.

The serenity of the picturesque scene was split by Anna's terrified screams and Don'ld's frantic barking. Hannah reached her first and scooped her into her arms.

Anna was still crying and babbling incoherently, but Hannah—terror stricken from Anna's first cry, could find no injury on the frightened child.

"What is it Anna?" She attempted to coax her into revealing what had frightened her so very much. She collapsed on a log with the now whimpering child, as her legs—weak from fright—completely failed her.

Don'ld was dancing around them, whining and pressing close to Anna.

"'Nake, 'nake," she cried between sobs and pointed toward the creek.

"Did it bite you?" Hannah questioned her as she frantically inspected Anna's arms and legs.

"Boot," she said pointing to a mark on her sturdy boots. "'Nake bite boot." She buried her head in the curve of Hannah's shoulder and continued to sob.

Hannah fumbled with Anna's boots and long stockings. Her fingers seemed to be all thumbs, as she frantically pulled and tugged at them.

Bernice hurried up panting from her race to the creek and the fear that something had happened to Anna. She examined Anna's legs and feet carefully. She could find no sign of snakebite. Anna had numerous mosquito and chigger bites, but nothing resembling a fresh snakebite.

Joseph rushed up from further down on the creek where he and Daniel had been watering the horses and mules, after hastily tying them to some trees along the shore.

After assuring himself that Anna had not been bitten, he examined her boots. The smooth leather had two tiny holes approximately three inches above the heel. He rubbed the inside of the boot to make sure the fang had not penetrated the tough leather. His forehead broke out with beads of perspiration as he contemplated what could have happened. Hannah was aghast as she considered little Anna's close brush with death.

Daniel appeared from the direction of the creek carrying a large black snake over a branch.

"It was a moccasin all right. It cannot hurt you now Anna."

Joseph picked Anna up and strolled with her to where Daniel stood holding the dead reptile. He began to give her an important nature and safety lesson.

"Anna, you are very fortunate." She buried her head in his shirt not wanting to look at the dreaded snake.

"Bad 'nake."

"Yes, Anna. This is a Cottonmouth and it is a bad snake to tangle with." He pried the mouth open with a stick. "Look at his white mouth. It looks like cotton, doesn't it? See the shape of his head."

Daniel slipped away while Joseph was instructing Anna. Her curiosity got the better of her and in a short time she was absorbed in her father's lecture.

"This snake is poisonous and can hurt you. You must always stay away from this kind of snake." He watched her closely to gage her reaction to what he was saying. He noted that she shook her head in agreement.

Daniel returned and handed Joseph a small green snake. "Now this little fellow would not hurt you for anything," Joseph informed Anna. He allowed the snake to move slowly up his arm. "Would you like to pet him?" She pressed her cheek against her father's shoulder on the opposite side from the snake.

"See this friendly fellow is the color of spring grass." Joseph continued talking about snakes and the different kinds they might encounter in Arkansas.

He then told her about a blue racer he had happened across as a boy. "I took off running and that snake ran after me." He related the story, laughing at the memory. "My father saw what was happening and called to me, 'turn around boy and chase him.' Well, I did just that and that old snake ran the other way."

Anna began to laugh at the picture in her mind of her father being chased by the snake and then chasing the snake in a game of tag.

"Would you like to pet this one now? Tentatively she inched her small hand closer to the bright green snake that was still making his way up his father's arm.

"Joseph, please don't make her touch it. Can't you see she is frightened?" Hannah's eyes pleaded for him to cease the nature lesson. Hannah twisted her dress in her hands apprehensively.

"No, Anna is not frightened of this little fellow," he assured Hannah. "She is just being cautious so she won't scare him. She is very good at petting snakes, only she must learn the difference between the snakes it is all right to pet and the ones she must give a wide berth too.

Anna was never to forget her father's knack of giving her the courage to do something she would have otherwise been afraid to tackle. Her frown was replaced by a look of pride and confidence, at her father's words. She touched the small creature and smiled up at her father.

"Oh! Feels nice. Feels like Anna's wizard." She became excited as she grew braver and let the small snake crawl onto her arm. "He's soft."

"Yes, they feel nice," Joseph encouraged her. "Would you like to keep him for a pet? Just for this evening of course. We really do not have room for more pets in the wagon and Don'ld might get his feelings hurt if we took him with us, but he probably won't mind if he just visits.

The near tragedy had been turned into an important nature lesson. This would be an oft-repeated event in their lives. Nature lesson or not, Hannah could not get to sleep that night. She continued to think of what might have happened to their precious Anna.

"Come lay down, Hannah." Joseph put his arm around her and gently pulled her back against him. She was sitting in back of the wagon looking out at the star-filled sky.

"I can't sleep." She turned a stricken face toward him, as she again pondered what might have happened. "What if she had been barefoot? It was a miracle she still had her boots on. She is always taking them off and she especially loves to wade in water."

"Hannah, there will be enough sorrow to push its way into our lives." He pulled her close to him and his voice was gentle. "We don't need to borrow trouble, by worrying about the might-have-beens. Tonight we should be praising God for the miracle, instead of worrying about the what-ifs." He kissed her tenderly and felt her begin to relax.

"We may have a lot of close calls during our summer travels, but let's not spend our time worrying about the bad times while we are in the midst's of the good ones."

Chapter Thirty-Three

They continued their trip the next morning without further incident. Anna's snake had escaped from his basket during the night and they were unable to find him anywhere. Joseph assured his daughter that the small creature had returned to his mama after he awakened during the night and grew homesick, but Hannah continued to keep a vigilant eye for a moving bright spring green object.

They traveled along the old de Soto Trail and Hannah told her small step-daughter stories of de Soto's adventures. Repeating the tales of his exploits often, until Anna was able to tell the story herself.

"Fust white man to come to Ar-kan-sas," she informed Don'ld. "Was wooking for gold in 1541." She petted Don'ld and he wagged his tail as she continued her instruction. "Wandered the wand." Don'ld jumped up and began prancing around her in circles, as Anna continued the story. "Up the mon'ans." She embellished the story by waving her hands high in the air. "Down in the baleys." And she swooped her arms toward the ground. Her audience barked enthusiastically. "Died of the bever," she completed her sad tale.

The adults enjoyed Anna's rendition of history and were delighted with the progress she was making in her studies since they had been on the trail.

Joseph had happily been able to add to his store of medicinal recipes from the many new friends along the way. But he made sure that he took time for a science or some kind of nature lesson with Anna each day.

* * *

Amity was the next town they visited. "The city of Brotherly Love, Charity and Good Will,' lived up to its name. They were welcomed into the home of a local doctor, who was delighted at the opportunity to discuss medicine with a colleague. Joseph accompanied him to his clinic and they made several house calls together.

The travelers spent a week in the lovely community that certainly lived up to its name. Everywhere they went they were welcomed as if they had spent their entire lives there. Anna enjoyed having children to play with again and Hannah was able to visit with other young mothers, sharing recipes and household hints.

Bernice discovered that the doctor's wife had also been a nurse during the war. She had moved to Amity from South Carolina to live with an aunt after the war, seeking a place of peace for her soul. She had met the doctor who was just beginning his practice and they had married after a few months of courtship. Bernice and the doctor's wife were delighted at the opportunity to share with one another, someone who understood what each of them had experienced during that terrible time. The memories were painful, but it seemed to help each of them. They were able to unleash feelings, which had been bottled up inside of them for years.

Daniel discovered a group of friendly young people through the church they attended with the elderly physician and his wife. One was a brown haired beauty named Mary.

Mary arranged a hayride for the young people in the area after Sunday service, to introduce him to the others. Daniel was made to feel right at home and was included in many of the local activities. It was the first time since he had left home that he really had time to relax for an extended period with others his own age.

The young people, most of whom, had never been further away from home than Hot Springs or Arkadelphia wanted to hear all about the journey from Georgia. They especially liked to hear stories about the old prospector who had joined them in Alabama.

The group was reluctant to leave the marvelously hospitable community. Sunday night after evening service and an impromptu social, they bid a tearful farewell to new but fast friends at the Community Church.

Daniel was able to muster enough courage to kiss the lovely Mary on the cheek, as he escorted her home from the social. He promised to write and vowed he would return as soon as he could. Out of all the adventures packed into the summer expedition, Amity was the highlight of the trip for Daniel.

Monday morning they resumed their journey. Hannah teased her brother about having a girlfriend at every little town they passed through. "What would Louise think about that?"

Daniel blushed, but he did not respond. He had taken Louise to several socials in the months before they had left on the trip, but he knew that at the age of sixteen, he was not ready to settle down with any one girl.

That night they camped just south of Glenwood, on the Caddo River. There was an excellent sawmill at Glenwood and Joseph obtained a brace for the wagon. He felt it was needed before they traversed the rest of the mountainous trail that they were following.

The lush green forests opened into hilly pastures where cattle grazed and gardens and fruit trees flourished. Wild flowers abounded along the trail with gentle mountain streams running across the trail in many areas.

They spent several days in the area before crossing the Caddo River. Then they turned in a more northerly direction, toward the gap in the mountains known as Caddo Gap.

It took two days to travel this six-mile stretch. When they arrived, they were delighted with the quaint little town nestled in the valley between the high hogback mountains.

Joseph's ledgers were bursting with the information gleaned from the hospitable folk they had encountered. It was hard for them to believe they had been traveling for over a month. The summer was swiftly fading.

Anna was tanned and healthy from her summer of camping and romping outdoors. She had grown taller and stronger. Although she missed Sheba and Joshua and frequently inquired about them, she enjoyed their delightful outdoor adventure.

Joseph spent many hours with Anna, teaching her about the animals they encountered, or sitting with her on a rock to admire a spider's beautiful creation. He taught her how to care for the animals and allowed her to help lead them to water and the abundant grass along the way.

A cut finger was an opportunity for him to share with his small daughter information about germs. While bandaging it with a clean cloth, he told her about organisms too tiny for her to see, but potent enough to make her sick if allowed entry into her body. She absorbed the lessons like a small sponge.

She also looked forward to her studies with Hannah each day. Hannah continually sought new methods of making the lessons interesting and exciting for the three year old. They sang songs, as they traveled about Arkansas, United States history, or characters from the Bible. They played alphabet games and Anna was delighted to learn that Anna and Hannah were both spelled the same backward as they were forward.

Hannah attempted to teach her to spell Savannah also, but that seemed too difficult for her. She was gaining more control over her tongue and was now able to form her l's and v's more consistently. Anna was soon spelling simple words and always shared her new knowledge with her faithful companion Don'ld. He seemed an adept pupil, wagging his tail eagerly at each lesson.

After another month of traveling through the Ouachita Mountains, they reached Crystal Springs. The journey had been productive. The family had spent two months together, sharing with one another, enjoying new sights and relaxing around campfires. Joseph and Bernice were able to add many folk cures to the ledgers while Hannah and Anna worked on informal lessons.

They had made many new friends along the way, adding to Bernice's correspondence. Daniel was especially pleased about the many acquaintances he had made, especially Mary of Amity.

Chapter Thirty-Four

They arrived in Hot Springs after another week of traveling along the mountain roads and had a joyous reunion with Sheba, Joshua and Rose. Joshua had grown so much that Anna had to be repeatedly reassured he really was baby Josh. When they parted at Malvern, he had been crawling everywhere, but now he was walking erect like a little boy.

"The baths were wonderful," Sheba informed them, as they sat down together beside one of the famous springs. "I have been more pain free and relaxed here than I have at any time since the accident. Even though I can't walk, I feel stronger in my arms and can do more for myself."

"Yes," agreed Rose. "She has worked very hard. She can transfer herself to her chair from the bed with only a minimum of assistance."

"Rose has learned a lot of the techniques they use." Sheba smiled at her companion and patted Rose's arm.

"At the Palace Bath House, they taught me how to continue her therapy. It is that one down the road there." Rose pointed toward an ornate, frame building, fronted by a low wall. "It is built right over the hot spring."

"Well that is certainly one way to save on fuel bills, I guess." Joseph chuckled as he looked up the street at the building Rose had indicated.

"We are so happy that the baths helped you." Hannah hugged Sheba and smiled at her, happy that they were all back together again.

"You can teach me the therapy and then I can help you with Sheba's treatment," Bernice offered.

The adults caught one another up on the highlights of the past couple of months, while Anna and Joshua played in the grass.

Anna discovered new playmates at the hotel where they were staying. She enjoyed the companionship of other children after the long time of exploring and had especially missed little Joshua.

* * *

"Why do you call your mother Hannah?" An inquisitive six year old asked her while they were playing with their dolls in the hotel garden.

"Mother?" Anna repeated perplexed. Hannah had always been Hannah. "Why?" she countered.

"She is your mother, isn't she?" The girl pressed.

"Why?" Anna asked again, not having a real answer to the bewildering question, but soon the children went onto something else and the question of Anna's mother was forgotten.

At lunch Anna decided she must unravel the mystery. "Hannah! Sheba is Josh's mother." It was a statement made while she stirred her vegetables around on her plate.

"That's right." Hannah agreed, not quite sure where the conversation was leading. "Sheba is Joshua's mother."

"Uncle Ben is Joshua's papa." Anna made the pronouncement while studying Hannah closely. The question of the golden skinned Joshua had also come up during play.

Hannah glanced at Joseph across the table. He nodded his head yes, as he listened to the conversation closely. Anna had directed the statements to Hannah, so he was reluctant to intervene.

"Yes, Anna. Your uncle Ben is Joshua's father and that makes Joshua your cousin."

Anna did not seem to have a problem with that, but her face was still wrinkled up in consternation. "Papa's my papa." She continued still addressing her statements to Hannah.

The adults were perplexed, not knowing what had prompted this conversation, but anxious to answer any questions she might have been pondering. Apparently she was seeking reassurance about something.

"Why aren't you my mama?" She studied Hannah closely, gazing intently into her eyes.

Hannah's blue eyes suddenly filled with tears, as she smiled at Anna. She was at a loss as to how to respond and she glanced at Joseph for assistance.

"Let's go for a little walk Anna." Joseph stood and walked around the table to where his daughter sat looking from one to the other. He picked her up and set her on her feet then taking her small hand in his large one they walked quickly from the room.

Hannah heard his reassuring response before they passed through the doorway. "Of course Hannah is your mama." They strode through the door hand-in-hand. "Would you like to call her mama, or maybe mama Hannah?"

"Mama," Anna repeated, testing the sound of it. "Why do I call my mama Hannah?" she asked repeating the question her new friend had asked her.

"Hannah has not always been your mama, honey. A long time ago, when you were a brand new baby, you had another mama. She was young and pretty like Hannah, but had black hair like yours instead of golden hair like Hannah's." He studied Anna, trying to gauge how much she seemed to understand of what he had said.

"Do you remember how Sheba carried little Joshua inside of her until he was big enough to live with the rest of us?"

"Guess so," she said wrinkling her brow. She was not really sure if she remembered that or not.

"Well anyway, you lived inside of your other mother, until you were big enough to live with us." He smiled down at her. "Do you remember what happened to de Soto?"

"He hunted for gold." She answered confidently, happy that she knew the answer to some of the questions.

"That's right, but when he did not find the gold what happened?" He continued to draw the information from her. He wanted to help her understand, by relating the unknown part of her life to a familiar story.

"He found Hot Springs and then he took a bath."

"You are probably right about that." Joseph could not help but chuckle at her answer. "Then what happened to him?"

"He died of the fever." Anna grew serious as she remembered how the story had ended.

"Yes, Anna." Joseph found himself choked up and he was finding it hard to continue. "Honey that is what happened to your first mama. She died of a fever."

"Don't be sad papa." She placed her hand comfortingly on his arm. "God sent us a good mama to take her place."

"Yes Anna," he agreed, fighting back tears that had filled his eyes and were determined to run down his cheeks. "God sent us a very good mama." He swiped at the tears with his large white handkerchief. It was a poignant moment that he would never forget. "Why don't we go tell her so?"

"Yes, papa." She put her hand in his and led him back to where the others waited at the table in the hotel.

She crawled into Hannah's lap and taking her face in both of her small hands, she looked into the blue eyes brimming with tears. "You aren't going to be Hannah anymore. You're mama now." Then she kissed her and jumped down to play.

She informed her inquisitor that afternoon after her nap that she no longer had Hannah, but she did have a mama. She was not sure how that arrangement was to work and was a little apprehensive; until she finally felt reassured she had not really lost a loved one. She had been unsure about a mother's role in her life.

* * *

Before they left Hot Springs, Joseph visited the famous Army-Navy hospital located there. It had an excellent reputation for discharging its patients cured or at least able to live more independent lives then they had when they were admitted. He was very impressed with the modern facility and the dedicated doctors he met at the hospital.

It was time to begin the journey home. Joseph decided they could make Traskwood in the wagon, in about a week. They would be able to board the train for Little Rock at that point.

Bernice would stay to assist Rose since they would have to change trains at Malvern. He thought Hannah might wish to join them. She had not seemed to be feeling well the past couple weeks of their trip. Hannah insisted she was fine and wished to remain with him, Anna and Daniel.

Joseph was very curious about the towns of Jones Mill, Magnet Cove and Butterfield. The narrow roadway through the mountainous region proved a beautiful route. They spent a lot of time walking behind the wagon and leading the horses and mules up the steep grades. This only seemed to add to their enjoyment. They loved being together and viewing the magnificent scenery.

"You cannot use compasses around here," Joseph informed Daniel when they reached Magnet Cove. "There are huge deposits of magnetic oar that nullify the compass readings. It is a fascinating place. Early explorers were mystified by the strange phenomena."

"I hope we can find some of the magnetic oar to take with us. I have always been interested in different kinds of rocks and minerals."

"They say the magnetic oar is healing for rheumatic disorders. I am anxious to learn more about it for the journal."

The railroad track ran through the valley at Cove Creek Station. As they descended the steep mountain trail, Hannah was delighted to rediscover the enchanting depot they had seen on their honeymoon. It was made of beautiful crystal and other decorative stones native to the area. The sun glistened on the wonderful building making it appear as if made from enormous precious stones, just as she remembered it from their earlier visit.

There were many amazing rock formations and semi-precious stones to be discovered in the fields and mountains surrounding the depot. They camped nearby to explore the open fields for samples of the stones, unique to the Magnet Cove area.

They found a wide assortment of small stones and Daniel collected samples of each specimen. He picked up several different varieties of crystal; the prized novaculite from which Indians made their arrowheads and spear points; slate; a couple beautiful pieces of black garnet; an opal and some cinnamon stone.

While they were in the area, they met the United States Geological Survey team. The team had been commissioned to make a thorough study of the minerals found in Arkansas. Daniel was fascinated with the work they were doing and listened intently while they explained some of their discoveries. They helped him identify the specimens he had collected and gave him a small sample of the magnetic oar.

They had to hurry on to Traskwood to meet the others. When they were reunited they all agreed it had been a marvelous summer. They not only had acquired treasures, but many treasured memories to share with one another throughout the rest of the year and years to come.

Chapter Thirty-Five

Back in Little Rock, the indomitable Peg greeted them. Amidst many grumblings, he informed them that some Eastern capitalists had purchased the Little Rock waterworks. Peg had missed the family and appeared on their doorstep bright and early the morning after their return.

"Sure and it's more carpetbaggers for 'Robbers Row' tis all it is." He began ranting about the blankety blank Yankees, as he paced restlessly up and down the Warren kitchen, his peg leg thumping on the floor as he moved about the room.

"We need good water, Peg," Joseph attempted to console him. "We certainly do not want to be faced with the problems Memphis had, with the yellow fever deaths and the city going bankrupt."

He allowed Peg time to consider the alternatives, before beginning to point out some of the merits of an adequate supply of good water for a city the size of Little Rock, regardless of who was responsible for supplying it.

"Little Rock is growing. More people are arriving every month and we must be ready for them. Planning for adequate facilities is very important; especially when you have the rapid growth we are experiencing right now. Water is probably the most essential of all the services the city is providing. Wells are not adequate when you have so many families living close together."

Peg went off mumbling to himself, but did not stay away long. On his daily visits, he began updating Joseph on the progress of the waterworks improvements and before long he sounded as if the entire project was of his creation.

* * *

The rest of the summer seemed to fly by and directly it was time for Joshua to celebrate his first birthday. Ben sent him a small wooden rocking horse, to commemorate the auspicious occasion. He rocked away many hours, while his smiling mother gazed fondly at him over her sewing. It helped time pass more pleasantly for her, watching the antics of her son, who was obviously happy and thriving. When Joshua was not riding his pony, he was usually toddling after Anna.

Anna was delighted to have someone to play with. She did not even complain when the inquisitive toddler pulled all the furniture from her dollhouse or dropped her china doll in a mud puddle, to see if it could swim. She patiently replaced the furniture and asked Bernice to clean up the muddy doll.

"Could have been worse," she said philosophically. "It would probably have broken if he'd dropped it on the hard ground."

The adults smiled as they watched the children play. Anna was like a little mother to Joshua and watched over him carefully whenever they played out in the yard. They were both healthy and active and kept the adults busy trying to keep up with them. Hannah made it a practice to take them both for a walk at least three or four times each week. They always went in the afternoon, because Hannah had not been feeling well in the mornings since their return from their summer trip.

"Come on Anna. You might need a sweater. It is getting a bit cooler out.

"Here Joshua, put your arm in your jacket." She instructed Joshua as she helped him into his jacket, while they waited for Anna.

"We will be back shortly," Hannah called to Sheba, as they hurried out the door.

"Don'ld!" Anna held the gate open for her special friend, as the dog pranced beside her his tail wagging cheerfully.

"Can you believe it was only a year ago that we found this house on one of our walks?" Hannah looked back at the house and then down at the children. "We brought Joshua here in the carriage. Do you remember Anna?"

"I think so," Anna wrinkled her brow in concentration and then began to smile, as she remembered her beloved swing. "I swinged. Then papa bought it for us and it was my swing." She looked down at Joshua. "It's Joshua's swing too," she added generously.

"Yes, that's right." Hannah smiled and refrained from correcting her English. They could discuss the proper word later when they did their lessons.

When they had walked several blocks, they sat down to rest under a large elm tree. Joshua crawled into Hannah's lap and Anna sat on her wide skirt.

"Anna, how would you like another baby to play with?" Hannah inquired nonchalantly, while brushing Anna's dark hair back from her face.

"Like Josh?"

"Well, a smaller baby. Small like when Joshua came home from the hospital last year."

"Can I help take care of him?"

"Of course, but the baby might be a girl."

"That's okay. We don't mind, do we Josh?" She had turned her attention to the toddler who had begun playing with golden leaves. "Josh, we are going to have another baby."

"Ba-by." Joshua repeated the word and continued playing in the leaves.

"Where we going to get him? Is Sheba carrying him for us?"

"No, this time, I am carrying the baby under my heart. Just like Sheba carried Josh." She patted her slightly enlarged middle.

That night at the table, Anna informed the rest of the family that she was getting another baby. The adults smiled at the forthright way she had made the announcement.

"Ba-by," echoed Joshua.

Everyone was looking forward to the new arrival. Anna helped make room for the new baby's crib in her bedroom. She wanted to help take care of him, so she did not mind giving up a little space. Her domain was the out of doors, not where she slept and kept her clothes.

* * *

That Christmas Ben sent two Appaloosa Indian ponies, one for Joshua and the other for Anna. Anna named her pony Patch and extravagantly showered affection on him.

She quickly learned to ride without assistance and spent part of each day riding around the backyard with Don'ld following along at the pony's hooves. Occasionally

Don'ld took a notion to jump up and nip at Patch's flowing tail, when Anna seemed to be ignoring him.

Daniel led Joshua around on his pony, which Anna had named Brownie, several evenings a week. Everyone agreed no gifts had ever been enjoyed more than the two ponies.

* * *

After the first of the year, Joseph read a pleasant announcement in the Gazette. President Harrison was bemoaning the predicament of five million dollars in surplus revenues left from 1889. The forecast for 1890 was an excess of eighty-three million dollars. He called for an examination of the present tariff laws with the intention of revising them, under the assumption that there was obviously something wrong, or there would not be so much money left over. The president directed congress to find means of utilizing these funds.

"Well," Joseph commented thoughtfully. "It is a sure bet that there will not be a surplus next year."

"I am afraid you are right Joseph. The politicians will find someway to spend the money and probably ask for more." Bernice looked thoughtful as she considered what they might decide to do with the funds.

"I would like to help him spend it. Perhaps I will send him some ideas. As citizens it is our responsibility to assist the lawmakers by providing them with helpful suggestions." The others agreed and all decided they would make up lists to submit to their senators.

* * *

In February, Hannah gave birth to a healthy baby boy. They named him Jeremiah. Anna and Joshua were delighted with the new member of the family and both were eager to help take care of him.

Joseph decided 1890 looked more promising then 1889 had begun, but his optimism was short lived.

* * *

That summer they chose to explore the central plains of Arkansas and were able to observe first hand the hardships the farmers were facing. Prices for farm products were falling drastically and depression was beginning to stalk the country. They found the farm families they encountered hospitable, but pessimistic about their plight. Most farmers were beginning to spend more to grow and harvest their crops than the market was paying them for the produce.

"I am having to pay dearly for the privilege of working from dawn till dark," complained the patriarch of one farm family. "I just don't know how long I can afford the luxury of feeding the rest of the country." These same sentiments were echoed wherever they went. It was time to write another letter to their senators.

During the summer, a site was purchased for the Old Soldiers' Home six miles southeast of Little Rock. A fifty-four acre farm had been obtained for the purpose.

* * *

Anna began first grade in September of 1890, even though she would not be five until December. She was able to keep up easily with the other students with all the tutoring she had been receiving from Hannah and Joseph. She was actually ahead of most of the other first graders. Hannah had been instructing her in the basics of reading, writing and arithmetic since she was old enough to talk.

Joshua missed her terribly while she was at school. After his nap each afternoon, he could be found sitting on the front steps of the wide porch, his arm around Don'ld—who felt equally neglected, as they waited for Anna to appear from the direction of her school. Jeremiah was not yet old enough to play with and he missed Anna tremendously.

For Joshua's second birthday, his father had sent him a pony cart. Now they could either ride on the ponies or behind them in the cart.

Anna had learned how to bridle the ponies by herself, which meant they could ride every day. They no longer had to wait for an adult to assist them. The only rule was they had to stay in the large yard.

Joshua loved to ride as much as Anna and eagerly looked forward to this special treat. He could not understand why Anna left him each day for the mysterious place called school.

Occasionally, Anna took baby Jeremiah for a ride, much to his delight and Hannah's numerous misgivings. She always hovered beside the pony when the baby rode with them, ever ready to catch him if the unthinkable happened and Anna dropped him—but of course she never did.

* * *

After the renovations, the Old Soldiers Home was opened for occupancy the first of December.

Four new states were admitted to the Union, making a total of forty-two by the close of 1890. December brought new troubles to the month old state of South Dakota, when hostilities rose among the Sioux and Cheyenne. Fifteen hundred warriors gathered and participated in ghost dances, in preparation for war. An outbreak at Standing Rock brought Federal troops to the area. Seven hundred braves were imprisoned at Porcupine and Pine Ridge, where Big Foot was leading the insurrection.

"More trouble for the native people of our great nation." Joseph was reading the news to the family. "I wonder where it will all end."

Hannah walked to her husband and laid her hand lightly on his shoulder. "They will have to learn to live with one another and respect each other as a people, before there will be any peace.

"Papa, why are they fighting?"

"Well Anna, one tribe probably thought the other tribe had more of something than they did. A bully picking on someone from the other tribe could have started it, or maybe one stole from the other. And of course it isn't impossible that some whites started it just to cause trouble among the tribes. Sure wouldn't be the first time. Chances are they do not even know what started it."

* * *

Peg's health was slowly failing and Daniel convinced him to move into the Old Soldier's Home after he declined their offer to live with them. He would get regular meals at the home and be able to fellowship with the other residents. Daniel promised Peg he would ride out to see him at least once a month.

Peg finally agreed to try it for a while. Daniel packed Peg's meager possessions into the wagon and drove him out to the house in the country.

Hannah was in the family way again, but this time she had trouble with her ankles swelling. Joseph insisted that she stay off her feet most of the day. Rose and Sheba looked after Joshua and Jeremiah while Bernice ran the household.

Her feet propped cozily on a hassock, Hannah spent her days reading and doing needle work. She made clothes for her family--especially the children and expected baby and did the mending for everyone.

Jeremiah toddled around at her feet, or attempted to keep up with the energetic Joshua and frolicsome Don'ld. They raced through the house from one adventure to another.

Hannah was able to empathize with Sheba's plight more in those last months of her pregnancy, than she ever had before. She vowed to do everything she could to make Sheba's days more interesting and exciting, when she was finally released from her own enforced confinement.

Hannah had nearly despaired of ever leaving the house again, when the baby decided to make her appearance. She was a delightful small pink bundle. They named her Carolyn Elaine after her grandmothers.

Anna loved the boys, but was absolutely captivated by her tiny sister. She seemed so much more delicate than the robust Jeremiah. She was unquestioningly feminine from the day she was born.

President Benjamin Harrison, his wife and a large entourage from Washington, visited Little Rock on April 17, 1891—a week after Carolyn's birth. Hannah insisted everyone go to the exciting event including Sheba and fourteen month old Jeremiah. Daniel even rode out and brought Peg in to enjoy the momentous event.

All of Little Rock was bedecked for the marvelous occasion. Red, white and blue ribbons streamed from electric poles and buildings throughout the city. The children loved the bands and the cannons, but Jeremiah held his ears at the loud noise. The cannons saluted President Harrison as he made his appearance at the State House before a crowd of fifteen thousand cheering citizens.

People clustered on roof tops, with the more adventuresome perched on limbs of tall trees, in order to obtain a better view of the President and his party. There were enterprising vendors that mingled throughout the crowd, selling patriotic ribbons and Harrison images.

The children were eager to share the excitement with Hannah when they returned home. She almost felt she had been there herself after their colorful and enthusiastic descriptions.

Each day, Anna hurried home from school to 'help mama' take care of baby Carolyn, before going out to bridle Patch and Brownie.

Joshua had learned to ride alone and riding his pony was the highlight of his day. He waited anxiously for Anna's return from school. Joshua was at first very put out with her for not going immediately to the stable. He could not understand why the birth of the baby should make such a difference, after all baby Carolyn could not play with them. All she did was eat, sleep and wet—and cry.

He did not see anything special about that. Before long he grew accustomed to the routine though and began helping Anna with whatever task she was performing for the baby. He eventually became interested in helping Aunt

Hannah with little Carolyn and the rambunctious Jeremiah during the day.

Chapter Thirty-Six

Joseph was reluctant to make the summer excursion with the new baby, but Hannah convinced him that baby Carolyn could make the trip without any problems.

"The boys and Anna will be devastated if we don't go Joseph. Joshua has talked of nothing but riding Brownie on our big trip. Anna has become very good on Patch and even does well on the big horses. It will do us all good. And besides," she persisted. "Sheba needs to get out. She has been cooped up most of the year with the heavy rains in the spring.

"Since the months I spent confined to a chair, I have a better understanding of how she feels being so restricted." Hannah picked up the Gazette to cinch her argument.

"Have you seen the paper?" she inquired. "The influenza epidemic is growing much worse. One day last week there were two hundred and twenty-seven deaths in New York alone. Can you imagine, in one day? You know it will be healthier for all of us out in the fresh air away from the city."

"I cannot argue with logic like that." Joseph laughed at his wife's attempt to convince him they would be better off camping than they would be staying in their home. *Woman's logic,* he dubbed it. Still something nagged at him about this trip, but he just could not put his finger on it.

"I must admit that I would certainly like to see the new pontoon bridge at Dardanelle. They say it is the longest pontoon bridge in the world that crosses running water. Can you imagine something like that, right here in Arkansas?"

"Admit it," Hannah teased laughing gaily. "You would have been absolutely devastated, if I had agreed with you that we should stay home this summer."

"I guess I would have at that," he agreed sheepishly. "Are you sure it will be all right? I will not risk your health or the health of one of the children, so I can traipse around the countryside." His demeanor was quite serious, as they continued to discuss the pros and cons about the summer excursion.

"You and the children are more important to me than anything else in this world."

"Joseph, we know that." She laid her small hand lightly on his arm and gazed lovingly into his eyes. It was still a shock to her sometimes that this wonderful man loved her and was her husband.

"We love our summer trips. I do think it is time to get another wagon though, our family has increased so much."

"I can't deny that." Joseph looked over their burgeoning family with a mixture of love and pride as he gazed at each one of them. "I'll order a new wagon right away and have a pulley lift attached, so we can raise and lower Sheba in her chair."

Thoughts whirled around in his head, as he considered the possibilities for making the trip more comfortable. He would have a small area portioned off in each wagon with a commode seat built in for the ladies. A bucket hung beneath the hole would allow them to empty it from outside the wagon. He had been concerned about the discomforts the ladies endured on their summer travels, especially after the unfortunate incident with the poison ivy the year before.

* * *

When the wagons were ready, he proudly displayed their modern conveniences to an admiring and grateful audience. He received a hug of gratitude from each of the women.

"This time we will be going a lot further," Joseph informed his family after supper. "We will be going all the way to Fort Smith along the old Indian trails that follow the Arkansas River. I have checked with people who have traversed it and they assure me that it is wide enough for the wagons and we should not have any difficulty during the summer while it is dry. Some of the area is impassable during the rainy season, but that should not affect us."

"Will we see Indians Papa?" Anna's large hazel eyes were opened wide, as she contemplated the possibility of encountering Indians along the trail.

"Weal Engines?" Joshua chimed in growing excited.

"Well! I don't think we will see any Indians and if we do they will be friendly Indians." Joseph assured the children, much to their disappointment. "We will load the wagons on barges for the return trip and float down the river, all the way back home to Little Rock. That will be an added adventure for us this year."

"A boat ride! We get to take a boat ride!" Anna grabbed Joshua's hands and the children danced around with joy.

Jeremiah attempted to keep up with them. "Boat—boat!" he chanted, as he danced around on his short legs.

"All right you Indians, simmer down." Hannah admonished them while trying to keep from laughing at their antics. "How far is it to Fort Smith, Joseph?"

""It is nearly one hundred and seventy miles. Fort Smith borders the Indian Nation so we may actually see real Native Americans when we reach Fort Smith. I have arranged to be away until the end of September. We will have nearly four months for the entire trip. You can tutor Anna, so she won't miss out on the first month of school."

"I cannot believe we are really going." Sheba had been listening intently to the discussion, enthralled with all that Joseph described. "It sounds wonderful." She had tears glistening in her dark eyes.

"Yes it does, doesn't it?" Bernice looked on enthusiastically, as she thought of seeing yet another new area. They would be right on the edge of the western frontier. "I almost feel like dancing with the children."

"Hannah you don't look very excited." Joseph glanced at his wife and noted frown lines creasing her forehead.

Hannah quickly replaced the frown with a smile and gave Joseph a reassuring hug. "It will be a wonderful trip. You know me. I always think of something to worry about. I know we will have a wonderful time and it will be a great educational experience for the children."

While she kept a smile on her face, she was unable to shake the feeling of foreboding that kept cropping up. It only seemed to grow stronger while they made the final preparations for the trip. Shake out of it she kept reprimanding herself. She was determined she would not diminish Joseph's anticipation of the trip; any reservations that he had at first seemed to have disappeared all together.

Chapter Thirty-Eight

They arrived in Fort Smith the middle of September. The adventurers were surprised to find the border city teeming with visitors.

"I knew that Fort Smith was one of the larger cities in Arkansas, but I can't imagine where all these people came from." Joseph looked around perplexed to find the dirt streets swarming with people. "I read something about another Land-Run into Oklahoma Territory, but never dreamed it would attract this kind of crowd. Surely there is not enough land available for all these people."

"I have never seen the streets of Little Rock this crowded. What a crush of people." Hannah looked around in amazement. There was hardly room for the wagons to move down the crowded streets.

"Man I guess so," Daniel agreed. "The mules are practically wading through the people." The wagons continued to make slow progress forward.

The air was swirling with thick dust and the noise was almost overwhelming from the milling crowds of people, horses and wagons. They all seemed to be moving restlessly through the town in anticipation of the Land-Run into Oklahoma Territory.

Joseph and Daniel maneuvered their wagons through the crowd of onlookers and land seekers, who appeared anxious to be a part of the historic event about to take place even if it was only from the sidelines.

The summer away from their regular jobs and responsibilities had been a respite the family had all needed, but they certainly were not prepared for the vast crowds of people they were encountering in Fort Smith. The pandemonium and cacophony of sound, after the relatively secluded back trails and county roads they had taken most of the trip, was staggering.

Joseph carefully drove the mules down the crowded street and Daniel followed cautiously in the second wagon, staying as close as he could to the back of the horses tied to Joseph's wagon. It would not do to become separated in the chaotic bustle that surrounded them. If they lost each other in this teeming crowd, it would be hard to find one another.

The two covered wagons, almost identical to every other wagon they passed, wove cautiously along the dusty streets through the disorderly crowd. They moved steadily in what they hoped was the direction of the river. The ponies tied behind Daniel's wagon, were getting skittish in the jammed roadways, as were the saddle horses in front of him.

"Whoa, whoa," Joseph called, as he reigned in the mules. A boy was squeezing between the wagon and a horse that rode beside them. The rider was so close Joseph was pretty sure he could reach over and touch the rider's saddle horn, if he were a mind to do such a foolhardy thing.

"Look sharp boy," he yelled. "You'll get stepped on if you don't step lively." The boy looked up at him sullenly. Joseph guessed he was about twelve, with the ruddy complexion of a Native American and his black hair hanging loose to his shoulders.

As another wagon pushed in close to the rider beside them, Joseph reached down and grabbed the boy's arm. The horse, in order to avoid the wagon crowding in beside him, was sidestepping right into Joseph's wagon and would have sandwiched the boy between them. The rider's attention was riveted on the other wagon and controlling his horse.

Joseph quickly hauled the boy up on the seat beside him, just as the horse slammed into the wagon.

"Boy, what are you doing? That animal nearly flattened you!"

The boy's angry retort died in his throat as he grabbed a firm hold on the seat, the very moment the horse and wagon made contact. Joseph's attention returned to his team. The jolt had startled the mules and he struggled to gain control. His hands gripped the reigns so tightly that the veins swelled large like thick blue cords across the top of his hands and up his tanned muscular arms. He was barely aware of the boy clinging to the seat, or Hannah trying to calm the baby, while being tossed about in the wagon. The mules strained one last time, before settling back down to a walk.

"That was fun," a voice said behind him. "Do it again papa." Small arms reached out from the wagon, between Joseph and the boy, and hugged his waist. Joseph gently squeezed one of the arms with his elbow, without moving his hands from the reigns. Joseph glanced quickly backward and winked at the face smiling up at him.

"You liked that, did you?" Joseph asked Anna. He smiled at his daughter's enthusiasm, before returning his attention to the mules.

"Who are you?" asked Anna, studying the stranger. The boy wore pants made of animal skin and his bare chest was covered with strings of bone and bright pebbles. Before he could answer, she blurted out, "I'm Anna."

He glanced at the young girl, who was smiling at him with an open and friendly pixie face. He found it impossible to maintain his surely scowl and hesitantly returned her smile.

"We're trying to get to the river." Joseph quickly took advantage of the boy's hesitation. "Can you direct us in the best way to get to the river? I am not sure I can find the way in all this crowd."

The boy reluctantly pulled his gaze away from the bright, hazel eyes of the little girl. With his expression softened by the child's friendly smile, he gave Joseph directions through the crowded frontier town to the banks of the Arkansas River.

"Just keep on the way you're headed. Take a right at the big oak. You'll pass a large red brick house. I think my mother calls it *Victorian*. Turn northwest there and the road will lead you direct to the river. You'll pass a two-story white brick house with narrow columns across the porch. It will be on your right. You should be able to see the top floor of the brewery off to your right as you get closer to the river," the boy instructed him. "You'll have a hard time finding a place to camp though."

Joseph noted a touch of bitterness in the boy's voice, but it seemed to soften whenever he darted furtive glances at Anna.

"Where did all these people come from?" Joseph asked. "Why, Fort Smith appears bigger than Little Rock. I never saw so many people in one town before. Atlanta streets weren't this packed."

"You must really be from the back woods, if you don't know what's happening. They have gathered in Fort Smith before moving through our land." The boy studied Joseph thoughtfully. "They've come to steal our land again. The government chased us off the rich bottomlands and fertile mountains. They forced us through the swamps where many babies and old people died and then they told us to stay in the dry land of the howling wind, because the white man didn't want it.

"Now they say they are crowded again and will take even this land which God has forsaken."

"Yes, I knew there was to be another Land-Run. I just didn't think it would attract this many people. I'm not sure it was wise to bring my family here at this time. Some of these people look pretty unsavory."

"They will have their race to confiscate our lands next week. That is what has brought all these whites and their wagons here. They've been gathering like vultures hovering over a wounded deer." He looked up at Joseph skeptically. "If you didn't come for the Run, why are you here?"

"It's a fun trip," Joseph responded lamely. "We have been learning about the state by visiting different towns. My family and I," he waved his arm to encompass the wagon he was in and the one following directly behind him. "We have been traveling around the western part of Arkansas this summer, to acquaint ourselves with the area and its history.

"We're fairly new to the state and thought this would be the best way to learn about different parts, looks like we didn't choose a very good time to come here."

He looked at the crowded street before him and then glanced back at the boy. "I'm sorry about this." He looked at the milling crowds, a frown creasing his handsome face.

"The government's been unfair to your people. I'm truly sorry," he repeated for emphasis. Joseph pulled the team to a stop, so the boy could climb down.

"Thank you for pulling me up on the wagon. I guess that horse would have made me a bit taller." He glanced at Anna to catch her reaction.

Anna smiled even bigger and leaned against her father to get a better view of the boy. Her long lashes outlined her large-hazel-eyes and with her friendly smile the dimples grew deeper in her pink cheeks.

Daniel had handed the reigns to Bernice and climbed down from the other wagon. He stood with one foot on the ground and one propped on the traces, casually studying the boy who was climbing down from the high wagon seat. Sticking out his right hand in a gesture of friendship, he said, "Name's Daniel Brown. Guess you've met my brother-in-law, Dr. Joseph Warren."

"I am called John T.B. Wolf-Hunter," the boy said, shaking Daniel's outstretched hand politely.

"That's an unusual name. What do the initials stand for?" he asked curiously.

"My full name is John The Baptist Wolf-Hunter," he replied, with a mixture of pride and challenge in his voice. "I am from the Aniwaya Clan of the Cherokee Nation." He almost seemed to dare Daniel to ridicule his name or heritage.

"That's a powerful name to live up to," Joseph commented reflectively. "What does Aniwaya mean?"

"Aniwaya means wolf. It is the clan of my mother. She used to work at the mission. She wished to honor both her heritage and her adopted faith. My mother is determined that one-day I will be a great leader of people in the likeness of John the Baptist. We studied about him in school and the preacher talks about him often on Sundays."

"It's a good solid name," Joseph said. "Daniel and I were both named after men in the Bible. Like your people, we left our home far away to seek a new home in Arkansas and now we are trying to learn more about it."

"But my friend," John replied perceptively, an edge creeping into his voice again. "I believe you left willingly, not with soldiers at your back." He caught sight of Anna standing behind her father. She was watching him curiously. "What's your name, Little Blossom?" he asked.

"My name's Savannah Elizabeth Warren, but you may call me Anna," she replied politely.   She thrust her hand toward him in greeting.

"That's a very large name for one so small. I think I will continue to call you Little Blossom. With your permission of course," he said politely. "You look to me like a beautiful bud about to blossom into a fragrant flower." He smiled at her and quite solemnly jumped up on the trace and clasped her hand in his. "I feel our paths will cross again." It was said almost as a promise. He jumped down and bid them good day and was soon lost in the crowd.

Joseph and Daniel exchanged surprised looks, taken aback by the boy's action and quick disappearance.

It had been a poignant moment between the ruddy-faced adolescent and the small raven- haired five-year-old. She watched him weave through the crowd until he was lost among the horses and men. "Papa, will we see John again? I like him."

"I would not be surprised if we did," Joseph said, ruffling Anna's shinny dark hair.

"You had better keep an eye on that one," Daniel said recovering first. He gazed at the spot where they had last seen John.

"I believe you're right, Daniel.

"This crowd is awful. Let's pull the wagons over and try to find rooms in the hotel, instead of camping in the wagons tonight."

"Sounds like that would be the wisest thing." Daniel agreed and quickly returned to his wagon.

It took them thirty minutes just to move the wagons over to the side of the road through the crowd. They tied the mules to a post and set the brakes on both wagons.

Joseph checked on Hannah and the children. Five-month-old Baby Carolyn was suckling at Hannah's breast and grasping at the ties dangling from her hat. The boys were playing in the back wagon with Sheba and Rose. Jeremiah and Joshua were playing with the stick figures Anna had painstakingly painted for them along the trail. She had used berries to paint eyes, hair and a mouth, on each of them.

"Daniel and I are going to see about rooms for the night," Joseph called to Hannah through the back flap of the wagon. "We'll catch a steamboat going down river tomorrow and get out of here. I'll take Anna with me, but leave the boys with Sheba and Rose in the other wagon. Daniel is tying up the other mules and Bernice is going to come up here with you.

"Do you need anything? I doubt if there is anything worth buying left in Fort Smith with this crowd. I have never seen so many people in one place before. Don't try to get out of the wagon," he cautioned. "Will you be all right?"

She wiped a hand over her hot forehead and brushed back a wisp of chestnut hair. "Yes, of course we'll manage.

I can't believe it is still so hot, this late in September. Do take Anna. She has been cooped up too long and will enjoy seeing something new."

Joseph and Daniel, with Anna taking turns riding on her father and uncle's shoulders, went to every hotel and rooming house in Fort Smith. They followed every lead they received, but were unable to find a single unoccupied room. Even the sheds and barns were filled with people. Tents were pitched in every vacant spot they passed.

They wearily and dejectedly made their way back to the wagons. Joseph dreaded having to tell Hannah they would have to spend the night in the wagons, camped in amongst such a rowdy bunch of cowboys and dirt farmers. He was sure that most of them were good folks with hopes and dreams of owning their own land next week and many others were just here for the excitement, but some of them looked pretty unsavory. Someone had estimated the crowd at over twenty thousand settlers plus the townsfolk and onlookers like themselves.

"I'm sorry Hannah," he said. "There just wasn't a bed to be found anywhere. We followed every lead we heard of, but there wasn't a single room not already rented. We checked the churches and people have paid just to sleep on the benches. Daniel even tried the dance hall and the gambling house," he said with a nervous laugh.

"I'm afraid we'll just have to spend the night in the wagons, but we'll leave first thing in the morning."

"We've been sleeping in the wagons all summer. Why would it be a problem to do so one more night," Hannah said, smiling at her husband in reassurance. She pressed a tin cup, containing some of their remaining water, into his hands.

"We'll be fine in the wagons." Hannah handed her brother a cup of the water before turning her attention back to Carolyn.

"You are wonderful." Joseph reached over and kissed her tenderly. "Don't get to close," he cautioned when she tried to snuggle closer to him. "I am drenched with sweat. I can't believe it has gotten so hot."

"You had both better wash up." She looked from her husband to her brother. Their faces were bright red and their clothes drenched. "You will feel cooler." She got up to prepare the wash pan.

"That's all right." Joseph motioned for her to sit back down. "I'll wait until we set up camp. I'll just get hotter and dirtier."

Joseph and Daniel drank thirstily of the lukewarm liquid. When Daniel put the dipper in the pail again, it made a scrapping sound as it scratched across the bottom. They had spent so much time trying to locate a room, that it would be difficult to find space for the wagons anywhere near the river. They might have to carry water for the horses, mules and the family from a great distance.

Joseph and Daniel climbed to the seats and guided the mules slowly and cautiously back out into the crowded roadway. The mules and wagons made their way toward the wild Arkansas River.

The crowds grew even greater as they neared the river. They had to pull the mules up frequently to avoid running over a pedestrian, horse and rider, or to avoid locking wheels with another wagon. It took all of Joseph's skill to manage the cantankerous mules. Finally they had moved as close to the river as they could and decided to set up camp.

"Back the wagons up to that scrub oak," Daniel shouted above the din around them. "I'll watch for you," he said as he swung down to the ground and quickly took up a position effectively blocking anyone from cutting Joseph off, as he tried to maneuver the team into position. When Joseph had his wagon backed up to the scraggly tree, he guided Daniel into place. This way they would be headed out in the morning.

They untied the horses and mules leading them through the throng to drink at the river. They had strapped their water containers on the backs of the mules, in order to fill them without making multiple trips to the river.

Joseph did not like leaving his womenfolk alone any longer than necessary. Most of the crowd was made up of decent folk, settlers looking for land to raise crops and families, but there was an element of rowdy roughnecks intermingled with the settlers.

Chapter Thirty-Nine

By the time they returned to the wagons, the sun was beginning to set and the western sky was glowing with soft oranges, yellows, pinks and purples. Most, of the people they passed, were cooking over campfires or had already rolled up in bedrolls.

Bernice had a fire going and was stirring something in a large iron pot that was hung from a hook over the fire, while Sheba prepared cornbread for the big iron skillet. Anna hung over her shoulder and insisted on knowing everything that would be put in the bowl. Sheba smiled at her patiently and let her measure out the ingredients and stir the mixture to be put into the pan.

Daniel tied the horses to the tree and the mules to the wagon on the other side. Hannah swung down from the wagon and filled a basin with water so Joseph and Daniel could wash up for supper.

"You'll feel better after you wash up," Hannah said offering Joseph a towel and a chunk of soap.

"We rinsed off in the river, but by the time we got through wrestling with the water barrels and fastening them back on the mules, we were as dirty as ever." Joseph laughed as he took the towel and soap from Hannah.

The men washed the grime from the trail and the dusty streets from their faces, arms and hands. With all the activity in the town, the dust seemed to roll up in a never-ending cloud. The water in the basin turned dirty reddish brown by the time they finished. As the last of the light dwindled in the west, they gathered around the campfire to eat the stew and cornbread.

"Daddy, I helped make the cornbread," Anna announced proudly. "Sheba told me what to put in and I measured everything and stirred it up for the skillet."

"Well, I believe this is the best cornbread that I have ever eaten," Joseph told her, picking up another piece and popping it in his mouth.

"We helped get kindling for the fire," Joshua announced proudly,

"Got kin'lin'," Jeremiah confirmed.

"You are all three very good helpers," Joseph praised the children. "What would we ever do without you?" He tousled the boys' hair and lifted Anna onto his lap.

"Rose, make sure the boys don't wonder from camp." Joseph's voice was low, but had a serious undertone. "We have seen some pretty rough looking folk wondering the area." Keep a close watch." He turned to the boys, placing a hand on each of their shoulders. "You boys mind now. There are so many people about that it would be easy to get lost. You are not to go anywhere without one of the adults with you."

The looks they gave him were pure angelic innocence, but he was not fooled. "I mean it now." He looked around. "I believe I see several cherry trees around wearing some very nice switches." He looked at them sternly to impress his words upon their inquisitive minds. They were not used to restrictions and had never been in a situation where someone might want to do them harm.

"Don't worry papa. I'll watch them," Anna promised. She smiled at the rambunctious boys. She had been helping look after them from the time they had each been brought home from the hospital and knew first hand how much trouble they could get into.

The adults smiled at Anna. They knew how carefully she watched over her brother and cousin, but they were also aware how fast the boys could get into trouble. Even as young as Jeremiah was, he could disappear in a flash if he wasn't watched every minute. It had been a long day and everyone was tired. It was time for all of them to get ready for bed.

Bernice helped Rose straighten up the camp, when they finished eating. The rule they traveled by was to always leave the camping area in the same condition they found it.

Hannah prepared beds for everyone in the wagons, as best she could. It would be crowded, but she was reluctant to have any of the women or children sleeping out under the wagons, as was their custom when out on the trail. Anna held her baby sister and the boys sat beside her as Sheba told them a Bible story.

The two men led the horses and mules to the river for another drink, before tying them up for the night. Joseph was concerned about the mules and horses, with all the people milling around. There was sure to be a certain amount of undesirables among them. The livery stables, like the hotels, were full.

"We will have to keep a close eye on the livestock, with this crowd around and the shortage of available animals." Joseph glanced around at the milling people, most of who were beginning to settle down.

Daniel agreed, as he carefully looked over the tents and wagons near them. In the distance they could still hear some revelers laughing and occasionally shooting in the air, their exuberance no doubt enhanced by the consumption of the jugs of moonshine they had observed changing hands.

The stars shone brightly in the moonlit sky when Daniel moved Sheba's chair to the lift at the end of the wagon. He hoisted it up and Joseph got inside and swung the chair into the wagon and lifted Sheba onto the pallet Hannah had fixed for her. Then he slipped out of the wagon to give them some privacy, while Rose helped her get ready for bed.

Anna and the boys finally climbed into the lead wagon and Bernice climbed into the other wagon with Sheba and Rose. Joseph helped Hannah up into the other wagon. He kissed Carolyn's golden hair, then handed her carefully up to her mother's waiting arms.

"I'll be there in a minute," he said smiling up at his wife. "I'm just going to help Daniel put the fire out." He turned back to Hannah's brother. "We need to stay alert tonight," he said, speaking low. "There's a lot of ruff looking men around, probably a lot of undesirables among them." They could still hear the rowdy laughter of men who had been drinking heavily.

"I plan to sleep under the other wagon," Daniel assured him. "I'll keep the shotgun handy, just in case."

Joseph nodded his agreement, before climbing into the wagon.

They slept fitfully with the noise of people, animals and babies crying at neighboring campsites. Camping, on the trail, far from towns and people, was very different from the hustle and bustle in which they found themselves.

The next day Joseph left to see about getting tickets on the steamboat, which would take them and their wagons downstream to Little Rock. Rose left to wash clothes on a rock down at the river. A couple men stopped to chat with her and she visited with them while she scrubbed the clothes for the family.

The boys chased each other around the wagons and Anna helped Hannah and Sheba with baby Carolyn. The day was clear and hot, but a breeze blew steadily from the West. The children grew hungry and tired from their play and Hannah fixed them a snack.

Most of the other campsites were empty; she could see the Arkansas River easily now. She could even see Rose, where she was washing out clothes. She smiled when she saw the two men hunkered down talking to her. *One of these days we are going to loose our Rose to some handsome fellow who comes by courting. We sure will miss her.*

Mid morning after he finished the chores, Daniel found he had time on his hands and decided to take Sheba for a ride in her chair. Bernice packed them a picnic lunch and placed the basket in Sheba's lap. It was nearly impossible to find a place anywhere close by that was not overrun with people.

He finally located a patch of woods running alongside the river. Daniel placed Sheba's chair behind some trees, so it would be hidden from the road and picked her up. He carried her to the riverbank and made her as comfortable as he could in a grassy recess, shaded by the overhanging tree branches.

"Thanks for bringing me here Daniel. The river looks so peaceful." She sighed deeply as she drank in the scene before her. Barges passed close enough for them to wave to men on the large sprawling decks that were laden with produce and merchandise headed southeast downriver.

"It's a nice spot, but don't kid yourself. There is nothing peaceful about that river." He thought about his experience in the river when Joshua had taken a header into the swiftly flowing waters. "We can still hear people milling around here, but at least there is no one to jostle us."

They watched the river activity and enjoyed the picnic lunch.

"What is that boat up-stream? It looks like it's going across the river."

"That's the ferry. That land over there is Indian Territory." Daniel pointed up river and across to the far bank.

"We're that close? I can't believe we have come so far west. I am a long way from the Atlantic Ocean." Sheba sighed deeply and gazed out over the water. Her tone was a mixture of amusement and wistfulness.

"You must miss it very much? I never got to Savannah myself, but mama was from there. She talked about the ocean a lot. Her folks died right after her and papa married, so we never had any call to visit. We were always going to, but with all the kids and work in the fields, we just never got around to it."

"The ocean's beautiful. Of course, I only saw it a couple times. The Savannah River is what flows right alongside the town. The Arkansas reminds me of it a lot." She laughed. "Of course there is no Spanish moss hanging from the trees and I haven't seen a single alligator, so it does lack some of the ambiance of the Savannah. I don't think the mosquitoes are quite as large either."

"Well, Peg swears there are alligators in the Arkansas, but I haven't seen one yet either." Daniel chuckled, as he gazed out at the river.

"This is a real treat to sit here under the shade of these trees and watch the river activity. You have been a good friend to me Daniel and it means a lot." She smiled at the young man with a trace of tears in her eyes.

"Well, of course I had to have an excuse to get off where it was quieter." Daniel feigned indifference to cover his embarrassment.

"And of course you couldn't have come off by yourself, I don't suppose?" Her smile grew wider. "What do you hear from all your lady friends?" She teased.

"Nothing since we left of course. I got a letter from Mary just before we left home and she said she missed me." His face lit with pleasure. "I plan to write Mary and Louise when we get back to the wagon, have to keep the ladies happy." Daniel laughed good-naturedly and Sheba swatted playfully at his shoulder.

"Well, I think Louise is pretty special, but Hannah said that Mary is real nice too. I wish I could have met her. Hannah said she was all starry-eyed over you when y'all were in Amity."

"That's me, the heart throb." Daniel grinned, but his ruddy complexion took on a deeper hue.

"We probably better get back."

"I am afraid you are right. I hate for this day to end. It has been so perfect. They will be wondering if we fell in a hole or something. We have been gone quite awhile."
Sheba gathered up the picnic items and carefully placed them in the basket and covered them with the cloth.

"I'll take you to the river for picnics when we get home," Daniel promised, as he picked her up and carried her back to the chair. *Ben's an idiot,* he muttered to himself. A scowl crossed his rugged face, as he thought of Sheba's husband.

The sun had moved far off across Indian Territory. They could barely see across the river, because the sun was directly in their line of vision, as they moved back to the camp.

Chapter Forty

The next day while Rose was assisting Sheba to bathe, she noticed blisters covering her legs. Sheba was also rubbing her hands together. Rose saw that they were covered with the same kind of blisters, as those on her legs. She called to Bernice to check them. Bernice confirmed her suspicions. Daniel had unintentionally set Sheba down in a patch of poison ivy. Sheba was covered with oozing, itchy, poison ivy blisters. Bernice quickly doctored her with one of Joseph's concoctions, but she was still very uncomfortable.

Joseph had not been able to book passage for them until the following day. Bernice told him it was probably just as well, another day would give Sheba's blisters a chance to begin to dry.

Joseph rode off to buy supplies and some ingredients for the medicine Bernice was using on Sheba. It took a lot of the solution to cover the numerous blisters and Bernice had to treat the poison ivy so frequently that they were getting low.

Daniel announced he had some letters to post and Bernice asked to accompany him.

"Hannah," he peered in the end of the wagon. "Bernice and I are going to post some letters. Do you have any letters to go?"

"Yes, wait a minute. I wrote a letter to the folks." She handed the letter and twenty-four cents for the postage to Daniel. She did not write to them often, because postage was so expensive, but she tried to write to them at least once a month.

They started off through the dense crowd to post their letters soon after breakfast, with Anna's dog Don'ld close on their heels. Most of their neighbors had left to start the trek into Oklahoma Territory to be in place for the Land Run.

"Anna, why don't you read to the boys in the wagon for a while?" Hannah suggested. "I'm going to feed Carolyn and put her down for her nap."

"Yes ma'am." Anna called to the boys and helped them climb into the other wagon, where Sheba was already resting. Rose was busy putting away the clothes she had washed and dried on bushes near the wagon. They could hear their mother begin to sing a lullaby to the baby.

Hannah watched the children climb safely into the wagon and then she looked around at the other campsites, still singing softly.

Carolyn began to cry and her attention turned to the needs of her infant daughter. When the baby drifted off to sleep, Hannah lay down beside her on the pallet in the narrow wagon bed. She had not slept much the night before and was soon sleeping soundly, cradling the infant in her arm.

"Sheba, would you mind if I go on a picnic with Carl? Rose's cheeks were pink with excitement. She had settled Sheba on her pallet and the children were all asleep.

They had enjoyed a busy morning playing and gathering kindling.

Sheba smiled at her companion. She knew that Rose had met Carl while she was washing clothes the day before. Apparently he was staying in a tent not far from their campsite with his brother, Zeke. Rose had been as giddy as a teenager ever since their first meeting and had told the others about the two men she had met. They had seemed to be quite attentive to her.

"Of course, enjoy yourself. Just keep out of the poison ivy," she warned with a grimace. "I hope you aren't planning on leaving us," she teased.

Rose blushed an attractive crimson. Giggling, she checked her reflection in a bit of dark glass. "I won't be gone long," she called as she climbed down from the wagon and waved. She hurried off to meet her new friend.

* * *

Joseph returned to the wagon about an hour after Hannah had fallen asleep. His saddlebags were bulging with purchases.

"What are you ladies up to?" he called, turning the canvas back.

Hannah rubbed her eyes and smiled at her husband. "Shhh," she whispered, holding her finger to her lips and motioning toward the sleeping baby. "Your youngest daughter is finally asleep." She moved to the back of the wagon, where Joseph was peering in and bent over to kiss him.

"Where did Daniel take the other wagon?" he asked, glancing at the spot where the other wagon had been sitting.

"Daniel and Bernice went to town to post some letters this morning. I don't think they have returned," she said following his gaze. The wagon was no longer there. "Joseph!" Hannah cried out in alarm and hastily scrambling from the wagon. "It was there a little while ago." Panic was rising in her voice.

"I watched the children climb into the wagon before I fed Carolyn. I fell asleep. I didn't hear anything. She ran to the spot where the wagon had stood, holding its precious cargo.

Joseph disappeared, but was soon back. "The mules are gone, all four of them. They were tied on the other side of the wagon. Did Daniel take the other horse?"

"No, they were walking when they left. Joseph, where could they be?" Her voice cracked with emotion. "How could I not hear someone untie the mules from the side of the wagon and drive it away from here?" Her voice was beginning to rise hysterically. "My babies, my babies," she cried, collapsing in a heap.

"Hannah, who was in the wagon?" Joseph asked, kneeling and gripping her shoulders firmly. She stared at him blankly, and he shook her slightly, repeating his question. "Who – was – in – the - wagon?"

"Anna and the boys, along with Sheba; they were taking a nap," she responded weakly. "Anna was going to read to them. They probably fell asleep. None of us slept well last night with all the noise.

"I looked over to check on the children when Daniel left. There was not a sound coming from the wagon." She ran to the spot where the wagon had been parked.

"Joseph where can they be? They are all babies." She was growing hysterical, as she looked around the camp frantically.

"What has happened," Bernice called, hurrying up with Daniel. They had heard Hannah's frightened voice before they could actually see the camp.

"Where's the wagon?" Daniel walked up and looked around.

"It's gone," Joseph said curtly. "Hannah was in the other wagon with the baby. Anna and the boys were in the wagon with Sheba." He started for his horse. "Come on Daniel, we have to find them." He glanced back at Hannah. "We'll find them and bring them home," he promised.

He looked around, as if counting heads. "Where is Rose? Was she with them?"

"Yes, no—I am really not sure. I think I heard her leave. She mentioned something earlier about Carl taking her on a picnic. You know the man she was talking about last night?"

"Bernice, please stay with Hannah and the baby." Joseph slid his foot in the stirrup of the tall roan. "We'll bring the children back," he said with conviction.

After a hurried conversation, Daniel strode back toward town and Joseph rode toward the border.

Bernice helped Hannah to her feet. "See about the baby. I'll ask along the river if anyone has seen them."

"I'll get Carolyn and we'll go in different directions," Hannah said firmly, willing herself to think calmly. "You go down river and I'll go up river. Ask everyone you see to help." Hannah quickly climbed into the wagon and retrieved the protesting baby, who had been sleeping soundly until her mother snatched her up in her arms.

"Here, help me with this," she said extending a large piece of cloth. They secured the baby to Hannah's back with a sling fashioned from the cloth and set out in opposite directions.

Periodically the women came back to the wagons, but neither had met anyone who could recall seeing the wagon or the three children. No one even noticed it leaving. Everyone promised to keep a look out. Some offered to watch the baby for her, but after the disappearance of the other children, Hannah was reluctant to accept any help with Carolyn. Hannah and Bernice took turns carrying the baby. It was as if Sheba, Anna, Jeremiah, Joshua and Rose had disappeared off the face of the earth.

When Joseph returned, his horse was lathered and sweat stained his clothes. His face was creased with worry and defeat. Daniel arrived back at the camp soon after Joseph. Bernice walked up with Carolyn.

"Where is Hannah?" Joseph looked around expecting to find his wife waiting in the wagon.

"We have been looking along the river banks, trying to find someone who might have seen something."

"Neither the Federal Marshall, or the army can help us," Joseph said. They said there are over twenty thousand people waiting for the Run, who are passing through Fort Smith and the law has more meanness than they can possibly handle. There is only enough land for one out of three of them. They are expecting a lot of attempts to cross early and claim the sites along the rivers and streams. The authorities have all their men watching the border. He did say he would send word to them to keep an eye out for the children, but it'll be up to us to find the children," he said resolutely.

"They took all four of the mules and one of the saddle horses. All we have left are the ponies and they sure cannot pull a wagon. There isn't a team of mules or horses to be had this side of Dardanelle. Men have bought up anything that could still stand."

"Which way do you want me to go, Joseph?"

"Check out every wagon up river, Daniel. I'll go back to town. Ask questions of everyone." Joseph's voice was breaking with the intense emotion he felt. "Someone has to have seen a wagon full of children pulled by four mules with a horse tied to the back."

"Start a mile beyond our camp site. Bernice and I have already covered this area. We will keep looking and fan out a little further on the way back. That way we will be sure to check the entire area." Hannah walked up and informed them.

"Hannah you can't go wandering around here by yourself in this crowd. I don't even like leaving you here at the wagon after what's happened," Joseph said firmly.

"Joseph," she replied in the same inflexible tone that Joseph had used. "My children and my friend are in that wagon and only God knows where it is by now. If you think I'm going to sit here sewing, or twiddling my thumbs, waiting for someone to bring us word, you have another think coming." Carolyn had begun to fret and Bernice helped her untie the cloth. "As soon as I feed baby Carolyn, we will be back out looking for the children."

Joseph took one look at his wife's determined face, mounted his horse and turned his head toward town. He cantered along the crowded road searching for the wagon and its precious cargo.

"Be careful sis." Daniel squeezed Hannah's hand and walked quickly up river in the direction of the ferry.

Hannah quickly climbed into the wagon and settled Carolyn to her breast. Bernice brought her bread and cheese, and a flask of water. She made sure Hannah ate and drank the nourishment while she nursed the baby, because she knew as soon as the little one was done feeding, Hannah would be back out hunting.

Hannah and Bernice wondered back and forth, stopping at each campsite. No one recalled having seen any sign of the wagon, Sheba or the children. They returned to the wagon occasionally to see if Joseph or Daniel had returned with any news and then started out again.

The river flowed north at the point where they were camped, then circled around the peninsula, which was about five miles across and seven miles deep. Joseph was afraid that who ever had taken the wagon would head across the river and deep into Indian Territory, as soon as possible. The chance of finding them after that was extremely slim.

They hunted until dark, without a clue to where the children had disappeared. No one they spoke to could remember seeing a wagon, mules or horse like they described. At dark Joseph returned to the wagon and instructed Hannah and Bernice not to leave the confines of their camp.

"It isn't safe for you to be wandering around and besides, Anna is very resourceful," Joseph said. "If she can manage to get away, she will try to get back here. Someone has to be here, if that happens."

Daniel, at Joseph's insistence, confined his search closer to camp, so he could check on the women frequently. Joseph coaxed Hannah into drinking some chamomile tea to help her sleep, before he climbed wearily back on Ginger to continue the search.

Both men returned to the wagon about three o'clock and slept fitfully until daybreak. The women hastily prepared biscuits, which they sliced and stuffed with eggs and bacon, and flasks of coffee for Joseph and Daniel to carry with them.

"Don't worry Hannah." Joseph tenderly kissed her, the weariness in his voice belying his words. "We'll find them." His voice lacked the assurance that might have instilled any hope, for those left behind.

They would have to get more help, if they were to have any chance of rescuing them. He stopped at the telegraph office and sent three messages, before continuing the search.

Chapter Forty-One

Anna awoke to the gentle rocking of the wagon. Jeremiah had crawled across her and was jabbering to a wooden toy. She glanced up at the bunk where Sheba was scratching her poison ivy in her sleep. Anna reached over and touched her shoulder gently.

"Sheba," she whispered, so as not to awaken Joshua. "You are not supposed to do that. Miz Bernice said it would spread."

Sheba opened her eyes and grinned at the child who was trying to mother her, in the same manner she used on the other children. "That is easier said than done," she whispered back. "This is a powerful itch." She rubbed one arm against the other trying to get some relief from the constant itching.

"I wonder where we are going. I hope we are headed home. I really don't think I like it here." Anna sat up and moved Jeremiah aside. She started toward the front of the wagon to ask her father if they were headed for the boat that would take them home, but was startled to hear unfamiliar voices coming from the driver's seat. Intuitively, she hung back and listened to the men.

"I don't know why we can't just dump them in the river come night fall, like we did the other one."

"May need them as a cover when we get to the run; one of us is going to have to go in at night, got to stake out a good section. The other one'll drive the wagon in."

The voices were rough and unfamiliar and what they were saying did not make any sense to Anna. Where were her parents and Uncle Daniel? She looked around. Rose wasn't here to care for Sheba and the boys. *And where was Miz Bernice?* Anna heard one of the men spit and then it grew quiet again. She still did not understand, but remained silent. She pressed up against the trunk that lay between where she crouched and the wagon seat, afraid to move.

"I don't like it," the first man said petulantly.

"Don't have to, Zeke. Just have to do what you're told." The voice was rough and harsh. "Use your head. If their men folk catch up to us, what they going to do so long as we got those kids of theirs and that cripple?"

Jeremiah had followed Anna to the front of the wagon and was beginning to jabber again. She placed her hand lightly over his mouth and whispered for him to be still. As quietly as possible, she picked him up and carried him back to Sheba.

"Sheba," she whispered. "I don't know how it happened, but we've been stole."

"What are you talking about child?" Sheba's voice carried a hint of disbelief mixed with panic. "Why are we moving? Who is driving the wagon?" Her voice was beginning to rise, as was her fear.

"I don't know." Anna was whispering, so quietly that it was hard for Sheba to hear her. "One of them sounds like Miz Rose's new friend, but I don't know who the other one is."

"Well maybe Joseph got him to drive the wagon to the boat, so he and Daniel could ride the horses," Sheba said a little relief creeping into her voice.

"I don't think so Sheba. It sounded like they were arguing about throwing us in the river." Anna's expression was quite serious and she appeared to be terribly frightened. Sheba again grew apprehensive.

"Eat!" Jeremiah demanded. "Hun'gy."

"Me too," Joshua chorused, sitting up and rubbing his eyes. "Hey we're moving. Daniel said I could help with the team." He jumped to his feet and rushed forward. Anna leaped to her feet and in a flying tackle landed on top of her cousin, her hand immediately covering his mouth as he tried to holler his protests.

"Come back here and be quite," Sheba hissed at her son, attempting to console Jeremiah who had begun to cry. She kept her voice low, but her tone held authority. Unconsciously, she rubbed at the worrisome poison ivy.

Joshua pushed Anna's hand away from his mouth and scowled at his cousin, but he shuffled back to where his mother sat holding Jeremiah. Sheba never spoke in a gruff manner, sometimes Rose scolded the boys, but his mother had never fussed at him about anything and he felt quite put out.

"What's wrong mama?" He stood before her a pout on his face.

"I'm sorry Josh." She turned to Anna again. "Are you sure?" She hoped with all her heart that Anna had heard wrong.

"Yes ma'am." She was on the verge of tears herself and her voice wavered as she sniffed quietly.

"Anna," Sheba said sharply. "You are not to start crying. We need you. You will have to be my legs. And if what you say is true, you are going to have to be very brave."

"Don't worry Sheba. Papa will come." Anna had absolute confidence in her father. "Papa and Uncle Daniel are probably already looking for us. They will find us pretty soon." She cut her eyes to the front of the wagon and tried to sound confident, but was unable to completely hide her fear.

"Papa," Jeremiah piped in. "Want papa. Where's Dan'l?" Jeremiah adored his Uncle Daniel. After papa and mama, Daniel was the first name Jeremiah had learned. Of course Anna and Sheba were usually 'mama' and sometimes Rose and Bernice also. Since Caroline's birth, it was to Anna that he usually scrambled for solace or Sheba if Anna was at school. He had been Anna's shadow all summer, but when Daniel was around camp, Jeremiah held his pudgy arms up to be held or for some rougher play with his doting uncle.

Anna picked her little brother up and nestled him on her lap. She smoothed his unruly blond hair back form his forehead and patted him gently.

"You must be real quiet, buba," she admonished softly. "We are going to play hide and seek and the drivers up front are it. We have to be real quite, so they don't find us." She had played hide and seek with the boys often and even little Jeremiah had learned to remain quite when he was being sought by whoever was 'it'.

"Anna, hand me Jeremiah and climb up in the back and look out. Looks like someone fastened the back flaps. That's why it is so dark in here." She reached for nineteen-month-old Jeremiah. "Maybe you can get down that way and go for help."

Anna handed her brother to Sheba and made her way quietly to the heavy canvas at the back. She tugged on it, but it had been secured tightly on the outside. She could see a hole over her head, so she climbed up on Sheba's chair. Peering cautiously through the small opening, she looked out over a sea of people. There seemed to be hundreds of people in every direction she looked. There were men on horseback, others in wagons and still more trudging by on foot.

Thick clouds of dust rose up and covered the entire area. It made its way through the small hole and it was all she could do to muffle several sneezes she could not prevent. Many of the wagons looked just like theirs. Several times she thought she saw the other wagon, her father or Uncle Daniel on one of the horses, but each time it was a stranger.

Her heart nearly stopped when she looked down and saw their second mule team tied to the back of the wagon, in which they rode. She climbed down and moved quietly to Sheba's side and reported all she had seen.

The wagon stopped and a noise echoed back to them from the front. They heard one of the men enter and make his way through the semidarkness of the interior. The children huddled together, clinging to Sheba as he approached. The heavy bitter stench of whiskey and dirty sweaty clothes permeated the wagon.

Anna's fear was so profound, she nearly cried out. Instead, she bit down on her lip until it bled. She had pushed Joshua behind her and was pressed against Sheba, who still held Jeremiah on her lap. Joshua was nearly smothered, so tightly was he sandwiched between his cousin and mother. Jeremiah began to wail and pressed his face into Sheba's shoulder.

"Shut that brat up," the big man hissed at them. "We may need some of you, but we sure don't need all of you." The man cursed and drew back his hand as if to hit the toddler. Anna moved to block him from her brother, still holding Joshua behind her.

The menace in the man's voice and the harsh words he had thrown at them were so frightening that Sheba felt light headed. *Dear heavenly Father,"* she silently prayed. *Help us. And Lord, give me the strength to see these children safe. Whatever happens to me precious Lord, please don't let these babies be hurt.* The uncontrollable fear began to ease and she faced their captor resolutely.

"What do you want with us?" she demanded firmly. "You don't need these children. Just put them out and Anna will see them safely back to her parents."

"Well now, don't you have a lot of spunk?" The man leered down at her, leaning so close that she could smell his whisky breath. "It might not be bad having a little colored gal around to keep things interesting." He spit a wad of tobacco juice on the floor at Anna's feet. She scrunched up her face, but did not utter a sound.

"We'll just see how much spunk you have—later." He leered at Sheba lustfully. "We're loading on the ferry so keep your trap shut and these brats quiet—if you want to keep them alive." His words were menacing enough, but his tone was even harsher. He glared at them viciously, before turning back toward the front of the wagon.

Joshua peeked around Anna, his dark eyes wide with fear, as he looked from his mother to Anna and then followed the man's progress back to the front of the wagon.

"Mama," he whispered, squeezing closer to her. "Who was that?"

"A bad man, Joshua, he is a very bad and evil man."

They felt the wagon begin to move and then could hear the sloshing of the river against the sides of the ferry. Before long they felt the gentle rocking as the ferry rose and fell gently with the current. They knew they were crossing the wide Arkansas River. Sheba and Anna looked at each other in despair. They realized it would be much more difficult for anyone to find them once they were lost in Indian Territory.

When they arrived on the other side, they felt the lurch as the team pulled the wagon off the ferry and up the steep bank. They could hear the man yell and crack the long mule whip. Soon they were pulling away from the river.

Anna cautiously made her way to the back and again climbed up on Sheba's chair. She peered through the small hole and watched the river grow smaller behind them. Tears trickled down her cheeks, but she was careful not to make a sound.

There were still a lot of wagons and men on horses, but now there was more space separating them. They were all traveling the same direction, away from the river and her family. She knew there were two men and she thought only one of them was on the wagon seat driving the mules. The other might be one of the men on horseback behind them, so she was afraid to make any kind of signal to anyone.

They continued on through the night. The four captives clustered together on Sheba's pallet; a woman of color, who had no use of her legs and who was covered with poison ivy, a girl not yet six, but who was intelligent and mature for her age, a three year old and a toddler just turned nineteen months.

Lord, how shall we ever get out of this? Send Your angels to surround these children and keep them safe, whatever happens to me. Keep my babies safe precious

Lord, don't let any harm come to them. Help Joseph to find us and rescue us. Her prayer invoked the urgency and desperation she felt.

Sheba knew it would be next to impossible for Joseph to find them in the vast territory, especially in the sea of wagons that all resembled one another. Turbulent, frantic thoughts kept tumbling through her mind, as she saw herself drowning in a pool of hopelessness.

Anna patted Sheba's blistered hand and whispered to her softly. "Don't worry, Sheba. I prayed and asked God to help papa find us. It will be all right." She spoke with the assurance of the young when turning their problems over to the Heavenly Father.

* * *

The children finally fell asleep and Sheba slept fitfully for short periods. She heard when the men changed places driving the team and the other climbed into the front for some sleep, but they did not come near her or the children.

Anna woke up during the night, trembling and crying out in fear. She had not had the nightmare in a long time, but their abduction must have resurrected the terror that had begun after she had become lost on the train several years before.

Sheba felt the old guilt creeping over her. She had held herself to blame for Anna wondering off and her frightening experience. *I have to get control of myself. I have to be able to think clearly, so we can take advantage of any chance of escape that comes along.*

She willed herself to compose her thoughts and calmed Anna with soothing words and gentle pats on her back.

They were still moving when a ray of sunlight pushed away the darkness from the small opening in the back of the wagon. Sheba glanced toward the front. It was still dark in that direction, so they were still headed west into unfamiliar territory. They would not know anyone, no one would know them or that they had been abducted and the children would have no idea how to get back to their family. The despair in her heart at that moment was darker than the blackest night.

Anna awoke and sleepily rubbed her eyes. She yawned and smiled at Sheba. Sleep had temporarily erased the plight they were in from her mind.

"Hush baby," Sheba whispered softly. She patted Anna's arm and pointed to the front of the wagon.

Tears sprang into her eyes. "I forgot." Fear quickly replaced the sweet smile that she had worn only moments before. "Where are we, Sheba?" She looked around and noted that it was still dark toward the front of the wagon.

"We are still traveling toward the west. It looks like we are joining the Oklahoma Run. We have been traveling all night. They have only stopped long enough to switch the mule teams and change places driving the team. They are pushing real hard; must be trying to get a good position for the run." She spoke so low that only Anna could hear. The boys were still asleep.

"I heard papa talking about it. He said there were a lot more people after the land, than there was land." She began wriggling where she lay. "You suppose it would be all right to use the bucket?"

"Yes, just be quite. It was probably emptied, so put some cloth down the hole into the bucket, so there will not be any noise. They probably can't hear it anyway with the noise surrounding us, but I don't want to draw any more attention to us than we can help."

Anna did as instructed and when finished poured some water into the bowl and washed up before returning to the pallet to help Sheba take care of her needs.

"The men must be anxious to get to a certain location and with the great crowds that might make them even more desperate. They will probably keep pushing until they get where they plan to be situated on the twenty-second."

It seemed to help to discuss the situation with Anna. She was only a child, but had always demonstrated an uncommon amount of common sense and intelligence.

"Sheba," Anna asked solemnly. "Will they kill us?" Her eyes were large with fright and she cut them toward the front of the wagon.

"No, precious." It was said with more conviction than she felt. "They need us alive," she assured Anna, but the smile she gave her was weak.

"Ungy!" Jeremiah announced sitting up. "Ungy," he repeated and began to whine.

"Hush buba," Anna soothed. "I'll find us something to eat." Anna slipped easily into the role of provider. She found some bread, which had been set aside and pinched off some for each of them. Joshua had awakened and although he was subdued, he glared toward the front of the wagon.

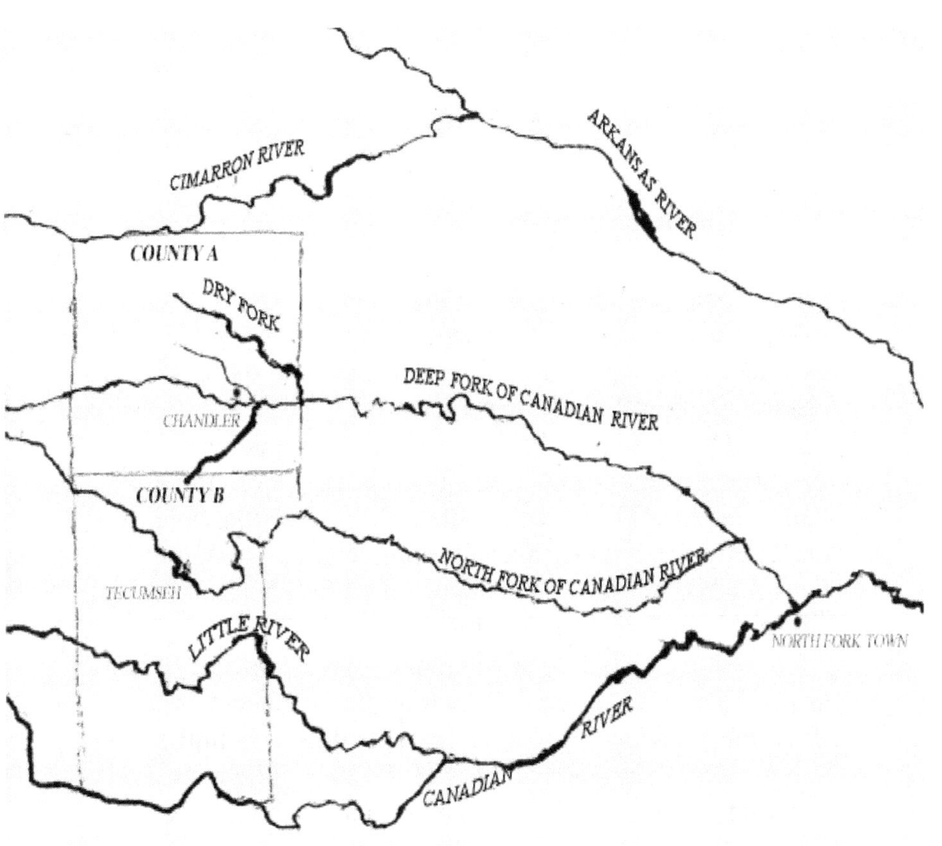

CIMARRON RIVER
ARKANSAS RIVER
COUNTY A
DRY FORK
DEEP FORK OF CANADIAN RIVER
CHANDLER
COUNTY B
NORTH FORK OF CANADIAN RIVER
TECUMSEH
NORTH FORK TOWN
LITTLE RIVER
CANADIAN RIVER

Chapter Forty-Two

They ate silently while they traveled ever further from their loved ones. They saw little of their captors. The two men were apparently taking turns driving the team and sleeping in the front of the wagon.

The area in the back where they huddled was beginning to smell of the unemptied bucket, even though Anna was careful to keep the door closed over the hole. Ordinarily when they traveled in uninhabited areas, the bucket was set aside. They had been in the wagon four days and still moved over the rolling prairie.

Sheba had no idea where they were. Once they had crossed a sizable body of water that she assumed to be a river, but her knowledge of Indian Territory was limited to it being west of Arkansas and north of Texas. The bucket of drinking water was getting very low and Sheba instructed Anna how to ration what was left.

The men had offered them neither water nor food since the nightmare had begun. Apparently they needed them as hostages, but were not particularly concerned about the condition of their health.

Inside the wagon, with the back flap closed except the small hole near the top, it felt like an oven and Sheba and the children felt they were slowly baking. There was plenty of water in the barrel on the side, but they could not get to it from inside the wagon.

They were hot and dirty with the September sun beating down on the wagon and dust constantly seeping into the wagon. Thirst was a constant problem. Joseph had preached to them constantly while they traveled about the dangers of not keeping hydrated. Sheba knew the children could become dehydrated quickly in this heat if they did not receive adequate liquid. She made sure the two boys were given water frequently, but Sheba was afraid there would not be any left for any of them before long. She worried about what would happen to the children when the water and food were gone.

Jeremiah began to fret in the unbearable heat. The man who was asleep in the front was awakened by his cries and made his way clumsily through the wagon, cussing and yelling. The intimidation in his voice and words were obvious and although Jeremiah was too young to understand the meaning of the man's words, his tone was enough to silence the toddler. He buried his face in Anna's shoulder. Anna began trembling and could not will herself to stop, no matter how hard she tried. Joshua gripped his fists tighter and stood his ground, in front of Anna and Jeremiah.

"Leave us alone," he shouted. "My uncles will fix you. What are you doing with our wagon?" he demanded.

Joshua did not see the big man draw back his fist to strike him quickly enough to avoid the blow. The sound of the man's large hand connecting with Joshua's head reverberated throughout the wagon. Anna crawled to his side, dragging a screaming Jeremiah with her. She cradled her cousin's head in her lap, oblivious to her own whimpering. Little Jeremiah clung to her like a leach, his little face buried in her side, his terrified shrieks muffled by her body.

"What's the raucous back there?" a rough voice called from the front of the wagon. "I thought I told you to keep those brats quiet not see how loud you can make them yell," the voice hissed. "There is a lot of other people around here so shut them up and get up here."

"One more sound from any of you and I'll tie your traps shut," the man threatened, leaning over them so close Anna could smell the rancid odor of stale whiskey on this breath. "You got me?" he demanded.

"Yes, sir," Anna whispered. She was trembling so much, Joshua almost slipped from her lap. She immediately turned her attention to her injured cousin. She had to find a way to quiet Jeremiah, before the man tied them up or hit him like he had Joshua. Anna was not sure if Joshua was even alive.

She pulled him over to where Sheba could scoop him into her arms, but he had not moved since his head hit the side of the wagon. She cuddled Jeremiah and whispered one of mama's lullabies in his ear, while she rocked him gently in her arms. His crying died down to a soft whimper that probably could not be heard outside the wagon.

* * *

That night she dreamed of her mama and her room at home, with its high, soft, feather bed. When she awoke, it was a new day and Jeremiah was crying for mama. She cradled him in her arms and looked over to where Sheba sat holding the immobile Joshua. A ray of sunlight pushed away the darkness from the small hole in the back of the wagon. It was still dark towards the front of the wagon. Anna tried to remember what papa had told her about the sun.

"The sun comes up in the east," she said, remembering. She looked back at the front of the wagon. They were headed west, west even further into Oklahoma Territory. Papa told her that across the river was Oklahoma Territory and they had crossed the river the first day.

Anna looked back at Joshua. She could see something on the side of his head. She set Jeremiah down and handed him his toy wooden horse. Uncle Daniel had carved it from a block of wood the night he was born. It was his favorite toy and temporarily distracted him. Anna quickly moved to where Sheba held Joshua. She touched him gently. The stuff was sticky. She raised her fingers to the small shaft of light. It was red. The sticky stuff was blood. She looked into Sheba's worried face.

"I need to wash it, Sheba. I'll have to wash the blood away." Her face grew very serious. "I won't drink any more water," she offered. "Not until we can get to the barrel."

"You have to drink some, baby. We will just have to be real careful. Wet a cloth and don't use any more water than you have to." Tears were streaming from Sheba's eyes and running down her cheeks. The situation was so desperate; she hardly even knew how to pray.

Anna grabbed a piece of cloth and wet it from the nearly empty water flask. Jeremiah was still playing with his horse. She moved quickly back to where Sheba held Joshua and started dabbing at the blood on the side of his head.

"I can do that, sweetheart; you find us something to eat." Sheba continued to swab the area being as gentle as she could, but Joshua did not seem to care. He stayed asleep, while she cleaned up his wound. When she finished, the entire cloth was red with his blood, but his head looked better.

"Doctor Joseph always says sleep allows the body to heal, we'll just let Josh sleep."

"Hu'gy 'nana," Jeremiah said, looking up at his sister with his large eyes. His golden hair was tousled and his face was streaked with dirt and tears.

"I'm hungry too, Jeremiah," she whispered. "You show your horse to Joshua while I find us something. Okay?"

Jeremiah picked his wooden horse back up and carried it to where Joshua lay so still. When he sat beside Sheba and Joshua and began playing, Anna started going through the food hamper. She was looking for something they could eat without cooking. All she found, in the still mostly dark wagon, was a couple small potatoes and some small hard biscuits nearly a week old. None of them had eaten much since they were abducted. They munched on the potatoes and biscuits ravenously. Anna was careful to put some back for Joshua. She slipped two biscuits in her pocket to give him when he woke up.

* * *

The wagon wheels rolled continuously and the distance from Arkansas lengthened. The men took turns sleeping, but stayed in the front of the wagon and left the children alone.

On the second day after the man hit him, Joshua woke up and asked for food. When both of the men were on the wagon seat, Anna looked more carefully for food. She retrieved some onions, a few green apples picked from trees near Dardanelle, and some very ripe peaches. They had picked them up from the ground in an orchard where they had spent the night in Johnson County. They also had bunches of purple grapes, a half loaf of very dry bread and more of the raw potatoes.

Not knowing how long they would have to live on these meager supplies. Anna hid what they did not eat for each meal. Her family had been at the end of their summer long trekking through back roads and trails. They were to have left for home already. Although papa had bought supplies in Fort Smith, they had expected to be home within the week. They were fortunate that they were in the provision wagon. They did have flour, cornmeal, sugar, and dry beans, but without a fire Anna did not think these things were edible.

Anna could hear one of the men occasionally ask for the red-eye or the scattergun. Then as like as not they would hear more cussing and every now and then a shotgun blast. This was seldom, but occasionally followed by, "Got em," or "he'll make an outrageous stew."

As they had traveled, papa had gone over books with pictures of maps to show them where they were in Arkansas. Sometimes the maps showed parts of Oklahoma Territory. Anna tried to remember what it looked like, but she could not visualize the land they were traversing in the wagon. Unfortunately all the books were in the other wagon. She thought they must have been getting near the Land Run starting point.

Mama and papa would expect her to help Sheba take care of the boys. She had been helping with their care since they were born. Anna was determined to take care of them and Sheba too, until papa and Uncle Daniel found them and took them home.

Joshua still slept a lot more than usual, but he claimed his head hurt less each time Anna asked. Sheba's poison ivy seemed to have spread in the terrible heat and Anna knew she was miserable, but she never complained.

The men had offered them neither water nor food, even though Anna was certain that sometimes they stopped long enough to cook something for themselves. They only had what Anna could find for them. Their water had dwindled to less than a half a cup and neither Anna nor Sheba was drinking any to save it for the boys.

They had talked about the possibility of finding an opportunity to empty the slop bucket and fill their water flasks from the water barrel fastened to the outside of the wagon, if they every stopped.

* * *

Finally the wagon wheels were stilled and the big man came back to where they were huddled. He leered menacingly at Sheba. The children huddled together. Jeremiah started crying. Joshua's hand moved involuntarily to the wound on his head. It was mending, but was still tender enough to remind him of what had happened the last time he had encountered this man.

"Not much longer to wait now," he sneered. "By tomorrow night we'll be on my quarter section and you and me can get better acquainted. Maybe the little dolly too." He smirked at Anna and laughed evilly, before he turned back toward the front of the wagon. He took a long drink from the leather flask tied to his belt, as he walked unsteadily through the wagon.

Sheba felt hate rise within her like she had never before experienced. She willed her legs to move, but they continued to lay on the cot, limp and useless. Sheba knew the man meant to ravage her, but she had to find some way to protect Anna and the boys.

"Anna," she turned to the child beside her. "You have to find a way to get yourself and the boys away from here. These men are pure evil and they mean to hurt us." Sheba was desperate. She knew she was asking too much of a child, but Anna was the only hope for any of them to survive.

"But Sheba," Anna began to cry.

"No buts," Sheba said sternly. "When the time comes you will have to take the boys and leave."

Joshua was still unsteady when he tried to stand and he complained of his head still hurting. They could hear the men talking outside the wagon. There were many people close by, but there was no way to know who would help them. Anna peeped through the hole, but did not feel she dared take the chance of calling to anyone.

Sheba had a plan, but knew it was weak. She would have to have an alternate in case the first one did not work. The further they got from Arkansas, the harder it would be for Anna to find her way back home.

"Anna, listen to me carefully." She was speaking so low that Anna had to practically put her ear to Sheba's mouth. "If the man comes back and acts as if he will stay with me, you will have to act quickly. Get the boys to the front of the wagon, climb down and get as far away as possible. Take the horse if you can. You will have to have water and food with you; when you have gone as far as you possibly can, ask someone for help. Do you understand?"

She was still crying, but nodded her head yes.

"You must not stop or seek help from anyone close by; because we don't know who might be with them and the men would probably lie and say you were their children. You have to keep going, until you cannot go any further. Hide and rest when you have to, but keep going as long as you are able to move. Remember," she added. "Your papa is looking for you and he will find you."

Anna brightened at that thought. She had forgotten that papa and Uncle Daniel would be looking for them and she knew that her papa would never give up until he found them.

Sheba willed Anna to be strong. The lives of all three children depended on this slight girl. *If only I could walk. Lord this isn't fair,* she cried. *You look after these babies; they are depending on you. Send your angels, Lord. Just surround these precious children with your angels and guide Joseph to where they are.*

"Sheba, you can come too. I can lower the chair and push you. You can hold Jeremiah in your lap and Joshua and I can both push."

"I can't baby. You could never push the chair over this rough ground with the two of us in it. I will have to make a diversion so you can get away with the boys. I'm sorry I won't be able to help you." Tears filled her eyes in spite of her effort to put up a strong front. "I will be praying for you. I promise I will pray."

Anna was very frightened at the prospect of leaving the sanctuary of the wagon. She knew that Sheba would not ask her to do it, unless it was absolutely necessary, but she was awfully scared. While the men were outside, she rummaged through the wagon for provisions.

They would not be able to carry anything very heavy and there was no way to know if they would be able to leave on one of the horses or mules. Chances were that they would have to carry anything they took. Even Jeremiah would be able to help with some of the supplies. Maybe she could strap it to his back someway.

She found an empty feed sack and a few canned goods in a box under the bunk. They had come five days east of Fort Smith in the wagon. She knew they were still headed east, because of the beautiful orange and pink sunset, with purple and magenta streaks straight ahead.

Even if they could hide from the men in the great crowd outside, she had no idea how long it would take them to walk out, carrying provisions and probably Jeremiah most of the time.

Sheba instructed the boys to find all of Joseph and Daniel's socks. Fortunately for them, Rose had left the laundry in their wagon while she had gone on her picnic. Anna put cornmeal, flour, dried fruit, beans and other grains in the socks. There were six empty water flasks. She would have to fill up the flasks, or they would not have a chance, to make it out on foot. Anna had no idea how far they were from a stream. Papa and Mama told them all the time to drink lots of water when it was hot outside. Even with the meager provisions she was able to find, she thought it would probably be impossible for the three of them to manage.

"Hide everything up in the front under something that you don't think the men will bother," Sheba whispered. "Be careful, you mustn't get caught." She took a hold of Anna's arm and stressed the importance of her words.

"I hope you will be able to take the horse or one of the mules, or even the chair would give you something to put provisions in." She let go of Anna's arm and lay back on the pallet exhausted. She quivered with fear when she considered sending the children out alone. She strained to hear what the men were saying, but they were talking softly and the noise around them kept her from making out all but a few words.

Anna resolutely hid her stores under some toys and extra tack near the front of the wagon. If the opportunity presented itself, she would take the boys and leave. She did not want to, but she had promised and would not let Sheba down.

The voices of the men grew louder in argument. "Why do I have ta go?" one man shouted angrily. It sounded like the one who had been terrorizing them.

"'Cause I can't trust you," the other man shouted just as loudly.

Their voices drifted further from the wagon and Anna could no longer make out their words. It sounded like one of them was going away, Anna thought to herself. One of the men had never ventured into the wagon where the children huddled in the back. She hoped it was the one who had hit Jeremiah that was leaving. The wagon rocked slightly and they knew one of the men was climbing up on the high seat at the front. They heard him enter the wagon and cringed as they listened silently to his loud breathing. He made his way carefully to the back of the dark wagon. The children huddled together.

The man stood over them, apparently satisfying himself they were all there and not going to cause him any trouble. He dropped some things beside Anna and then returned to the front of the wagon and lay across the opening. Anna tried to see what the man had dropped beside them, but it was too dark. She felt for the objects with her hands.

There were two things. One was a flask. She carefully opened the top. There was no smell. She dipped her finger cautiously into the liquid and tasted it. It was water.

She eagerly turned to the other bundle. It was something tied up in a cloth. She carefully unwrapped it. She still could not see what it contained, but it felt like food. She broke off a piece and tasted a bite. It was meat. She did not know what kind, but it was cooked meat. The children had not had any meat since the night before the wagon was taken. She eagerly handed it to Sheba to divide while she gave each of them a long drink from the water flask. There were also some solid biscuits in the cloth. They ate ravenously.

"The man is lying across the exit. There is no way you will be able to get out. Go to sleep, I will wake you if I think you can get away."

With their bellies full for the first time in nearly a week, the children settled down to sleep. Anna held Jeremiah in her wiry arms, rocking him back and forth and singing to him gently. He was soon asleep, his thumb stuck comfortably in his mouth. Joshua lay in his mother's lap and fell asleep listening to Anna's songs.

Chapter Forty-Three

In and around Fort Smith, the four frantic adults hunted desperately for the wagon containing Sheba and the three children. It, along with its precious contents, seemed to have utterly vanished. No one they encountered near the river or in town recalled having seen the wagon, the missing children, or the disabled woman, who would have stood out even in the crush of people.

The family continued to search, but Hannah had become so disheartened that her milk was drying up and baby Carolyn began crying and fretting most of the time. Joseph could not ascertain if the cause was inadequate nourishment or the depression that seemed to affect all of them. He sought someone with a milk cow in order to assure that there was an adequate supply of milk for his small daughter. He did not think any of them could bear to have anything happen to their remaining child.

The hotels had plenty of rooms to rent now, so he had procured rooms for all of them. When Hannah was not out hunting for the children, she sat in a chair before a window that looked out on the dirt street in front of the hotel.

Dejectedly she stared at the people who passed outside, only becoming animated when the baby cried or she spotted a child walking past that she thought might be one of their precious missing children.

A week after the disappearance Fort Smith was beginning to return to normal, but unfortunately the combined efforts of the law and the despondent family had been unable to unearth a single clue regarding their whereabouts. Joseph purchased another horse and he and Daniel rode out each day in search of their family. He was forced to accept the conclusion they had been taken into Oklahoma Territory. Hannah was inconsolable, as she considered the entire situation her fault. She just knew that everything would have been all right if she had only checked on them more frequently. The fact that they were in the wagon right next to hers and with Sheba and she had thought Rose would be back to check on her charges, did not ease her mind in the least.

When Bernice was in the room to watch the baby, she would walk the streets for hours, asking everyone she encountered if they had seen anything of her missing family. At night, Joseph and Daniel spent many hours pouring over maps of Oklahoma Territory. He sent telegraph messages to every law enforcement officer within a couple hundred miles, hoping someone would spot and detain the abductors or find his family.

An especially low point for all of them was when Rose's body was discovered downstream by a fisherman. They had a brief memorial service for her in Fort Smith, before sending her body downstream on a barge headed for Little Rock. They grieved over the young woman who had become like a family member and sorrowed over not being able to be with her relatives when she was laid to rest, but they had to continue their search.

A few days after this sad occasion, reinforcements began arriving. Ben arrived from Chicago and Donald from Birmingham, where he had returned after seeing the family across the river. The four men poured over the maps of western Arkansas, Indian Territory and Oklahoma Territory together. They realized their missing loved ones could be anywhere by this time, but decided to concentrate their search in the area recently opened up in the land run. It was the most likely place to find them.

The majority of the men involved in the Run were young farmers with families. No one Joseph discussed the bizarre affair with could shed any light on why murderers and thieves would be involved in the Run, unless they thought it was a good place for a hideout for nefarious activities. The Indian Territory had been the stomping ground of criminals for many years, especially the mountains in the southeast. Why any outlaws would want to hamper themselves with a covered wagon, mules, children and a disabled woman, was a mystery to everyone, unless they did not know they were in the wagon when it was taken.

"They must have needed to travel inconspicuously across Indian Territory for some reason." Joseph looked at Ben, as he speculated the abductors reasoning in hampering their flight with a wagon full of children and Sheba. The men were in Ben's room, so they could talk openly without the women overhearing them. Joseph's face was haggard and his hair was graying, as the events of the past couple weeks were taking a heavy toll.

"If he wanted to establish a safe place for a hide out in the middle of Indian Territory, he might have joined the Run. It would give the appearance of being homesteaders and he could even pass Sheba and the children off as his family." Ben hit the table hard with his fist.

"He better not harm them." Tears formed in his eyes, but his expression showed the terrible anger and guilt that was consuming him. "He had better hope the Indians find him before I do, if he harms a single hair on any of their heads." Ben spoke with the fierceness of his anger.

"Sure and it's a possibility, Joseph." Donald, who had been quietly studying the map, joined the conversation. "I think we must search every inch of the area opened up by the Run."

"Two counties have been established. There is a town opening up in each one, the marshal told me." Joseph pointed out the locations to them on the map; "Chandler, here in the north in County A and Tecumseh, in the south in County B. We can use the towns as our base, with two of us going to each of the counties."

"Sounds good," Ben was pacing up and down the room. "When do we leave?"

"Joseph, we prob'ly need to keep someone in Fort Smith and 'tis equally as important to have someone at the house in Little Rock. If there is a way under God's blue heaven for my wee bairn to get loose, those might be the only two places she would head for."

"But Donald, how can we do that? I hesitate to separate the women, with all that has happened, especially in Hannah's present state. I guess I could hire another nursemaid, but that would take time that we really do not have." He seemed to be talking to himself as he pondered how to solve the problem. "You are right of course. There probably is not anything else that makes sense."

"Donald is right, Joseph. We have to make sure everything is covered. We cannot take a chance of missing them anywhere." Ben continued his pacing as he spoke forcefully.

Daniel looked apprehensive about leaving Hannah alone with just the baby, as distressed as she was over the abduction. He knew she blamed herself, even if she had done everything possible to watch out for the children.

"Joseph, I sent a telegraph to Peg. He is not strong enough to go with us, but I have asked him to bring horses up from Little Rock and he would be here to stay with which ever of the women remains in Fort Smith, or could escort the other one back home. He could then stay at the house with her instead of returning to the Old Soldiers Home." Daniel looked at his brother-in-law, not sure how his suggestion would be received. "He should be here any day.

"I told him to be sure and make inquires along the river about the children and Sheba. One of the women will still be alone, though."

"No they won't," Ben interjected. "Father will be here any day. He can stay in Fort Smith with whichever woman stays here and with Peg escorting the other one back home that should take care of your concerns, Joseph."

"Hamilton is coming?" Joseph was astonished that his father-in-law, who was well into his sixties, was making the long trip from Savannah.

"The very one! I received a wire a couple days ago that he was in Memphis."

"But is he well enough to travel? Last I heard he was not feeling well." Joseph's concern for his father-in-law was genuine, as he had always admired him.

"Yes, but that was before his grandchildren were abducted. As soon as he got the telegraph he was on his way. He isn't in any condition to travel around the Territory on horseback, but should do fine staying here. He insisted on coming, I was afraid he would just be in the way, but as it turns out he will have an important job to do. He can even continue to scour this area during the day. He is still a forceful orator and if there is any information to be had in this town, he will ferret it out."

"Joseph, sure and it seems as if all the angles are kevered. Yea must prepare the women for what's ahead, while we obtain provisions for the trip. It will be hard for them being left behind, especially for the one who is bid to return home."

Joseph returned to the room he shared with Hannah and Carolyn after first stopping at Bernice's room and asking her to join them. He pulled Hannah into a chair and while holding both of her hands, gently explained what the men had decided. She was visibly upset at being relegated to what she considered a non-participating role in the hunt for the children.

"Hannah, you don't have to be the one to return home. You can stay in Fort Smith with Hamilton and Bernice can go back to the house." He glanced to where Bernice sat across from them. "I just thought it would be easier for you to care for Carolyn at home."

"But my children are here somewhere. I would be going even further away from them. I won't really be contributing anything. You just want me out of the way." The accusation in her voice stung Joseph.

"Never!" He gathered her in his arms and rocked her back and forth as if she was one of the children. "It grieves me for you to have to go, but what if Anna makes her way back home and no one is there to greet her. What would she do then?"

Hannah sat there with tears streaming down her cheeks. "You are right of course, Joseph. It was selfish of me to decline my part. I am just so frustrated with our efforts to find them not being fruitful and I am so afraid for all of them. We don't know what they are going through." She looked up at him through tear stained eyes. "I have prayed constantly for their return. It is like God isn't listening."

"He is listening, all right. And we are going to get them back," he said forcefully. "With God's help, Sheba and Anna will take care of the boys. You know how resourceful Anna is, she probably has her captors tied in knots by now." He smiled through his own tears, as he dried his wife's cheeks.

"Is it agreed then, as soon as Peg gets here, you will return and Bernice will stay in Fort Smith with Hamilton?" He looked at both women for a sign of assent.

"Yes, Joseph. Don't you worry about anything here. You just go find our family." Bernice stated with confidence.

Peg arrived the next day with six horses, so each of the men would have two mounts. After being assured that he would be helping them greatly in their effort to locate the children, he readily agreed to escort Hannah and baby Carolyn back to Little Rock and stay with her instead of returning to the home. He would have naturally preferred accompanying the men into Oklahoma Territory, but knew he was not up to the arduous travel. Joseph explained how important the responsibility he had been given was and that seemed to placate him.

Had Peg not been failing in his health and advancing in age, the hunt would probably have proved too much for the seaman anyway. He was accustomed to the rolling deck of a boat, not the broad back of a horse. On the trip from Little Rock, one of the large saddle horses had bit him and another had tried to kick him. They had certainly not endeared themselves to the old seaman. He had not been able to learn anything from the boatmen he had encountered that would aid in their search. Some had heard about the search for some children, but there was not as much as a rumor about their whereabouts.

Peg actually welcomed the opportunity to get back into town. The Old Soldiers home was too far out for him to get down to the docks and visit with his cronies. Staying at the house would afford him that opportunity and he could continue to quiz everyone he met if they had seen any sign of a disabled woman of color and three wee children.

Joseph planned to send the wagon back with them also. Bernice and Hamilton would stay at the hotel and it would just slow the men down. They planned to travel fast and light.

Bernice made arrangements to work with a local physician in his clinic, on a temporary basis. She spent hours each day after work, walking the streets of Fort Smith with Hamilton Earl. They asked questions and searched the face of each child they saw for a glimpse of the missing children. They asked people in stores and strangers they encountered on the street if they had seen anything of them, but no one had.

A tearful Hannah boarded the train on October 1, 1891. She carried six-month-old Carolyn and was assisted by their friend Peg. The old seaman seemed to have more spring in his step, given his new purpose and responsibilities.

Joseph was hopeful they would take care of each other and find something to keep busy, so the time would pass more quickly. He knew that his lot was easier than Hannah's. He had a mission, a definite plan of action to keep him occupied, but she had to sit and wait, the hardest job of all. He knew that if it were him forced to wait at home for word of the fate of the children, he would not hold up as well as she was. He could easily empathize with what she was going through.

The next day as they prepared to leave from the stable, John T. B. Wolf-hunter approached Joseph and asked to be allowed to join them. Daniel had come across the lad while searching one day and asked him to keep a look out for Sheba and the children. When he realized it was the small girl he called Little Blossom that was missing, he had hunted for the children every day.

The twelve-year-old, who was familiar with the territory they were about to enter, had become intrigued with the bright little girl with the large green eyes and friendly smile and he wanted to help find her.

"I have hunted in the area many times and know many of the places where water can be found and someone might try to hide themselves."

Joseph quickly obtained permission from John's mother for him to accompany them. Joseph had not sent the children's ponies back and it was decided they would serve well as his mounts. He could ride Anna's Patch and have Brownie as his back-up mount.

They decided the three most probable routes for the thieves to have gone were: up the Arkansas River, the Canadian River, or due west from Fort Smith across the rolling plains.

Chapter Forty-Four

Oklahoma Territory
September 22, 1901

Dawn broke with noise and confusion. The soft gray light of first dawn penetrated the wagon and pushed the darkness gently aside. Anna sat and rubbed her eyes, as she sleepily glanced around. At first, she wandered where she was. Then she remembered and looked toward the front of the wagon. The man no longer lay across the opening, but she could see him perched on the high seat leaning forward.

Suddenly, she heard shots being fired. The boys awoke with a start, jumped up and looked around, their wide-eyed expressions showing their fear. Sheba screamed and grabbed at the boys, but could not reach them.

Anna quickly pushed them back down and lay across them. Without warning, the wagon jolted and sprang forward. The children clung to one another in a terrified embrace and Sheba scooted close to them and flung her arms around all three. Jeremiah began to cry, but this time both Sheba and Anna were too frightened to respond to his plaintive wail.

They heard men shouting and urging horses and mules forward. The grating squeak of wagon wheels turning rapidly and horses and mules racing across the rolling prairie echoed around them. They raced on for what seemed an eternity to Sheba and the children, bouncing and jolting in the back of the wagon. They clung to each other, to keep from being tossed about and injured seriously.

Finally the wagon stopped. They could hear men shouting angrily. Anna scrambled up on Sheba's chair to look through the hole in the back. She saw great clouds of dust. The sky appeared almost blackened by the dust rising skyward. Wagons emerged from the curtain of dust and seemed to be scattered all along a gully in the distance.

The thick dust permeated the wagon and all four of them began to cough. "I have to go to the front of the wagon. I can't see anything for the dust." Anna quickly climbed down from her perch. "Hold Jeremiah," she said as she picked her brother up and thrust the toddler into Joshua's small arms. "Don't let him follow me." The command was sharper than she intended, but in their situation it was important that Joshua do as he was told, regardless if it was Anna or Sheba doing the telling. She was determined to protect the boys, whatever the cost.

Joshua was holding his throbbing head in both of his hands, but he reached out and pulled Jeremiah into his lap and held him tightly with one hand. When Jeremiah began to wail, he firmly clamped his other hand over the little one's mouth and handed him to Sheba to console.

Anna made her way to the front and climbed up where she had a better view. She remained there balanced on her tiptoes, concealed behind the great gathered canvas that surrounded the front opening. She was balanced precariously when she felt something touch her leg. She grabbed the canvas and steadied herself.

"Joshua Benjamin Earl, you scared me half to death," she hissed, holding her hand over her fluttering heart and trembling like a leaf.

"I just wanted to see."

Anna glared at him and climbed down on unsteady legs and made her way stealthily back to where Sheba still held tightly to Jeremiah. Joshua sheepishly followed in her wake.

"There's a small stream in front of us. They've taken the mules to water. It looks nearly dry. There's only a little water running in it," she quickly reported. "Both men are out there, plus another one. The big one was arguing with the newcomer. The man said he got here first, but the big man said he did and pointed at his stakes, already in the ground. The other man called the big man a dirty thieving sooner. The big man knocked him down and told him to get off his land. Said he'd put him in a pine box, if he ever saw him again."

The boys were wide eyed and spellbound by Anna's narrative. "Then what happened," Joshua asked excitedly.

"The man left," Anna responded matter-of -factly. She sat down and unwrapped the remains of last night's meal. She gave Sheba, each of the boys and herself equal shares, before starting to munch on the meat and bread.

"What's a Sooner," asked Joshua, beginning to eat the meager breakfast.

"I heard papa tell Uncle Daniel that some people try to sneak in early when there is a Land Run. They call them Sooners," Anna explained. "I guess its bad manners or against the law or something to start early, kind of like breaking in line at the store."

The voices grew loud again and Anna climbed up to look out the back. "They've got guns strapped to their sides," she whispered to Joshua, who asked permission this time before he climbed up behind her on Sheba's chair. He was as careful as a three-year-old boy could to be quite.

"One of them is on one of our horses and the other is riding one of our mules," Anna whispered. "It looks like they're leaving. They're going in different directions." She kept watching, but did not see anyone around the wagon.

"Sheba, I am going up front and see if I can see anything," she whispered. "Joshua you stay here with your mama and help her with Jeremiah." Not waiting for a reply, she ran to the front and cautiously climbed out and up on the high seat.

The cloud of dust still hung heavy in the sky. It was so thick that it obscured the sun, giving the appearance of twilight instead of mid-afternoon.

She had no way of knowing how long the men would be gone. Anna knew the three of them on foot would be no match for two men on horseback. *Maybe I can at least empty the bucket and fill our water flasks from that little stream.* She looked around carefully again, before looking back into the wagon. She could barely see the anxious faces that stared back at her.

"Joshua," she called in a loud enough voice to carry back to them, but hopefully not loud enough to hear far from the wagon. "Quick! Bring me all the water flasks." She started climbing down, as soon as she saw Joshua grabbing up the flasks and start her way. She ran around to the back and peered up under the wagon. The bucket was suspended underneath and she would have to slide it out and then lift it down. It would be tricky, because it was very full.

She crawled under and tried sliding it, but quickly found it was too heavy for her. She motioned for Joshua to join her and between them they got the heavy bucket loose, their muscles straining as they tried to control it. They were as careful as they could be not to splash the contents on themselves, but in spite of their solicitousness some of the contents splashed out on Anna's dress. In spite of her soiled dress, she held steady and did not drop it as they eased it out from under the wagon.

The two children struggled with the heavy bucket and its smelly contents until they got it to where Anna decided it was a safe enough distance from the wagon. They found a small crevice and dumped the contents into it and then covered it up as best they could. She knew they should dig a hole and bury it, but that task was beyond them at the moment.

Joshua ran back and got the flasks from where he had thrown them over the side of the wagon. Scooping them up in his arms, he ran right to the little stream. The two children had to wade around to find a deep enough pool to fill them. When they were done, Anna carried the bucket down stream and rinsed it out, before returning it to the grooves under the wagon. The children quickly decided they would go to the bathroom in the trees and only use the bucket for emergences. Of course Sheba would have to use the bucket, but with only one using it the bucket would not fill up so quickly. Joshua began making trips to the wagon with the water flasks, while Anna took care of the bucket.

"Anna, Anna," Sheba called frantically from the wagon. "The baby got away from me."

"Down! Down!"

Anna looked up to see Jeremiah perched up on the high seat, holding out his arms for her to lift him down. He was used to jumping off the porch into their papa's arms, so she knew he would not stay on his precarious perch long.

"Jeremiah Hollis Warren," she said sternly, climbing as fast as she could. "You know you are not allowed to climb on the wagon seat. She picked him up and kissed the top of his curly blond head. Tears of relief stung her eyes, as she hugged him to her and quickly moved to the back of the wagon. Anna placed her baby brother into Sheba's waiting arms. "Now you stay with Sheba while Josh and I get the water. Don't you move! I promise I will come back and get you as soon as I can." Anna hurried back to the front and climbed down.

The two children laboriously hauled all six of the water flasks up into the wagon and took them back to where Sheba held tightly to Jeremiah. She was afraid to let him loose while the children lugged the water up, for fear he would fall out of the wagon. It took them all of thirty minutes to finish the task. Joshua lay down on the floor, seemingly exhausted from the task.

"Anna, I can't do another thing," he whined, sure she would find another task for them.

"I am sorry to hear that. I thought maybe we could take us a little dip in the water before the men return, but if you're too tired…"

Joshua jumped up as if he had all the energy in the world. "Let's go." He quickly headed for the front of the wagon.

"Wait! We need to take Jeremiah with us. I think we can get him down if we tie a rope around his waist and lower him."

"Anna, what if the men come back? Maybe you should just leave Jeremiah here with me. You may not be able to get him back up."

"We can, can't we Josh?" She turned to her cousin for confirmation.

"Sure we can. We took care of the bucket and got the water didn't we?" The pride in what they had accomplished was clear in his voice.

"That you did. Be very careful though. If you hear them returning, get back up here quickly. Maybe you should just try to get away." Concern marked her face, which like her body had become drawn and dehydrated from lack of nourishment and water. She had been giving most of her ration to the children, trying to protect their young bodies and keep them as healthy as possible.

"I don't think it is time Sheba. They probably won't be gone long and they are both mounted and have guns." The children moved to the entrance and Joshua climbed down. Anna carefully lowered Jeremiah with a rope tied to the inside of the wagon, so they could use it to haul him back up. Joshua caught him and lowered him to the ground.

The water was shallow enough in a pool beside the shore that they let Jeremiah play and splash, while they played in water up to their waists. They washed themselves and their clothes and for the first time began to cool off. They started splashing one another and enjoyed their refreshing play in the water, temporarily forgetting their peril.

Suddenly Anna threw her finger to her lips and said, "Shh, I hear something." They heard the drumming of hoof beats. Anna grabbed Jeremiah and hollered at Joshua to get to the wagon.

They ran as fast as they could. Anna tied the rope around Jeremiah and scrambled back into the wagon. She pulled Jeremiah up while Joshua pushed from below, as soon as she had Jeremiah in; she helped Joshua scurry into the wagon. They untied Jeremiah and all three scampered to the back beside Sheba, just as the horse and rider reached the campsite. The children hovered in the very back of the wagon, hiding their water behind them.

After a while, they heard the second rider return. Neither of the men came into the wagon where the four inhabitants remained fearfully quiet. The men were arguing again and before long the children could smell food cooking over a campfire. None of the food was brought to them and Sheba was afraid to have Anna approach the men.

At sundown, one of the men climbed up into the wagon. It was the smaller of the two, the one who had earlier brought them food and water. He again moved to the back of the wagon and deposited a container and a flask.

"I was watching you today," he said looking straight at Anna and then at Joshua. "Remember, I will always be close enough to see you, so don't try anything, just because you think we are gone."

The children trembled, as they thought of all the vile things that might have happened to them if they had tried to get away when they thought they were unobserved. When the man returned to the front and lay down, Anna checked the contents of the container the man had left. It was cold stew. It tasted wonderful to the hungry group in the wagon, even with the congealed fat floating on top.

The next morning, the two men again rode out in different directions. The children ate the rest of the cold stew and drank from the water flask. Again they helped Jeremiah over the side and played in the water. After cautioning Joshua to watch Jeremiah closely, Anna returned to the wagon. She climbed up on the outside of the wagon, at the back and tried to find a way to loosen the rope, which held the back flaps secure. It would not budge.

"I can't get it loose, Sheba," she cried in desperation.

"Get a knife or the scissors from Bernice's sewing basket," came the muffled response from inside. "Just be real careful."

Anna rushed around to the front, climbed up to the seat and slipped inside. She quickly located a sharp knife in the kitchen supplies.

"Be careful Anna." Sheba's voice was frantic. She felt so helpless, just having to lie there while the child, who had been her responsibility since birth, took all the chances. "Toss the knife down; don't try to carry it while you climb."

Anna threw the knife to the ground and scrambled over the side. She picked up the knife and walked to the back of the wagon. She slipped the knife up on the platform built on the back for Sheba's chair and then climbed up on the wheel and eased herself onto the platform.

"Cut away from you, Anna. Remember your safety tips." Sheba's muffled voice cautioned from inside the wagon.

Anna carefully laid the blade against the rope, which held the canvas fast and started sawing on the heavy hemp. Back and forth, back and forth, she sawed on the rope, until finally it gave and the heavy canvas flapped open in the gusting wind. It nearly knocked her from her precarious perch, as the canvas flew outward and a breeze swept through the wagon.

It was the first time in a couple weeks that Sheba had any relief from the stifling heat. She took a deep breath of the beautiful fresh air.

Chapter Forty-Five

Sheba knew there was no way the children could lift her and the chair down to the ground. The pulley system Joseph had installed worked very well, but it took a strong man to work it and usually Daniel and Joseph coordinated it together—one on the inside and one on the outside working the pulley.

If I can let myself down on the rope, maybe Anna and I can lower the chair. I have to get outside so I can cook for the children. How will I ever get back into the wagon, once I get out, or even pull myself up into the chair? That creek will just have to be forded when we get to it. I am sure you will come up with something, Lord. I am putting this problem in your hands. It is certainly beyond mine, she prayed softly to herself.

Sheba pushed and tugged the chair until she was able to get it out on the platform. She lowered her useless legs over the side and held on with her arms. She was weak from the two weeks she had been shut up in the oven-like wagon with very little water to drink or food to eat. The poison ivy that seemed to cover her entire body certainly had not helped her situation. *I need a little help here, Lord.* She looked upward at the cloudless sky, as if seeking a response to her pleas.

Here we go. She maneuvered her legs to the edge of the platform and then lifted them over the side with her arms. Just this much was a long tedious task and she lay back completely spent gasping for breath. She could hear Anna's encouragement from below, but it was some minutes before she was able to respond in any way. She lay on the platform with her legs dangling out in space and her lungs heaving as if she had climbed a mountain. *I guess in someway I have,* she considered when she was able to put a coherent thought together.

When she was able to proceed, she flopped over on her stomach and edged herself off the platform, an inch at a time. As she got close to the edge, Sheba gripped the platform with her hands and worked her body completely off the edge, with her useless legs dangling like a rag doll caught in the wind. Her fingers were slipping and she calculated she was about as close to the ground as she was going to be able to manage and turned loose. As she fell, she attempted to twist so that her hands and arms would take most of the blow. The ground seemed to rise up and slam against her back and pain shot through her body, causing her to cry out in agony.

One of the men rode up on the horse and began yelling at them. "What you think you're doing? You can't run anywhere out here. I told you I'd be watching you." His voice was gruff, but for some reason he sounded more frightened than mad.

Sheba struggled against the pain. "I am trying to cook for the children." Her breath was coming in gasps as the piercing pain shot threw her. She struggled to regain the breath that had been knocked out of her when she landed on the hard ground. Her voice came across much calmer than she felt.

"They have not had a descent meal in a week. If you will lower my chair and sit me in it, I will fix a meal for all of us." Just maybe if she cooked for the men also, they would let her fix meals for the children.

Sheba spoke slowly and cautiously, hoping the man could not see how she was trembling. It would not do for him to guess how very terrified she actually was.

The man advanced toward her. He looked up and saw how the pulley apparatus worked and lowered the chair, after assuring himself she actually could not walk. In her condition it would be impossible for her to run away and he did not think the children would attempt to go anywhere without her. He knew they would never make it out of this dry land on foot, not alive anyway. After watching Sheba for a couple minutes as she struggled across the ground, pulling herself with her arms and making slow progress toward the chair, he suddenly moved to where she lay, picked her up and carelessly shoved her into her special wheeled chair.

"Thank you." She said it through clenched teeth, but got it out. It would not do to antagonize him. "Thank you, Jesus," she murmured softly, recognizing this as another answer to one of her prayers.

"Anna, get the boys. I will need you'll to help me." She smiled at Anna weakly though her pain. "Go on! Hurry now."

Anna raced to the creek to fetch the boys. They were having a wonderful time playing in a shallow pool. Jeremiah did not want to leave the water and put on his clothes and he resisted Joshua's attempts to drag him from the water. He lay face down and began to kick, coming up spitting, having swallowed water while throwing his little fit. Anna had to wade in and pick up her screaming brother and carry him to the bank. The children each took one of the toddler's hands and half dragged him to where Sheba sat watching.

"Joshua, you and Jeremiah will need to gather wood for a fire," Sheba said in a no-nonsense tone. "Anna, fetch me some flour, meal, salt, soda and the lard bucket. I will need the big black skillet and the bread-oven. You and I are going to make some cornmeal. Slice off a little of that ham and I'll fry it up too. We will have a feast tonight."

Sheba knew the survival of the children might depend on what they learned to do for themselves; she was afraid what little strength she had left would not last much longer. Tears filled her eyes as she considered their desperate situation. If it were not for her strong faith in the Lord, she would probably just give up. She watched the man ride off; apparently satisfied their captives would not try to escape.

Anna got the boys started gathering wood, before going to the wagon to fetch the sack full of ingredients. She picked up a long stick that had fallen from a near-by tree and took everything to Sheba. When the boys returned with the kindling, Sheba instructed Anna how to build the fire, so there would be hot coals to cook over.

While the boys went after more wood, Anna stirred the coals of the campfire the men had used and placed some of the dried kindling near the hot coals, with larger pieces of wood on top. There was a small grove of cottonwood trees along the stream and soon the boys had a sizable pile of wood beside Sheba's chair. The coals were finally ready. Anna brought the large, iron, bread-oven from the wagon and Sheba leaned over and placed it over the white-hot coals.

"Anna move me back from the fire a little." Sheba was getting pretty hot and sure did not want to catch her dress on fire. *The Lord does expect me to use the brain he has given me,* she admonished herself. Joshua and Anna pulled the chair back a couple feet from the fire.

"Now you children watch. We are going to make up some cornbread and then we will fry the ham." She took the wooden bowl Anna handed her. "You must get the oven and lid hot before you put the bread inside to cook. We will mix the dough in the bowl and when it is about ready we will put some lard in the bread-oven to melt. Then when we pour the cornmeal mixture in the oven, we will stir in the melted lard." She watched carefully to try and discern if Anna understood the instructions.

"First scoop up four handfuls of meal; that's good, now pick up two handfuls of flour and add it to the cornmeal. Okay, you are doing real well. This time only use your fingertips. Pickup just a little salt first and after you put that in, add a little soda the same way. Excellent! Now brush your hands off real good and cup your hands. That's right. Joshua," she instructed. "Pour water into Anna's hands until they are full." She watched him, barely breathing as her son tilted the flask up and poured Anna's hands full of water. "Now, Anna put that in the bowl and Joshua, pour another handful of water. We have to use water, because we don't have any buttermilk," she explained, when the children cut their eyes at her as if she was daft.

"You are doing wonderful. Now you have to stir it real good."

When it was stirred to her satisfaction, she took Anna's hand. "This is the hard part. You have to remove the lid with a towel and set it aside, while you add the lard and stir it around, real carefully, so you don't burn yourself.

Do you think you can do that?" She looked at the child trying to access her understanding of the task.

"Yes ma'am. I have watched mama and Bernice do it, lots of times." She saw the worried frown on Sheba's face. "Don't worry. I will be very careful."

Anna removed the lid cautiously and set it on a rock, while Sheba held onto Anna's skirt, so she would not accidentally fall into the fire. Anna put a scoop of lard in the pot and moved it around with a big wooden spoon. Next Sheba instructed her to sprinkle some meal in the pot and then pour the batter they had prepared into the oven and stir it into the lard.

When all that was completed, Sheba told her to use the towel and place the lid back on the oven. Then she told her to take a flat board and scoop ashes up and place them on top of the lid.

"Be careful you don't burn yourself," she cautioned.

"You did so well," she praised Anna when the cornbread was baking. "Now when that is done, we will place the skillet on the coals and fry the ham."

Anna's face was streaked with perspiration and she had a small burn on one finger, but otherwise she was unharmed. She grinned proudly at Sheba's praise.

"Joshua, run fetch me a piece off the burn plant that's hanging in the wagon."

When Joshua returned with the green spike, Sheba placed Anna's hands in hers to put the juice on the burn. She was horrified when she saw the open blisters on the palms of the child's small hands.

"Gracious, child, we may have to use the entire plant on these hands." Carefully she squeezed the liquid on the blisters as well as the small burn.

"Anna while the bread is cooking, you and the boys run and play in the stream. I'll put more medicine on your hands after you play. You have all worked very hard." She blinked back her tears, as she praised their efforts. The children were being so brave and doing so much.

"Leave your clothes on, they will dry quickly enough in this hot wind and they will get a good wash."

"I could wash all of our clothes," Anna offered.

"Not today, sweetheart. We will have more cooking to do later. You can wash the clothes tomorrow, or the next day." Anna was so eager to help and had not made a peep of complaint. *Lord, I don't know what I would do without this child. I would wish her anywhere but here, but since she is here, I thank you for her. I know you will help her get the boys away when the time is right.*

She watched from her chair, as the children played in the water as carefree as if they were home in their back yard.

When she felt the cornbread had cooked long enough, she called for Anna to come take it off the fire. Anna hurried to her, clothes clinging to her slim body. *She looks so thin,* Sheba thought sadly. She had to fight against the tears brimming in her eyes trying to spill out.

"What's wrong Sheba? Are you hurting?" Her face was scrunched up in concern.

"No, baby, the smoke got in my eyes is all. Rake the ashes off the lid and then use the towel to remove the lid," she instructed, holding Anna's skirt back from the fire.

Anna did as she was instructed and soon had the heavy pot sitting on the ground beside Sheba's chair. Sheba looked at the golden brown cornbread and pronounced it the best she had ever seen. A tantalizing aroma wafted up from the oven.

"Now put the skillet on and put those slices of ham in the pan."

When the ham was done, Anna removed it from the fire. She passed the flask of water around for the boys to get a drink and then they enjoyed a feast of fried ham and golden cornbread. It was darker brown and crispy on the outside, but golden, rich and crumbly inside. They decided it was the best meal they had ever eaten. It was their first hot meal in over a week.

Anna looked at Sheba and the boys eating the food she had prepared. She figured that mama and papa would be proud of her.

"Anna set some of the bread and ham aside for the men. We have to keep them happy so they will let us continue to cook. Hide the rest for our breakfast."

Anna carefully placed the remaining bread and ham in two cloths. She sent Joshua to the wagon with one bundle and left the other near the fire.

"Now take the pans to the stream. Use sand to scrub them clean. Tomorrow we will put on a pot of soup. It needs to cook longer, so we will put it on the first thing after breakfast. Maybe the men will have some meat when they come back and we can put some in the soup with the vegetables from the wagon."

She would give most any thing if she could wash the pots instead of Anna's poor blistered hands, but she did thank the Lord that He had let her live long enough to be here with the children and at least instruct them what to do. She shuddered to think what would have happened to them if they had been by themselves in the wagon when the men abducted them.

Joshua helped Anna carry the pots to the water and they made a game of seeing which one could clean their pot the quickest. Jeremiah, sleepy and fussy, crawled into Sheba's lap. He was soon fast asleep.

* * *

When the children had their fill of playing in the water and the day was turning dusky, Sheba called Anna over and instructed her how to put the fire to bed. "Cover the coals with ashes to preserve them until morning." She watched closely while Anna did as she had instructed. Sheba again held Anna's dress back from the fire, to prevent it from catching fire and so she could jerk her back if she lost her balance over the hot coals.

Sheba did not know how she could get back into the wagon. She did not relish the idea of having to spend the night out in the open. *I guess I could have Anna make me a pallet under the wagon and not worry about getting in and out. I sure don't like the idea of being separated from the children or spending the night down here in plain sight of those men all night.* She studied the back of the wagon and tried to determine the possibilities.

She knew that Daniel and Joseph were able to lift the platform alone. The other one just stayed in the wagon to lift her out of the chair and put her on her pallet. She was afraid that even together, Anna and Joshua were not strong enough to haul the platform up with the chair and it would be impossible with her on it. Even if she left the chair out here, it would be difficult. The platform itself was quite heavy. She did not think it was possible for her to pull on the rope herself, while she was on the platform. But she might have to try.

"Anna, It's time to put the boys to bed."

"I'll put you to bed little gal." The big man had come up behind her and was leering down at her. Sheba tried not to show her fear, but knew she was trembling and could not seem to stop.

The smaller of the two men walked to her chair and pushed her to the back of the wagon. Without comment, he picked her up and placed her on the platform, hauled it up and secured the rope to the wagon. She was trembling with fear when he turned and walked away. *Thank you Jesus! Thank you Jesus!* Her problem had been solved. Slowly and laboriously she arm crawled into the wagon, oblivious to how the wood tore at her poison ivy blisters.

Anna hurried to her and helped her move to the pallet and then she cleaned the blisters and put some medicine of her papa's on them. The children curled up beside her and they all fell into a restless sleep after their busy day.

* * *

The next morning after they had eaten the rest of the cornbread and ham, Sheba again crawled to the platform and hung out over the side in preparation for the dangerous drop to the ground. Just as she was about to let go, she was grasped around the waist from behind and roughly shoved into her chair.

"Thank you," she murmured, gripping the arms of her chair willing the pain to pass. She watched as the man strolled off without a word, saddled the horse and rode across the creek and headed north. The children, who were still huddled in the wagon, peeked out the back and watched until he rode out of sight. One of the mules was gone, so they figured the other man was gone also.

"It's all right." Sheba looked from where she had been watching the man, to the children. "Boys it is time to get kindling. Anna bring me potatoes and vegetables. Joshua, you need to fill the big iron pot about three-fourths full with water. Carry it in the water bucket, because the pot will be too heavy to carry with so much water in it. Anna I will need the dry vegetables first." She glanced in the direction the man had ridden. "I sure hope he comes back with some game for the pot, if he returns."

The boys gathered kindling and Anna built the fire as Sheba had showed her the day before, all the while Sheba sat in her chair close enough to watch every step. When the coals were hot the big iron pot was set over them and Joshua began filling it with water, while Anna held him securely around the waist and Sheba held her skirts, to prevent any tumbles into the fire.

Anna had found dried peas and okra and that was put into the pot. Then she brought potatoes, onions and carrots, which the children carefully washed in the stream. Sheba cut them up into bite size chunks and Anna added them to the pot of water. Everything went into the pot except the outer skin of the onions; even the carrot tops were used to add greens to the soup.

"We cannot afford to waste anything that is edible," Sheba admonished, when Joshua protested the use of the carrot tops. "Now Anna, put the lid back on the pot." She watched as Anna cautiously set the heavy lid on the pot. "It's a little crooked, honey. Straighten it up." Anna moved it with a towel until it slid in place, while Sheba firmly gripped the back of her dress. "That's good. Great job! What would I ever do without my helpers? Push my chair a bit further from the fire and bring me my crocheting and then you can all three go play in the water. Watch Jeremiah real close. Even though the water is shallow, he could loose his balance and fall in head first."

The children hollered their delight with the prospect of playing in the stream again. Joshua had a wooden boat that Daniel had carved and he ran to get that, while Anna guided Jeremiah to a shallow pool.

Sheba watched them play happily in the water. It was still warm enough for them to enjoy the water, but the nights were beginning to turn cool. She was satisfied the children were learning well the lessons they would need to survive, when she was no longer with them. Absently she rubbed at the poison ivy, which had become infected and was oozing yellow fluid from open blisters. Even though they had more to eat and plenty of water for hydration now, the week of depravation had taken a harsh toll on her body. Sheba did not expect to be with them much longer.

She was concerned about the approaching cooler weather and the strong, unobstructed winds that continuously blew across the prairie. Their food supply was limited and the pitiful stream that trickled past their camp would dry up completely if the rains did not come soon to replenish the life giving water.

The smaller of their two captors seemed to have a bit of compassion in him and even brought meat sometimes for the soup. But she would not put anything past the big man who leered at her every time he got within sight. *If the children wait very long before they try to leave, the prairie could become treacherous for them,* Sheba considered. *Even here in the wagon, if Joseph did not find them before it grew cold, their chance of survival was quite slim; about as slim as their being found in this barren land at all,* she could not help think despondently.

Chapter Forty-Six

Donald set out alone. He followed the Arkansas River north to the Cimarron River then west to the Northwest corner of County A. It took him nearly three weeks to make this journey, but by the time he reached the northern boarder of the county he had information on nearly the entire outlaw element that was presently working within that part of Indian Territory and some of the surrounding area.

He began systematically crisscrossing the northern part of County A. Whenever he came across settlers, Donald stopped to palaver. He squatted around many campfires; discussing the weather—dry and windy, worst drought they had ever seen; he chatted with new settlers beside numerous dugouts; and lifting logs for several rough one-room cabins that were being hastily erected before the winter storms descended on the plains.

* * *

Ben, Daniel, John and Joseph traveled together along the north bank of the Canadian River until they reached North Fork Town. By following the river, they had traveled nearly one hundred and fifty miles. When they arrived in the small frontier town it was time for them to split up. Ben and Daniel headed northwest, with Ben following the Deep Fork of the Canadian and Daniel riding along the North Fork of the Canadian. Joseph and John continued to follow the Canadian River to the west.

Ben followed the general course of the Deep Fork of the Canadian northwest until he reached the western boarder of County A. He then began a north-south searching pattern. His area took in parts of the southern half of County A and the northern half of County B, between the Deep Fork of the Canadian and the North Fork of the Canadian. He traveled from north to south, occasionally dipping as far south as Tecumseh and as far north as Chandler to check for messages.

He followed along the river a short distance before dropping down as far as the North Canadian. Frequently he spent the night around the campfire of newly arrived settlers. Occasionally he came upon some rough looking hombres, who allowed him to bed down. On those nights, he made sure he slept light and with his hand on his gun.

* * *

Daniel followed the North Canadian across Indian Territory to the southern boarder of County A, only touching the river, which had the appearance of a long snake making its way lazily across the dry land, at brief intervals. Then he rode along the northern third of County B. His inquires took him as far south as the new city of Tecumseh.

He questioned everyone he saw, but no one had seen anyone meeting Sheba or the children's description. In Tecumseh he was told of some settlers about five miles out who had three children and he rode out to check on them. It turned out that the children were adolescents and all girls at that. They did not want him to leave and encouraged or begged him to perform one chore after the other to get him to prolong his visit. The entire family urged him to stay with them.

The father of the girls took Daniel aside and encouraged him to marry one of his daughters and file a claim on an adjoining property. The elderly settler who had staked a claim on the land had died right after staking his claim and his wife was returning to Indiana to live with a married daughter.

Daniel decided a quick retreat was called for and while assuring the man that anyone would be proud to marry his daughters, he explained his urgency in continuing the search for his family. As he mounted his horse to leave, the girls were teary eyed and the settler called to him that he would always be welcomed back. As he waved his hat in farewell, he felt that he had barely managed to escape that encounter still single.

* * *

Joseph and John rode west, following the Canadian River. They parted company at the Little River in mid October. Joseph continued as far west as the southwestern corner of County B along the Canadian River. He had much further to go than either Daniel or Ben, about one hundred and ten miles all-together, but he was following a well-traveled trail. He reached his destination a couple of weeks after leaving Ben and Daniel. The trail took him slightly north of the river and he made actual contact with the river only at a few locations.

At Little River, twelve-year-old John headed northwest following the river that was barely flowing after the long dry spell. He arrived at the western boarder of the county; a day after Joseph reached the Southwestern corner. They had agreed before hand that John would wait at the river until Joseph made his way north to the Little Canadian so they could search together.

Several days later, Joseph joined John. Sheba and the children had been missing over a month. Joshua and John had been traveling hard and rested only when their horses needed food and rest and they could hardly hold themselves in their saddles. The area they were about to search was twenty-three miles across and a little over fifteen miles deep. They decided to work a half mile apart, with each of them heading south talking with everyone they encountered. Allowing two days for the trip, they arranged to meet along the South Canadian in a couple days. They planned to compare notes before starting north the following day.

* * *

When John joined Joseph, they felt they had covered the area very well. Despite all of their diligence in interviewing every one they came across, neither of them had talked with anyone who could help them. Starting north, they again traveled a half-mile apart, but moved a quarter mile to the east before they began. Joseph was determined to cover every inch of ground if necessary, to find his family. In his heart he knew they were still out there somewhere and that they would find them if only they were thorough enough.

* * *

Donald followed up on every lead, however slim, but was unable to uncover any useful information to help them locate Sheba or the children. No one had seen anyone even faintly meeting their description. Some had seen a child or two, but when Donald threw Sheba, a woman of color who was disabled to the point of being unable to walk, in to the discussion, no one could or would admit to having seen anything of her or the children.

All they had to go on concerning the abductors were the names Carl and Zeke. Carl was the name of the man the nursemaid named Rose had been with when she had disappeared and Hannah had heard him call his partner or brother Zeke.

They really did not know for sure that was who had abducted Sheba and the children, but after finding Rose's body they had decided they were the most likely perpetrators. Donald finally got lucky when he stopped at one settlement and asked his usual questions about Sheba and the children. When he asked if the man had ever heard of any one named Carl or Zeke, in the area, he got a positive response.

"Is Zeke a large man, a crude, bully of a man?" The man's face had grown red with rage as he spit out his question and a chaw of tobacco that barely missed Donald's feet.

"Sure, and I don't rightly know what the mon looks like. Tell me about this Zeke.

"Well, I hear even the outlaws give him a wide birth. A bully of a man, he cut down a friend of mine for nothing but saying 'watch it' when this Zeke bumped into him. You need to talk to the marshal in Chandler about him. He can tell you plenty, I'd wager."

"And its thankin' yea I am," Donald said doffing his hat.

He continued his search pattern, not wanting to take a chance at missing them because he did not cover all the ground carefully. But the next time his search took him into Chandler he sought out the marshal and asked him about an outlaw named Zeke.

"All I can tell you is, if it is the man we have been looking for, he and his partner are wanted by the authorities for questioning in several territories, for murders, robberies and worse. Those two are bad news and Zeke is worse than his partner. Think the partner's name is Carl.

"Ah, sure and I believe it would be the same two. We think they are the pole cats what absconded with our wee children and Mistress Sheba." Donald gave him all the details.

The marshal rummaged in his desk and brought out a flyer about the abduction that Joseph had printed and sent across the territory. "Yes, I heard about that woman and children. I have kept an eye out for any sign of them." He looked down at his desk instead of into Donald's eyes.

"You know, that if those two have them, there isn't much chance you will find them alive, or undamaged."

"Me Anna will be found alive and the rest with her, if it be possible, for I know the Good Lord be looking after her even though we can't be right now. We'll find her and the rest of them too." He paused until the marshal looked up at him.

"Sure, and you will be getting your outlaws too, I'm a thinken." Donald left the marshal's office but from that time on, he concentrated on asking if anyone had any knowledge of the whereabouts of Zeke or Carl.

His next trip through Chandler, he ran into Ben and related the information he had gotten from the marshal.

Chapter Forty-Seven

The trees were becoming clothed in bright yellows and oranges, as the leaves donned their autumn foliage. Anna did not think they were as pretty as the brilliant colors of an Arkansas fall, which she thought resembled leaping tongues of fire scattered across the hills and mountains. But still she wished at times that she could capture the scenery with paints like the pictures she had seen in museums.

The trees near their camp, in the dry, windy, almost grassless land, were much shorter than what she was used to. Some of the trees were hardly larger than a good size bush, but they were hardy enough to stand up to the formidable tempests that blew across the plain. The thin prairie grass had begun turning from a dull sage color to a dusty golden hue. The stream they played in each day was barely trickling as the dry October weather continued. Anna longed for home and her family.

Why doesn't papa come? God, where is my papa?

Fierce winds kicked whirlwinds of dust into the air; sometimes they could barely see in front of the wagon the dust was so thick. The water in their barrel was empty and the water they filled their flasks with each day was muddy.

"Hurry, Anna. Take the lid off the water barrel," Sheba called to her, when they finally got a little shower. They would have to catch every drop of rainwater they could. "If the air stays as dry as it has been, the little stream might dry up completely. We cannot survive without water and you must keep all the flasks filled each day, in case the opportunity arises for you to get away."

Anna looked solemn as she hurried to do Sheba's bidding. She contemplated the fearful prospect of leaving the camp for the wide empty spaces surrounding them. She did not know how she would manage to leave Sheba, but the boys depended on her and Sheba expected her to take care of them, as would mama and papa.

Sheba continued each day to instruct Anna and Joshua in the things that might help them survive out in the open. Anna found some of the edible wild plants her father had introduced her to, during his many nature lessons, but they were scarce.

She was unable to locate an abundance of foliage nearby, like she was accustomed to finding in the woods near their home, or out on the trail. Then again, they were not usually out in the wagon this late in the year. By this time, papa would be practicing medicine and have little time for their nature lessons. She was unsure of some of the fall plants that she came across. *Did papa go back to Little Rock to his practice? Has he forgotten about us?*

There would not be many places for them to hide after they left the shelter of the wagon and she would not be able to protect them. It would be essential for them to get as far away as possible, as quickly as they could. Sheba knew that their chance of making it without the horse or one of the mules was very slim indeed.

Each day, Sheba set aside some time for school lessons with Anna and Joshua. Little Jeremiah listened nearby. It reminded Sheba of the little schoolhouse in Thomasville, when Anna was about the same age as Jeremiah. It had been a wonderful time for all of them.

She thought of Ben and wondered if he was aware of their plight, or if he even cared, if he did know. These thoughts depressed her even more and she despaired of their ever being found. She would have been surprised if she had known just how much he did care and how hard he was trying to find them.

* * *

Several weeks after their arrival, Sheba was awakened to the sound of violent arguing. She could not make out what was being said, but gathered the smaller man was leaving.

Although neither man had spoken kindly to them or assisted them with cooking or gathering wood or water, the smaller of the two had silently and a bit roughly put her back on the platform each night. He had begun pushing her chair under the platform after depositing her on it. It allowed her to drop into the chair instead of having to fall all the way to the ground. She was sure the gesture had kept her from breaking a bone or two.

Sheba sensed that he didn't really liked being a party to their abduction and keeping them there. Not like the other man who leered at her and Anna whenever he drew near.

She dreaded being left at the mercy of the coarse bully, called Zeke. She had caught him watching her and Anna on numerous occasions in a way that made her skin crawl with revulsion and terror. *I'll have to go over again a plan of escape with Anna. They will have to leave. It will be better for them to parish out on the plains, than at the hands of that monster.*

The next day, Sheba decided she would stay in the wagon. She barely had the strength to crawl out on the platform and let herself down to her chair anyway and she decided it was better to conserve what remaining strength she could muster.

"Anna, come close." She spoke low, so her voice would not travel beyond the confines of the wagon. "When you have to leave, try and take one of the mules. The horse is gone, so that is not an option. They keep them hobbled so you can probably catch one of them. All three of you can ride on one of their broad backs and still take food and water wrapped in a blanket.

"They must have sold a couple of the mules, because I have only seen a couple around the camp. If you can manage to get away with both of them, it will take longer for them to find you."

The alarm was very evident in Anna's small face. Her hazel eyes were large and round and her expression fearful. She listened attentively to all that Sheba told her, even though her insides were trembling in apprehension at the thought of being parted from Sheba.

"Anna, do you remember where you first see the sun in the morning?"

"Yes ma'am." Tears were beginning to spill over and run down her cheeks. "It's that way." She pointed downstream.

"That's right Anna. Now that direction is east. The stream probably flows northeast part of the way and southeast part of the way, so it is the sky you will have to watch. East is back to Arkansas. East is home.

"Can you remember that Anna? The direction we first see the sun of a morning, is east. Do you understand Anna?" She repeated her question, while holding Anna's small hands in her own and looking into the girl's eyes.

"Yes ma'am. If we go in the direction the sun comes up, we will get home."

"Now at noon it will be right over head, so that will be a good time to rest, so you won't get turned around. In the afternoon, the sun will be at your back. Now listen closely. You have to stay close to water to refill your flasks, but you cannot follow this stream very far, because that is what they will expect and it will be easier for them to find you.

"We crossed a river when we came, so I know if you go south you will come to a river. It will be bigger than the one we are on and have a better water supply. You must go south until you reach that river. If that is east," Sheba pointed toward the east. "Which way is south?"

Anna thought a minute looking around. "If downstream is east and the sun is in our face to the east, when we go south it will be on our left side in the morning and our right side in the afternoon. It is that way." She pointed due south.

"Good girl!" Sheba praised her and gave her a big hug. "Get your slate and I will draw how I think the area is laid out."

Anna handed her the slate and some chalk. Sheba drew the stream where they were camped. Then she drew a dotted line going south, then a river flowing east that connected with a larger river.

"I wish I knew the area better, but we could not see anything on the way here. I believe if you can follow that river it will take you to the Arkansas River. And the Arkansas River will take you home."

When Anna had studied the drawing, Sheba erased it clean with her sleeve.

"We live on the Arkansas River."

"Yes, we do. Now when you do get to the Arkansas, you will travel with the flow of the river—downstream. Do you understand?"

"Yes ma'am." Anna was beginning to take a real interest in the expedition that would take them to the Arkansas and home to mama and papa."

"Now when you first leave, you should probably walk in this little stream for awhile before you head south. You don't have to hide your tracks, if they see them in the mud every once in awhile that is all right. Maybe they will continue to follow the stream.

"When you get out of the stream, try to make sure the ground is hard so they won't see the mule's tracks."

Sheba was terrified at the prospect of the children striking out on their own, but was even more afraid for them if they stayed. She was positive that Joseph would never give up looking for them. His chances of just him and Daniel finding them however, in this vast sparsely inhabited country--so very far from where they were abducted, was extremely remote. In the time they had been there, no one had even passed within sight of their camp.

She prayed she was doing the right thing, by making them leave. Anna looked so small and frightened. Anna would not even be six-years-old for a couple more months. How could she possibly lead the other two children out of this dry prairie—back to their family in Arkansas?

There were all kind of impediments to her making it: if they did not find water before the water in their flasks was gone, they would die of thirst; if they could not find more food, they would starve to death; they might run into renegade Indians and be abducted again; their current abductors might catch up with them; Anna might get confused and head in the wrong direction. So many things could happen to three small children traveling alone. Tears filled her eyes as she considered all they might be up against.

All these things were whirling around in her mind, when she seemed to hear God's voice chastising her. "If I am concerned about the flowers in the fields and the birds in the air, how much more do you think I will be concerned for the welfare of three of My children?"

You are right Lord. I am putting these children in your hands. Guide them each step. They are so small, but I know that You will walk with them. Help Joseph and Daniel in their search. Amen.

"I don't want to leave you, Sheba." Anna spoke low, but tears streamed down her deeply tanned cheeks. "Why can't you go with us? You could ride the mule and we could walk." Her face was stricken with fear, as she thought about being alone on the prairie and responsible for the welfare of not only herself but also the boys.

"Honey, listen to me." Sheba kept her voice calm. "I need to stay here and create a diversion if I can. That's a big word. Do you know what it means?"

"I think so. It means to keep their mind on something besides us."

"That is exactly what it means, to distract them, so they won't come after you. That will give you time to get away. "Zeke may come in the wagon with me; if he does you must leave then. I want you to get your supplies and water out to that groove of cotton wood trees. Have the boys take them out as they gather wood.

"You will need to leave as fast as you can and get as far away as possible, before the men realize that you are gone. Do you understand?" She spoke as sternly as she could manage with her own tears choking her voice. Anna stood beside Sheba silently crying, but she nodded her head yes to let her know that she understood.

"Anna, you must promise me, that no matter what happens to me or what you hear coming from this wagon that you will leave and take the boys. Do you promise?" Sheba grasped both of Anna's arms and forced her to look into her eyes.

"Yes ma'am." The promise was given in a very low voice and came from a face stricken with grief, but it was given.

"Now go fix breakfast like always. Keep Joshua and Jeremiah with you everywhere you go. Use the open iron pot to start dinner. That should keep Zeke off guard. Only put a few vegetables in the pot, if you can find some greens, any kind, fill the pot up with them, so he won't get suspicious. Wash the oven after you fix the bread. If you are able to leave on the mule, take it with you. But if you have to walk out, don't try to carry it. The iron pot would be much too heavy and slow you down. Hide as much of the bread as you can in the socks, because you will not be able to stop and build a fire until you reach the river.

"If Zeke wants to know where I am, tell him I'm sick. That sure won't be a lie." She lay back on the pallet exhausted. She felt like she did not have a grain of strength left.

"'ick," Jeremiah echoed. "Beba 'ick." He leaned his arms on her legs and looked sorrowful into her eyes. "Poor Beba."

"That's right, little one." Sheba smiled at the toddler. "I am sick." Her eyes were brimming with unshed tears, as she pulled him into her arms and hugged and kissed him. "Now you have to be a good boy and mind what Anna tells you. Can you do that for Sheba?"

Jeremiah smiled and nodded his agreement. Joshua moved to her side and gave her a big hug and kiss. He did not understand everything that was happening, but he knew it could not be good or his mama and Anna would not be crying.

The children scrambled from the wagon, but not before Anna had stuffed socks filled with food under their clothes. They went about their routine chores, which included filling the flasks with water and gathering wood from the groove of trees for Anna's fire. Each trip to the trees they deposited a flask of water or sock filled with provisions, which had been concealed on their person, by the enterprising Anna.

Anna carried a bucket of water from the stream to the wagon. She set it in Sheba's chair and then climbed into the chair. Then she carefully lifted the bucket of water onto the platform, only spilling a bit on herself. She quickly climbed down and hurried around the front where it was easier to climb into the wagon. She retrieved the bucket and set it within Sheba's reach, hugged her tight and then left to finish breakfast.

Anna was growing stronger with the daily lifting of the heavy pots on and off the fire. *She is going to need that strength to survive the ordeal ahead* reflected Sheba, as she watched Anna's progress. *Lord go with her each step. Send your angels to surround her.*

Sheba's poison ivy had nearly cleared up. The ugly infected blisters had kept the men at a distance, so they had stopped treating the sores right after their capture. She still had some blisters and turned her sleeves up to expose them, anything was worth a try.

Zeke questioned the children about why Sheba had not come out of the wagon, while they ate breakfast within hearing of where Sheba lay. Anna had brought her some bread and ham earlier, whispering that the oven was washed and hidden with the other supplies in the woods.

"Beba sick." Jeremiah was quick to inform him.

"Yes," Anna confirmed. "She is very sick." She was so frightened she could hardly get the words out.

Zeke looked from one of the children to the other. It figured that they would be upset if they thought she was dying. *Doubt the little brat could make it up,* he considered looking at Jeremiah. Still he watched them skeptically.

"You leave my mama alone!" Three-year-old Joshua's bold demand was yelled with his hands on his hips and his feet firmly planted in a wide stance. He glared at the big man, as he shouted his ultimatum.

"Your mother huh, so, I won't be her first white man then?" His evil laugh terrified the children.

They clung together, too frightened to move, as they heard him climb into the wagon.

"Sick are you? I'll show you sick." He stumbled through the wagon, back to where Sheba lay on her pallet and lunged at her.

She struggled with the man, but was no match for him and would not have been even if she could have moved her legs. *Run, Anna. Run with the boys.* Her thought flew to the children.

Anna heard Sheba scream once, a popping sound like something hitting something and then all they heard was the rough voice of Zeke. Grabbing Jeremiah and the rest of the bread, she ran for the groove of trees to retrieve their hidden stores.

"Joshua, we have to get the mules. I promised Sheba I would get you away." Tears streamed down her cheeks and sobs chocked her voice.

"I didn't promise!" Joshua grabbed up a shovel and ran for the front of the wagon. Quickly he scrambled up onto the seat and made his way through the dark interior. He found the man so engrossed in what he was doing, that he did not hear the child's furious charge.

Joshua swung the shovel over his head as hard as he could right at the man's head. It dazed the big man, but did not render him unconscious. He uttered a string of curses as he turned on the boy. Joshua did not have time to swing again, so he jabbed the shovel at the man in defense. Zeke's pants were down around his ankles and his feet got tangled in them causing him to fall forward. His weight and momentum forward bore him down hard across the end of the shovel. Blood spurted everywhere. Joshua stood looking at the man, unable to move.

Anna's head popped over the wagon. She saw the immobile Joshua standing in the back near Sheba, but had to climb in and get further to the back before she saw the large man lying in a pool of blood. Sheba seemed to be unconscious. She moved cautiously around the man's body and leaned over Sheba. She shook her shoulder, but she did not rouse. She laid her head on Sheba's chest like she had watched her papa do and was relieved to hear the faint sound of her beating heart.

"Joshua! Joshua come here and help me get your mama out on the platform. We will have to tie her across one of the mules and take her with us.

"Joshua," she called. "I said come help me." She turned to her cousin, who still stared at the man without moving. She raised her voice and yelled at him again, before he looked up at her with stricken eyes.

"I didn't mean to kill him. Anna I'll go to hell for killing a man."

"No you won't. Besides," she lied, deciding he could learn the truth latter when papa could explain it to him. "He is just knocked out like your mama. I need your help. Help me get her out to the platform and then we'll bring the mule right under it and push her on top of the mule.

"You will have to sit on the mule and help me lay her across his back and then we'll tie her on. I'll put some blankets on the mule to cushion it as much as possible."

The children heard Jeremiah crying outside the wagon, while they struggled to pull Sheba out on the platform. While Joshua sat with his mother, Anna climbed down, moved the chair to the side and ran for one of the mules. She unhobbled it and led it right beside the platform. Anna climbed up to the platform and Joshua climbed out on the mule. Jeremiah stood beside the large animal, looking up at the activity on the platform, one thumb in his mouth, the other hand patting the mule's long leg and tears streaming down his face.

They struggled for what seemed like forever to the young children, but finally had Sheba lying on blankets over the broad back of the mule. Anna went through the wagon and picked up some more food they had left and quickly climbed down.

"I am going to get the other mule and load our stuff on him. You stay on the mule with your mama; you can ride with her. Jeremiah and I will ride the other one with the supplies." She did not wait for an answer, but scooped her brother up and headed for the other mule.

Jeremiah put both arms around her neck and almost chocked off her breath his grip was so tight. The mule did not attempt to move away from the girl who had brought him sugar and apples many times during the long summer trip. He allowed her to loop the rope in his halter, while he sniffed for a treat.

She set Jeremiah on top and admonishing him to hold on tight, she led the mule back to where Joshua waited, gently patting his unconscious mother's arm. Anna quickly tied all their supplies on the mule, by standing on Sheba's chair and then boosted herself up. She admonished Jeremiah to hold tight to the mule's mane. Anna had ridden him many times on her pony, but the mule seemed about twice as high.

"We have to get as far away as possible before the other man comes back. We were supposed to start out in the creek, but I am going to head directly south. We have to get to that river before we run out of water." She made her explanations to the boys while she moved forward in the direction she knew to be south.

The sun would be directly overhead in several hours so they had to get as far from camp as possible before that happened. They would not dare move while she could not distinguish her directions. The mules moved off at a steady pace in what Anna hoped was the direction of a river that if followed downstream would take them to Arkansas.

Chapter Forty-Eight

They continued over the parched ground, with Anna keeping a weary eye on the sun to make sure they were headed in the right direction. Anna guided the amiable mule, which they called Old Joe, with gentle urging from her heels and the rope tied to the halter.

Their supplies were secured across the mule's broad back. Anna sat on the edge of the tote bag, which held the socks filled with food and flasks of water, to make sure it would not slip to the ground.

If something fell off they would be in big trouble, because there was no way she could get back up without standing on something.

* * *

The children rode for several hours until the sun was high over their heads. Jeremiah fell asleep with his head pillowed on the mule's neck. Anna gripped his shirt in one of her hands, to make sure that he would not fall off.

She began to watch for a sheltered place to rest. Just as she spotted a groove of trees, Jeremiah awoke and began crying for Sheba and something to eat. This new game was getting old to the toddler. He was ready to return to the comfort of the wagon and Sheba. Anna glanced at the other mule where Sheba's head bounced face down against the broad side. She had not stirred since they left the camp. Joshua rode the mule with one hand on the rope attached to the halter and the other reaching behind him to pat his mother, as if trying to sooth her.

"We had better stop and feed him, Josh. The sun is overhead anyway and we aren't supposed to travel when I can't tell which way south is. There are some trees over there." She pointed toward the grove of spindly looking trees.

"Head for the trees. Maybe the mules can find some grass. We will have to hobble them while we eat and rest."

As they rode near the trees, Anna stopped her mule, cautioned Jeremiah to hold tight to the mane and slid to the ground. Her feet hit first and then she abruptly landed on her bottom. Quickly she hobbled the mule and then walked to the side of the large animal.

"Jeremiah, you have to jump. I'll catch you." She looked up at her brother, the apprehension she felt clearly visible on her face. "Don't jump hard, just kind of slide down, okay? Hold tight to Old Joe's mane, until I tell you to let go." Jeremiah moved his right leg over the broad back to join his left leg. While still holding tightly to the mule's mane he slid down the side.

"Okay! Let go. I've got you." She held her arms up to receive him. Jeremiah let go and slid quickly down the mule's side into her waiting arms. Unfortunately, his weight knocked her off her feet and they both sprawled in the dirt. He puckered up to cry until he saw his sister laughing and rolling in the dirt. He jumped on her and laughed too.

"'gen, 'gen." He shouted, grasping the mule's leg and attempting to climb back up.

"Oh! We'll do it lots of times Jeremiah. Right now I have to get Joshua down and fix us something to eat." She took some of the food and water off the mule and set it down with Jeremiah under a tree, before she walked over to where Joshua sat the other mule.

"I'll help you get down Josh."

Tears were brimming in his eyes, as he looked down at his mother. "What about mama, Anna?"

"We can't get her down, Josh. If we did, we would never be able to get her back up on the mule. I'll hobble him and let him graze some before I tie him under a tree, so she will be in the shade. I'll try to give her a drink before we eat though."

He thought about it a minute and then decided that her response seemed reasonable to him. He lifted his right leg over to the left side, turned around and slid down like Jeremiah had. He was taller and was able to drop further before he let go, but also weighed more, so again Anna went sprawling in the dirt.

She got up and dusted herself off. "We have to find a better way to do that, before you two kill me."

She did not know how long they had been riding, but it seemed like forever to the young girl. She knew from the position of the sun that it was around noon. They would have a couple hours to eat and rest before they had to find a way to get back on the mules and head south again, with the sun on her right shoulder.

Anna pried open a can of beans. They ate hungrily of the contents and some of the leftover bread she had baked that morning. She passed around a water flask, making sure that both boys got a good drink before she gulped some down. It was warm, almost hot from the sun, but it was wet. Sheba had warned Anna over and over that they must drink lots of water.

She used her finger to scoop up some of the juice in the can and forced it in Sheba's mouth, while Joshua held his mother's head up as high as he could reach. Then she slowly poured some water into her parched mouth. Most of it trickled out of her mouth and fell down to the ground, but Anna thought she had successfully gotten some of it actually inside Sheba.

She could still see a small flutter of the pulse in her neck, so even though she remained unconscious, Anna was sure she was alive.

"Do you think he kilt her?" Joshua looked at his mother uncertainly.   He looked over at Anna, his large dark eyes brimming with tears.

"No, Josh. I promise your mama is still alive. See that movement in her throat?" She pointed out the slight movement of Sheba's pulse. "As long as her heart is beating, we can feel it there in her neck." Her answer seemed to satisfy him.

"We have to get to the river and then head east towards the Arkansas. We need to rest for a while and then get back on the mules and head south. I can angle a little east, but mostly south. We can't miss the river." Joshua helped her pick up everything, including the empty bean can, so they would be ready to leave as soon as the sun was hitting on Anna's right shoulder. They led the mule into the shade of the trees and put him on a long enough tether so he could reach the sparse grass.

They slept a couple of hours and then Anna looked around for a fallen tree that she would be able to climb on and get back on the mule. When she found one, she put all the supplies on the tree and took a flask of water to where Sheba lay over the mule. Again she tried to get some water between her parched lips. Then she poured some in her pot and gave each of the mules a drink, before giving the boys and herself a long drink.

Joshua, you lead my mule over to that tree. Jeremiah and I will climb up into the tree then I will lift him up on Old Joe, put the supplies up and climb up myself. When we get up on Old Joe, you untie your mule and give me the rope. I'll hold the mule near the tree while you climb on, do you think you can do that?"

"Sure I can do it." He had all the bravado of any three-year-old male demonstrating how big he was.

Anna pushed Jeremiah up on the mule's back and he promptly started to fall off the other side. She grabbed his pants, nearly pulling them off, but the feisty toddler grabbed the mule's mane and held on tight. Anna got him settled securely enough to put the supplies up and climb on herself. Joshua followed her instructions and soon they were on their way.

The sun was on their right and slightly to their backs. Anna knew they were headed south and she figured maybe a little east, hoping that would get them to the Arkansas a little more quickly.

Anna did not know how long she could keep things together out here, with the unconscious Sheba and the two boys. She was very afraid.

Chapter Forty-Nine

The sun was going down. They would have to stop before she could no longer tell in which direction to travel. The children were tired and sore from riding all day. They were used to riding their ponies for long stretches, but they were smaller and wore saddles, which made for a much more comfortable ride than sitting on the hard backbones of the mules.

It was with great relief they slid off the back of the mules, even if they did land in a heap on the hard ground. The children again shared the flask of water and ate what remained of the bread. She gave the mules a drink before hobbling them for the night. She attempted to give Sheba a drink, but could not get her lips opened.

The faint pulse that she had been checking in her neck did not seem to have any movement. She felt it cautiously with her small fingers, but was unable to detect a beat. The children curled up together on one of the blankets and covered up with another that had been wrapped around the supplies. The rest of their blankets were under Sheba.

Coyotes howled nearby, while curious rabbits and prairie dogs inspected the sleeping children. Old Joe stood over them or grazed nearby, a gentle guard watching throughout the night, while the other mule, carrying Sheba, wandered in a wide circle around them.

* * *

The next morning they ate some dried meat and fruit and drank from their dwindling supply of water. Both mules stopped grazing and made their way slowly back to the children.

Anna poured all but a little of the remaining water in the oven for the mule. After the mules drank their ration of water, Anna carefully dried the heavy iron pot with her skirt and packed it back in the feed sack.

Sheba had told her that if they took the animals they would have to share their water ration with them, or the mules would not be able to continue and they would end up afoot.

They started out again in a southeasterly direction with the morning sun still low on the eastern horizon. The children saw more animals and birds than they had the day before.

" 'orses, 'orses," Jeremiah cried excitedly.

"No Jeremiah, those are deer." Anna laughed at her baby brother's excitement. "See it's a mama, a papa and a baby deer."

At the mention of mama, Joshua looked behind him where his mother lay still over the back of the mule. Tears formed in his eyes and slid quietly down his cheeks.

The children watched the deer grazing peacefully, as they passed. The buck raised his head and sniffed the air, as the wind carried the scent and voices of the children toward him. Apparently satisfied they were quite harmless; he soon resumed grazing with his family.

Anna glanced around frequently to check for any sign they were being pursued. Once when a cloud of dust to the north frightened her, she urged the mules to pick up their pace. It proved to be merely a heard of antelope.

They passed a lazy rattlesnake occasionally and Anna was reminded of her close brush with the cottonmouth by the creek. She could barely remember the episode, but her parents and Sheba had frequently told her the story. Whenever she spotted a snake that she considered one of the dangerous ones, she gave it plenty of room. If a snake bit one of the mules, they would be in a desperate strait. The three children might be able to ride on one mule, but she knew there was no way that one of the mules could carry all of them and Sheba too.

As they had the day before, Anna looked for some shelter when the sun was straight overhead, so they could eat and rest. They saw some black jack trees and headed in that direction. They ate, took care of the mules, attempted to get water into Sheba's mouth and then lay down to sleep for a couple hours. They were exhausted; so fell asleep as soon as they lay on the hard ground.

* * *

There was no fallen tree this time, but Anna tied Old Joe to a tree and was then able to climb up into the tree. Joshua pushed Jeremiah up to her. She set him on the mule and then Joshua handed the supplies up to her. She leaned way over, while hanging on with one hand and managed to snag the sack, pull it up and secured it on the back of the mule. Then she let her self down on top of the mule's back, while Jeremiah clung tenaciously to the mane.

Joshua gave her the rope for the other mule and she held it while Joshua climbed the tree and slithered out onto the mule's back, settling just in front of his mother.

* * *

It was late afternoon of the second day when Joe picked up his step and turned in a more easterly direction. Their water was gone. They were hot, tired and dirty.

Anna had not noticed the subtle change in direction, until she realized the sun was beating down more on her back than it was on her right side. She attempted to turn Joe, but he continued on in the direction he had chosen. They were into an area of higher rolling hills and did not see the river until they topped a rise.

"It's the river!" Anna almost toppled off the mule in her excitement. "Look Josh! That's why Old Joe came this way. The river curves to the south just west of here." Anna pointed to where the river curved away from them upstream. "If we had kept going straight, it might've taken another day to get to the water."

She was crying and laughing as she slid to the ground and helped the boys down. They rushed to the water. The mules waded in and drank long and thirstily. The children not only drank the cool water, but also splashed at the edge of the slightly muddy but refreshing river. Sheba had been right. This was much larger than the stream where they had left the wagon.

Anna stood in the cool water, her wet clothes clinging to her body. Jeremiah held tightly to her hand, because the current seemed to pull at his short legs in an attempt to tip him over.

She gazed at the wide river that seemed as wide as the Arkansas to the young child. She knew that no one could walk across the Arkansas; it was much too deep. Papa had frequently cautioned about the treacherous currents in the wide river. She just could not remember how big it actually was.

It seemed like a long time since that had been camped on the banks of the Arkansas with their family. That thought brought more tears to her eyes, but these were not happy tears. She felt small and alone. She knew she had to cross the river, or they would be on the wrong side when they reached the Arkansas and never be able to get back to the family.

They would probably be safer on that side also, because if their abductors came this way they probably would not expect the children to cross the river.

Anna stood at the edge and studied the river. She doubted that they could walk or swim across; she remembered Joshua's experience in the Arkansas. Horses could swim, so she figured the mules could. *Mules are part horse, so they should be able to do whatever a horse can,* she reasoned.

I have to find a shelter where I can leave Sheba and the boys and see if I can get help for Sheba. She was not at all sure if Sheba was still alive, but if she were Anna would have to find someone to help her.

The children found a big rock and climbed back up on the mules, which had been happily grazing along the riverbank. Anna held onto the rope dangling from the halter from the other mule and urged Old Joe out into the water.

The current grew stronger as they moved out to the center, but because it had been so dry it was still shallow enough for the mules to walk across most of the way.

"It's all right Old Joe, you can do it." She urged him forward with trembling voice, as the water rushed against his side.

Joshua could still remember his close call in the Arkansas River, near the pontoon bridge when he had flown over his pony's head and landed in the rushing river. He began to cry for his mama and begged Anna to get them out of the water.

"Hold tight Josh. Hold tight Jeremiah. We are almost there." Tears streamed down her cheeks and she shook with her own fear, but held tight to the mules' ropes. They were all drenched from the splashing of the mules' powerful legs as they churned in the swift water, but they finally reached the other side and started climbing out on the south bank.

They tumbled off the mules on wobbly legs and lay in a grateful heap looking back across the way they had come.

"We did it! We did it!" Joshua shouted as he looked at Anna with awe.

Anna smiled at her cousin and scooted up on legs that threatened not to hold her upright, as she moved to the side of the mule and checked on Sheba. Because of her position lying over the mule, Anna knew that Sheba's face had been underwater for some of the trip across. She again felt for a pulse, but there was no movement that she could detect.

They had finally reached an abundant supply of water, but food and shelter would still be a problem. The children hugged each other in triumph. They had made it to the river and managed to cross safely to the other side.

"We have to find some kind of shelter. I need to leave you boys and see if I can find someone to help Sheba. When I leave, I'll mark my trail so I can get back to you and I won't go more than one day away. If I don't find help within one day's ride, I will turn around and come back and we will just keep going.

"Joshua do you think you can watch over Jeremiah that long?"

"You find someone to make mama well. I'll watch Jeremiah." He looked as if he was on the verge of crying, but was equally determined to do whatever necessary to help his mama.

They climbed back on the mule with the aid of a fallen tree and made their way downstream. The sun was already dipping low in the west when they headed east along the riverbank.

It was dusky when they stopped beside a hill. Anna knew they would have to find someplace soon. She felt she should go back up stream to find help and she did not want to get so far from the boys that it would be hard to find her way back.

When dark caught them still on the mules, they slid off and found shelter in a small gully. It would be out of sight of any passersby. She wanted to make sure when she found help that it would be someone who would not hurt them, but actually be a helper.

The next day they began hunting for a place to camp. They hunted on foot, always staying within sight of the river. Anna had almost despaired of finding anything, when they came across an abandoned dugout in one of the rolling hills.

Anna looked in cautiously, but screamed in terror when a rabbit darted between her legs. Jeremiah began to cry and Joshua grabbed Anna, frightened by her sudden scream.

"It's...all...right," she stammered breathlessly. "It was only a rabbit." She looked at the boys sheepishly. She was ashamed of herself. After all the times she had warned the boys to be quite, she had screamed like a banshee at the sight of a rabbit dashing out of the cave-like structure. She figured anyone within a hundred miles could have heard her.

They entered the dark structure, which had been dug out of the south side of the hill and was not visible from the river.

I think you will be safe here. Someone lived here once." She looked around at the small dirt room cautiously, checking for snakes or other less harmful wildlife. "I think who ever lived here has been gone for a long time."

A few broken pieces of homemade furniture were scattered on the floor of the dugout, but there was nothing else inside. She discovered a hole in the roof, above a circle of stones, where the previous occupants had cooked.

"I'll bake some bread and then put on a pot of soup. That way you will have food while I'm gone. Tomorrow morning early, I'll take Old Joe and head back up stream to see if I can find anyone. I think we probably better cut your mama off the mule and drag her into the dugout. It will be easier to try and get some water or soup into her."

She looked at Josh. Anna knew once they got her off the mule, they would never be able to get her back on without help.

Josh shook his head up and down in agreement with the plan. After Joshua and Anna managed to get Sheba down off the mule and pulled into the dugout, the boys went out to gather some kindling. Anna brought the supplies in and began stirring up some cornbread.

When the boys returned with their arms loaded with small branches and dried grass Anna started the fire.

"Joshua, you have to keep the fire going after I leave, but not too hot. We don't want a lot of smoke billowing out of the hole to announce our presence."

When it was done, Anna gave each of the boys some cornbread and dried meat then she started the soup cooking over the fire. She sat some of the cornbread aside to take with her and left the rest in the pan for the boys to eat while she was gone.

The soup cooked throughout the night while the children slept next to Sheba. The next morning, they ate soup and cornbread. Anna attempted without success to get some down Sheba.

She poured some of the soup in one of their flasks to take with her and made sure the fire was banked sufficiently to keep the soup warm for the boys. She only filled one container with water to take with her, because she planned to stay close to the river.

Anna knew if she wondered far from the river there would be a very real danger of getting lost and being unable to return to where she left the boys.

She filled the other flasks with water from the river for the boys. If at all possible, she did not want them going down to the river while she was gone.

"Now Joshua," she admonished. "Be careful when you get water. You should have enough with what I have left, but if you need any, be careful you don't fall in. Don't let Jeremiah out of your sight. He was used to playing in the shallow stream, so don't even let him near this river." She was torn between trying to get help for Sheba and staying with the boys. She was not sure which her papa would want her to do.

Joshua led Old Joe beside the dugout and she climbed halfway up and jumped onto the broad back of the mule. Tears streaming from her eyes, she did not turn around and look at the boys, but waved to them as she rode west along the river.

Chapter Fifty

Anna followed the river upstream, moving much faster without the load the mule had been carrying, when she had all the supplies and Jeremiah. She was determined to get back to the boys as soon as possible.

She could not be gone more than a couple of days, or they would be out of cooked food. The boys could grow afraid and anything might happen to them while she was searching for help.

She had gotten her clothes wet while she filled the flasks from the river, but the hot sun on her back and the wind that never seemed to stop, quickly dried them.

The river twisted and turned, but she was afraid to cut straight across and get far from it. If she got lost and could not get back to the boys, they would probably all die. Anyway, she reasoned that her best bet to find settlers was along the river. Anyone making his or her home in this arid land would have to have water to survive.

She saw dust rising in the distance toward evening. There was a high bank with a slight overhang, so she led Old Joe into the water and huddled under the overhang. She spoke soothingly to Joe trying to keep him quite, as they waited for the rider to pass. Anna peered up through the brush close to the riverbank. She tried to get a better look at whoever it was, before calling out.

She continued to see the dust, but never got a good look at the rider. She could not tell if it was one of their abductors, but was determined that no one would prevent her from getting help and returning to the boys.

When she could no longer see well enough to safely proceed, she pulled Old Joe up and slid from his back. She led him to the water, watching wearily for anyone who might be up to no good. After they had both drank from the river, she led Old Joe back a ways from the river and hobbled him. Wearily she ate some of the cornbread that she had brought with her and lay down under a bush.

* * *

The next morning a rider cantering up on a large brown mare rudely awakened her. She sat up terrified that one of their abductors had found her.

"What are you doing here child?" The man was dressed in gray homespun pants and shirt. Black suspenders held the rather baggy pants up around his slender waist. He stared at the frightened child and looked around cautiously to make sure some adult didn't have a bead on him with a shotgun.

"Downriver," she answered softly. "I came from downriver. I…I was out looking for berries, but I came too far." Anna knew better than to tell lies, but she did not know what this man's intentions were.

"Where are your folks?"

"They're back that way." Anna pointed to the east back downriver. She figured that was not a lie. Her folks did live in that direction.

"Well, the misses has breakfast ready. You better come back to the cabin and eat. After we eat I'll go back with you to make sure you don't get lost.

Anna was so relieved to hear that the man had a wife and a cabin nearby that she jumped up quickly. She looked around for something to climb on, but there did not seem to be anything handy.

"Mister, could you give me a boost up, please?"

The man slid to the ground in one smooth motion and grabbed Anna around the waist. He quickly had her seated on top of the mule, but instead of handing her the rope, he held onto it and led the mule behind him.

Anna followed the man to the lean-to, where his wife and three children greeted them. A cabin was under construction nearby. The oldest girl was about Anna's age. The children were delighted to have another child as their guest; they had not seen any other children since they had come to Oklahoma Territory to settle.

"That is where are cabin is going to be." The girl informed Anna. She hesitantly reached out for Anna's hand and drew her over to the log structure. "We are just making-do until the cabin's done." It was obviously something she had heard her parents tell her repeatedly.

The children were thin and wiry. They wore patched, threadbare clothes and curious expressions, as they looked Anna over carefully. The younger children were boys and their bare feet kicked up tiny whirlpools of dust, as they stared at the newcomer.

The two adults appeared old and tired. Anna guessed them to be around mama's age, but they looked older. She kind of wished she had brought the boys with her. They would have loved to play with these two that looked like they could get into every bit as much mischief as her brother and cousin.

The woman retrieved another metal pie pan from the lean-to and split up the food she had already put on the five plates. There were real eggs and thick slices of bread with butter. It was then that Anna saw the chickens walking in and out of the lean-to and the cow in a rail pen off to the side.

The woman was adding vegetables to the inevitable pot of soup, but Anna noticed their soup had real chunks of meat, as well as vegetables. Anna's mouth watered as she watched the meat floating in the pot of rich soup.

The child's reaction was not lost on the woman and she sent her daughter after a piece of meat they had left from the night before. She added that to Anna's plate.

The woman looked at her husband questioningly. He pulled her to the side and spoke softly for her ears alone. "Found her along the river. Said she was berry picking, but I didn't see any berries. I'll take her back to her folks after we eat." The man assumed she could not have come far.

The women watched curiously while Anna divided her meat into three pieces, popped one in her mouth and stuffed the other two in her pocket.

They walked back to the fire and sat down to eat. He introduced his family to Anna.

"I'm Jed Johnson. My wife's Beth and these kids here are Janie, Joel, and Harry."

"I am Anna, Anna Warren from Little Rock. My first mama's name was Beth, but I didn't know her." She responded as politely as possible while munching on the delicious meat.

"Little Rock? How on earth did you get here?" the woman asked in astonishment.

"We were abducted. I have to get back to my brother and cousin. My aunt is hurt real bad and I need help for her."

"Abducted? Who abducted you?"

"Some bad men and they are probably trying to find us. Well one of them anyway. I think maybe Joshua killed one with a shovel and his mama may not be alive either. I can't find a pulse."

"A pulse is it." The woman smiled at the child with the sad tale. They were not sure she was not making all this up as well as the tale about getting lost picking berries. More than likely she had got in a fuss with her folks and took off on the mule then got lost and could not find her way back. "What do you know about pulses?"

"My papa is a doctor and he taught me a lot about that sort of thing." Anna was obvious indignant about being questioned about her knowledge of medical things.

"What kind of soup is that?" She did not intentionally change the subject, but she could not take her eyes off the pot of soup.

"It's just soup." The woman shrugged her shoulders and leaned over to stir the soup in the big iron pot, "Taters, onions, venison, beans and the like."

"That's deer meat." Anna knew that venison came from deer. " My Uncle Daniel brought venison home for mama to cook, but I haven't had any for a long time."

"My man provides for us right smart." The woman's voice, as she smiled at her husband was filled with both pride and love.

After they had finished, Anna offered to clean the big iron skillet in which the woman had fried the eggs.

"Sakes child, that pan is much too heavy for the likes of you." She smiled warmly at the child who had appeared at her door. The couple questioned her about her family. They were especially curious as to why she had not been eating meat.

"Don't your father know how to hunt?" They had not accepted her tale of abduction and thought she was just spinning a yarn. "Deer are pretty plentiful around here."

"Papa is probably too busy looking for us, too have time to hunt," she responded indignantly.

The couple looked at one another and then the man went after his horse and Old Joe. He wanted to get the girl back home and get back to building his cabin. Cold weather was just before moving in and he did not want his family suffering through the winter in just the lean-to. Besides, it was not safe to leave them unguarded. There were still some hostile Indians in the area and cutthroats seemed to abound.

"I have some venison already cooked inside. I'll send it home with you. It will help out until your father gets back.

Her husband followed her into the lean-to. "You know, I thought I knew all the settlers up and down the river, but I can't place her family."

When he walked back out to where Anna stood beside the horse and mule, he looked Old Joe over carefully.

"You know a mean looking varmint rode by here the other day. Said he was looking for someone what stole his mule. Kind of looked like this one, as he described it."

"And had you seen someone with a mule?" Fear replaced the good feeling she had about these settlers.

"Well, if I had, I wouldn't have told him. Looked like a shiftless sort to me. Of course if I had something that belonged to someone like him, I sure wouldn't want him catching up with me." He looked at the child cautiously.

"I believe I saw somebody riding off on a mule upstream," Anna lied. Unfortunately she seemed to be getting better at it. "You might tell them that. If you run into them again, that is." She glanced up at the man with wide eyes, as innocent as she could make them.

"I'll keep that in mind." He smiled as he boosted her up on the mule and climbed on his horse. This time he let her hold the rope she used for reigns. The girl appeared young and innocent, probably not older than his Janie, but he knew she was lying to him.

Beth walked to the child's side with some food tied up in a cloth. "Tell me the truth child. How many people you feeding?"

"There are four of us, but Sheba hasn't eaten anything for a long time. She's Josh's mother." The woman shook her head in disbelief, but walked to the lean-to and brought out another bundle of food.

"That should keep you for awhile, maybe until your papa comes home anyway."

"Thank you." She smiled at the woman, but knew that she did not believe her.

They made their way along the river, headed east toward the boys. It was getting dark and she judged they were still a ways from where she left the boys. The man seemed to be getting edgy about returning to his family.

Anna did not really think that Sheba was still alive and she had been gone for two full days. She promised the boys she would be back, but she knew there was little chance of her finding the dugout in the dark. She had food for the boys and that was more than she expected to accomplish when she had started out.

"I know you need to get back to your family. It isn't far too where I left the boys, but I won't be able to find the dugout in the dark. You go on back to your family. I'll just stay here until morning and then I'll go on to where they are. I am thankful for all your help, especially for this food." She slid off the big mule in her normal unceremonious plop to the ground.

The man watched as she expertly hobbled her mule and waved good-bye to him. Reluctantly he turned back toward home and urged his horse back up-stream. He knew his wife would be worried, but he hated leaving the child. She seemed to know what she was about though. No telling what she had gotten herself into.

Anna fell asleep immediately curled up under a bush, with her head pillowed on her arms. She did not even notice the cold, as exhausted as she was. She dreamed of home and the security of her papa's arms.

Chapter Fifty-One

In the morning she awoke to Old Joe nipping at her hair. The sun was barely peeking over the eastern horizon, but she quickly got up and nibbled on a piece of bread in the poke the woman had given her.

There was nothing for her to step on to get up on Old Joe, so she led him downriver, plodding along still tired and discouraged that she could not do anything for Sheba.

Joshua would be crushed when she did not bring help back, but she could not in good conscious make the man leave his family unprotected when she was sure that Sheba had already gone on to heaven.

"Please Lord, help me find the boys." Tears streaked down her dirty face, as she searched for a familiar landmark. She knew from the angle of the sun that she had been walking for hours.

Have I passed up the dugout? "Papa, where are you. Don't you love me anymore?" She felt totally abandoned, by God and her family. Gently Old Joe nudged her forward and she started walking again.

* * *

After she had walked about thirty minutes more and could barely put one foot in front of the other, she looked up to see two riders sitting on spotted ponies across the river. Her eyes grew wide with fear. They were Indians and they were watching her.

She started running, but in her exhaustion she stumbled over a rock and fell face down in the dirt.

The Indians quickly crossed the river and rode to where Anna lay in the dirt crying, unable to move. The younger of the men swung down from his pony and scooped the terrified child up in his arms, carried her to where Old Joe stood stoically munching on some grass and placed her on the mule.

He handed her the rope and they galloped back across the river without uttering a word.

Anna sat on Old Joe's back and stared open-mouthed at the departing Indians, while tears still streamed unchecked down her cheeks. She was convinced forever more that they were two 'angels unawares' that she had been hearing about in Sunday school all her life.

She seemed to be revitalized from her encounter with the men and urged Old Joe forward with renewed faith that she would find her way back to the boys.

The sun was high overhead, but she knew that all she had to do was follow the river downstream and she would find the dugout where Joshua and Jeremiah waited for her.

About thirty minutes later, she saw a tree weaving back and forth. Suddenly she realized that it wasn't a tree at all, but Joshua standing on top of the dugout waving his arms at her.

She urged the mule forward at a faster clip and began shouting. "I brought food, Josh. I brought food."

When she reached the dugout, she quickly slid from the back of the mule. Jeremiah came out of the cave-like structure crying and holding his arms up to her.

"What's wrong buba?" She sank to the ground exhausted and gathered her brother in her arms. She kissed his wet cheeks and wiped at his dirt-streaked face with her equally dirty dress.

"He's hungry. Soups gone. Just keeps crying." Joshua looked at the toddler disgustedly. "Told him you'd feed us. He wouldn't hush."

Joshua walked to where Old Joe was happily munching on some dry grass and quickly began to hobble him as if it was a perfectly normal chore that he was expected to do every day.

"I'm sorry buba. I got back as soon as I could." Tears were forming in her eyes and threatening to spill over when suddenly she thought about the provisions she had brought with her and immediately brightened.

"But I have food. I met a family and they gave me food." She hurried to the mule and retrieved the poke of meat and vegetables the woman had given her. There was even a jar of homemade prickly pear jelly and some oatmeal cookies. The children had not had such a treat in a month.

Anna pulled out a piece of meat for each of them along with a raw wrinkled potato. They snapped off the white roots, which were beginning to protrude from the potatoes, sat at the mouth of the dugout and happily munched on the stark fare as if it were a banquet.

Between bites, Anna told them about the family she had encountered. Joshua wanted to know everything she could tell him about the two boys in the family.

Jeremiah sat in her lap and held to her skirt with one hand, while he stuffed food into his mouth with the other.

When they had exhausted the tale of the family, she told them about the two Indians who had found her.

"I think they were angels." She confided, a very serious expression on her face.

"Anna! Why didn't you bring them back to help mama?" Joshua looked at her accusingly. "Why didn't the man come? I tried to get water and soup down her. She just wouldn't eat or drink. I couldn't get her mouth open. I tried to pour it into her. Honest I did Anna."

"I'll go check on her." Anna got up and solemnly walked into the dugout. She had been dreading this moment.

She walked over to where Sheba lay on the blankets they had used to pull her into the cave. She felt for the pulse in her neck. There was no beat there and she felt cold and unresponsive.

Joshua had piled blankets on top of her to try and warm his mother's lifeless body. Anna pulled the blanket back and the sight made her immediately retch. She scrambled to the opening and lost the rest of the contents of her stomach, while the boys stood and watched open mouthed.

"Are you sick?" Joshua looked at his cousin curiously. "Was mama all right? I tried to warm her up? She was really cold."

When she finally stopped gagging, Anna looked up at Joshua with a grief stricken face. Thinking it was true was an entirely different thing then the reality of seeing someone who had been dead for many days. Outside of the outlaw Zeke, which Anna was not really sure if he was dead or not, Anna had never seen a dead body before. And she had certainly never seen anyone who had begun to decay.

"Josh," she said sorrowfully. "Your mama has gone onto heaven and we have to bury her." She looked around at the hard ground. "I don't know how, but we have to do it."

Tears were streaming down his face. In his heart he had known his mama was no longer with them, but it was a hard reality to face for a three year old.

"Can we have a fu'nal?"

"Of course we can. We'll read the Bible and everything." She looked around some more. "I sure don't know how we are going to dig a grave."

Joshua carried water from the river and Anna cleaned Sheba up as best she could, dry heaves wracking her small body all the while. Then she rolled Sheba in the blanket she was laying on and Joshua helped her tug their precious burden out of the dugout and over to a small tree.

Sheba had lost so much weight during their month of depravation that she did not weigh much more than Anna. All three children found sharp stones and began digging in the hard dirt, while their tears wet the dry earth.

Suddenly Joshua looked up from his task and stared wide eyed behind Anna. She looked behind her and her sad dirty tear streaked face blossomed into a smile of welcome.

Anna's black, dirt caked hair, wet with perspiration, was plastered to her head and face, as she looked into the dark eyes of her 'two angels'. The two Indians were standing directly behind her.

Without hesitation she looked at them and asked, "Can you help us? My aunt has died and we can't dig the hole." She motioned to where they had been scratching at the earth with the stones and over to the blanket wrapped body.

The two men motioned for the children to go into the dugout and wait. Without a sound, Anna took the hands of the boys and walked solemnly toward the dugout. When she looked back, she saw the younger of the men retrieve what looked like a hatchet from his pony.

The children huddled together in the dugout for what seemed like a very long time.

Finally the younger of the men came to the opening and motioned for them to come out. Anna picked up Sheba's well-worn Bible and followed by the boys, she walked to where a small mound of dirt had become the resting place for her beloved aunt.

Anna solemnly read the Twenty-third Psalm, which she knew was a favorite of Sheba's and then the children, sang Jesus Loves Me. The men stood behind the children quietly paying their respects, as much to the courageous children as the woman lying in the grave.

"Bye, bye mama," Joshua said, tears streaming down his cheeks and wetting the dirty shirt he had worn since they had left camp. "I'll see you in heaven." Anna took both boys in her arms and hugged them tight.

The Indians left the children to their mourning, but that evening just before dusk the younger of the two reappeared with a brace of rabbits, cleaned and ready for the pot.

Anna thanked him and sent the boys for kindling so she could get the rabbits in the pot to cook over night. They would have a feast the next morning.

* * *

When they awoke the next day, they found the rains had finally come to Oklahoma Territory. It was getting colder and the wind howled fiercely outside the dugout. Their cook fire kept them warm and they had the hot nourishing rabbit to eat. They were subdued, but not uncomfortable in their cave-like structure.

"Anna the kindling is about gone. We walked until we could barely see the dugout. Over there is what is left." Joshua pointed at the small pile of sticks beside the entrance.

"Yes. It's time to move on; we have to get to the Arkansas River. Tomorrow morning we will leave, even if it is still raining. We will have to fill all the flasks. Miss Beth gave us cooked meat. We have that and the vegetables. There is some bread left, but it is beginning to look a bit green. There is nothing to keep us here. I think it would be very hard for papa to find us in the dugout, so we have to keep moving east."

"They probably think we are dead. I'll bet they quit looking." Joshua's lower lip protruded so low it nearly touched his chin. Anna jumped up and threw herself on him and began to pummel him with her small fists.

"Take it back, Josh. You take it back. Papa will never give up looking for us. Don't you ever say that again." Josh lay on the floor of the dugout protecting his face with his hands, until Anna lay back on the floor beside him, her anger spent.

"I'm sorry Josh. Did I hurt you?" She looked him over solicitously, ashamed of her outburst.

"Naw, I'm okay. I shouldn't have said it."

Early the next morning, the children solemnly packed what remained of their supplies, including the rest of the rabbits. The rain had become little more than a mist, but the air was cold.

Anna fashioned a cross with two of the pieces of kindling, tying them together with a bit of twine and Joshua put it in the ground over his mother's grave. Anna said a short prayer and they were ready to leave.

She tied the supplies to Joshua's mule and after setting Jeremiah on Old Joe and helping Joshua on the other mule, she climbed up behind Jeremiah. The children fashioned their blankets over them for what protection they could manage and started downstream, along the river, headed in an easterly direction. If they went far enough and stayed close to the river, they would reach the Arkansas.

Chapter Fifty-Two

It was the day before Thanksgiving when John reached one of the branches off the Little Canadian and found an unexpected surprise. The wagon he saw sitting beside the dry stream looked like the one he had seen in Fort Smith, but it was hard to tell because nearly all of the wagons transporting settlers to Indian Territory and across the plains looked much the same.

He watched cautiously from the protection of a grove of trees for any sign of movement in the camp. The ponies were becoming restless when after an hour he tied them to a tree and stealthily approached the wagon. The stones surrounding what had been a cook fire were cold and the camp appeared deserted.

Guardedly he crept up to the back of the wagon. Discarded on its side lay the chair Dr. Joseph had described as having belonged to the one called Sheba. Then he knew that he was in the right camp. He peered into the dark interior, but was unable to make out any movement. He pulled himself stealthily up on the platform and entered with his knife drawn. The smell almost overwhelmed him. A body lay face down in the middle of the wagon. It was covered with maggots and would be impossible to identify. From the clothes, he determined it was a man and not one of those he sought.

He forced himself to search the entire wagon, but did not find any sign of either the disabled woman or the three children. Climbing back outside, he shot his gun into the air three times. It was the signal all four of the searchers used to alert the others that they had found something significant. Joseph should be able to hear the sound over the unobstructed land.

The signal given he began to search the surrounding area for any sign of the children, the woman, or missing animals. Everything was gone and from the looks of things had been for quite some time.

Joseph had been traveling parallel to John's search area and heard the faint sound of the three shots. He knew approximately where John would be, so quickly rode east to join him. When he arrived, he found John squatting on the ground, looking for any sign of the missing children.

The young Indian boy had spotted horses hooves circling the camp before they headed north, but he considered that to be more likely one of the abductors than anyone trying to escape. Reluctantly, he searched for any sign of graves, not wanting to miss anything.

"It looks like they went that way." John informed Joseph, pointing toward the south. "The trail is very faint, but looks like maybe two mules carrying heavy loads."

Joseph looked around, but would have to take the boy's words as fact, because his tracking know-how was only the little he had picked up from the boy and his limited hunting experience.

They found ample evidence the children had been there, a toy of Jeremiah's in the wagon, discarded cooking utensils and bits of clothing that Joseph recognized.

"All right, John. If the kids got away on the mules and it looks like they might have. I don't even want to think how that man in the wagon was killed; I can only hope it was in a fight with one of his cohorts," Joseph added softly, shaking his head. He shook off the depression that came over him when he found himself face-to-face with the possibility one of the children had actually had to kill someone to get away.

He took a deep breath and continued. "We can't miss them!" His expression had turned almost fierce. "And we have to let the others know the direction we think they have gone.

"Since you are better at tracking, if you will begin crisscrossing the area south of here all the way to the Canadian River, I'll ride back to Tecumseh and send a wire to Chandler for Donald and Ben and leave word at Tecumseh for Ben and Daniel.

"Ben will be traveling between both towns; so will check both places for messages every time he passes through. They will be checking in at the telegraph offices whenever they get near the towns while they are hunting.

"We need to get everyone looking in this direction. Cover the area as well as you can. I'll meet you south of here on the Canadian. When I get there, I'll wait for you to find me."

John agreed it was the best plan. They quickly buried the dead man after Joseph briefly examined his decaying body for the cause of death. As soon as they had finished and washed in the meager water in the stream, they parted.

Joseph rode north to Tecumseh to send the wires and John watching for sign as he rode south.

* * *

Joseph got to Tecumseh after dark and had to get the telegrapher up to send the messages. He found a room in a boarding house for the night but was headed south at first light the next morning.

* * *

John did not stop until it was too dark to see and he was afraid he would miss them or some sign of them. A layer of dust had covered most of their tracks, but he picked up some sign every few miles that made him feel he was still on the right track.

He continued to crisscross the area so he would not miss anything. It was not until the next afternoon that he reached the river. He studied the area carefully, trying to determine, which way they had gone, but could not pick up any sign of the mules or children.

He started east, the most likely direction for them to go if they were trying to get back to Arkansas. John dismounted and led both ponies, the one that carried his supplies and the one he had been riding. He wanted to make sure he did not miss any sign.

* * *

At dusk when he could no longer see well enough to locate sign if it was there, John stopped and looked across the river. He studied the current and tried to gauge the depth.   Surely it was not possible that three small children and a woman unable to walk had crossed that river, even if they were on mules.

"Little Blossom," he whispered. "Where are you my brave little friend?"

* * *

The next day he rode another day's journey east without spotting even the remotest sign that mules or children had traveled that way. After spending a restless night, he turned back to the west and followed the river in that direction.

When he grew near the place where he had started, he spotted a campfire. He was relieved to see that it was Dr. Joseph and he had hot coffee on a flat stone and a roasted rabbit on a spit over the fire. It was a good greeting to the hungry and tired twelve-year-old.

"Any sign of them?" Joseph stood when he heard the ponies approach.

"No. I don't believe they went that way. Maybe she got turned around and went west."

Joseph shook his head. "It is possible of course. I have worked with her on directions a lot and Sheba would have instructed her if she were able. We can't afford to miss them though, by making conjectures that might be wrong." He looked desperate and weary.

"She is so small, how will she ever manage under such odds?"

"But she is bright and resourceful. You have said so yourself many times as we have searched. I think she will not give up no matter what." John turned toward the south and silently gazed across the river.

"What are you thinking? Surely you don't think they could cross the river?" Joseph's eyes followed the boys. The thought of his little Anna trying to get Sheba and the boys across that river made his skin crawl. *Surely she would not do that.*

"The mules could swim. It isn't impossible that she did attempt to cross. I think we should go back up stream and one of us should cross the river and look on that side, while the other goes inward maybe a quarter of a mile, following the river downstream.

"I have already been along the riverbank and have not seen anything. If either of us find anything, anything at all that would give us a direction to search then we fire three shots and get back together." He looked at Joseph as the man obviously was mulling over the plan.

"Okay, we'll do it. Which way do you want to go? Daniel and Ben should catch up with us in a few days. It might take a little longer for Donald. I told them to spread out and crisscross the area between the Little Canadian and the Canadian."

"I will go west and cross the river whenever I find a place suitable for crossing. When the rains start it will be more difficult to cross." He glanced at the clouds moving in from the west.

Chapter Fifty-Three

The next morning as the sun barely peeped over the horizon in the east, John started west and Joseph turned his horses north. Joseph rode until he gauged himself about a quarter-mile from the river and then headed east.

John rode slowly west looking for sign and a way across the river. The ponies were shorter than the horses, but should be able to swim if he put in at an area where the river was not flowing so swiftly.

* * *

Just before dusk, he spotted a settler's lean-to and a cabin going up across the river. He decided it was time to get to the other side, so he took the ponies reigns and led them into the river. Patch did not hesitate, but the one called Brownie balked when he came to the edge of the water.

John had to work patiently to coax the reluctant pony into the water and to move forward.

He led them out as far as he could walk and then swam beside them, encouraging them with soft Cherokee words and sounds. The current carried them downstream about an eighth of a mile, but finally they made it to the other bank and struggled up onto dry land.

John lay on his back, still holding to the ponies reigns, while they nuzzled his shoulder, as if to say, "Come on, it's time to go." When John caught his breath from the strenuous swim, he decided to wait until daylight to backtrack to where he had spotted the settlers.

They might not take kindly to having an Indian come into their camp after dark. Even a boy could startle them into shooting first and checking later to find out if he was friend or foe.

* * *

As soon as it was light, John headed for the settler's camp. He approached cautiously, not wanting to get himself shot while he was seeking information.

When he got close enough to see people stirring, he called out, to let them know he was approaching their camp.

"Hello, I'm looking for some friends and wondered if you might have seen them."

The man moved to his gun, but when he saw that it was just a boy he held the gun loosely in his hand. Still he instructed his family to go inside and stay until he told them it was all right to come out. He stood in front of the lean-to as the Indian boy rode up to him.

John dismounted slowly, leaving his own gun in his bedroll. "My friends and I are looking for some lost children."

At the mention of friends, the settler looked around cautiously. "Haven't seen any children, how'd they get lost?"

"They were abducted in Fort Smith. We tracked them to a small stream off the Little Canadian, but we think they must have come this way.

"Dr. Warren, Anna's father, is searching on the other side of the Canadian and I crossed over to see if they might by some miracle have gotten across to this side.

"Joshua's father and another friend of the family are hunting for them also and they might show up here."

The settler turned as he heard the rustling of his wife coming up behind him.

"He said the girl's father was a doctor. She told us she had been abducted, we just didn't believe her." John did not miss the woman's whispered words.

"I told you to stay in the lean-to," he said turning slightly but keeping his eye on the boy.

"Please, if you have seen the children or know where they are, we have been searching for them since the middle of September.

"Anna is a young girl about six and has black hair and huge hazel eyes. She is about this tall." He held his arm up about chest high.

"How do I know you aren't one of her abductors?" The man asked suspiciously. "She weren't no Indian girl."

"No. Anna is not Indian. I am just trying to help her father find her and the other children. She is white; she comes from Arkansas.

"Anna, her cousin, and little brother were abducted along with her aunt, while the children were visiting Fort Smith with their family. Her aunt is a light skinned woman of color, who can't walk. Anna's father is a doctor.

"We found the camp where they had been held. One of her abductors was there, but he was dead. There is no telling how many of them there were, but we believe there was at least two.

"If you will shoot your gun in the air three times, her father will come if he is still within the sound of it. He is on the other side traveling east, but sound carries pretty far out here."

"How do I know that's not a sign to a group of renegades to ride in." The man looked at him suspiciously.

"Oh for heaven sake, Carl, can't you see he is just trying to find the child?" She pushed herself around her husband.

"We haven't seen any of them but Anna. She was here—my, it's been at least a month and a half ago. Anna told us she and her kin had been abducted, but we didn't believe her." The woman looked sorrowful.

"I know she was feeding others. We gave her a sack of food and my husband took her back to her camp.

"She was a polite little thing. She offered to help me clean up after breakfast, even wanted to wash the big skillet. For all the dirt and raggedy clothes, I knowed she was from educated folk, from her speech." She looked up at her husband expectantly.

"Did you see the others he described?"

Her husband looked down at the ground, shame written across his face. "I didn't take her all the way back. She said she knew where she was and I was afraid to leave you and the children alone any longer.

"She had told us so many different stories; I didn't know what I would be getting into in her camp. I left her beside the river at dark and made my way back home. I hated to leave her," he defended himself. "But I couldn't leave you and the kids unprotected. She said she knew where she was," he added weakly.

"How far down river did you go?" John turned to the man excitedly. This was the first real proof they had that Anna was still alive, or at least had been alive and had made it all the way to the Canadian River. *And had actually crossed it*, he thought with awe. It was too much to just be a coincidence. It had to be her.

"We left right after breakfast, she was bent on leaving. We traveled 'til dark. There was a full moon or I would never have been able to get back home myself. It took me till near daybreak to get back here."

A little girl about Anna's age peeped around her mother's skirts. "Anna said she lived in a dugout; back a ways from the river. Said her aunt, cousin and brother were there waiting for her to get back."

Another head popped out from behind their mother. "Are you a real Indian?"

"Yes, I really am." John chuckled, as the boy's eyes grew large. "I am Cherokee. My people came from the great mountains to the East." He turned to the man and woman.

"Thank you for helping us. Her family will be grateful."

"She was on a mule. She called him Old something-or-other. Before she came, a man came along looking for a stolen mule. That's another reason it was hard to believe her tale—thought she might have stolen it.

"If we had knowed she really was abducted, we would have got the others and kept them here with us. First she told me she got lost berry picking, then she told us that wild tale of being abducted and we just thought she was making it all up. I am as sorry as I can be; if there is anything I can do, just let me know.

"We're good Christian people and we would not have just abandoned them, if we had known their need."

"The help you gave them is appreciated and this information is most welcome. If you would fire your gun in the air three times for Dr. Warren, it would be helpful.

"Your shotgun will be louder than my pistol and maybe Joseph will hear and cross the river. Thanks for all your help. We appreciate you giving her supplies.

"That could make the difference in finding them alive or dead." He quickly remounted and rode swiftly downstream.

He was relieved to hear the three shots fired in succession, before he was out of sight of the camp.

* * *

Every hour or two he stopped to fire his gun three times, hoping Joseph was near enough to hear and join him on this side of the river.

* * *

Before nightfall he found where she had stopped for the night. He began to ride south about a quarter mile, crisscrossing back and forth from the river to about the same distance south. When he could no longer see, he stopped and waited for day to break, if they were in a dugout anywhere near the river, he would find them.

As soon as Joseph heard the gunshots, he turned and headed back upriver.

He had not gone far before he saw two Native Americans, who were watering their ponies on the south bank. He attempted to call to them across the river and ask them if they had seen Sheba or the children. They did not seem to understand what he was yelling at them.

They looked at him quizzically and then turned and continued in an easterly direction along the south bank. *Well, it's unlikely they have come across the children.*

Yet he was sorry he could not question them. If John had been with him, he might have been able to communicate with them.

* * *

It was growing dark and he waited until morning to cross over to the south side, before he continued west staying close to the banks of the Canadian.

* * *

John finally rode across a dugout about mid-morning. He looked around cautiously. The unshod hooves of ponies were evident nearby. Spotting the grave with its simple cross, he nearly cried, in his fear they had come to late to save the children. On closer inspection, he found moccasin tracks as well as the tracks made by small bare feet around the grave.

"Yes!" His shout echoed over the river. The tracks were three different sizes. He was certain that the grave did not hold the small bodies of the children.

He went into the dugout and made a thorough search. They had cleaned their area well, but signs still remained of barefoot children and a cold campfire, surrounded by rabbit bones.

There was no way to tell who lay in the grave, or how they had managed to dig it in the hard soil, but more than likely it was the one called Sheba. There was some sign a hatchet had been used. If it was the woman in the grave, the children were now alone, unless the ones belonging to the moccasin tracks had taken them.

They could be friendly Choctaw or even Chickasaw. He looked around and judged himself to be approximately at the boundary of the two nations. Then again they could be renegades from those or other tribes.

John scoured the area for tracks and finally picked up tracks from the two mules headed downstream not far from the bank. But he also found sign that the unshod ponies had gone the same direction. He signaled with his gun again and sat down with some dried meat to wait for Joseph to catch up with him.

The ponies needed a rest. He had been pushing them hard for the past couple months.

* * *

"Are they with you?" Joseph called urging his horse along swiftly as he spotted John. He pulled up beside the boy and quickly dismounted.

Spotting the dugout, he ran to it and ducked down to enter the dark dirt structure. Not seeing anyone inside he retreated to where John stood holding his horses.

"Where are they? Have you seen them?"

"No, I have not seen them, but others have." John related what the settlers had told him and how he had found the spot where Anna had slept under the bush.

He showed Joseph the grave and told him whom he thought lay beneath the earth, showing him the bare footprints of the children. Then he told him about the moccasin and unshod pony tracks he had spotted. Joseph listened attentively, as John told him everything.

"Do you think the Indians that were here are friendly?"

"There is no way to know?" His response was given sadly and reluctantly. "But the children had rabbits to eat and I think it unlikely that Anna caught them, no matter how resourceful she is.

"The settlers told me what they gave Anna and they didn't mention rabbits. I think the People might have been feeding the children."

Chapter Fifty-Four

After running into Donald at Chandler, Ben began questioning everyone he met about Carl and Zeke, and finally he got lucky close to the end of November.

His family had been missing over two months. He rode into a camp along the trail one night just at dusk. The men around the fire eyed him suspiciously, their hands hovering over their guns. Cautiously he slipped off his horse with his hands staying in plain sight.

"Smelled your coffee, mind if I have a cup?" He walked slowly toward the group by the fire, spotting a couple more standing in the shadows at the edge of the trees.

One of the men beckoned him forward and he walked to where the grizzly looking man sat on a log pulled close to the campfire. He was careful to hold his hands out where they could see them.

The man handed Ben a cup of coffee. Ben accepted the dirty cup without flinching, took a long drink of the strong, black liquid, which was hot enough to scald his throat all the way down.

Oh well! There shouldn't be any of the germs that Joseph is always telling us about left alive on the cup, he consoled himself as the hot liquid continued to burn his throat.

Then he squatted by the fire and told the men that he was hunting for his wife, son, niece and nephew, who had been abducted in Fort Smith over a month before.

It was the same tale he told everywhere he went. Ben asked them if they had seen anything of them, or two men named Zeke and Carl.

The youngest of the group sidled up to him importantly. "I ain't seen that lady or kids, but I know that Zeke and Carl you're asking about. That Zeke is a mean one. Shot my brother for no reason a tall. That Carl he runs with, he ain't much better."

"Where did you last see them?" Ben's interest had certainly peeked.

"There's a settlement not over a half day's ride south of here. An old fur trader has built himself a saloon of sorts there. I saw Carl there, wasn't a week past.

"Zeke weren't with him and I didn't ask about him. Think Carl frequents the place. If you hold up there, you're bound to run across him."

"I am mighty obliged to you. If it's all right with all of you," Ben looked around taking in all of the men, including the ones who had remained in the shadows. "I'd like to throw my bedroll down near your fire and then I'll head south at daybreak." The men nodded their acceptance.

This was the first real break that Ben had in his search and he found it hard to fall asleep. He knew he would never find the place he was headed in the dark, so finally he settled down to a restless sleep.

* * *

The next morning he was up with first-light and after politely accepting another cup of the worst coffee he had ever tasted, he headed south with the directions he had been given. The bitter tang of the awful brew kept him company a long way.

* * *

As soon as he could, Ben stopped and sent a telegraph for Daniel, hoping he would get it and meet him at the saloon.

* * *

After finding the makeshift saloon, he waited three days before luck shown on him. The proprietor made it plain when he first entered the rustic one-room building that if he did not drink, he could not stay.

Fortunately the owner had a ready supply of homemade sarsaparilla and Ben figured he had drunk a lifetime's supply of the non-alcoholic beverage, in the three days he was there.

On the third day, a man resembling the description and poster he had seen of Carl entered about sundown. He sidled up to the bar looking around at the sparsely populated room and ordered a whisky.

The man downed it in one swallow and put his glass down for a refill. Ben moved up to him.

"Don't think we've met. Let me buy you a drink." He looked at the owner and pushed Carl's glass toward him, motioning for him to put his drink in Carl's glass.

"I'll have my usual." The proprietor knew Ben was up to something, but didn't figure it was any of his business as long as he continued to pay for drinks.

He poured the shot glass full of sarsaparilla and poured another full of whiskey, placing the second one in front of Carl.

* * *

Ben continued to buy whiskey for Carl while he drank sarsaparilla, until Carl was in a talkative move. Talk moved from the exceptionally dry weather to the Land Runs.

"I hear some people actually moved in early to claim prize lands. I forget what they called them."

"Sooners! They called them Sooners. I sent my partner in," the man said winking. "Yep oh Zeke didn't want to go, but he did. Got a good piece of ground on a creek, we did—just what the boss ordered."

"You don't really look like a farmer to me."

"Won't catch me plowing no fields, just doing a job is all."

"Oh, you were hired to block off a piece of the stream, huh?"

"That's right. We each got a section, gave the boss a couple more than he could get for himself." He nudged Ben in the ribs. "Who's going to expect anybody to hold up on settler's land?" He laughed uproariously and drank another whiskey.

"I'll bet it is close to a town site too." Ben lifted his glass of sarsaparilla in a salute, encouraging the man to continue.

The man laughed and winked his acknowledgement, enjoying the company of this stranger, who seemed willing to buy drinks all night.

"Ben smiled at him conspiratorially. "Guess you left Zeke back on the spread, to plow and such."

"Thet shiftless skunk never plowed a furrow in his life, less it was to bury his mother." The disgust in Carl's voice was evident. That black-hearted devil deserved what he got. Should have shot him for I left the first time." Carl's gaze was glassy, "Probably attached that woman and girl as soon as I was out of sight."

Ben's face flashed red with anger at the startling statement. *If Zeke is dead and Carl is hanging around here, Sheba and the children must be close—if they are still alive, anyway.* He shook his head as if to clear it. *I can't think like that. They are still alive and this wretched piece of trash knows where they are.*

He relaxed his stance, giving his anger and anguish time to clear before he spoke again.

"Had a woman and girl with you did you?" He was careful not to add any information to the man's story, but it took every ounce of restraint he could muster not to demand to know where the boys were.

"Yea. She was crippled. Couldn't defend herself. Kid was kind of cute. Did most of the work. I told him to leave them alone, but knowed he wouldn't."

"Your wife and child?" Ben could barely suppress the desire to flatten the man where he stood.

"Naw. Just some folk unlucky enough to be in the wagon we took. We knew the kids would be there. Kids make good hostages. Didn't know about that crippled gal though."

"Where are the woman and children now?" Ben put his arm around the man's shoulders and began moving toward the door.

Suddenly the man's whisky fogged brain registered that his new benefactor was questioning him about the woman and kids. A warning signal went off somewhere in his befuddled brain, as he attempted to recall what he had admitted doing.

"Don' know nothing bout no woman and children." Sullenly he tried to pull away from the man who had a firm grip on his shoulder and was steering him to the door.

Before he knew it there was another man on the other side of him and they were moving him forward. The other man took a firm grip on his arm and they practically dragged him outside and around to the side of the building where the only light was the little shining from the moon.

The man's alcohol drugged mind was quickly clearing as adrenalin surged through his system. He knew he had said too much, but could not remember exactly just what he had said.

"I want to know everything you know about the whereabouts of that woman and the three children." While Ben interrogated him, Daniel leaned his arm firmly against the man's throat, letting up just enough to allow him to answer.

"We can have this little talk here, or with the marshal. Which would you prefer?" Ben had not raised his voice, but the deadly calm was much more intimidating than if he had been shouting.

"What do you want to know?" Carl knew he did not have a chance against the man who stood a good six inches above him and the shorter but stocky younger man.

"We want to know where our family is and what condition they are in." Ben's voice was still low, but had a deadly quality to it.

"I don't know where they are and that's God's own truth. I went back to camp and found Zeke half dead in the wagon and the woman and the kids were all gone. I don't know what happened to them. I looked around, but couldn't tell you which direction they went from there.

"The mules were gone, so I figured they took both of the mules we hadn't sold yet. I shot Zeke—put him out of his misery and left him there, don't know what happened to the woman and kids. They were just gone."

"Why did you shoot Zeke?" Ben was curious at this turn of events.

"Found him cut pretty bad with his pants down in the wagon where the woman had been. Decided he didn't deserve to live. That little girl probably got them all out of there. She was a smart little thing. Did most of the cooking herself and her no bigger than a minute."

Ben got the directions to the camp and then both of them stepped back and let the man sink to his knees. "We ought to string you up, but probably owe you a medal for shooting your partner," Ben said disgustedly. They left him there, but sent word to the marshal where he was holed up.

They sent telegraph messages to Chandler and Tecumseh for the others about what they had learned from Carl. Then they began working their way toward the location of the camp by continuing to crisscross the county. They planned to concentrate their search in County B. There was still no telling where they had gone when they left the camp, so they would have to continue to conduct a wide search.

* * *

It was getting dark and Daniel pulled alongside Ben, so they could discuss what to do next.

"Ben, why don't you head for the camp? I can go on to Tecumseh and send a wire to Joseph and Donald to meet us there. Since we know the children have already left the camp, keep a lookout along the way, because we don't know which direction they went.

"I should catch up with you within a couple days." Daniel knew Ben was raring to go. This was the first concrete news they had gotten from anyone.

"Thanks Daniel. I'll meet you at the camp and see if I can find any sign they might have left. Wish we had John with us. He seems to be pretty good picking up sign." Ben mounted his horse and following the stars rode another hour before making camp for the night.

Chapter Fifty-Five

Daniel received Joseph's telegraph message when he rode into Tecumseh to send his own messages. He sent a message to Donald just in case Joseph had not notified him and another to Hamilton, to let him know the abductors had been found, but not Sheba or the children.

He would leave it up to him whether or not to notify Hannah. They really did not have anything firm about the children's whereabouts and he was not sure if the news he did have would make her feel better or worse.

* * *

Ben reached the campsite where the wagon stood--a lone sentinel on the bleak landscape, in a day and a half.

The fresh grave drew his attention like a magnet. He knew the grave was recently dug. Carl had not said anything about burying his partner and this grave looked too fresh to have been there very long. He spent the day and a half that he waited for Daniel searching the area for any clue of where his family had gone, or been taken.

* * *

As soon as the messages were sent, Daniel headed south to join Ben. He switched back and forth between his horses, in order to rest them as much as possible.

* * *

It took him a day and a half to find the camp. Joseph's message was terse, only stating that the children had been at the campsite on the small tributary off Little River and John had picked up their trail heading south toward the Canadian River.

Joseph's message instructed them to head due south until they reached the Canadian River and they would meet them there. He had not mentioned finding anyone dead, or burying anyone.

Daniel related Joseph's message to Ben before he even dismounted. They decided the grave was probably Zeke's, because they found the blood in the wagon and no sign of the outlaw's body.

Besides the grave was unmarked and they knew that if Joseph had buried Sheba or one of the children some sort of marking would have been placed there.

After eating a quick bite, they again headed south.

* * *

It was midday of the following day when they reached the Canadian. There wasn't any sign of Joseph or the young Indian boy John.

Daniel rode upstream and Ben rode downstream looking for any sign they had been there and left any kind of message. Daniel had not ridden far, before he found a white handkerchief waving at him like a flag of surrender. It was tied to a tall branch stuck into the soft earth near the river.

He quickly retrieved it and discovered it was one of Joseph's. Hannah had embroidered his initials in one corner of the smudged white handkerchief. The message, made with a stick and some kind of berry juice, instructed them to cross the river and head east. At the bottom of the message it stated, "Anna has been spotted."

Daniel whirled his horse around and headed back down stream after firing off three shots.

He met Ben galloping toward him and quickly rode along side him and handed him the note. It had been raining off and on for the past few weeks and the Canadian was running fast. He didn't see how the children had gotten across this river, but he figured as dry as it had been earlier, the river would have been shallower then and not as swift as it was running now.

Daniel replanted the message for Donald and then Daniel and Joseph urged their horses into the water. They swam the horses across from the north bank. Letting them drift with the current downstream, they angled across to the south bank.

The note had instructed them to head east, so they figured they might as well get a head start in the water. They let the current help them instead of wearing the horses out fighting the strong current.

The horses plowed their way up the bank on the south side of the river about a quarter-mile downstream from where they had begun. They had not ridden far, before Daniel spotted the grave and then the dugout.

Finding the grave here, they knew there was little chance that it wasn't the resting place for one of their loved ones. They again stood over a grave, but this time they bowed their heads.

Daniel, hat in hand, began to pray. "Dear Lord, I don't even know how to make this plea, because I love everyone of those children and Sheba as much as I do my own brothers and sisters.

"And Lord, You know that Ben is seeking his wife and son. But dear Lord, if you would just do me the favor of sparing the babies, I'd be eternally grateful."

The grave was larger than would have had to be dug for a small child. They were also aware that it was unlikely that Sheba with her limited physical mobility had survived the two months of captivity and the harrowing escape from their abductors.

If her body didn't lie back at the wagon campsite, it surely lay here along the Canadian River. The simple cross showed that whoever lay there had been sent off with love and prayers.

Ben fell to his knees and cried great wracking tears of grief and shame. There was little hope that someone very dear to him didn't lie in the grave and it was probably his wife.

The wife that he had abandoned and now it was doubtful he would ever be able to ask her forgiveness and make up for the heartache he had caused her the past four years.   The wife he had left because he was ashamed to be married to a woman of color. The wife his father had told him was too good for him and he had been right.

* * *

After paying their respects at the grave, they quickly remounted the still wet horses and started following the river east. They rode hard because their goal now was to catch up with Joseph and John and join in the search along the Canadian.

* * *

Two days after leaving the dugout, they saw riders ahead of them, watering their horses at the river.

* * *

Donald pulled into Chandler on the seventh of December. He went to the telegraph office as soon as he reached town, because he planned to keep going to the east until nightfall.

There were two telegraph messages waiting for him, one from Daniel, about the information they had obtained from Carl and the other from Joseph, telling him they were on the trail of the children and to head south to the Canadian River and then follow it toward the Arkansas.

The Canadian was about twenty-eight miles due south of Chandler. It was all open country, because his route would take him east of Tecumseh.

He figured that Ben and Daniel would probably get their messages in that new frontier town, so although he was much further north, he would hit the Canadian a little east of where they would.

Donald started out at once.

* * *

Since he was further east, he did not pass through either the camp where the wagon sat, or the site where the dugout and grave rested along the river.

He made good time and reached the Canadian in three days. Donald immediately crossed and headed east along the south bank. On December twelfth, nineteen hundred and one, he saw men on horseback ahead of him and knew he had rejoined the hunt.

* * *

John was leading the search by staying along the riverbank and checking for any sign of the mules. The rains had obliterated much of the tracks he had been able to follow earlier, but he looked for crushed grass, broken brush and signs of their campfire.

The other men fanned out a quarter mile apart. They would be able to hear any shots and sporadically they caught site of one another in a flat land area, although they were beginning to get into the rolling hills of east Oklahoma.

Chapter Fifty-Six

The children had been traveling for two months. It
had rained off and on, sometimes heavy and the wind, which
was always strong, occasionally blew so hard it was hard for
them to stay on the backs of the mules.

Some days they barely made a half-mile and a couple
times they were so tired that they got turned around and
retraced their steps heading west instead of east.

Cold and tired, they barely had strength to continue
to urge the mules or themselves forward at all. The food
they had brought with them and that they had gotten from the
settler and his family was long gone, but each night when
they stopped one of Anna's 'angels' would show up with a
rabbit, piece of venison or some kind of fowl.

Anna cooked it over their campfire and after they ate
their fill, she wrapped what was left for their breakfast the
next day. Sometimes there would be bread and at least once
a week a container made of animal skin and full of sweet
milk would be propped against a stone near where Anna
slept one arm around each of the boys.

Anna no longer could muster the strength needed to
wash the tin pans in the river, so they ate with their fingers

directly from whatever food had been brought to them. They had begun to stop earlier and earlier in the day from sheer exhaustion and hunger.

They were making little progress in their quest to get to the Arkansas River, which meant the same as getting home to the children. Anna knew if the Indians had not been bringing them food each night they would all three have died of starvation.

"Co'd Anna. I'm co'd." Jeremiah stood beside the fire wrapped in a blanket, with tears streaming down his dirty face. His blond hair was so dirty that it looked brown instead of its natural golden blond.

Anna pulled him onto her lap. "I know buba. I'm cold too." She was unable to stop the chattering of her teeth. She held the toddler close to her body and wrapped the blanket around both of them. Joshua sat across from them, listless and shaking.

"I don't know how long we have been out here, seems like we would be getting close to the Arkansas, pretty soon." Anna noticed Joshua's tears and motioned for him to sit beside her.

"Are you hurting Josh? The energy it took to ask the question was almost more than the child could manage.

"I'm not hurting. It's just this trip is too long. Anna how long have we been gone from the dugout? Do you know how to get back to the dugout? You think we could go back?" he asked hopefully. "It was warm in the dugout." His little face showed his despair, as he squatted by the fire, his arms hanging between his legs and his head drooping.

"I know Josh, but we have to keep going or we will never get home. And besides it would be cold there now too.

"I don't remember how long we have been gone, but it has been a very long time. If we can just keep going, we will get to the Arkansas and then we can follow it on into Fort Smith. Even if our folks aren't there, we will be able to get word to them. There are lawmen in Fort Smith. They will help us."

She looked at her cousin until he lifted his head and looked up at her. "We have to get home, Josh. We have to. And the only way we can do that is to keep going."

"But what if your angels stop feeding us? We'll starve before we get there."

"God won't let that happen. Why would they just abandon us after staying so close all this time?" Her argument sounded reasonable to her, but she could not imagine what would happen to them if the Indians did not continue to supply them with nourishment.

God, I know You have sent them to us. Thank you, dear Lord. Mama and papa didn't come. Why Lord? Why didn't papa come for us? Doesn't papa love us anymore?

* * *

The next day they saw a small river coming in to the big river they were following on the north bank. Joshua saw it first and began shouting that they had reached the Arkansas.

"No Joshua, that is much too small to be the Arkansas. Don't you remember how big it was when you fell in?"

It was hard for him to remember anything as tired as he was all the time. He even had to study to remember mama's face. The thought caused tears to trickle down his cheeks in dirty rivulets.

Each time they stopped it was harder for the children to muster enough energy to gather wood and start a fire.

* * *

Anna's hands were chapped and cracked from the cold and Joshua had nearly fallen off his mule before she had called a halt with the sun just starting to move to her back.

Neither Anna nor Joshua had the energy to build a fire or even look for the kindling that was needed and Jeremiah lay where Anna had deposited him when she had pulled him down from Old Joe.

They huddled together under a dirty damp blanket and fell asleep.

* * *

When Anna awoke a couple hours later it was to a warm fire and a wild turkey roasting on a spit. She looked around, but Joshua was still asleep. There was no sign of anyone else, or that anyone had been there.

"My angel's have been here." She sat up and rubbed her eyes completely accepting that her "angels" had taken over when she no longer could manage. The boys woke when she stirred and looked at the fire.

"'ungy, 'ungy," Jeremiah cried crawling over to inspect the bird. He no longer seemed to have enough energy to stand on his short legs.

Anna quickly moved between him and the fire and swiftly removed the cooked bird from the spit.

She brushed a rock off and pulled pieces of the hot bird off for the baby and laid them on the rock to cool.

"It's hot Jeremiah, so you will have to wait a minute to eat it. Joshua had retrieved the slightly grungy tin pie pans they had previously used for plates and helped her tear pieces of the bird off for each of their plates.

* * *

When they had eaten their fill, Anna again wrapped what was left for the next day and the children lay back down. They slept through the night with their bellies full of the hot turkey.

* * *

For the next week as they moved continually northeast with the river, their food was not only provided but cooked and ready for them. They would find it waiting when they awoke from their restless exhausted sleep. The children had been slipped into a deep sleep as soon as they stopped.

It was becoming bitterly cold, as the northern winds and cold rains bombarded the children and mules. It seemed to the three small children they would never be warm again.

* * *

Anna spotted another river coming into the big river from the northwest. This one was larger and she thought they had reached the Arkansas.

The children shouted excitedly, bouncing up and down on the mules with renewed energy when she announced they had finally reached their goal and Fort Smith must be just around the bend. Even the mules picked up their pace as the children eagerly urged them on toward their home.

* * *

After they traveled two more days and could see nothing but the river and hills stretching out in front of them, they returned to the melancholy that had gripped them for the past week.

Still each day their food was provided and they had an abundance of water, so they continued to follow the river downstream.

Anna thought of her family and had come to the conclusion that they had gone on with their lives and had not even tried to find them. She reasoned that if they had not cared enough to come after her, they might not want her back at all.

Surely, they would have been here long ago if they were looking for us. She did know that God was still looking after them; because He had not failed to send His angels a single time they needed them.

* * *

John reached the North Fork of the Canadian River on December twentieth. The children's trail had been easy to follow, even with the rains. They had not traveled far each day, before making camp.

He had seen signs of the unshod ponies trailing them and hoped he was right about the People looking after the children.

* * *

Two days later he came across an ancient Indian and his son. After greeting them in the Cherokee tongue and not getting any response, he tried Choctaw.

He questioned them about the children. "Chipota," (young children) he asked in his limited Choctaw. The younger man confirmed through sign and the words that John was able to follow that they had been trailing the children and supplying them with food.

He informed John that Amoshuli (to have courage), Nitushi (young bear) and Hanan (small Eagle) had grown weak and they were all suffering from the weather and exhaustion.

John asked them about the grave and by what they were able to impart to him, he learned what he had already surmised for himself. It was Sheba's body that lay in the grave.

But now he was sure that the children were alive and had been cared for by the two Choctaw, who obviously had much respect for the three small children who had demonstrated great courage during their adversity.

He thanked them for their help and offered them some of the gold that Joseph had given him to use for expenses, but they declined. They explained that the children were only a half a day's journey ahead and would probably stop soon as was their custom. The People then turned back toward the west and were soon lost over a hill.

John switched to Patch and hurried the pony forward after shooting his gun in the air three times to single the others.

* * *

He reached the children's camp before dusk and found them asleep. They were bundled together tightly for warmth. John removed his bedroll and covered them with that, before building a fire.

The People he had met had presented him with two rabbits they had killed to take to the children. He soon had a spit fixed and the rabbits roasting over the campfire.

When Anna awoke, she thought she was seeing things. It was not her angel's squatting before the fire, but an Indian boy. He looked a little familiar. Before she could speak, she heard other riders coming into camp.

Chapter Fifty-Seven

John turned and looked at the bedraggled children. They were scrawny and filthy, but all three were alive.

"Little Blossom." He moved toward her offering her a piece of the rabbit, as the four men rode into camp and dismounted.

Anna sat up and stared blankly at the Indian boy who approached her with the meat offering. Her large hazel eyes dominating her dirt streaked face. Her long dark hair was caked with mud and tangled with twigs and leaves. He could not help reflecting that what had been the most beautiful hair he had ever seen; now somewhat resembled a squirrel nest. John squatted in front of her and held the rabbit to her mouth.

"Little Blossom, do you remember me? I'm John. We met in Fort Smith." Tears filled the young warrior's eyes as he looked from one child to the other. It was nothing short of a miracle that they had survived their grueling trip.

Anna stared at him without acknowledgement. "Did God send you?

"Papa didn't come." She looked so desolate and her voice was so flat that John quickly gathered her in his arms.

"Yes, Anna. I believe with all my heart that God sent us, but your papa has been hunting for you from the moment they discovered you missing."

He turned and held her up to Joseph, who had heard what she had said. Tears rolled unobstructed down his cheeks as he bundled Anna in his arms and walked to where the other two children still lay in an exhausted sleep.

Daniel and Donald took care of the horses while Ben ran to his son and gently picked the sleeping child up and hugged him close to his chest. All four men were unabashedly crying, as they assured themselves that the children were indeed all alive and although they suffered from malnutrition, exposure and were unbelievably filthy the older two appeared to not have any lasting physical effects from the ordeal.

Joseph squatted on the ground still holding the unresponsive Anna and scooped Jeremiah up with his other arm. The toddler awoke and began to cry weekly and grasped Anna's torn dress. His eyes were glazed and he seemed to be burning up with fever.

Joshua opened his eyes and looked into the matching eyes of his father and let out a terrified yell.

"It's all right Josh. He's just Uncle Ben. He's your papa." Anna soothed her cousin in a flat monotonous voice, while trying to quiet her brother.

When the boys quieted, John brought each of them food. Anna slipped her hand into his and held tight while she munched on the tasty rabbit. Every time John started to move away to retrieve something, her eyes grew large with fright and she began to tremble.

While she allowed Joseph to hold her, she remained rigid in his lap all the while watching John anxiously as he moved around the camp.

With their stomachs full the children fell to sleep huddled under the blankets their fathers lovingly tucked around them.

The four men and the boy sat around the fire discussing what action to take first. Joseph had examined all three children and then they had bathed them as well as they could with water heated from the river. The children quickly fell into an exhausted sleep holding tightly to one another.

John sat with his legs crossed on the ground beside them with Anna clutching his hand until she joined her brother and cousin in deep sleep.

"We have to get them home as soon as possible. They are malnourished and suffering from exposure, but Anna and Joshua otherwise appear to be healthy.

"Jeremiah is running a pretty high fever from the exposure and we have to get a lot of fluid down him. I mixed up herbal tea that should help, but we need to get him to a medical clinic as soon as possible. "

He nodded at John. "John told us about the Indians who were following them and bringing them meat. Anna called them 'the angels,' but she didn't know how long they had been with them.

"She obviously has taken care of the boys ever since they were abducted.

"Her birthday is today. Six years old." Upon that pronouncement he broke down in sobs. "How did a child not yet six get all three of them from that camp and keep them alive?"

"Sure and Doctor Joseph you know the answer to that. 'Twas all the prayers that have been bombarding heaven on their behalf these past three months."

"Amen to that," echoed Daniel.

Ben bowed his head into his folded hands. "Thank you Lord for looking after our children. Thank you for sending your angels to look out for them and feed them when they could no longer do it themselves. Forgive me for the way I treated my family. If you will give me the opportunity to make it up to my son, he will never have reason to be ashamed I am his earthly father." Ben prayed and cried as he looked to where his son lay asleep with his cousins.

"I thank you Lord for my little niece Anna and the summer trips that taught her how to survive. And Lord, if Sheba is looking down on us, let her know that I love her very much. I have always loved her Lord, I just hope she can forgive me for the way I treated her and our son. I promise I will use the rest of my life to make it up to him."

There was a chorus of "Amen's" when he finished praying.

"Sure and we have to decide how best to proceed. We can't ride hard with the babies, but the wee one must get quickly to care and those we left behind must be notified as soon as possible, as there is no doubt they are worried sick, especially our precious Hannah—they have suffered long enough."

"You're right Donald, those are exactly our priorities. Ben if you will hold Josh and," he looked worriedly at his sleeping daughter. "And John if you think you can hold Anna and ride one of the horses, she seems to have bonded with you.

"Daniel you go on ahead and send a wire to Hannah to catch the next train to Fort Smith and let Hamilton and

Bernice know that we have found them and Jeremiah will need immediate medical care. Then I'll bring Jeremiah as quickly as I can.

"I will have to travel fast, but still get fluid into him as we ride. Donald that will leave you with the ponies and mules and extra horses, do you think you can manage all of that?"

"Sure, and I'll just tie the buggers all together. Don't worry about me. You just get those wee ones back to Arkansas as swiftly as you can.

The next morning before the sun had even begun to peep over the eastern horizon, Daniel and Joseph left camp with Jeremiah lying limply in Joseph's left arm while he guided the horse with his right hand. They took the swiftest of the horses. Joseph looked to where Anna still slept before kicking his horse into a fast trot. He did not see her sit up and watch sorrowfully as her papa, holding Jeremiah, left her behind.

The others quickly fed Anna and Joshua and taking the children up in their arms, Ben and John rode toward Arkansas, with Donald trailing with the spare horses, mules and ponies.

The young Indian boy tried several times to engage Anna in conversation, but finally gave up and began to relate the events of the hunt to her in hopes that would reassure her that she had not been abandoned. But seeing her father ride away with Jeremiah that morning had seemed to completely crush her.

She rode with her face buried in John's chest and stoically remained silent for the entire trip to Fort Smith. When John put food in her mouth she chewed and swallowed. When he put the canteen to her mouth she drank. When they stopped to rest the horse, she clung to him fiercely. Other than that, she made no attempt to communicate or respond to her surroundings in any manner.

* * *

Daniel arrived first and sent wires to Hannah and their parents. If he knew his sister, she would be on a train heading west that very day. Then he sought Hamilton and Bernice.

Bernice immediately went to the clinic and prepared to receive the ailing toddler, while Hamilton checked to see when the next train left Little Rock and arrived in Fort Smith. They knew that Hannah would be on it and he wanted to make sure someone would be there to meet her and get her quickly to the children.

* * *

About three hours later, Joseph rode in with the baby and rode directly to the clinic. He had to stop frequently to get dribbles of water into the baby to fight the dehydration and exposure that was causing his high fever.

Chapter Fifty-Eight

It was the next morning before Ben and John arrived with the other two children, about the same time that Hannah was arriving with Carolyn and Peg from Little Rock.

Hamilton took them directly to the clinic where Joseph and Bernice were working frantically to save Jeremiah.

Hannah had been afforded celebrity status on the train from Little Rock after other passengers learned she was the mother of two of the missing children.

Hamilton had put advertisements in the papers about the children and all of the family remaining in Arkansas had been interviewed several times. The worried grandfather had felt the more people who knew about the missing children the more likely they would be found.

He had put posters up describing Sheba and the three children throughout the Fort Smith area and had followed up on every lead regardless of how remote it seemed. They had all worked tirelessly to do whatever they could to see the children safely home.

Many of the passengers confided that they had prayed daily for the safe return of the children. News spread quickly that the children had all been found alive, even though the mother of one of them had not survived.

Hamilton held Carolyn while Hannah rushed into the room where little Jeremiah lay listlessly in Bernice's arms. She was systematically spooning dribbles of sugar and salt water into his small mouth.

Hannah rushed to her son and Bernice held him up to her. She nuzzled him to her breast. Tears streamed from her eyes, as she held him close and looked around the room.

"Where are the others? Where are Anna and Joshua?"

"They just rode in. Ben has taken them to the hotel to clean them up and feed them. They are slightly malnourished and have suffered from exposure, but do not seem to be in any danger. I'll go to the hotel and check them as soon as I am sure that Jeremiah is out of danger."

"Hannah," Bernice took the child from her and began again administering the sips of the liquid. "Do you want to stay here with Jeremiah and pour the sips of water into his mouth, or go to the hotel and care for the other two?

"We can't both stay with Jeremiah when the others need care also. From what Joseph has said, Anna feels she was abandoned. Her physical needs are not as extensive as the baby's, but I am afraid her emotional needs are much more severe."

Hannah looked at Joseph, not sure what to do. She loved both of her children equally and did not think she could choose between them. It did not matter that Anna was not her birth child, she had raised her since she was seven-months-old and loved her as much as Carolyn and Jeremiah.

"Why don't you go back to the hotel and take baby Carolyn? Maybe the baby will bring her out of her stupor. Anna needs her mother now more than Jeremiah. We will take care of him and soon we will all be together again. Can you do that?" Joseph knew how difficult it would be for her to leave Jeremiah as sick as he was.

"Yes, of course I will," she said between sobs. "You will let me know if there is any change?"

"Yes, I promise."

"Good or bad," she stated staring into Joseph's eyes.

"Good or bad," he promised, as he walked her to the door, followed by Hamilton and Peg, who were also wiping tears from their eyes.

When Hannah reached the hotel, she went first to Ben's room to check on Joshua. She knew that once she got in the room with Anna, she would not want to leave her for anything.

Ben sat in a rocker, gently rocking the three year old, holding him close to his heart.

He looked up at Hannah with tears in his eyes. "Do you think he will ever forgive me for leaving him and his mother?"

She patted his shoulder as she looked down on the sleeping child, who had obviously been freshly bathed and wrapped in one of his father's large shirts. "Yes, he will. You aren't the same man that left them," she said intuitively.

"I'll be seeing about Anna, but you send for me if you need me for anything." She turned and quickly left Ben's room to go to Anna.

When she opened the door, she was startled to see an Indian boy sitting on the floor holding Anna snuggly in his arms. She was asleep. But even in her sleep, she gripped his hand. He sang to her softly in a tongue Hannah was not familiar with.

As she moved closer, she recognized John as the young Indian boy who they had met when they entered Fort

Smith, three long months ago and who had helped in the hunt for the children.

"Is she all right?" Hannah whispered as she drew closer. Anna still wore her almost shredded filthy dress. Hannah grimaced as she looked at the pitiful state of her wonderful and much loved Anna. She handed Carolyn to Peg and he followed Hamilton out of the room, before both men dissolved in tears at the sight of the bedraggled child.

"I have sent for my mother to come and bathe her. I did not know how long before you arrived. I did not think it proper for me to do it, but she will not turn loose of my hand. We rode all the way like this. Even when she ate she would not turn loose of my hand. She seems to be very apprehensive and will not speak."

"My poor baby," Anna's eyes flickered open at the sound of her mother's voice, but she did not smile; her countenance remained flat and unresponsive. Hannah thought her heart might break at the sight of her precious child. She picked her up in her arms and cuddled her close, but Anna held herself stiffly.

"Oh Anna, I prayed so hard for all of you, but especially for you because I knew my brave girl would have to take care of the boys. I've missed you so." Other than one tear that spilled over beside her nose and trickled down her cheek, Anna made no response.

There was a tentative knock on the door and John moved to answer it. Anna stiffened in Hannah's arms as he moved away from her, but did not cry out.

John ushered into the room a petite woman with long black braids. The braids were lightly streaked with silver and hung down her back to her hips.

He introduced his mother to Hannah. All the while, Anna did not take her eyes off her rescuer.

"Miz Hannah, this is my mother. She is called Raven."

"I am very pleased to meet you, Raven. This is Anna." Anna reached her hand tentatively toward John, her face revealing her apprehension.

"Perhaps you would help me bathe her, Raven? I brought some new clothes for her that I made while I waited for Joseph to bring her home. I knew how she was growing and that she would need something new on her return." This was said more to reassure Anna of her confidence that they would be found, as it was to inform the others.

"Certainly, my son tells me she is a very brave child. I will be honored to assist you. I will prepare her bath." Without hesitating, she moved to the bathing room next door and began filling the tub with warm water, gathering towels, soap and a washcloth.

"John, if you would hold Anna for a few minutes, I will get her clothes out of my trunk. I think they will fit her. They will be close anyway."

Anna went willingly into John's arms and he sat back on the floor cuddling and crooning to her, as she hid her face in his chest.

Hannah quickly retrieved the new clothes, a hairbrush and ribbons and took everything next door to the bathing room.

She had no more gotten the door closed, when she collapsed on the stool beside the tub. Great wracking sobs tore through her body as she let her sorrow out. Raven gathered her in her arms and crooned to her, as John had been doing with Anna.

"Oh Raven! How shall we ever make up to her what she has gone through? She is so distant and unresponsive. My Anna was so bubbly; she was like a refreshing spring that couldn't be extinguished. And now she doesn't even speak."

"She is a strong child. She will recover with time and love. Right now all she can think of is her sorrow, but when she realizes how hard everyone searched for her and that she was not abandoned she will recover. You must give her time."

Hannah began to wipe her eyes. "Thank you, Raven. Your encouragement has helped me. Pray for us, I am afraid we will need much prayer to get through the next months and reach her again."

"You can be assured of our prayers. My John is very fond of the little one. I was reluctant to let him go on this long hunt, but I could see how important it was to him."

"He's a good boy, my John. The children seem to be very attached to one another. He told me of the special child he had met before she was abducted.

"Their paths will cross again," she predicted, as they prepared to bathe Anna.

"Yes, yes he is. I thank you for your sacrifice in allowing him to go. His tracking ability is what made the difference." Hannah wiped her eyes and splashed water on her face to erase the evidence of her tears, before returning to the room to fetch Anna.

"Come on darling," she gently coaxed, as she leaned over to scoop Anna into her arms. "Let's get you cleaned up." Anna held tenaciously to John's hand. He gently removed her fingers while continuing to croon to her.

"When we get you all cleaned up, you can come back and see John." Anna's eyes were large with the fear she felt at being separated from the boy who had come to mean security to her, but she allowed Hannah to hold her and move to the bathing room. Her eyes remained on John, until Hannah shut the door behind her.

While Hannah held Anna on her lap, the two women stripped off the filthy ragged clothes. Hannah caught her breath as she saw Anna's scratched and bruised body. Raven looked at her with a warning glance and Hannah nodded and kept her voice light and airy as she prattled on about Carolyn and Don'ld, Anna's beloved dog, while the two women bathed her.

When they had finally scrubbed her hair and body clean the water had turned a muddy brown. Hannah stood her in the tub, while Raven poured warm water over her to rinse away all traces of dirt and soap. Anna stood stoically enduring the procedure.

Hannah toweled her dry and carefully brushed out her now clean but still very tangled hair. "Oh Anna, we may have to cut your hair short. I don't think I can get all these tangles out."

Anna actually looked at her mother for the first time. "It will be all right mama. It will grow back," she said solemnly. They were the first words she had spoken since her papa had ridden away with Jeremiah.

Hannah hugged her close and tears of joy spilled from her eyes. "Well, then. That is just what we will do." They dressed her in the new clothes and Hannah took her hand and led her back to her room where John stood waiting in front of the window. He had gone to Ben's room and cleaned himself up while they were busy with Anna.

"Well John, what do you think of our girl now?"

He smiled at the child, who was now clean and dressed in an emerald green dress with a matching ribbon in her still tangled but clean hair. Anna's tentative smile, as she looked up at the boy who had found her and the boys, was her first animated expression.

"We are going to cut her hair short, but as Anna said, it will grow back."

"No, please. I will untangle her hair."

And for the next hour, he patiently brushed and combed all the tangles out until her hair lay smooth as silk. Then with remarkable tenacity he braided the waist length hair in two long braids. When he had finished, Hannah, who had been sitting in the rocker nursing Carolyn while tears streamed unchecked down her face handed the baby to Raven and tied a large green ribbon to each braid.

"I think it is time for us to gather everyone up and go to the dinning room to eat." She looked proudly at her daughter and held out her hand to her. Anna slipped her hand cautiously into her mother's and all of them made there way to the dining room downstairs.

Chapter Fifty-Nine

Jeremiah was gradually improving under Bernice and Joseph's vigilant care. By the close of the third day, he began taking liquid on his own and no longer had to have it dribbled into his mouth around the clock by one of his indefatigable caregivers.

By the fourth day his fever had come down and was staying down. Joseph took him to the hotel the fifth day, because by then he was crying for Anna.

Everyone had taken turns visiting with him and helping with his care, even Anna, who needed the assurance that he was going to be all right.

Joshua had responded quickly to the food, rest and love showered on him by his father and the rest of the family. Hamilton enjoyed taking his grandson to the river to watch the barges and people picnicking on the shore. The three-year-old's sunny disposition quickly resurfaced, along with his sweet smile. The most prominent after effect he displayed from his traumatic experience on the plains, was his insistence upon carrying food in his hand or pocket at all times, regardless of how much he ate at a meal. He even slept with a piece of bread or a handful of dried fruit conveniently under his pillow.

He confided to his father, "I might get hungry."

Ben did not try to dissuade him from holding onto the food that he invariably secreted on his person when they left the table after each meal. He felt this would eventually become a matter of trust that food would be provided whenever it was needed.

At first they had to watch that the children did not over eat and make themselves sick. They wanted to taste everything they saw. And it was obvious that they were not sure there would be another meal, so they had to eat as much as they could hold while food was available. It took a lot of coaxing and assurance on the part of the adults to get them away from the table without eating so much they made them selves sick.

It was Anna that had them all concerned. Her eyes remained unresponsive and wary. When she was held by anyone but John, she did not relax, but held herself aloof. Her muscles were constantly tight as if ready to run at the faintest provocation. It was only when John held her that she snuggled against him and held tightly to his hand.

Joseph held her frequently and spoke of familiar things, but nothing seemed to penetrate the wall she had built around herself. He wondered what horrors she had experienced during the three months they were gone, to so completely shut out everyone except the three boys.

Hannah was no more successful in cutting through the barrier Anna had erected than Joseph was. Anna did begin to respond to Donald, after Jeremiah came home. She had loved the small man dearly when he traveled with them—before they had arrived in Arkansas. Anna would sit on his lap and eventually begun to cling to him as she did John.

She would sometimes bury her face in his rough shirt, but she would not talk of her long nightmare, even to him or John.

John spent as much time as he could with Anna and the boys, but after his long absence, his mother had many chores for him to do. She took in laundry to support her family and picking up and delivering the baskets of clothes had been a real hardship for her without John to help her.

He knew this family he had grown so close to would soon leave for their home in Little Rock. John would miss them, especially the little girl who had become so dear to him, who he called Little Blossom. The months he had spent helping this family look for the children had drawn him close to all of them. He was reluctant to see them leave.

As he approached the hotel after delivering some laundry for his mother, he met Daniel sitting in a chair on the wide porch.

"How are the children today?" he greeted him. He squatted on his haunches beside Daniel even though there was another chair on the other side of Anna's uncle.

"Joshua is doing great. Of course he is trying to eat everything in sight." Daniel chuckled as he thought about the youngster stuffing everything he could in his mouth. "He has begun to chatter to everyone within his hearing and always has food with him. He even smiles a lot. But he does not mention the time in Oklahoma Territory.

"Jeremiah is much better. He also has begun to eat whatever his little hands can grab. He has even started filling out some. Of course three months was a long time in his short life and he doesn't seem to remember anyone.

"He is happiest when Anna rocks him, but lets his parents hold him now without screaming like he did at first. If he wakes up crying, only Anna can sooth him."

"And Little Blossom, what about her?"

"To tell you the truth John, she isn't doing very well. Anna is having terrible nightmares. She wakes up in the night screaming, but she turns away from whoever tries to comfort her. She just stares at us unresponsively and turns toward the wall with her knees drawn up.

"Usually Jeremiah is sleeping with her and he starts crying when she does. It is pretty bad. Everyone has tried to reach her.

"Sometimes, Donald sleeps in a chair beside her bed and when she awakes with one of her nightmares, he holds her and rocks her until she calms, but she won't even talk to him." Daniel looked sad as he related this to John.

"Maybe if you go in and try to get her to talk about the last three months, she will be able to start recovering from the ordeal. I tell you, I just can't stand seeing her this way and Hannah and Joseph cry almost all the time they aren't right in the room with her. It's like she really hasn't been rescued yet.

"The boys have, but Anna is still out there alone somewhere enduring a tortuous existence."

John nodded and made his way to the room where Anna stayed with her parents, brother and sister. He knocked on the door and as Joseph opened it, he saw her small face glance fearfully at the opened door.

When he entered, he walked directly to where she sat on a short stool holding her baby sister. John turned to Joseph and asked permission to take her for a short walk. Outside of a couple trips to the clinic to see about Jeremiah, she had not been out of the hotel.

"If she wants to," Joseph said hopefully, as he glanced down at his daughter.

"Would you like to go for a walk in the hotel garden, or maybe down to the river?" John held his hand out to her as Hannah took baby Carolyn from her.

"The wind is not so strong here and the sun is shinning. No rain, just sunshine, although it is a little cool."

She appeared to relax a little and obediently rose to her feet. She allowed Hannah to slip a light coat over her warm dress and adjust a knitted hat over her shiny dark hair.

The only emotion she demonstrated was when her eyes darted around the room, checking on the activities of Joshua and Jeremiah. The boys were playing together with wooden wagons and horses made by Donald.

Seemingly assured they were safe, she held her small hand out to John and allowed him to lead her out the door, down the wide staircase and out onto the porch.

"Where would you like to walk? We can go into the gardens and sit on a bench and visit or even walk down to the river and watch the boats."

Her face grew fearful as she looked in the direction of the river and then she gently tugged on his hand and drew him toward the garden. It was winter and the only flowers blooming were camellias, but there were evergreens to brighten the pathways and inviting benches throughout the garden.

The two children mature far beyond their years, walked along the paths for a few minutes. Before long John felt the small hand, which had gripped his so tightly, begin to relax.

He pointed out small animals and birds scurrying around looking for food, which was not as abundant as the New Year approached. They had been lucky that the weather had been mild up to that time. So far Arkansas had not yet experienced any of the snow or ice that was possible at any time during December and January.

John shuddered when he thought of what might have happened if the children had been lost in Oklahoma Territory in harsh winter weather. *Thank you Lord for holding your winter back.*

They strolled around a bit more before settling on a bench that faced the river. As Anna looked out at the wide river, even from this distance, she began to tremble. "Little Blossom are you cold?"

"The river," she whispered so low he could barely here her.

"Yes, that is the Arkansas river." John squeezed her hand in assurance. "See the barges?" He pointed to where several barges made their slow progress down the river.

He knew she must have been thinking of how they were camping beside the river when they were abducted. He attempted to bring other thoughts of the river to her mind.

"Your parents tell me that you live near the Arkansas River, in Little Rock. I think it would be fun to watch the barges float down the river and bring supplies. Sometimes I just sit on the riverbank and watch them float by and wonder where they will go, maybe as far as the big sea."

"It's bigger than I remembered," she said softly, studying the river while holding firmly to John's hand.

"Yes, the Arkansas is wider and deeper than the other rivers you saw. Of course they all feed into the Arkansas and contribute to the great size. It is much deeper here than the Canadian River.

"What's the Canadian?"

"That is the river you and the boys crossed. Of course it had been real dry and it was much lower in September than it is now, since all the rain."

"Oh! I didn't know its name. Thank you for telling me." Her responses were all very low and polite. She had stopped trembling and was beginning to appear more curious than the frightened expression she had worn when they first spotted the river.

"You are most welcome. Would you like to walk down to the river and watch the boats?" He stood and gently tugged on her hand. She held back at first, but eventually began to move with him toward the river.

John picked up a multicolored stone from the gravel path that was shaped roughly like a heart. It was worn smooth, probably from years of the swift water rushing over it and had been dumped on the path with a load of gravel hauled from the river.

They walked to a spot beneath a tree, bare of its leaves, but with branches that spread out like sentinels standing guard. John spread a quilt on the ground that Hannah had sent with him. They sat down on it and then while she watched, he began to patiently and cautiously drill a hole in the top of the heart shaped rock. He used a sharp pointed rock and his knife. Anna watched his every move, fascinated as a hole began to appear in the odd shaped rock.

"This is where we were camped, isn't it?" Anna was looking around, a frightened expression on her small face.

"No, I believe it was up river a bit towards the ferry." John gestured to a spot further up river where a small grove of trees hung out over the river. He resumed his drilling on the rock.

"Anna, did the men hurt you?" He kept his eyes on the rock, but felt her hand grasp his coat. She was silent for a long time. He continued to drill the hole in the rock.

Chapter Sixty

"No, not really, one of them, the smaller one, even brought us some food until we got to the camp and could cook." She stared out over the river before resuming. "Zeke hurt Sheba. She started screaming, but I couldn't go back. I had promised, but Josh didn't. He went back. I think he killed Zeke."

"No, Little Blossom. Josh didn't kill him. His partner came back and shot him. Your father and I buried him. He was shot and his partner told your uncles that he was the one who shot him."

"That's good. Joshua worried he had killed a man and God wouldn't forgive him."

"His father has told him of this. He knows he did not kill him, but Our Lord would have forgiven the act. He is a loving Father and Joshua acted in defense of his mother. God would never have held that against him."

Anna looked up at John solemnly. "Yes! I told him that, but he still worried. The Bible says 'Thou shall not kill.'"

"Yes, you're right. The Bible does say that, but I don't think God means for us to stand by and watch while one person hurts another."

"Sheba never woke up after Zeke hurt her, but we took her with us. She was alive, but I let her die."

"No! Don't you think that. You kept her and the boys alive. All those months, you did all you could possibly do.

"Was it after Sheba died that the People came to bring you food?"

"You mean the angels God sent?"

"Yes, the two men who look like me."

"Yes, God sent his angels to bury her and feed us. I wish Sheba didn't have to die." She started sobbing and buried her head in his arms. John lay down his knife and the rock and held her, rocking slowly back and forth crooning to her softly.

"Sheba is in heaven. And you made her so proud taking care of the boys like you did. You were very strong and did more than most adults would have been able to do."

"When I went for help, Jeremiah was crying when I got back. I had not fixed them enough food to last and he was hungry," she related despondently. "I didn't take good care of them. Jeremiah got sick. He almost died. I heard people talking. He didn't get enough water. That was my fault. I promised Sheba that I would take care of them."

"Oh Little Blossom, you took very good care of them. You were very brave."

"Sheba was covered with worms," she confided in a voice so soft he had to lean closer to hear. "I threw up, over and over. When I finished, I washed them away—the worms. Then we wrapped her in a blanket.

"Josh and I pulled her out of the dugout, but we didn't have anything to dig a hole with. That was when the angels came back and dug a hole with a hatchet."

"They had been there before?" John tried not to show the horror he felt at all this child had gone through. No wonder she had closed herself off. The memories were too horrible for her to face.

"Yes, after I left the settler. I couldn't get back on Old Joe. One of them lifted me up on his back. That was the first time they came. After that, they came whenever we needed them. They buried Sheba and brought us food along the trail. If God had not sent the angels, we would have starved."

"The People value children. I spoke with them. They thought you were very brave. They had names for each of you. They called you Amoshuli. It means to have courage. Joshua they called Nitushi, young bear and Jeremiah was Hanan, meaning small Eagle. They had great respect for you and the boys and yes, they were doing God's work by seeing to your needs. Often God asks us to minister to others. They were obedient to God."

Anna looked up at John in wonder at all he told her. "What did they call me?" Her voice was filled with awe at the news that John had actually met and talked with her angels.

"Amoshuli. They named you that because they could see the courage with which you cared for the boys and struggled to get them home. Never think you failed in your task. You were very brave. And you brought the boys home alive and safe.

"I want you to also remember that not for a minute were you and the boys forgotten. Many were searching for you and many more, probably hundreds were praying for you. You were never alone."

Anna began crying again, but this time her tears were not the harsh sobs from before. She seemed to relax in his arms and even glanced back out at the river. "But papa didn't come for us. I looked for him forever, but he didn't come."

This was said so desolately, that John could not retain the tears that filled his eyes. Surreptitiously he wiped them away, before looking down into her upturned eyes.

"Oh Anna!" In his anguish at this child's misery, he used her name instead of Little Blossom. "Your papa began looking for you the very minute they discovered you missing and he would be out there yet if we had not found all of you when we did.

"Everyone was looking for you. It took a long time, because we did not know where you had been taken. Your uncle Ben came from his home in the north, your grandfather came all the way from the great ocean to the east and Donald came from a place called Alabama to look for you.

"Your papa, your uncle Daniel and I also hunted for you. Your mama went to the house in Little Rock, just in case you got back there. Miz Bernice searched here in Fort Smith with your grandfather.

"Everyone searched. We would never have given up until we had found you. Your parents and the rest of the family love you very much. You are most precious to them."

Anna looked at the youth who had been the one to find them. She wanted to believe his words, but the waiting had been so hard and the cost had been so high.

"Truth John?" Her hazel eyes bore into his dark brown eyes.

"Anna, I will never lie to you." It was a solemn promise and he did not flinch from her steady gaze.

"You found us." The response was matter-of-fact and her gaze held steady.

"Yes, I found you, but the others were close behind. They were not with me only because they crisscrossed the area to make sure we did not miss you and I went in a straight line. Everyone looked very hard. We covered a lot of territory in the three months you were gone.

John had continued to drill the hole through the red, heart-shaped rock. When it was completed, he broke off several strands of wiregrass and braided them tightly. He fashioned a strong thin chain and threaded it through the hole he had so carefully drilled in the rock—forming a necklace. Then he knelt before her and ceremonially placed it around her neck, tying the ends at the back of her neck under her thick black braids.

"This gift from me to you is my solemn pledge that I will never tell you anything but the truth. Let this stone be the symbol of our lasting friendship. There is no one braver or more beautiful in the entire world than you are, Little Blossom."

Anna fingered the stone, slowly tracing the heart shape and holding it up for the sun to catch the beautiful colors that intermingled against the background of the mostly red stone.

"It is very pretty. I will keep it always." She smiled for the first time, the radiant smile that had first drawn him to the child. Anna felt a special bond with the youth, who had been the one to find them after their long arduous ordeal. She fingered the stone and again looked to him for the answer to the thing that troubled her most.

"John, do you really think papa and mama still love me?"

"Yes! They love you very much." He held both of her hands and looked into her eyes. "Would you like to go and tell them how much you love them? I know they are very worried about you and it would mean much to them to hear the words from your mouth."

"I think that is a good idea," she said solemnly. She stood and brushed off her skirt, while John picked up the quilt and shook it out.

They hurried back along the path and were soon joined by Daniel. He had followed them at a discreet distance. The family trusted the young Native American completely, but Anna was in such a fragile state that they felt someone should be nearby in case John needed help.

Anna might have broken down from the stress she was under, or someone might have interfered with an Indian boy walking alone with a young white girl. Daniel was insurance against any additional unpleasantness occurring.

When they reached the hotel, John said he had to go help his mother, but he would return later that day. Daniel took Anna up to the room she shared with her parents. After seeing her safely into the room, Daniel returned to the porch where he saw John disappearing in the direction of his home.

He quickly caught up with him and as they walked along, John related all that Anna had told him about her ordeal in Oklahoma Territory. He felt her family needed to know some of what she had been through to better understand her suffering.

Perhaps then they would be able to help her recover. Both had tears in their eyes, as they spoke of the courage of the child.

* * *

Anna walked up to her father. "Papa, John says you still love me."

Joseph's eyes were swimming in tears as he looked back at his daughter. These were the first words he had heard her speak, since they had found the children.

"John is certainly right. I love you very much." It was hard speaking through the lump in his throat. He knelt down and picked her up in his arms.

"You are my Anna. And I will always love you, even when you are grown and have children of your own."

"Well, I love you too papa," she replied solemnly. "John told me you couldn't find us, but you kept looking. He said you would have looked forever until you found us."

"That's right. We would have looked forever." He studied his daughter's serious face and was not sure what else he could say to reassure her. Joseph knew it would take a long time for her to get over the events of the past three months, if she ever actually could.

"Papa, I didn't think you loved me anymore. I wasn't sure you would want me to come home. I let Sheba die. I was going to leave her there with that bad man and take the boys away.

"I promised Sheba I would papa. I didn't want to. When I saw you leave with Jeremiah, I was sure you didn't want me anymore." Anna hung her head and tears ran down her cheeks.

"Oh Anna," his heart was breaking at his daughter's words. He held her close and prayed for the right words to reassure her of his love. "Jeremiah was very sick. I had to get him more medical attention than what I could provide on the trail. I wanted to tell you, but you were still asleep when I left.

"It wasn't because I loved him more than you; he was just sicker and needed immediate care." He held his daughter to him, so tightly that soon Anna began to squirm.

"I'm sorry I let Jeremiah get so sick." She hung her head and refused to look at him.

"Anna," Joseph put his finger under her chin and raised it so that she was looking into his eyes.

"You did a wonderful job of taking care of the boys. It was because Jeremiah was smaller and younger that he got so sick. It was not anything you did. You were very brave and took very good care of the boys."

Chapter Sixty-One

The family prepared to return to Little Rock on the train. Daniel had related the tales that John had told him of Anna's time away from them. Joseph was horrified at what his small daughter had endured. It had been more than most adults could have survived. It was only through the grace of God that the children had been returned to them.

Reluctantly they bid goodbye to John and his mother. The four men had grown to respect and become fond of John after the three months on the trail and his expertise in tracking, plus he was the one that had begun Anna's healing with their talk by the river.

The women had also visited frequently with Raven, whenever her busy schedule allowed for it. But no one would miss John more than Anna.

She could not understand why he had to remain behind in Fort Smith. They had been collecting new family members as long as she could remember, why not John and his mother.

"Come home with us," she pleaded. "You can go to school with me."

"My family needs me Little Blossom. I promise to come see you. I will write often."

He cupped the stone she wore around her neck in his hand. John continued to reassure her, while looking into her large eyes. Her expression changed from sad to hopeful.

"This will be the bond between us. Whenever you are lonesome or afraid, rub the stone and whisper a prayer. Your guardian angel will send a message to mine and we will be close, however far apart we are. I will feel your presence and you will feel mine." He kissed her lightly on her cheek and stepped back as Daniel picked her up and lifted her up on the train.

She hurried to her seat and pressed her face against the window so she could continue to watch him, as the big black engine started pulling the train from the station. All the while she rubbed the heart-shaped red stone. John represented safety. It was frightening for her to have to leave him standing beside the depot, waving goodbye, while the train carried her away from him.

As she rubbed the stone, she whispered a prayer. "Keep him safe guardian angel. Bring us together again."

Joseph was sitting across from her. He was very concerned about his daughter's reaction to being separated from John. The boy obviously represented a safe haven for her. The youth had become very important to her and was the only one who had been able to draw from her the terror of her abduction and escape.

"We'll see John again," he promised. "If he can't come to Little Rock, we'll come back to Fort Smith to visit."

"He'll come see us," Anna replied confidently. "I'm going to marry John when I grow up." Her parents looked at one another in amazement that such a thought had even occurred to her.

"You could not choose anyone better." Daniel told her with a big wink and a smile. "By the way I have an announcement to make. I have asked Louise to be my wife and she has said yes. I got the reply just before we left."

Everyone congratulated him and began teasing him, which helped lighten everyone's mood.

Anna smiled to herself. The adults had treated her announcement as the musings of a child, but she knew that one day she would be Savannah "Little Blossom" Wolf-Hunter. She contentedly rubbed the stone and pictured John sitting beside the river braiding grass for the chain.

* * *

It was a picture she visualized during the days and nights at home whenever the nightmares returned or the memories of Oklahoma started to trouble her conscious thoughts. There were no doubts in Anna's mind. She would see John again. They would walk together again, beside the river.

www.ingramcontent.com/pod-product-compliance
Lightning Source LLC
Chambersburg PA
CBHW070730120726
47910CB00001B/46